As varied as it is vast, the India in these selected stories throbs with vivid color and intense heat. Whether it serves as the setting or exists only in a character's memory, the country is a conundrum, at once backward and modern, democratic and hierarchical, spiritual and secular, rural and urban. It flaunts enormous riches and cries out from dire poverty. But at their core, the selections in *Passages* speak to the universal human condition: the desire to understand the motives of others; the many ideas we absorb as we grow up in a particular culture; identification of the strong thread that connects us. Suffused as these stories are with arranged marriages, the intricacies of the caste system, the omnipresence of poverty-stricken servants, the unrelenting heat, street vendors, and monsoons, *Passages* highlights how powerfully a culture can influence an individual and his relationships to others.

T0200912

Barbara H. Solomon is a professor of English and Director of Writing at Iona College. Her academic interests include twentieth-century American literature and women's studies. Among the anthologies she has edited are *The Awakening and Selected Stories of Kate Chopin*, *Other Voices, Other Vistas*, *Herland and Selected Stories of Charlotte Perkins Gilman*, and *The Haves and the Have-Nots*.

Eileen Panetta is an associate professor of English at Iona College. Her teaching focuses on the modern British novel and nineteenth-century American literature. With Barbara Solomon she is the editor of *Once Upon a Childhood* and *Miss Lulu Bett and Selected Stories of Zona Gale*.

Passages

24 Modern Indian Stories

Edited and with an Introduction by
Barbara H. Solomon and Eileen Panetta

SIGNET CLASSICS

SIGNET CLASSICS
Published by New American Library, a division of
Penguin Group (USA) Inc., 375 Hudson Street,
New York, New York 10014, USA
Penguin Group (Canada), 90 Eglinton Avenue East, Suite 700, Toronto,
Ontario M4P 2Y3, Canada (a division of Pearson Penguin Canada Inc.)
Penguin Books Ltd., 80 Strand, London WC2R 0RL, England
Penguin Ireland, 25 St. Stephen's Green, Dublin 2,
Ireland (a division of Penguin Books Ltd.)
Penguin Group (Australia), 250 Camberwell Road, Camberwell, Victoria 3124,
Australia (a division of Pearson Australia Group Pty. Ltd.)
Penguin Books India Pvt. Ltd., 11 Community Centre, Panchsheel Park,
New Delhi - 110 017, India
Penguin Group (NZ), 67 Apollo Drive, Rosedale, North Shore 0632,
New Zealand (a division of Pearson New Zealand Ltd.)
Penguin Books (South Africa) (Pty.) Ltd., 24 Sturdee Avenue,
Rosebank, Johannesburg 2196, South Africa

Penguin Books Ltd., Registered Offices:
80 Strand, London WC2R 0RL, England

Published by Signet Classics, an imprint of New American Library,
a division of Penguin Group (USA) Inc.

First Signet Classics Printing, May 2009
10 9 8 7 6 5 4 3 2 1

Introduction copyright © Barbara H. Solomon and Eileen Panetta, 2009
(*Author copyrights and permissions can be found on pages 337–39.*)
All rights reserved

 REGISTERED TRADEMARK—MARCA REGISTRADA

Printed in the United States of America

For Naomi Levinson,
cherished cousin and good friend

and

Ann Blanchette,
sister and courageous woman

Acknowledgments

We wish to express our gratitude to Tracy Bernstein at NAL for her enthusiastic support and helpful guidance as well as to Florence B. Eichin of Penguin's Permissions Department for her valuable aid in locating and securing materials.

At Iona College, a great deal of assistance was provided by Edward L. Helmrich of Ryan Library's Interlibrary Loan Program and by Elana Fara Grabowski, Department of English Graduate Assistant.

Contents

x   Contents

Introduction

Because the contributors to this collection live in India, or were born or raised in India, or their parents are Indian, these selections dramatize insights about life in a vast and intriguing nation, one that is backward and modern, democratic and hierarchical, rich and poor, spiritual and secular, rural and urban. They employ details of a very distinct and traditional culture as well as depicting the experience of immigration, of the wrenching experience of leaving relatives and friends and adapting to a foreign way of life. While many of these stories are very culture specific, some speak to the human condition that is universal and, with only slight changes, could be set in almost any location.

Unlike most Western countries, India is not unified by a single national language. Among the sixteen major regional languages are Assamese, Bangla, Bengali, Gujarati, Hindi, Kannada, Malayalam, Tamil, and Telugu. Each of these is the mother tongue of millions of Indian citizens. An important publisher, Penguin India, releases more than sixty volumes every year in languages such as Hindi, Malayalam, Marathi, Punjabi, and Urdu. Although much of India's literature read in the West appears in translation, a number of talented authors write in two languages. For example, Manoj Das has published more than forty volumes in English and another forty in Oriya, the language of Orissa, his home state.

Ironically, English is the language of business and political life in contemporary India. Brought to Indian shores by the hated conquering British Raj, it was long the language by which these foreign rulers with their military power governed a people for whom they often had contempt. The prestige associated with fluent English is closely connected to the high value placed on a British or American education. Thus, children of affluent and ambitious families are encouraged—or at least allowed—to study abroad at Cambridge, Oxford, and numerous American universities.

The families at home have to cope not only with the great distance that separates them from their sons and daughters, but also with well-founded fears that their children will be irrevocably changed by their Western experience, seduced by new freedoms, different customs, and broader perspectives. In "Her Mother" by Anjana Appachana, an Indian mother meditates as she responds to the first, and very unsatisfying, letter from her daughter, Rani, who is a graduate student in America. The letter the mother writes is filled with advice to Rani to be true to her Indian roots, to oil her hair instead of using shampoo, to avoid foreign diets, to pray each morning, and to keep the silver statue of Ganesha close to her. Rani's mother, not unexpectedly, advocates arranged marriage and suggests that her daughter meet with a young man known to the family. She expresses her hope that Rani won't marry an American.

Some of the particulars of life in India are either referred to in passing descriptions or as conditions that the characters acknowledge without particular comment. Among such background details are common references to arranged marriages; to the legacy of the caste system; to the employment of servants who are very poor and poorly treated by middle-class as well as upper-class families; to the labor-intensive preparation of highly spiced vegetarian dishes; to the comfort of eating rice with one's fingers; to the crowds on city streets; to the numerous street vendors of food; to the heat, which in certain areas regularly reaches temperatures of 110 to 116 degrees Fahrenheit each day; to the droughts, which destroy crops and result in a severe lack of clean running water in large areas; to the common power shortages; and to the yearly three-month cycle of daily monsoon rains, which supply much-needed water, but also flood streets and buildings, swelling wooden doors and cabinets, and releasing colonies of insects.

The political history of India and the powerful religious divisions in the country sometimes appear as casual elements in the stories and are sometimes at the crux of the fiction. For example, in Saadat Hasan Manto's "The Assignment," set in the 1940s, a Muslim family has remained behind in their home in a Hindu area although all of the other Muslims have fled because of the rioting that has been escalating around them. The father of an eleven-year-old son and seventeen-year-old daughter, Mian Abdul Hai has misjudged the danger. With fires raging throughout the city and uninterrupted looting, his prediction that all will soon return to normal is merely wishful thinking. The historic hatred between the two religious groups, which led to Partition in 1947, continues to haunt Indians and Pakistanis alike.

In "Dharma," Vikram Chandra describes Major General Jago Antia, a much-revered and decorated war hero. A member of India's Paratrooper Brigade, he had lost a leg at the age of thirty during a battle with Pakistani troops for the city of Sylhet. A legendary hero, he severed the leg himself after being gravely wounded by a mine explosion and realizing that none of the men around him was capable of doing it. Now, after twenty years, he is driven to take a medical leave and return to his childhood home because of the mysterious and extreme phantom pain in the missing limb. In one way, his exemplary service to his country reflects magnificence, but there is more than one way that he can view his life.

The continued bitter religious conflicts both within India and with Pakistan are a fact of Indian life. Paradoxically, India is home to many millions who embrace an array of Eastern religions such as Hinduism, Islam, Jainism, Sikhism, and Buddhism. Deeply embedded in its daily life are practices connected to yoga, Zen, and meditation as well as the chanting of prayers first thing each morning. Yet the practical result of this pluralism has often been distrust, hatred, and violence.

Woven throughout numerous stories are references to

prayers to the Hindu gods and goddesses along with regular visits or pilgrimages to temples and shrines and holy
men or special journeys in times of crisis. In "Two More
Under the Indian Sun," Ruth Prawer Jhabvala describes
Margaret, an Englishwoman and widow of a British official, who has lived in India for many years and would
never leave it. The religious life of the country engages
her and she is proud to have been told by many people
that in her last birth she was an Indian. A social activist,
she welcomes "holy men from the Himalayas, village
welfare workers, [and] organizers of conferences on spiritual welfare" who stay at her large house in Delhi for
weeks or months. Margaret tells her young friend Elizabeth about the best time in her life, when she lived in
the ashram of Swami Vishwananda. Her experience
there was of extraordinary freedom and joy, and when
the Swami sang, she wept with happiness.

On the other hand, in "Ajji's Miracle" Anita Rau
Badami depicts the cynical exploitation of people's belief
in prayer and sacrifice by Ajji, a widow who lives with
her son and daughter-in-law. Ajji expected to run their
household, but she spends her days plotting vengeance
against her daughter-in-law, who clearly despises her and
mistreats her. The scheming old woman takes advantage
of a medical problem of her granddaughter, Tara, using
the girl's situation to regain the power she once had in
the family. Although a surgical procedure that is commonplace in the West would bring Tara relief, Ajji convinces her family to put their faith in prayer and she
offers to undertake a well-publicized fast. Tara's humiliation and suffering count for nothing in her grandmother's quest for power and pleasure.

The poverty of India is notorious, with images of the
beggars on the streets of Calcutta or Delhi abounding
throughout the Western world. In her introduction to
Out of India, Ruth Prawer Jhabvala observes "that a
very great number of Indians never get enough to eat.
Literally that: from birth to death they never for one
day cease to suffer from hunger." In Rohinton Mistry's
"One Sunday," though Francis has lost his job as a furniture delivery boy, he continues to sleep on the street,

under the store's awning—his habitual home. Now, he performs odd jobs for the tenants of the apartment house across the street. Paid with small sums and leftovers, he is well aware that he must ask for work humbly. On the Sunday of the story, he has not had anything to eat for two days, and a widow who had spoken to him about some work has gone off for a visit for the day.

In "A Horse and Two Goats" by R. K. Narayan, the elderly Muni is the poorest man in his tiny Tamil village. With no provisions in the house to prepare dinner, his wife sends Muni on a futile trip to the store to purchase "dhall, chili, curry leaves, mustard, coriander, gingelley, oil, and one large potato," but the shopkeeper refuses to extend Muni credit. The likable old man is humiliated as he tries to deal with the shop owner in front of other customers: "Muni thought helplessly: My poverty is exposed to everybody. But what can I do?" Fortunately, on this day a chance encounter with an affluent American tourist will bring unexpected relief to this philosophical villager.

In "Biju in America" (chapter ten of Kiran Desai's *The Inheritance of Loss*), the poverty of India is mirrored in the poverty of an illegal Indian immigrant in New York City. Although his father, a cook in India, is filled with illusions about Biju's American success, in reality the son has endured a series of the lowliest jobs at restaurants in which the middle- and upper-class patrons dine in attractive surroundings upstairs while immigrants from around the world struggle in crowded and dirty basements, oppressed by employers who distrust and resent them. The owners of an Italian restaurant who hire Biju had hoped to be able to employ European workers because "At least they might have something in common with them like religion and skin color. . . ." From basement kitchens, Biju returns to a basement place in Harlem where illegal immigrants camp out "near the fuse box, behind the boiler, in the cubbyholes and odd-shaped corners that were once pantries, maids' rooms, laundry rooms, and storage rooms at the bottom of what had been a single-family home."

Interestingly, while several stories of childhood and

old age are enriched by details of life in India that add texture to the tales, the essential insights about the characters and situations are not necessarily linked to the elements of Indian culture and, instead, express universal experience. In Chitra Banerjee Divakaruni's "The Forgotten Children," the first-person narrator, Didi, recalls her situation with a brutal father who regularly abuses both of his children and his wife. A belligerent factory worker and alcoholic, the father is fired from one job after another. The family lives in increasing poverty and fear of him. Didi refers to her mother's broken arm, to her own hiding of a bruised thigh, to "discolored finger marks left on a forearm" and the "pink ridges of a forehead scar." Divakaruni insightfully depicts the typical cycle of domestic violence as the father, while in a calm mood, contritely acknowledges his hurtful behavior or brings home gifts for his wife, entertaining her and his children with snatches of songs. But his good moods never last long and his fury is vented on a loving wife and vulnerable children. The story is set in an oil town in Assam, but its essential events could and do occur any place.

In "Field Trip," by Githa Hariharan, Krishna, a ten-year-old city boy, is spending his summer vacation visiting his aunt, Parvati Mami, and uncle, Sundaram Mama, a strong and understanding farmer of considerable consequence in the village. With Sundaram's help, he can overcome his fear of six bullying local boys. They taunt him with being a "sissy" because he doesn't know how to swim and becomes dizzy when he tries to climb a tree. There can be no doubt about the manliness of his strong and respected uncle, who has become his hero. There is, however, one disquieting element in this story of an overnight visit to a tenant farmer. Sundaram refers to the tenant farmer and his family as "peasants" who need him, and to himself as a "Big Master." The hospitality that the boy and his uncle enjoy is actually the obligation of subservient workers very conscious that they depend upon the property owner for their livelihood.

In Shashi Tharoor's "The Five-Dollar Smile," an orphan's poverty in India is the background fact of all the events, though such poverty is a common element of life in orphanages around the world and figured prominently in Charles Dickens's depiction of forlorn children in nineteenth-century London. Joseph Kumaran, who is about eleven years old, is aboard a plane that will take him from the orphanage where he has spent almost all his life in India to America for a month's visit with an American couple. He is a poster child for HELP, the Catholic relief organization that cares for orphaned or abandoned children. Joseph's plaintive photograph on ads for the organization has helped to raise significant sums through a program of "adopting" a child by sending a contribution of five dollars a month. The well-intentioned nuns who run the orphanage employ caning as punishment for disobedience. They have no idea of a child's deep longing for a small pleasure such as seeing a movie or a once-monthly treat of "crisp papadams" added to the usual daily fare of gruel. In fact, they have written to the American couple hosting Joseph's stay to warn them against spoiling the boy.

Two stories about older women depict the emptiness and marginalization that can accompany growing old, though in very different circumstances. Amitav Ghosh's "Grandmother Retires" (an excerpt from the novel *The Shadow Lines*) dramatizes the quick decline of a sixty-year-old grandmother who decides to retire from her position as headmistress of a girls' school in Calcutta. Her colleagues arrange for an elaborate ceremony and dinner in her honor as well as an impressive going-away gift. But as her loving grandson observes, his vibrant and involved grandmother soon undergoes a sad transformation. He explains: "Once I pushed open her door and saw her sitting by the window staring blankly at her cupped hands. I shut the door quickly. I knew what she had in her hands. Time—great livid gouts of it; I could smell it stinking." The woman who was once so central in the household has now withdrawn to her room.

In Manoj Das's "Miss Moberly's Targets," the octogenarian Dolly Moberly lives in an old age home called "The Rest." She has outlived her friends, and has no relatives to visit, but she gains considerable pleasure from throwing crusts of bread to the three roaming dogs that regularly stop in the street before her. When she entertains three guests, she is certain that they will admire the skill with which she aims the scraps of cake and bread for the dogs from her balcony, but they denigrate her achievement. Self-centered and insensitive, they have no idea how disappointing and even insulting their comments have been to a lonely old woman.

In "My Father's Trees in Dehra," Ruskin Bond brings together descriptions of old age and youth as the first-person narrator encounters a seventy-year-old peddler who knew his grandparents. The narrator, the son of an English couple, lived in Dehra when he was a boy and has returned for a sentimental journey. The peddler struggles to earn his living carrying his large pack of notions and stationery items from house to house as he has always done. He describes the curse of a long life that has become burdensome, of outliving his family: " 'Your friends, your loved ones, all go before you, and at the end you are left alone. But I must go too before long. The road to the bazaar seems to grow longer every day.' " On the other hand, for the narrator in his thirties, the sight of his grandparents' home makes him rejoice in memories of his boyhood possessions—such as a pocketknife and RAF badges—and in his close relationship with a wise and imaginative father, who has left him a precious legacy.

Four stories, Ambai's "Yellow Fish," Anita Desai's "The Farewell Party," Vikram Seth's "The Committee Meeting" (an excerpt from *A Suitable Boy*), and Shashi Deshpande's "A Day Like Any Other," explore with subtlety the widely differing relationships of a personal, social, and marital nature. "Yellow Fish" begins as a meditation on the colorful scene of the arrival of fishing boats, laden with a variety of fish. The narrator's attention is drawn to a yellow fish discarded on the sand as the men sort through the catch. She notes its color, "that palest yellow that comes before the withering and falling of leaves" as she watches it shuddering and gasping, desperate for the sea. The woman makes a powerful connection between this unvalued fish and a painful memory that it brings to life. Clearly, the haunting memory is only just below the surface, lying in wait and readily summoned by any chance circumstance, creating an unusual relationship.

In "The Farewell Party," Desai dramatizes the relationship between a socially inept couple with the acquaintances who are certainly not their friends. Bina and her husband, Raman, are leaving a small provincial town to move to Bombay because his firm has transferred him. They are well aware that they are outsiders in a snobbish community of corporate executives and their wives. They have four children, one of whom is disabled, and their care for this child has made them generally indifferent to the usual social and sporting activities of the town. Self-conscious and ill at ease, they have attempted an elegant evening lawn party that they are not quite up to giving. Raman knows that since he doesn't work at a British or American company, but only at an Indian firm, his social position is low in the hierarchy. But now that he and his wife are leaving and won't have to be invited to parties or to play golf or bridge, their guests can afford to be sentimental about their parting.

"The Committee Meeting," an excerpt from *A Suitable Boy* by Vikram Seth, depicts a relationship between two very different men. Dr. Pran Kapoor, a young university lecturer, attends a meeting of the English Department's syllabus committee with Professor O. P. Mishra and two other department members. Professor Mishra, whom he loathes, is the department head and is used to having his way. Clever and powerful, Mishra will decide who is to be promoted to the position for which Pran has applied. At the meeting, Pran proposes, as he has for the last year, that James Joyce be added to the list of twenty-one writers whom the students must read in order to earn a B.A. in Modern British Literature. Pran's admirable love of a great author and professional convictions are more important to him than pleasing a manipulative administrator who enjoys the power he has over those beneath him.

In Shashi Deshpande's "A Day Like Any Other," the

relationship that is threatened is that between a wife and her husband. The wife and mother of three young children learns that her husband is having an affair with his secretary. Interestingly, most of the wife's (and reader's) anger is directed toward the malicious woman who tells her of her husband's infidelity.

Two stories that demonstrate that a character's perspective means everything are Khushwant Singh's "The Bottom-Pincher" and Ginu Kamani's "This Anju." Both are told from the points of view of first-person narrators whose lack of self-knowledge and appropriate responses makes them comic figures of misguided actions. In "The Bottom-Pincher," the narrator is an affluent, outwardly respectable middle-aged man who is obsessed with women's bottoms. He longs to touch the buttocks of the numerous females he sees every day on the streets of Bombay. Having resisted this overwhelming temptation, he becomes obsessed with a man much like himself, except that this well-dressed and well-connected "gentleman" walks through the streets doing the pinching that the narrator so longs to engage in. He becomes fascinated by the respected family man, a double perhaps, who has been so successfully pursuing his own fantasy with such impunity.

In "This Anju" by Ginu Kamani, a lonely and possessive mother describes her anger at the young woman who has been dating her oldest son, Sanjay, for two years. Sanjay's mother bitterly resents the relationship and is (almost comically) disturbed by what she considers a shameful reversal of gender roles. In her own marriage, which she considers to be normal, her husband is the powerful one, scolding while she cries. The mother's list of Anju's faults is reminiscent of the Duke's list of his wife's unbearable flaws in Browning's dramatic monologue "My Last Duchess." Anju, who has a graduate degree from an American university, doesn't use makeup, desire jewelry, wear the traditional sari, engage in gossip about TV actresses, or act with humility. Powerless in her resentment, Sanjay's mother is a study in blind devotion to a flawed son and parental folly.

If there is one subject that is particularly Indian and

pervasive in fiction about family life both in India and
abroad, it is the issue of arranged marriage. An en-
trenched institution, it is a far-reaching economic, social,
and religious force that results in disdain for females and
an emphasis on the desirability of male offspring. First,
the family with a daughter will experience an enormous
financial drain at the time of her marriage. There is the
cost of a dowry, often consisting of jewelry and expensive saris as well as money and household objects. Since
the bride traditionally goes to live with her husband's
parents, she brings wealth from her parents' home to
that of her in-laws. Next, the weddings of middle- and
upper-class couples, also the responsibility of the bride's
family, are elaborate occasions of large feasts and gifts.
Finally, there is always the fear that if the daughter is
not sufficiently attractive or there is no money for a
dowry, her parents will be unable to find a suitable husband, one from a good family and with the right religious, social, and economic background.

In Shauna Singh Baldwin's "Nothing Must Spoil This
Visit," Janet, a Canadian, has been married for five
years to Arvind, a Sikh whom she met while he was a
student in Montreal. While Janet spent a pleasant week
with Arvind's parents at the time of her wedding, she is
meeting Arvind's younger brother, Kamal, and her
sister-in-law, Chaya, for the first time during this trip to
Delhi. Janet is shocked to discover that Chaya was first
engaged to Arvind, an arranged marriage between two
childhood playmates, before being married off to Kamal.
When Mumji discusses how it all happened, she uses the
words "Gave her. Took her. As though Chaya were a
thing." Janet discovers that her in-laws, who seemed so
genial and welcoming in Canada, are secretive and judg-
mental; Arvind's father even becomes openly nasty. The
visit, which she anticipated would be so wonderful, has
revealed the gulf between her beliefs and those of his
Sikh family.

Rehana, a beautiful young woman, arrives at the British Consulate on a Tuesday to arrange for a permit to
travel to London as "Good Advice Is Rarer Than Rubies" by Salman Rushdie opens. She needs this permit

because her fiancé of many years, Mustafa Dar, has finally sent for her. Her marriage was arranged by her parents when she was nine years old, and in all this time telephone calls from abroad have been her only contact with Dar. The women who are interviewed on Tuesdays are dependents or relatives of men living in England, and their answers to very personal questions must match exactly the answers previously given by those men, a humiliating experience. Rehana is approached by Muhammed Ali, a gray-haired old fraud who preys on the desperate "Tuesday women." He generally offers to arrange for an official at the consulate to process their papers for a bribe of money or gold jewelry, but of course this is a scam. Rushdie depicts an arrogant British system in which the "sahibs" can pretty much do what they like regarding the powerless supplicants.

Both Jhumpa Lahiri's "The Third and Final Continent" and Bharati Mukherjee's "A Wife's Story" depict couples in arranged marriages, in which one spouse has been living in America. Lahiri explores two themes. The first is the growing love of a husband and wife who, complete strangers when they wed, must come to understand and care for each other. The second concerns the strategies by which poor Indian immigrants from an enormously different culture learn about, negotiate, and triumph in creating a new life and new home far from all that has been comfortable and familiar. In this story, an arranged marriage can lead to tenderness, compatibility, and love.

Panna Bhatt, in "A Wife's Story," describes the circumstances of her marriage in an offhand manner: "My parents, with the help of a marriage broker, who was my mother's cousin, picked out a groom. All I had to do was get to know his taste in food." She has been living in New York while she studies for a Ph.D., adapting to life in America so well that she now refers to "trucks" instead of "lorries." Her husband arranges to visit her for a vacation, but he has trouble making himself understood in Manhattan and she negotiates such transactions as purchasing their tickets for a guided city tour. He is frustrated and jealous when she exchanges even casual remarks with any man, and he announces, " 'I've come to take you back. I have seen how men watch you.' " Panna realizes, though her husband does not, that his problem is not with other men's unwanted attention, but with the effects of his wife's liberating American experience.

These stories of India, or of the lives of those who have left India for the West, bring us vicarious experience from a vast land many of us have never seen and, possibly, will never travel to visit. But as all literature can do, they can provide us with the opportunity to use critical judgment about human behavior and values anywhere, to feel disdain or disgust for characters who act with insensitivity or cruelty, to understand the needs and motives of others, and to enable us to feel sympathy for those who face problems that may be very different from our own or who have endured painful events and tragic losses. These tales make us aware how powerfully a culture can influence an individual and our relationships to others, how many minor and major ideas we absorb as we grow up in a particular culture, as well as how strong is the thread that connects us.

—Barbara H. Solomon
and Eileen Panetta
Iona College
New Rochelle, New York

Passages

AMBAI [C. S. Lakshmi]

Ambai (C. S. Lakshmi) was born into a large family in the Indian state of Tamil Nadu in 1944. She received a doctorate from Jawaharlal Nehru University in the 1970s. Currently, she directs the Sound and Picture Archives for Research on Women (SPARROW) in Mumbai. Over a lifetime of writing, her work has been characterized by an intense commitment to women's lives and issues. *Siragugal Muriyum,* her first collection of short stories, was published in 1976, and the second collection, *Veettin Muulaiyil Oru Samayalarai,* in 1988. In 1984 she published a critical work in English, *The Face Behind the Mask,* a study of the images of women in modern Tamil fiction by women writers. She also writes scripts for the films of her husband, Vishnu Mathur. Her most recent work includes *A Purple Sea: Short Stories by Ambai* (1997), and the edited volumes *The Singer and the Song: Interviews with Women in the Arts* (2000), *Mirrors and Gestures: Conversations with Women Dancers* (2003), and *The Unhurried City: Writings on Chennai* (formerly Madras) (2004).

She was the recipient of the Narayanswami Aiyar Award for her fiction, which is described as varying from gemlike prose poems to fantasy and surrealism and to realistic psychological explorations.

Yellow Fish

High summer. Already the sand feels hot. It will not hold its wetness. Away, to the left of the shrunken sea and spent waves, the sand spreads like a desert. Yet the eye is compelled by the sea alone. Now the white

boat has arrived. This is the forerunner. Its appearance
is the signal that the fishing boats are returning. It floats
ashore like a swan, swaying from side to side. Far from
the shore, bright spots begin to move. The fisherwomen
make ready to welcome the boats ashore. Bright colours:
blinding indigo, demonic red, profound green, assaulting
blue. They stand vibrant against the white boat upon a
faded blue and ash grey sea.

Now it is possible to see the other boats. Walking
further, quite close to the boats you may see the fish
filling the nets. Bodies and hands darkened by the salt
wind, the men will spread their nets and start sorting the
fish the minute the boats come in. Now the fish splash
into plastic troughs, round eyes wide open. The unwanted ones are thrown away. There is a general murmur of tired voices, rising for a split second, then falling.

Black hands. Brown wood of the boats. Between the
meshes of the nets, white-bellied fish. Crowding near,
the colours of the saris press upon the eyes gently but
firmly. Painted troughs. Dry sand. An extraordinary col-
lage of colours, on the shores of the wide-spread sea. A
composition that imprints itself on the mind and memory.

A yellow fish is thrown away on the sand.

Of that palest yellow that comes before the withering
and falling of leaves. It has black spots. As I stoop to
watch, it begins to shudder and leap. The mouth gasps;
gasps and closes. It shudders and tosses on the hot sand.

The men carry on sorting their fish quickly and
efficiently.

That mouth closes; closes and opens, desperate for
water. Like Jalaja's mouth.

Too hasty infant Jalaja. She pushed and bumped her
way out into the world. Her name had already been
decided. She who rises from the waters. Lotus. Jalaja.
They had to put her in an incubator. I stood outside that
room constantly, watching her. Her pale red mouth. Her
round eyes. Sometimes she would open and close her
mouth, as if sucking.

The ashes which Arun brought back from the electric
crematorium were in a small urn, a miniature of those

huge earthenware jars of Mohenjodaro and Harappa. Its narrow mouth was tied with a piece of cloth.

"Why is the mouth closed?"

"What mouth?"

"The mouth of the urn. Open it."

"Anu. It contains only ashes."

"I want to see. Open it."

"Anu."

"Open its mouth. That mouth . . ."

Loud racking sobs. The cloth was removed to reveal the urn's tiny mouth.

The ashes were in this very sea.

The sea is at some distance. The yellow fish leaps hopelessly towards it. Its mouth falls open, skyward. Lifted from the hot sand, it falls away from the fingers, heaving and tossing. It falls away again from a leaf with which I try to hold it.

A fisherboy is on his way back from splashing in the waves.

He comes when I summon him in Marathi,

"Ikkade e, come here."

"Will you throw this yellow fish back into the sea?"

A quick snort of laughter. He grabs the fish firmly by its tail and starts running towards the sea. I run after him. He places it on the crest of an incoming wave. For a moment it splutters, helpless, like a drunk who cannot find the way home. Again it opens its mouth to the water, taking it in. Then a swish of the tail fin. An arrogant leap. Once again it swishes its tail and swims forward. You can see its clear yellow for a very long time. Then it merges into the blue-grey-white of the sea.

ANJANA APPACHANA

Born in Madkeri in Kodaga, India, Anjana Appachana cites her parents—her mother was a schoolteacher and her father a paratrooper—as among her greatest influences. She was educated at Scinda Vidyalaya, Delhi University, Jawaharlal Nehru University, and Penn State University. In 1984 she left India and now teaches at Arizona State University. Her first book, *Incantations and Other Stories,* was published in England in 1991 and in the United States in 1992. The stories in the volume are set in India of the 1980s and focus on the domestic rather than the political realities of the decade. One of them, "Sharmaji," was included in *Mirrorwork: Fifty Years of Indian Writing,* a collection edited by Salman Rushdie and Elizabeth West. She received a $200,000 creative writing fellowship from the National Endowment for the Arts, and her first novel, *Listening Now,* was published in 1997. In the novel, six women tell the story of two lovers, Padma and Karan, over a sixteen-year period.

Appachana received an O. Henry Festival Prize for the story "Her Mother," which also appeared in *The 1989 O. Henry Festival Stories.* Appachana states that she has found her work as a writer easier to pursue in the United States. She argues that it is not enough to have a room of one's own: "Unless you prioritize your writing, no one else will."

Her Mother

When she got her daughter's first letter from America, the mother had a good cry. Everything was fine, the daughter said. The plane journey was fine, her professor

who met her at the airport was nice, her university was
very nice, the house she shared with two American girls
(nice girls) was fine, her classes were OK and her teaching was surprisingly fine. She ended the letter saying she
was fine and hoping her mother and father were too.
The mother let out a moan she could barely control and
wept in an agony of longing and pain and frustration.
Who would have dreamt that her daughter was doing a
Ph.D. in Comparative Literature, she thought, wiping
her eyes with her sari palla, when all the words at her
command were "fine," "nice," and "OK." Who would
have imagined that she was a gold medallist from Delhi
University? Who would know from the blandness of her
letter, its vapidity, the monotony of its tone and the in-
difference of its adjectives that it came from a girl so
intense and articulate? Her daughter had written promptly,
as she had said she would, the mother thought, cleaning
her smudged spectacles and beginning to reread the letter. It had taken only ten days to arrive. She examined
her daughter's handwriting. There seemed to be no trace
of loneliness there, or discomfort, or insecurity—the
writing was firm, rounded and clear. She hadn't mentioned if that overfriendly man at the airport had sat
next to her on the plane. The mother hoped not. Once
Indian men boarded the plane for a new country, the
anonymity drove them crazy. They got drunk and made
life hell for the air-hostesses and everyone else nearby,
but of course, they thought they were flirting with fi-
nesse. Her daughter, for all her arguments with her parents, didn't know how to deal with such men. Most men.
Her brows furrowed, the mother took out a letter-
writing pad from her folder on the dining table and
began to write. Eat properly, she wrote. Have plenty of
milk, cheese and cereal. Eating badly makes you age
fast. That's why western women look so haggard. They
might be pencil slim, but look at the lines on their faces.
At thirty they start looking faded. So don't start these
stupid, western dieting fads. Oil your hair every week
and avoid shampoos. Chemicals ruin the hair. (You can
get almond oil easily if coconut oil isn't available.) With
all the hundreds of shampoos in América, American

women's hair isn't a patch on Indian women's. Your
grandmother had thick, black hair till the day she died.

One day, two months earlier, her daughter had cut off
her long thick hair, just like that. The abruptness and
sacrilege of this act still haunted the mother. That evening, when she opened the door for her daughter, her
hair reached just below her ears. The daughter stood
there, not looking at either her mother or father, but
almost, it seemed, beyond them, her face a strange mixture of relief and defiance and anger, as her father, his
face twisted, said, why, why. I like it short, she said.
Fifteen years of growing it below her knees, of oiling it
every week, and washing it so lovingly, the mother
thought as she touched her daughter's cheek and said,
you are angry with us . . . is this your revenge? Her
daughter had removed her hand and moved past her
parents, past her brother-in-law who was behind them,
and into her room. For the father it was as though a
limb had been amputated. For days he brooded in his
chair in the corner of the sitting-room, almost in mourn-
ing, avoiding even looking at her, while the mother murmured, you have perfected the art of hurting us.

Your brother-in-law has finally been allotted his three-
bedroomed house, she wrote, and he moved into it last
week. I think he was quite relieved to, after living with
us these few months. So there he is, living all alone in
that big house with two servants while your sister continues working in Bombay. Your sister says that commuting
marriages are inevitable, and like you, is not interested
in hearing her mother's opinion on the subject. I suppose
they will go on like this for years, postponing having
children, postponing being together, until one day when
they're as old as your father and me, they'll have nothing
to look forward to. Tell me, where would we have been
without you both? Of course, you will only support your
sister and your brother-in-law and their strange, selfish
marriage. Perhaps that is your dream too. Nobody seems
to have normal dreams any more.

The mother had once dreamt of love and a large
home, silk saris and sapphires. The love she had got, but
as her husband struggled in his job and the children

came and as they took loans to marry off her husband's sisters, the rest she did not. In the next fifteen years she had collected a nice selection of silk saris and jewellery for her daughters, but by that time, they showed no inclination for either. The older daughter and her husband had had a registered marriage, refused to have even a reception and did not accept so much as a handkerchief from their respective parents. And the younger one had said quite firmly before she left, that she wasn't even thinking of marriage.

The mother looked at her husband's back in the verandah. That's all he did after he came back from the office—sit in the verandah and think of his precious daughters, while she cooked and cleaned, attended to visitors and wrote to all her sisters and his sisters. Solitude to think—what a luxury! She had never thought in solitude. Her thoughts jumped to and fro and up and down and in and out as she dusted, cooked, cleaned, rearranged cupboards, polished the brass, put buttons on shirts and falls on saris, as she sympathised with her neighbour's problems and scolded the dhobi for not putting enough starch on the saris, as she reprimanded the milkman for watering the milk and lit the kerosene stove because the gas had finished, as she took the dry clothes from the clothes line and couldn't press them because the electricity had failed and realised that the cake in the oven would now never rise. The daughter was like her father, the mother thought—she too had wanted the escape of solitude, which meant, of course, that in the process she neither made her bed nor tidied up her room.

How will you look after yourself, my Rani Beti? she wrote. You have always had your mother to look after your comforts. I'm your mother and I don't mind doing all this, but some day you'll have to do it for the man you marry and how will you, when you can't even thread a needle?

But of course, her daughter didn't want marriage. She had been saying so, vehemently, in the last few months. The father blamed the mother. The mother had not taught her how to cook or sew and had only encouraged her and her sister to think and act with an independence quite uncalled for in daughters. How then, he asked her, could she expect her daughters to be suddenly amenable? How could she complain that she had no grandchildren and lose herself in self-pity when it was all her doing? Sometimes the mother fought with the father when he said such things, at other times she cried or brooded. But she was not much of a brooder, and losing her temper or crying helped her cope better.

The mother laid aside her pen. She had vowed not to lecture her daughter, and there she was, filling pages of rubbish when all she wanted to do was cry out, why did you leave us in such anger? what did we not do for you? why, why? No, she would not ask. She wasn't one to get after the poor child like that.

How far away you are, my pet, she wrote. How could you go away like that, so angry with the world? Why, my love, why? Your father says that I taught you to be so independent that all you hankered for was to get away from us. He says it's all my fault. I have heard that refrain enough in my married life. After all that I did for you, tutoring you, disciplining you, indulging you, caring for you, he says he understands you better because you are like him. And I can't even deny that because it's true. I must say it's very unfair, considering that all he did for you and your sister was give you chocolates and books.

When her daughter was six, the mother recalled, the teacher had asked the class to make a sentence with the word "good." She had written, my father is a good man. The mother sighed as she recalled asking her, isn't your mother a good woman? And the daughter's reply, daddy is gooder. The mother wrote, no, I don't understand— you talk like him, look like him, are as obstinate and as stupidly honest. It is as though he conceived you and gave birth to you entirely on his own. She was an ayah, the mother thought, putting her pen aside, that was all she was; she did all the dirty work and her husband got all the love.

The next day, after her husband had left for the office, the mother continued her letter. She wrote in a tinier handwriting now, squeezing as much as possible into the thin air-mail sheet. Write a longer letter to me, next time, my Rani, she wrote. Try and write as though you were talking to me. Describe the trees, the buildings, the people. Try not to be your usual perfunctory self. Let your mother experience America through your eyes. Also, before I forget, you must bathe every day, regardless of how cold it gets. People there can be quite dirty. But no, if I recall correctly, it is the English and other Europeans who hate to bathe. Your Naina Aunty, after her trip to Europe, said that they smelled all the time. Americans are almost as clean as Indians. And don't get into the dirty habit of using toilet paper, all right?

The mother blew her nose and wiped her cheek. Two years, she wrote, or even more for you to come back. I can't even begin to count the days for two years. How we worry, how we worry. Had you gone abroad with a husband, we would have been at peace, but now? If you fall ill who will look after you? You can't even make dal. You can't live on bread and cheese forever, but knowing you, you will. You will lose your complexion, your health, your hair. But why should I concern myself with your hair? You cut it off, just like that.

The mother laid her cheek on her hand and gazed at the door where her daughter had stood with her cropped hair, while she, her husband and her son-in-law stood like three figures in a tableau. The short hair made her face look even thinner. Suddenly she looked ordinary, like all the thousands of short-haired, western-looking Delhi girls one saw, all ordinarily attractive like the others, all the same. Her husband saying, why, why? his hands up in the air, then slowly falling down at his sides, her son-in-law, his lazy grin suddenly wiped off his face; she recalled it all, like a film in slow motion.

I always thought I understood you, she wrote, your dreams, your problems, but suddenly it seems there is nothing that I understand. No, nothing, she thought, the tiredness weighing down her eyes. She was ranting—the child could do without it. But how, how could she not think of this daughter of hers, who in the last few months had rushed from her usual, settled quietness to such unsettled stillness that it seemed the very house would begin to balloon outwards, unable to contain her straining.

Enough, she wrote. Let me give you the news before I make you angry with my grief. The day after you left, Mrs. Gupta from next door dropped in to comfort me, bless her. She said she had full faith you would come back, that only boys didn't. She says a daughter will always regard her parents' home as her only home, unlike sons who attach themselves to their wives. As you know, she has four sons, all married, and all, she says, under their wives' thumbs. But it was true, the mother thought. Her own husband fell to pieces every time she visited her parents without him. When he accompanied her there he needed so much looking after that she couldn't talk to her mother, so she preferred to go without him. With her parents she felt indulged and irresponsible. Who indulged her now? And when she came back from her parents the ayah would complain that her husband could never find his clothes, slept on the bedcover, constantly misplaced his spectacles, didn't know how to get himself a glass of water and kept waiting for the postman.

With all your talk about women's rights, she wrote, you refuse to see that your father has given me none. And on top of that he says that I am a nag. If I am a nag, it is because he's made me one. And talking of women's rights, some women take it too far. Mrs. Parekh is having, as the books say, a torrid affair with a married man. This man's wife is presently with her parents and when Mrs. Parekh's husband is on tour, she spends the night with him, and comes back early in the morning to get her children ready for school. Everyone has seen her car parked in the middle of the night outside his flat. Today our ayah said, memsahib, people like us do it for money. Why do memsahibs like her do it? But of course, you will launch into a tirade of how this is none of my business and sum it up with your famous phrase, each to her own. But my child, they're both married. Surely you won't defend it? Sometimes I don't understand how your strong principles co-exist with such strange values for what society says is wrong. Each to her own, you have often told me angrily, never seeming to realise that it is never one's own when one takes such a reckless step, that entire families disintegrate, that children bear scars forever. Each to her own, indeed.

Yes, she was a straightforward girl, the mother thought, and so loyal to those she loved. When the older daughter had got married five years ago, and this one was only seventeen, how staunchly she had supported her sister and brother-in-law's decision to do without all the frills of an Indian wedding. How she had later defended her sister's decision to continue with her job in Bombay, when her husband came on a transfer to Delhi. She had lost her temper with her parents for writing reproachful letters to the older daughter, and scolded them when they expressed their worry to the son-in-law, saying that as long as he was living with them, they should say nothing.

The mother was fond of her son-in-law in her own way. But deep inside she felt that he was irresponsible, uncaring and lazy. Yes, he had infinite charm, but he didn't write regularly to his wife, didn't save a paisa of his salary (he didn't even have a life insurance policy and no thoughts at all of buying a house), and instead of spending his evenings in the house as befitted a married man, went on a binge of plays and other cultural programmes, often taking her younger daughter with him, spending huge amounts on petrol and eating out. His wife was too practical, he told the mother, especially about money. She believed in saving, he believed in spending. She wanted security, he wanted fun. He laughed as he said this, and gave her a huge box of the most expensive barfis. The mother had to smile. She wanted him to pine for her daughter. Instead, he joked about her passion for her work and how he was waiting for the day when she would be earning twice as much as him, so that he could resign from his job and live luxuriously off her, reading, trekking and sleeping. At such times the mother couldn't even force a smile out. But her younger daughter would laugh and say that his priorities were clear. And the older daughter would write and urge the mother not to hound her sister about marriage, to let her pursue her interests. The sisters supported each other, the mother thought, irritated but happy.

Yesterday, the mother wrote, we got a letter from Naina Aunty. Her friend's son, a boy of twenty-six, is doing his Ph.D. in Stanford. He is tall, fair and very handsome. He is also supposed to be very intellectual, so don't get on your high horse. His family background is very cultured. Both his parents are lawyers. They are looking for a suitable match for him and Naina Aunty, who loves you so much, immediately thought of you and mentioned to them that you are also in the States. Now, before losing your temper with me, listen properly. This is just a suggestion. We are *not* forcing you into a marriage you don't want. But you must keep an open mind. At least meet him. Rather, *he* will come to the university to meet you. Talk, go out together, see how much you like each other. *Just* meet him and try and look pleasant and smile for a change. Give your father and me the pleasure of saying, there is *someone* who will look after our child. If something happens to us who will look after you? I know what a romantic you are, but believe me, arranged marriages work very well. Firstly, the bride is readily accepted by the family. Now look at me. Ours was a love marriage and his parents disliked me and disapproved of our marriage because my *sister* had married out of the community. They thought I was fast because in *those* days I played tennis with other men, wore lipstick and bras. I wonder why I bore it. I should have been cold and as distant as them. But I was ingratiating and accommodating. Then your father and I had to marry off his sisters. Now in an arranged marriage you can choose not to have such liabilities. I am not materialistic, but I am not a fool either. I know you want to be economically independent, and you must be that, but it will also help if your husband isn't burdened with debts. I am not blaming your father. Responsibilities are responsibilities. But if you can help it, why begin married life with them? Now don't write back and say you're sick of my nagging. You think I am a nag because it is

I who wield the stick and your father who gives those wonderful, idealistic lectures. Perhaps when you marry you will realise that fathers and husbands are two very different things. In an arranged marriage you will not be disillusioned because you will not have any illusions to begin with. That is why arranged marriages work. Of course, we will not put any pressure on you. Let us know if it is all right for the boy to meet you and I will write to Naina Aunty accordingly. Each day I pray that you will not marry an American. That would be very hard on us. Now, look at your father and me. Whatever your father's faults, infidelity isn't one of them. Now these Americans, they will divorce you at the drop of a hat. They don't know the meaning of the phrase, "sanctity of marriage." My love, if you marry an American and he divorces you and we are no longer in this world, what will you do?

When the milkman came early this morning, he enquired about you. I told him how far away you are. He sighed and said that it was indeed very far. I think he feels for us because he hasn't watered the milk since you left. I'm making the most of it and setting aside lots of thick malai for butter. When the postman came, he said, how is the baby? I replied, now only you will bear her news for us. He immediately asked for baksheesh. I said, nothing doing, what do you mean, baksheesh, it isn't Diwali. He replied, when I got your baby's first letter, wasn't it like Diwali? So I tipped him. Our bai has had a fight with her husband because he got drunk again and spent his entire salary gambling it away. She is in a fury and has left the house saying she won't go back to him unless he swears in the temple that he will never drink again. Your father says, hats off to her. Your father is always enraptured by other women who stand up for themselves. If I stood up for myself he would think he was betrayed.

Betrayal, betrayal, the mother mulled. His job had betrayed him, his strict father had, by a lack of tenderness, betrayed him, India herself had betrayed him after Independence, and this betrayal he raved against every evening, every night. He told her that sometimes he felt

glad that his daughter had left a country where brides
were burnt for dowry, where everyone was corrupt,
where people killed each other in the name of religion
and where so many still discriminated against Harijans.
At least, he said, his daughter was in a more civilised
country. At this the mother got very angry. She said, in
America fathers molested their own children. Wives
were abused and beaten up, just like the servant classes
in India. Friends raped other friends. No one looked
after the old. In India, the mother said, every woman
got equal pay for equal work. In America they were
still fighting for it. Could America ever have a woman
president? Never. Could it ever have a black president?
Never. Americans were as foolish about religion as Indians, willing to give millions to charlatans who said that
the Lord had asked for the money. She was also well
read, the mother told her husband, and she knew that
no Indian would part with his money so easily. As for
discrimination against untouchables in India—it only
happened among the uneducated, whereas discrimination against blacks was rampant even among educated
Americans. Blacks were the American untouchables.
The mother was now in her element. She too had read
Time and *Newsweek,* she told her husband, and she
knew that in India there had never been any question
of having segregation in buses where Harijans were concerned, as was the case in America, not so long ago.

Don't rant, her husband told her, and lower your
voice, I can hear you without your shrieking. The mother
got into a terrible fury and the father left the room.

The mother wrote, you better give us your views
about that country—you can give us a more balanced
picture. Your father thinks I'm the proverbial frog in the
well. Well, perhaps that is true, but he is another frog
in another well and Americans are all frogs in one large,
rich well. Imagine, when your aunt was in America, several educated Americans asked her whether India had
roads and if people lived in trees. They thought your
aunt had learnt all the English she knew in America.

The mother made herself a cup of tea and sipped it
slowly. Her son-in-law hadn't even been at home the

night her daughter had left. It upset the mother deeply. He could have offered to drive them to the airport at least, comforted them in their sorrow. But he had gone off for one of his plays and arrived a few minutes after they returned from the airport, his hair tousled, his eyes bright. He stopped briefly in the living room where the mother and father sat quietly, at opposite ends, opened his mouth to say something, then shrugged slightly and went to his room.

Selfish, the mother thought. Thoughtless. The daughter hadn't even enquired about him when she left. Had she recognised that her fun-loving brother-in-law had not an ounce of consideration in him?

The two months before her daughter had left had been the worst. Not only had she stopped talking to her parents, but to him. It frightened the mother. One can say and do what one likes with parents, she told her silent child once, parents will take anything. Don't cold-shoulder him too. If he takes a dislike to you and your moods, then you will be alienated even from your sister. Remember, marriage bonds are ultimately stronger than ties between sisters. The daughter had continued reading her book. And soon after, she had cut off her hair. Rapunzel, her brother-in-law had said once, as he watched her dry her hair in the courtyard and it fell like black silk below her knees. Rapunzel, he said again, as the mother smiled and watched her child comb it with her fingers. Rapunzel, Rapunzel, let down your hair. Oh she won't do that, the mother had said, proud that she understood, she is too quiet and withdrawn, and her daughter had gone back to her room and the next day she had cut it off, just like that.

The mother finished her tea and continued her letter. Let me end with some advice, she wrote, and don't groan now. Firstly, keep your distance from American men. You are innocent and have no idea what men are like. Men have more physical feelings than women. I'm sure you understand. Platonic friendship between the two sexes does not exist. In America they do not even pretend that it does. There kissing is as casual as holding hands. And after that you know what happens. One thing can lead to another and the next thing we know you will bring us an American son-in-law. You know we will accept even that if we have to, but it will make us most unhappy.

Secondly, if there is an Indian association in your university, please join it. You might meet some nice Indian men there with the same interests that you have. For get-togethers there, always wear a sari and try to look pleasant. Your father doesn't believe in joining such associations, but I feel it is a must.

The mother was tired of giving advice. What changed you so much the last few months before you left? she wanted to cry, why was going abroad no longer an adventure but an escape? At the airport, when the mother hugged the daughter, she had felt with a mother's instinct that the daughter would not return.

There had been a brief period when her child had seemed suddenly happy, which was strange, considering her final exams were drawing closer. She would work late into the night and the mother would sometimes awaken at night to hear the sounds of her making coffee in the kitchen. Once, on the way to the bathroom she heard sounds of laughter in the kitchen and stepped in to see her daughter and son-in-law cooking a monstrous omelette. He had just returned from one of his late night jaunts. An omelette at one a.m., the mother grunted sleepily and the two laughed even more as the toast emerged burnt and the omelette stuck to the pan. Silly children, the mother said and went back to bed.

And then, a few weeks later, that peculiar, turbulent stillness as her daughter continued studying for her exams and stopped talking to all of them, her face pale and shadows under her eyes, emanating a tension that gripped the mother like tentacles and left the father hurt and confused. She snapped at them when they questioned her, so they stopped. I'll talk to her after the exams, the mother told herself. She even stopped having dinner with them, eating either before they all sat at the table, or much after, and then only in her room.

And that pinched look on her face . . . the mother jerked up. It was pain, not anger. Her daughter had been in pain, in pain. She was hiding something. Twelve years ago, when the child was ten, the mother had seen the same pinched, strained look on her face. The child bore her secret for three days, avoiding her parents and her sister, spending long hours in the bathroom and moving almost furtively around the house. The mother noticed that two rolls of cotton had disappeared from her dressing table drawer and that an old bedsheet she had left in the cupboard to cut up and use as dusters had also disappeared. On the third day she saw her daughter go to the bathroom with a suspicious lump in her shirt. She stopped her, her hands on the trembling child's arms, put her fingers into her shirt and took out a large roll of cotton. She guided the child to the bathroom, raised her skirt and pulled down her panties. The daughter watched her mother's face, her eyes filled with terror, waiting for the same terror to reflect on her face, as her mother saw the blood flowing from this unmentionable part of her body and recognised her daughter's imminent death. The mother said, my love, why didn't you tell me, and the child, seeing only compassion, knew she would live, and wept.

The omniscience of motherhood could last only so long, the mother thought, and she could no longer guess her daughter's secrets. Twelve years ago there had been the disappearing cotton and sheet, but now? The mother closed her eyes and her daughter's face swam before her, her eyes dark, that delicate nose and long plaited hair—no, no, it was gone now and she could never picture her with her new face. After her daughter had cut her hair, the mother temporarily lost her vivacity. And the daughter became uncharacteristically tidy—her room spick and span, her desk always in order, every corner dusted, even her cupboard neatly arranged. The mother's daily scoldings to her, which were equally her daily declarations of love, ceased, and she thought she would burst with sadness. So one day, when the mother saw her daughter standing in her room, looking out of the window, a large white handkerchief held to her face, the mother said, don't cry, my love, don't cry, and then, don't you know it's unhygienic to use someone else's hanky, does nothing I tell you register, my Rani? And her daughter, her face flushed, saying, it's clean, and the mother taking it out of her hand and smelling it and snorting, clean, what rubbish and it isn't even your father's, it's your brother-in-law's, it smells of him, and it did, of cigarettes and aftershave and God knows what else and the mother had put it for a wash.

The mother's face jerked up. Her fingers' grip on the pen loosened and her eyes dilated. Her daughter had not been crying. Her eyes, as they turned to her mother, had that pinched look, but they were clear as she removed the handkerchief from her nose. It had smelled of him as she held it there and she wasn't wiping her tears.

The mother moaned. If God was omniscient, it didn't seem to hurt him. Why hadn't He denied her the omniscience of motherhood? Oh my love, my love, the mother thought. She held her hand to her aching throat. Oh my love. The tears weren't coming now. She began to write. Sometimes when one is troubled, she wrote, and there is no solution for the trouble, prayer helps. It gives you the strength to carry on. I know you don't believe in rituals, but all I'm asking you to do is to light the lamp in the morning, light an agarbatti, fold your hands, close your eyes and think of truth and correct actions. That's all. Keep these items and the silver idol of Ganesha which I put into your suitcase in a corner in your cupboard or on your desk. For the mother, who had prayed all her life, prayer was like bathing or brushing her teeth or chopping onions. She had found some strength in the patterns these created, and sometimes, some peace. Once, when her husband reprimanded her for cooking only eight dishes for a dinner party, she had wanted to break all the crockery in the kitchen, but after five minutes in her corner with the Gods, she didn't break them. She couldn't explain this to her child. She couldn't say, it's all right, it happens; or say, you'll forget, knowing her daughter wouldn't. If you don't come back next year, she wrote, knowing her daughter wouldn't, I'll come and get you. She would pretend to have a heart attack, the mother said to herself, her heart beating very fast, her tears now falling very rapidly, holding her head in her hands, she would phone her daughter and say, I have to see you before I die, and then her daughter would come home, yes, she would come home, and she would grow her hair again.

ANITA RAU BADAMI

Anita Rau Badami was born in 1961 in Rourkela, Orissa, India. Her father was an engineer who designed trains, and she and her family moved frequently around India before she was twenty. Both of her parents spoke different Indian dialects, so English became the bridging language. As a child she was immersed in the myths and cultures of her parents and various multilingual railway workers, and these stories inform her work.

She was educated at the University of Madras and Sophia College in Bombay. In 1991 Badami emigrated with her husband to Calgary, Canada, where she earned an MA at the University of Calgary. Her master's thesis there was the basis for her first novel, *Tamarind Mem* (1997). Though she sees herself as "suspended between two worlds," she has said in an interview, "I don't think I could have written a novel if I had not left India. I find that the distance gives me perspective and passion" (cited in *Book Browse*). Her 2001 novel *The Hero's Walk* won the Commonwealth Prize for the Caribbean and Canadian region and a number of other awards. Her third novel, *Can You Hear the Nightbird Call?*, was published in 2006. She is the recipient of the Marian Engel Award given to an outstanding Canadian woman writer at midcareer.

Badami lives with her family in Montreal.

Ajji's Miracle

These days the old woman, Ajji, hobbles around the house so full of herself that if you poke her with a pin she might explode. She shouts orders, bullies the

22

servants, eats enormous meals and then farts painfully through the night. She makes such a racket screaming, "Amma, Amma, Ammamma!" before every resounding expulsion of gas, that nobody else can sleep. Her daughter-in-law Rukku, who was the queen of the house just a few months ago, can only watch sullenly, her mind full of vicious thoughts against Ajji. Sometimes she finds it difficult to believe the way things have been turned upside down in her own home. As for poor young Tara, she can do nothing but pout and cry a little and wait for Ajji's miracle to occur. After all, if it had not been for her, Ajji would still have been sitting in a corner of the house like a pile of old clothes, begging her grandchildren for love or, if not that, at least a piece of jaggery.

This is how it all changed.

There was a time when Ajji used to sit quietly in the verandah, peering at a religious book or staring out at the road. At twelve o'clock she would summon her younger grandchild, a boy of six, and say, "Go and tell your mother that you can hear Ajji's stomach grumbling. Go, go, my putta, my sweet lump of sugar."

She was too scared to approach Rukku herself. Who knew, if she was in a bad mood, she might make Ajji wait till two o'clock for her lunch. But the little boy now, he was different. He was his mother's pet, anything he said was law. Quite different from her attitude toward her daughter Tara. This caused a lot of friction in the house, naturally, for Tara was Ajji's favourite. She was the one who stole little bits of bella for Ajji when the old woman was overcome with a craving for something sweet, and it was she who always listened patiently to Ajji's rambling stories of gods and goddesses.

"Oh Ajji," the dear child would say, "tell me again about Lord Krishna and the snake," or, "Ajji, my favourite Ajji, tell me the one about Lord Ganesha and the moon."

In this lonely world full of loud-mouthed daughters-in-law and limp-as-pyjama sons, Tara's attentions made Ajji feel like she still existed. Toothless and fleshless Ajji was, but not a corpse yet. Oh yes, she still had her wits

about her! And all her jewellry, without which Ajji
might not have been able to maintain her precarious
position in this household. She thanked her good sense
often for having held on to her gold chains and rings
and diamond earrings and nose-studs, her bangles and
armbands. When her son Kitta was newly married, she
had been tempted to give her chains and earrings to
Rukku, so pretty and innocent she had looked. Lurking
under that charming exterior, however, was a screeching
rakshasi. Oh yes, how she had simpered and smiled and
worn those tight little blouses. How she had wrapped
her husband's eyes with ribbons of desire, until Kitta
was so drunk on her body juices that he willingly turned
over every penny that he earned to her. Not his mother,
mind, not like he used to, and with that pay packet, with
that little slip of a chèque, slid Ajji's power in the house
that her husband had built. In the blink of an eyelash
Rukku had usurped her throne, had become maharani,
the whip, Queen of England. Within a month of her
arrival, she had kicked Ajji out of her room into the
smallest chamber with one little window high in the wall,
right next to the noisy street. In front of Kitta though,
Rukku behaved like a respectful daughter-in-law, but as
soon as the fool left for work, she was transformed. No
use complaining to the besotted fool either. Yes, Ajji
admitted that her only son was an idiot, men never did
understand the currents that ran through a household
full of women. Only knew how to shift from one pair of
breasts to another. That's all, that's all, hunh! Ajji cursed
her own dead husband for leaving her in the shadow
of her son's cowardly frame, for leaving her to tolerate
Rukku's tyrannies.

The old woman had her own ways of taking revenge
though. Guerrilla style she would launch sneak attacks
and then retreat to her corner to sit there innocent as
an empty sky. Rukku's favourite sari would develop a
sudden tear, one of her slippers might disappear, the
screw of her gold earring would get lost, forcing her to
spend for a replacement. Ajji's favourite act of vengeance was to go to the neighbours' homes and ask for
food. "I should have died long ago," she would say,

wiping her eyes with the end of her sari. "I don't know what my past sins are that this body still exists. How much trouble it causes everybody, I can't bear to think about it."

At this point the neighbour might say kindly, "Come now Ajji, why are you so bitter today?"

And Ajji, wiping the wet off the end of her nose would reply, "Ah what can I say? I don't want to be accused of eating the salt from a house and then cursing it. Though, to be honest, that is all I get to eat these days you know, just salt and a bit of rice. Oh my sinful past, to have reduced me to this sorry state! Oh, oh, oh!"

The neighbour would pat Ajji on her shoulder and say, "It's all right Ajji. Why don't you come inside and eat something, you do look like you haven't eaten all day, poor thing."

And Ajji again, hiding her triumph, "I can't lie, may god bite my tongue if I do, I can't lie and say that I have eaten. But then she is my daughter-in-law after all, I chose her myself from a lineup long as this road for my son, so I must bear my sorrow in my own belly."

The old woman went to a different house each day. That way all the neighbours knew that Rukku was ill-treating her mother-in-law and, even better, Ajji got to taste so many different types of cooking—the rasam in the house next door was wonderful, the govardhan-kai palya in that one there was amazing, and nothing to beat the rich taste of puliyodarey from that one across the road.

When the girl Tara was born Rukku cried with disappointment at not having had a male child. But Ajji, lamenting her own fate in bearing only one son (who had turned into his wife's tail), immediately declared that her diamond earrings and three of the fat gold chains strung about her parchment neck would go to Tara when she was married. "Of course," she added, "it all depends on whose side of the family she takes after. I covered my daughter-in-law with gold when she stepped into this house and see where that has left me!"

Rukku could do nothing more than curse mentally and

say in her most ingratiating voice, "As it is I am wretched, instead of an heir for my husband I have produced a burden. Without your help how can we manage?" She gave Ajji a sweet smile and added, "See, the girl looks just like you. Promises to be a beauty!"

"Her eyes are like a pair of lotuses," agreed Ajji. "And her nose like the stem of a jasmine. I'll have to rub it with almond oil every day to keep it that way, like my own grandmother did for me you know." The next day when she did her lunchtime rounds of the neighbours' homes, Ajji said with a sigh, "Thank the lord Krishna she did not take after her mother. A nose like a cauliflower would have been her fate."

If the girl grew up the way Ajji wanted her to, the old woman reflected after the day was done, she would get a pair of diamond earrings. They were Ajji's most precious possessions, so heavy that they had pulled the holes of her earlobes out of shape and now hung on a thin slice of brown skin. Ajji had seen Rukku eyeing those earrings. Let her hunger for them, she thought, she isn't going to get them anyway. But by promising them alternately to Rukku and to Tara, Ajji knew that she could wring a fairly decent life for herself in this house. Yes, it was a good thing that a girl-child had crawled out of Rukku's womb.

When the boy-child was born, Tara receded even further in her mother's affections. She became a ghostly being who might have faded into nothingness if it had not been for Ajji's exuberant attentions. It was Ajji who sang to Tara when she was a baby, revelling in the sound of her own voice from which music had fled many years ago. "Jo-jo, laali mari, may sugar sprinkle your dreams, tender pink lilies touch you to sleep," she carolled, rocking and soothing and petting little Tara to sleep.

Every Sunday the grandmother massaged the girl's thin body with oil before giving her a hot bath. "Now that will make your arms flow like lotus stems," Ajji would say, kneading and slapping Tara's arms in the hot sun of the courtyard. "And that will make your face smoother than honey."

While Tara grumbled and cried as the sharp mustard oil stung her skin, and Rukku from inside the house yelled to the world that the old witch was giving the child an inflated sense of her importance, Ajji's hands coaxed lustre out of her grandchild's skin.

"Lucky for you your old granny is still alive to look after you," she said, twisting and wringing Tara's arms, grunting as she rubbed her back. "That mother of yours doesn't care. She is only waiting for the day some man will come for you, that's all. But I, I won't let you go anywhere, my pet, I will always be here for you." She would wait expectantly, her hands stilled and then smile when Tara said sulkily, "And I will always be here for you, my darling Ajji."

It was as if Tara's existence lent power to the old woman. So what if Rukku screamed and complained? As long as the girl was there, Ajji had a little corner in the house. The ritual continued even when the girl turned sixteen, grown taller, but still as slim as a bamboo shoot.

So it was that Ajji was the first to notice that Tara's breasts were developing unevenly. While the right one had attained the right size, the left remained flat. At first Ajji kept quiet about it, rubbing oil onto Tara's chest even harder, hoping to stimulate the force that lay beneath the skin and made breasts grow. When coconut oil proved ineffective, she spent her own money and bought castor oil, hoping the denser fluid would work better. Nothing at all. Ajji hobbled to the ayurvedic doctor down the street. She trusted him far more than she did the posh new fellows with modern ideas and foreign degrees who made you pay through your nose, cut off a part of your body and then sold it to somebody else for a fortune. Yes, yes, Ajji had heard all about those big hospitals and the things that went on in there. Why, just yesterday, the temple priest's sister was telling her about her aunt's grandson who went to the hospital with a sore throat. Only a sore throat, see? But he made a mistake going to a big-shot hospital. The priest told him not to but who listened to their elders these days? The smart suit doctor sent the boy to another doctor who sent him somewhere else and before he could say aan or oon, they had him on an operating table. Took out his appendix, they said, but who knows what else they pulled out? The boy had been married six years now and still his wife's belly remained flat! Worse, who knew what they had put in? These foreign-trained doctors did all sorts of inauspicious things, put monkeys' hearts in humans, pigs' kidneys, dogs' eyeballs, anything they could lay their hands on!

Ajji came away from the doctor bearing a large jar of malam from Singapore. The doctor had assured her that it contained nothing but the best herbs and berries, ancient ones that did not grow in India anymore.

For the next few weeks Ajji religiously massaged Tara's chest with the ointment. She also forced the girl to eat large balls of fresh butter—perhaps, she thought, the child was not getting enough fatty foods. The jar of malam was almost empty and Tara's left breast remained indifferent to the attention.

It was time, Ajji felt, that Rukku be alerted to the problem. "I don't want to try anything else," she reflected. "Then if something happens, all the blame will be on my head. No, I will tell that stupid woman, Tara is her daughter after all."

She went on the offensive right away. "Enh, Rukku, do you know anything that is going on in this house? Your own daughter, that too? If my eyes, old but still good, hadn't noticed, god only knows what would have happened!"

"What? What is it?" demanded Rukku, her mind racing over all the things that could have happened to a girl. "Is it the pimply boy in Number 65? I have told that wretched Tara not to go by that house. So many different roads to school and still she will go that way only. That loafer sits there ogling girls all day. What has he done to Tara?"

"If your daughter was like you then you would have to worry," replied Ajji in a sly voice.

"What do you mean, you evil old gossip? Eat my food and spread rumours about me!" Rukku screamed.

"You think these old eyes haven't seen what goes on in this house? You think I haven't seen how you talk to that cousin of yours? Oh my, he is like a brother, you said, oh my! But leave all that for now, perhaps he is like your brother, my eyes might be worse than I thought. Let us worry about your daughter now."

"Enh, old woman, you want to lose your corner in this house?" Rukku said, fiercely tucking the end of her sari pallu into her waistband. "Maybe you want to take your gold chains and earrings and all and buy a room somewhere else, enh?"

Ajji sucked in her teeth and filled her eyes with tears. "How quickly you get angry, my dear. Didn't I say that my eyes were bad? I am an old woman, sometimes my tongue gets jumbled up and then, who knows what not falls out. Eh, all I worry about is your daughter."

Rukku was silent although she ached to hear what the problem was.

"Maybe you can try on my red-stone bangles this Deepavali," bargained Ajji. "Of course that will be possible only if I am still in the house."

"Ajji, you are like my own mother," Rukku said, already thinking of a sari to match the bangles. "I know that you have our welfare at heart always. Now tell me what is wrong with Tara."

They would start with prayer, they decided, the two of them, Rukku and Ajji. Over the next couple of weeks they covered all the temples in the city. For good measure they appealed to the Muslim and Christian gods as well. God was god, so what did it matter? They went to the big mosque in Fathima Bazaar and tied little wish threads onto pillars that were already covered with thousands of coloured ribbons and paper messages, all addressed to Allah the merciful.

Ajji was a bit doubtful about this method. "Suppose the Muslim god finds it difficult to read Tamil?" she asked.

"No, no," assured a woman next to her. "The almighty one is wise in the language of all beings."

Another day they pushed through the throngs into the

Basilica of Mary and Jesus. That was Rukku's idea.
Every day in the papers she had seen messages from the
devoted thanking the infant Jesus for a variety of favours
granted. At the gates of the basilica, Ajji and Rukku
bought a tin cutout of a female torso to deposit in the
prayer box along with money. Cutouts of various parts
of the body were available here. If you were lame you
bought a foot or a whole leg. There were eyes, noses,
ears, heads. This god, Ajji thought, was just like Lord
Venkateshwara in Tirupathi—words were not enough to
tell him about your problems!

"But how will this baby god know which breast isn't
growing?" she asked, ever alive to the various misinter-
pretations even a god could put on earthly messages.

Rukku solved the problem by marking off the afflicted
breast with a dab of kumkum liquid that she carried in
her purse. It wasn't indelible, but Rukku had faith that
the mark would stay long enough for the infant Jesus to
see it. Besides, wasn't god omniscient?

A whole month went by and the two women noticed no
change in Tara's anatomy. Rukku decided that it was
time to tell her husband about this family crisis.

"What can I do?" he demanded irritably. "This is a
woman's matter. What do I know about all this? I am a
busy man, so much work in the office and then I have
to come home to solve your problems too?"

"Is she my daughter only?" demanded Rukku. "Did
I produce her like Kunthi? Simply held out my arms to
the sun and said give me a child and a child I got?"

"Okay, okay," said her husband, defeated by the noise
that Rukku was creating. "I will ask the company doctor
and see what happens."

The doctor had so many suggestions that Rukku's husband came home with his head abuzz with strange medical terms and a worried feeling that a lot of money was
involved. He also got the name of a specialist in the
field, who was, as the company doctor put it, "world
famous in all of South India for his thorough knowledge
of the subject."

*   *   *

Ajji insisted on accompanying the family to the specialist's office despite her fear of doctors. She was certain that if he was a fraud, she would be able to spot him straightaway.

The specialist examined Tara and said that the only option was surgery. A Silastic percutaneous tissue-expander would be inserted. This object with a pompous name was only available abroad. Rukku's husband said that they would think things over and hustled his family out.

"See?" Ajji said triumphantly. "He wants to put rubber bands inside my child's body. I told you these modern fellows are no good. But who wants to listen to me?"

Tara started to weep noisily. Her life appeared to have been reduced to two consuming problems—the breast and how to get her married before the world noticed its absence. Nobody tried to comfort her. Rukku was busy thinking of inexpensive solutions, and Ajji, excited by the smell of problems and conflict, wondered if she could ask the taxi to stop at Grand Sweets for a moment. The thought of their fresh sugar-soaked janghris made her stomach yearn.

"Only abroad you can get this elastic thing," Rukku said thoughtfully. "I will write to my cousin Ramu. He will surely help. After all, my grandfather was the one who set his grandfather up in business. So their family fortunes are really due to the goodness of my grandfather."

Cousin Ramu replied almost immediately from New York. He offered his sympathies but was noncommittal about sending the tissue-expander. It was a product that had been banned in the US, he said, due to possible side effects. And if he did manage to procure one, there was the added complication of cost. A tissue-expander was expensive, and although Cousin Ramu would be only too happy to bear the cost for his beloved cousin, he didn't think it was a good idea to endanger her daughter's health with the product.

Rukku was disappointed with the letter. She had expected her cousin to mail the tissue-expander by return mail. It also gave Ajji the chance to snipe about Rukku's family. "Now if it was my cousin," the old woman remarked complacently, "he would have sent the elastic immediately. But of course only the blessed have such families."

"So what do we do now?" Rukku asked, ignoring Ajji's comments. "Not only do I have a daughter-headache, but a daughter with a problem."

"Don't worry, I will go on a fast," Ajji declared impulsively. "Such a strong fast it will be, I tell you, the very heavens will shake. The only things that I will eat are fruit and popcorn."

"What kind of fast is that?" Rukku asked. "For a strong fast you should not even touch water."

"I am too old for that," said Ajji. "The gods will understand that I am doing the best that I can. Even Gandhiji ate bananas when he was fasting and he got independence for the country."

Ajji hadn't planned to fast for more than a week. She thought that her son would decide on an operation before the week ran out. But Kitta was not willing to spend the money yet.

"So what are we going to do?" demanded Ajji, whose stomach was making urgent demands for spicy sambhar, jackfruit-seed curry and lemon rice. This fast business did not agree with her at all.

"I will break a few more coconuts at the Venkateshwara temple and you keep your fast. God will surely listen to two helpless women," Rukku said.

Ajji grumbled under her breath and included potato chips fried in ghee, sago uppuma, and ice cream in her list of foods that could be eaten during a fast. She told all her neighbours about the fast and the sacrifices that she was making for her granddaughter. Now that everybody on the street knew about the missing breast, poor Tara couldn't leave the house without somebody asking about it. She stopped going out altogether.

"Why did you tell everybody?" she raged at Ajji, who merely patted her on the head and went out to meet a neighbour. Life was finally becoming more interesting than it had been all these barren years and Ajji was not about to let Tara's wounded feelings get in the way of her own enjoyment.

The neighbour had brought some guava jelly for Ajji. "I know you are fasting, Ajji," the neighbour said. "But you can keep this and have it later."

"Oh but this is fruit after all," Ajji said. "It is allowed."

The neighbour, puffed up with the idea of having a major fast like this happening right next door, told everybody she knew about Ajji. "Her determination is as terrible as Parvati-devi's," she said, carried away somewhat. "Sometimes when she is totally immersed, I can even feel the ground shudder!"

Drawn by the spectacle of a girl without a breast, people from other streets stopped by to see Tara and ended up touching Ajji's feet. The old woman thrived on the fruit and ice cream that she ate every day even though it upset her digestion a bit. She loved all the attention, even though the original aim of it all was Tara, who refused to show her face outside her room. She demanded fresh lime juice every afternoon and insisted that Rukku squeeze it herself.

"What is the need for all this drama?" Rukku wanted to know, goaded beyond endurance.

"Drama? I am only doing this for your daughter. Now that everybody in the city knows about her problem, only a miracle can find her a groom." She turned tragic eyes upon her audience of neighbours who had started trickling in. "After all this penance I am doing my ancient body needs a little sugar. But if my daughter-in-law cannot afford this small indulgence then I will do without it. What is the worst that will happen? I will die of thirst, that is all."

Naturally one of her neighbours offered to bring her a jug of lime juice every day and Rukku could only grind her teeth and yell at the servant maid. She was bitter about this turn of events. She still had Kitta's pay packets but the power in the home had shifted to Ajji. Wasn't the old witch supposed to be fasting for the sake of her granddaughter? Everybody appeared to have forgotten this small fact. A month had gone by since that visit to the doctor, Tara's breast remained flat, but Ajji's eyes sparkled with all the food that she was eating. Yesterday it was potatoes roasted in ghee, today she said that Lord Shiva had appeared to her in a dream and ordered her to eat puli-shaadam on his behalf.

Well, thought Rukku, the old woman had better enjoy this state of affairs. It would surely not last very much longer. Once Tara was tied to some man, things would swing back to normal here. Now with Ajji's growing fame the family prestige had gone up several notches. They were getting offers for the girl's hand. To be connected by marriage to a divinely inspired grandmother was considered an advantage. Perhaps, thought Rukku, they would settle on that boy from the Parthasarathy family. How did it matter if he was so much older than Tara? Till the marriage though, Rukku would have to tolerate Ajji with her ordering and her pretending and her heckling, her eating and farting through the night. But Rukku could wait. She had the patience of a vulture.

In the verandah, Ajji shut her eyes and rocked happily. Her brain clicked busily. She wondered how she could prevent the match from the Parthasarathy family. She couldn't say anything about the horoscopes, she didn't even know which end of it was the right way up. But perhaps she could find an inauspicious mole or twitch on the boy's face and play it up. Tara could wait a bit to get married, Ajji had never had such a good time in her life. Who could have imagined the turn that her old and hitherto miserable life had taken? Truly it was a miracle.

SHAUNA SINGH BALDWIN

Shauna Singh Baldwin was born in Montreal in 1962, grew up in India, and now lives in Milwaukee, Wisconsin. She holds an MBA from Marquette University. She started out as an independent radio producer, hosting *Sunno!*, an East Indian–American radio program.

Baldwin began her writing career as the coauthor of *A Foreign Visitor's Survival Guide to America* (1992). Her first short story collection, *English Lessons and Other Stories* (1996), received the Friends of American Writers Award. Her bestselling first novel, *What the Body Remembers* (1999), about the lives of two women in a polygamous marriage during the 1947 partition of India, was awarded the 2000 Commonwealth Prize for Best Book. Of the novel the *London Times* wrote, "The characters shimmer with life. . . . [T]heir individual psychological journeys are instantly recognizable . . . open up another world and yet offer a glimpse of humanity that is both intimate and universal." The novel has been translated into eleven languages. *The Tiger Claw* (2004), a novel set in Vichy, France, which chronicles a Sufi Muslim woman's search for her beloved, was nominated for Canada's prestigious Giller Prize. A second short story collection, *We Are Not in Pakistan*, was published in 2007.

Currently, she and her husband own the Safe House, an espionage-themed restaurant in Milwaukee.

Nothing Must Spoil This Visit

"Watch it!"

Janet winced as the Maruti swerved onto gravel to avoid another overburdened truck. She turned to glare at its driver, but all she could see were the words painted on the back: "Horn Please OK TA TA." In Toronto he'd have been stopped for speeding, not wearing a seat belt, reckless endangerment, driving on the wrong side of the road, you name it.

"Relax," unflappable Arvind said. "Pretend you're on a ride at Canada's Wonderland."

"I'm trying."

"Wait till we get off the GT Road—the climb to Shimla is fabulous. You'll love it."

A rose-silver dawn edged out the dark and Janet peered at the parched barren flatness of the north Indian plain. A slow tickle of sweat began its daily crawl at her temples. Soon, the sun knifed the sky and a fine dust jetted from the car's useless air conditioner and began to settle thick on her contact lenses. She leaned forward and turned it off. Arvind had begun another lesson in Indian history.

"We're passing through Panipat. Three battles were fought on those fields." He pointed, but all she could see were roadside shacks, three-wheeled tempos carrying loads cloaked in jute bags, men on bicycles, always more bicycles. She rolled down the window, unfettering the hot breath of May; it flattened her into the black vinyl.

"Want some sunscreen?" She offered him the plastic tube she'd thought to buy at Shoppers Drug Mart; Arvind waved it away as he wove the car between plodding bullock carts and listing, vomit-streaked buses.

India, up close. Ugliness, dirt, poverty, people. Janet closed smarting eyes.

At the white-marbled Indira Gandhi International Airport a week ago, they had been met by Kamal and his wife, Chaya. Janet had expected the brothers to be more demonstrative after ten years apart, but they'd given one another a ritual hug, no more. She'd said to Kamal, "I didn't expect you to be taller than Arvind—he always calls you his little brother."

She hadn't been able to tell if Kamal's reply was sarcastic or just overly formal. "Arvind is shorter only because he no longer wears a turban."

Chaya had sparked to life briefly under that fluorescent glare—and never since. Bedecked and a-jingle with gold bracelets, gold anklets and gold chains for their four a.m. arrival, she had first held Arvind close and then scanned Janet with a curiosity that took in her travel-crumpled jeans, clear-plastic-rimmed spectacles and the remnant of a perm in her brown hair.

"She's very fair," she said to Arvind.

"She'll get a tan on this trip!" he replied.

Janet found herself snapping at Arvind, "Come on, let's get going."

Chaya still held Arvind's arm.

They followed Kamal's jeans and kurta and let his glowering intensity cut through the press of the crowds. He hailed a darting brown uniform to carry the luggage, which was full of 220-volt appliances Arvind had bought in Little India, and took custody himself of the duty free liquor bag, saying to Arvind, "Doctor-sahib still drinks all Papaji's whisky."

Janet could not imagine spry, gallant Papaji ever needing a doctor, but during their week in Delhi she'd realized Doctor-sahib was Mumji's buddy. He dropped in punctually at seven every evening to ask about Mumji's blood pressure and to lean his coconut-oiled head on the back of her crimson velvet sofa, swirling a two-inch Patiala-peg of prohibited pleasure.

Mumji was as youthful and charming and gracious as Janet remembered her from that week in Montreal at their wedding five years ago, petite and perfumed in a starched cotton sari, her hair-netted bun of black hair firm at the nape of her neck, her Nina Ricci sunglasses and a solid silver box of sweet-smelling supari always within reach.

Really, Arvind's family had been welcoming and kind. At the sandbagged black-and-white-striped blockade at the Punjab border, Arvind wasn't questioned after the AK-47-toting policeman looked at his brown skin and mustache through the driver's window. He didn't volunteer his Canadian passport when Janet's was requested for a check of its special visa for the state of Punjab. The policeman raked her bare legs with a lecherous eye and permitted her, finally, to return to the car. He spoke briefly to Arvind in Hindi.

"What did he say?" Janet asked.

"He said I picked up a mame." He grinned at her.

"Aunty Mame?" Surely the policeman couldn't have seen that film.

"No. A mame is a contraction of mem-sahib."

"Not meant as a polite term, I'm sure."

"It's what they call all white women."

"Why didn't you show him your passport?" Her sense of fairness was offended.

"He didn't ask."

"Why not?"

"He took me for a Hindu, since I no longer wear a turban."

"Why didn't you correct him?"

Arvind slowed for bright orange Escort tractors rainbowed with the turbans of farmers, but he didn't answer.

It wasn't a bit like him and it wasn't fair to her—she wasn't some ignorant tourist who'd read just one guidebook; she was a woman who'd learned to make perfect samosas for him from Mrs. Yogi Bhajan's cookbook and who'd studied the art and the history of India.

"Why didn't you correct him?" she repeated.

Arvind still didn't answer.

"Look! Stop, Arvind! There's a pottery stall."

Arvind pulled over and watched Janet bound out of the car, rupees at the ready. Those gaudy Hindu idols weren't the calibre of the artifacts she worked to restore at the Royal Ontario Museum, but they would feed her thirst for the exotic for a while. He checked the car's water level while he waited—what Janet called his engineer's tinkering was all the meditation or prayer he ever needed. Anyu, strange old Hungarian bird, had waited till Janet was ten to break the news about Santa Claus, but she'd never taught Janet to pray.

"Arvind, come see the baskets. Such beautiful baskets."

Janet didn't wait for him anyway. She, who wouldn't trust herself to bargain with a Yonge Street junk dealer, would bargain in broken Hindi for baskets, as if a dollar here or there would make a difference to their life.

She was as excited in India as he'd been when he first arrived in Montreal. He'd met her the month after he'd bought his first Jaguar. She'd read to him from her art history textbooks while he lay, asphalt cool at his back, under the car, and she'd trusted he'd take her someplace beautiful . . . eventually. He'd tried to show her the rhyme and the reason of that Jag's engine, but she couldn't find beauty under all that dirt and grease.

How could he expect her to understand why he hadn't shown the policeman his passport with the visa permitting him to enter his home state, the visa so stamped and official? There she was, aglow in that inviolable cocoon of Canadian niceness. Whereas he and the policeman were like the twigs of those baskets in the stall—woven together, yet tense with a contained rebellion. You couldn't pull one twig from those baskets without unraveling the whole. He couldn't talk about possible danger and unpleasantness if it were obvious he was a Sikh, couldn't remind her about the articles she'd clipped from the paper for him—articles on the massacre of Sikhs at the Golden Temple just two years ago, articles that referred to all Sikhs as terrorists. Honesty may be the best policy when you're faced with a Mountie, but here . . . nothing must spoil this visit.

"How much is pachas rupaya?" The shopkeeper's English vocabulary was proving as limited as Janet's Hindi.

"Fifty," he said. Somewhere between Montreal and Toronto, he'd given up arguing against her belief that people all over the world are the same, just with different languages, art and music. When they'd abandoned his turbans and left long arcs of his brown-black hair on the floor of a Greek barbershop in Montreal, a city become hostile to his English, hadn't she suppressed her French, ignoring Toronto's bilingual road signs? She who spoke Hungarian on her Sunday long-distance phone calls to Anyu now called herself an anglophone.

"Can we fit these in the back seat?" Janet beamed, a basket under each arm.

In Montreal, Janet had been enchanted when he had bent his (then) turbaned head over a sitar, cross-legged on his sole item of furniture, a mattress. It must have been Anyu who'd made her daughter this seeker of beautiful things, past and present. Anyu, who must have taken a vow on arriving in Canada to fashion her Janet's life into a procession of perfect, agreeable, beautiful experiences. Somehow, Anyu had protected her daughter's illusions through the seventies, and now he had the job.

"Move the garment bag, would you?" Janet's triumph was palpable.

But he knew Anyu still warned from Montreal, "Don't have children yet, it may not work out." Janet hadn't told Anyu yet (and neither had he) that it wasn't a matter of choice.

Looking out at earth-tone people blending into earth-tone villages—some with TV antennae rising from thatch—Janet remembered how enthusiastic she'd been about this trip. She wanted to experience India with him, his India, the India he'd told her of so many times. As soon as they'd arrived at his parents' home, Arvind had changed from pants and a jacket and tie to a white kurta-pyjama and sandals. When she'd worn a sari, thinking to please Papaji, the whole family had applauded.

Only Chaya remarked, "She walks so funny in a sari."

It was true, of course. Arvind tried to teach her to glide a little more gracefully, but she'd reverted to pants and a T-shirt the next day.

Mumji, always so charming, had tried to persuade her to return to the unaccustomed garb or at least try a salwar kameez, murmuring, "The best clothes for heat and modesty have been tested over centuries, dear."

Arvind had come to her defense. "Janet comes from a young country, Mumji. Women in Canada believe in learning by experience."

She'd seen Kamal then, looking over at Chaya as

though afraid this remark was inappropriate for her ears, but Chaya sat with her vacuous smile, stroking her son's handkerchiefed topknot.

Mumji had coaxed everyone back into harmony with a teasing smile at Arvind.

"Not everything needs to be reinvented, even by engineers." She had gone on to admire the width of Janet's hips, venturing the ever-so-gentle reminder that it was "high time" she provided Arvind's family with grandchildren. Mumji was right—like Arvind, Janet was four years away from forty—but. . . . Now Janet told herself she should expect Mumji's gentle intrusions, and anyway, Mumji was in Delhi, probably fanning herself in the languid dark of her air-conditioned bedroom with one of her *Femina* magazines. Janet imagined herself telling Anyu that her daughter had poured mustard-seed oil on a wood threshold and touched the feet of her husband's mother. Anyu, who had lived under Communists, would say, "You start bowing your head once, it gets easier and easier."

Outside Chandigarh, Arvind stopped at a roadside Government Milk Bar, but Janet was wary of germs in the chilled bottles of sweetened spiced milk. At Kalka, he waded through a throng of indolent men in white kurta-pyjamas to get her a bottle of Campa Cola to wash down the dust. She wiped the top of the bottle with a fastidious white tissue and shook her head when he offered to throw it from the car window when she was finished.

The car began to climb the Himalayas. Cooler air released them from the frenetic pulse of the plains. The scent of pine logs mixed with black diesel truck fumes as the little car screeched up winding roads that gripped the mountain "like a python's coils," Arvind said, laughing at her shudder.

He pointed to the precipitous drop to the valley below.

"That drop is called the khud," he said.

"Kud." She could not aspirate the consonant, even after five years of marriage. And anyway, she wasn't planning to use Hindi or Punjabi in Toronto.

At Solan, he stopped to buy beer as though it were a normal adjunct to driving—he even took a swig before getting back in the car. She would not remonstrate. This trip, this pilgrimage, was too important. Nothing must spoil it. Besides, the cool peace of the terraced mountains etched against the afternoon sky, the ebbing of crowds, and the absence of Papaji, Mumji, Doctor-sahib, Kamal and Chaya had lulled her to a dreamy calm. She waved at Tibetan refugee women chiseling stone from the mountain, sleeping babies slung upon their backs, and was rewarded by smiles tinged with slight puzzlement, but never a wave.

Chaya knew Kamal was pretending to be asleep as the morning preparations for Arvind and Janet's leave-taking were conducted in whispers outside the door. She left him alone long after the car had sped away up the next flyover on Ring Road; she wanted this time after Arvind was gone, this unaccustomed silence before any servants began their morning racket in the kitchen and before Papaji's Hindu tenant's wife began ringing her little bells and chanting the daily Aarti, to dream. What if, ten years ago, she had married Arvind instead, as everyone had intended?

It was planned so: Chaya would bring him a heart pure as Shimla snow, brimming with love, and he would take her to Canada, where she would bear many children.

After their engagement, she had grown suddenly shy of the boy Arvind whom she had known all her life. Everyone had permitted—expected—her to give him her love. When he left a month later, she had written him letters in her round, convent-educated hand. "How are you? By the grace of God your Mumji and Papaji and Kamal are well . . ." But Arvind wrote back about the vast number of books in the library at McGill, the underground shopping malls and cars in Montreal, how he'd bought a new hair dryer to dry his long hair, how he burnt two cups of sugar to caramel trying to make parshaad for the Gurdwara . . . as though Chaya had been his younger sister.

Mumji hadn't returned to bed, either, and Chaya

could hear her in the bathroom, filling a plastic water bucket for her morning bath. The tap sounded hollow-dry at first, then she heard a sputter, and the thin stream rose in pitch as the water began rising in the bucket. The mame had used two buckets of water yesterday and there had been none left for Chaya to bathe. Today Mumji would "forget" to leave enough water for her to wash her hair. But Chaya told herself she didn't mind; Arvind was gone with his pale, large-boned wife.

She unlocked the doli in the kitchen for the day, taking a mental inventory of the sugar and checking the level of the milk in the covered steel pan on the rack in the shaky old fridge. The cook used too much milk and sugar in his constant cups of tea till there wasn't enough left by evening for Chaya to make yoghurt. Had Mumji noticed Arvind had married a woman who didn't like yoghurt?

She counted the eggs. The dishwasher boy stole at least two a day and Mumji said Chaya just wasn't firm enough. But at least Mumji said it lovingly; her old college friends said there were worse mothers-in-law.

As far back as she could remember, when she and Arvind and Kamal were grubby playmates in Shimla, Mumji and she had recognized one another as Destiny. Mumji had treated her like a daughter, shielding her from Arvind's teasing and making Kamal apologize for pinching her stick-thin arms. When the time came, Mumji had taken a four-man rickshaw up the hill to her father's home. There, over a game of rummy and in sight of the langurs from the monkey temple at Jakhoo, she had personally, though obliquely, asked her father for his motherless daughter, to be married to Arvind. Chaya could still hear her father's belly laugh of triumph—such an honor from a good Khatri Sikh family, with land to inherit besides.

As she entered her son's room to wake him for school, Chaya wondered anew why Janet had denied herself and Arvind children to comfort them for all the things in life that might have been.

A practice chukker before the sun scorches the polo field, thought Kamal. Get rid of this, this . . . anger. He pulled on his breeches and the T-shirt with a Ralph Lauren polo player. Copied in India, but it would maha impress the other players at the Polo Club, anyway. Image—doesn't have to be real. None of the bloody buggers in America who wear forty-five-dollar shirts like this ever lift a polo stick. Image, yar, image. That's all there is.

He put a large brown finger through the brass rings on the boot trees and watched the pale wood slide from the leather. He always felt better around horses, booted and spurred, whip in left hand, mallet in right. A horse must have speed and obedience, and a mallet should be whippy. He took one from the rack in the corner of the room and centered its handle in his palm, testing its spring against the floor. This one was perfect—fifty-two inches. Better take a couple, even for practice; sometimes they broke under the force of his stroke.

Playing polo, he was in control. No one demanded his obedience. He had bought all four horses himself (on his allowance from Papaji). He played pivot on most teams, the player ready to hurtle into the fray to change the direction of the game, unzipping the air with the cut of a backhand or an under-the-neck thwack of bamboo upon bamboo. In the thunder of hooves and the sweating, clashing, knee-to-knee ride-offs he could pretend he was Raja Ranjit Singh and forget he was Kamal.

He heard Chaya in the kitchen and thought he would shout to her to bring him a bottle of cold water. But she would be slow and he was anxious to leave. She was always slow. It really didn't matter—she came from good blood and she had given him a son. What more was there? At least she wasn't like Janet, brash and talkative, asking questions as though she had a right to the answers.

What did Arvind see in Janet? A woman who appeared not to need a man. These foreign women, though, they talk their heads off against male chauvinism, but they really like it, they like surrendering to a real man. Look at their movies—full of gaunt red-lipped women thrusting their come-hither pelvises at every eye. No sweetness, no kindness, no softness. Unbroken fillies.

And Arvind. He was the one who'd had all the advantages. The one who'd removed himself so easily from the responsibilities of love and obedience. Sent abroad to study after acting like an idealist idiot, organizing a protest against Mrs. Gandhi's dictatorship . . . now he's a hotshot engineer, come to show off his white wife. What did he want Kamal to do, fall down and admire him? Forget it, yar.

Kamal gave a final tug at the last spiral of his partridge-coloured turban, clumped down the stairs and folded himself into Papaji's Fiat.

Woodville Hotel was cool, gracious and Victorian, but Arvind couldn't wait to walk down the hill the next morning to Knollswood, his grandfather's home. Janet watched him over the rim of a chipped teacup at breakfast in the wainscoted dining room; she hadn't seen him so oblivious to his surroundings since the last time he played the sitar.

"Are we taking the car?" she asked.

"We can't. Only VIP's cars can drive from here to the Cart Road."

Really, Arvind looked quite exotic in his Indian costume—he'd be offended if she called it a costume out loud—but he'd be cold in that thin muslin. She put on her sneakers and a Marks and Spencer sweater over corduroy pants.

He stopped her at the Cart Road above the spur. "Look for the red roof and the apple orchard beside it." The hundred-year-old house sprawled on the knoll with the green-brown khud falling away on one side, but its red roof was peeling and the tin-sheet grey showed through. Between the columns of pines she saw only row upon row of concrete government flats cantilevered between a few sorry apple trees.

They skittered down the steep dirt road, roots of trees offering them natural steps, pine needles crunching underfoot.

"There are the water tanks my grandfather built in the seventies so we would have running water."

Then Knollswood loomed before them, Arvind's days

of playing cricket with Kamal but a moment in its memory. This house, he told her, knew solar-topeed Britishers and the mem-sahibs with their white parasols, their corsets and their pallid cheeks. And then the brown-skinned imitations of the British that followed.

Janet said, "Wouldn't it be beautiful if it were remodelled? I can see bay windows in place of those casements, and a driveway in place of the rickshaw circle there."

Arvind shook his head.

"How about a gazebo under that weeping willow," she went on. "And that flowerbed would look wonderful with geraniums."

Arvind walked away into the house, and she was left absorbed in the shushing peace of the Shimla wind in the pines.

For Arvind, this was the house in which he grew up. He half-expected it to be unchanged, with people transfixed like the people of Pompeii, everything just as he left it when he spun westward, slick-reeled in by Promise to a science-fiction continent of chrome, plastic, manicured lawns and vast uncultivated spaces. This was the house he took with him, carrying the worn magic of every room aloft on its Persian carpets. This was the house he reassembled halfway around the world in a Toronto suburb called Scarborough—Rajasthan miniatures, silver-framed photos, Brewer's dictionary, ivory and ebony chess set, Wedgwood dinner plates and all.

Once a Muslim lived at Knollswood—he bought it from the Britisher who saw the end of his Victorian world coming. The Muslim broke a wall so that Knollswood would open towards Mecca; ever since it had been like a woman, with two mouths for entry.

Arvind had told Janet's uncle, a contractor in Scarborough, that he wanted a house with two entrances, and Janet's uncle had said, "A front door and a back door— it is in the plans." But no, Arvind had said, "Build me a house with two front doors, and one must face Mecca, though," he'd hastened to add, "I am not a Muslim." Janet's uncle had given him a Hungarian shrug (shoul-

ders lifted, corners of the mouth pulled downward, eyebrows raised, head shaking).

Once, an amber monkey climbed through the skylight
and found a perch atop a jangling chandelier in the main
drawing room. Arvind stood in the spot where his grandfather's old cook had stood below the wide-eyed langur,
offering his bright blue turban so the jabbering mass
could land.

He had bought a chandelier just like that one in an
antique shop on Cumberland Street, but it had no memory of any amber monkey.

In the room where the apples used to be brought in
from the orchard for sorting by hand, Arvind's charpai
still stood—but it sagged slightly.

On the nightstand, a portable oblong with a 45-33-78
lever had played the songs from *My Fair Lady* and *Kati
Patang* for hours. Once a parrot alighted on its felt turn-
table, flipped the switch with a wing and sailed round,
bewildered as an immigrant on a new continent.

He was looking for other things in this house, things
he might have forgotten to recreate in the Scarborough
house, "home," as the realtors would say. He had
bought cut-glass vases and Victorian figurines on Bay
Street—a lady in a blue bonnet with her tiny filigreed
basket of lavender.

Now that he looked closely, he saw that the one he
bought was not as delicate as this one.

In the dining room was the ten-foot table where his
grandfather sat at one end, his grandmother at the other,
and each taught him different manners: manners for
eating English food and manners for eating Indian food.
At this table, he and Kamal sat straight-backed with
Mumji and Papaji, legs dangling as they listened to tales
of India's struggle for independence and their grandfather's hopes for the independent Republic of India.
When he was older, the men had gathered for chess
every night at this table, often till two in the morning,
and neither he nor Papaji nor Kamal ever beat the old
man once.

That brass samovar and sink where everyone washed
their hands before eating would be impractical; neither

he nor Janet would bother polishing all that elegant metal to the mirror shine he remembered.

In the kitchen, there should have been servants who would respond to his imperious shout and there should have been jute sacks of grain in the stone-flagged store-room. But there was only brown bowlegged Kaluram, the gardener-become-caretaker, who swatted with a rag at spiders in the mildewing cupboards.

In his grandmother's dressing room were the powders and creams of a woman who crimped her hair like Bette Davis and painted her lipstick over her lips to make a Cupid's bow. Checking the dressing table drawer, he found the flaking yellow pages of one of the Georgette Heyer novels she always read in secret, and he hid it away again. Everyone has things that should remain private.

He stood in the large bathroom remembering when the thunderboxes were taken away and old rickshaw men turned construction workers laid pink and white tile for his grandfather's lavatory, the day the posters from his grandfather's 1972 trip to England were hung on its walls and his grandmother blushed for the shame of those women. And how, after all the expense of install-ing a shower, the old man ordered a servant to bring in his brass basin and chowki to save water.

Arvind strained, almost believing he could hear the lilting recitation of the Asa di Vaar punctuated by the splash of the two-cup-size garvi rising and falling from the brass basin to his grandfather's body, but it was only the voices of the middle-class multitudes rising from the new government flats in the valley, voices carried to his ears on a gust of mountain wind.

Kaluram doddered up behind him. Loyalty was all this old fellow had to give now and Arvind fell back into feudal superiority, ordering him to bring tea for the mem-sahib.

Janet wandered through drawing rooms curtained in fad-ing raw silk, touching the white cotton dust covers. The bric-a-brac was mostly reproductions, and of the several volumes she examined in the library, not one was a first edition. The huge dark paintings with their ornate gilt

frames were copies or prints of European paintings. She
began to examine the black and white photographs that
dotted the rooms. Arvind's grandfather, young as Arvind
was now but carrying himself prouder. Wearing a metic-
ulous turban, a custom-tailored three-piece suit and
sporting a cane, he stood behind Arvind's grandmother,
seated, slender as a nymph, in a chiffon sari. Other couples, just like them. Serious-faced family poses—Papaji
and Mumji, Arvind and Kamal.

And a later one in colour, Arvind looking about
twenty-five and Chaya in a sari, smiling up at him, smiling an adoring smile.

This she took with her, footsteps creaking on the
wood floors out through the double doors onto the veranda. Kaluram brought them glasses of steaming tan-
coloured tea.

Kamal and Papaji began arguing so loudly at breakfast
that the cook and the dishwasher boy could hear them
in the kitchen and Mumji was becoming distraught. All
for nothing, she said, no reason whatsoever.

Chaya came out of the bedroom with a housecoat over
her petticoat and an untied sari on her arm. "Please.
Mumji will be upset. She cannot stand this fighting."

Kamal rounded on her. "You stay out of this. Go
shopping or something."

But Chaya listened anyway, retreating behind the bedroom door. She stored the little bits of themselves that
people give away when they are angry; it helped her
avoid causing displeasure.

"What will Arvind do with Knollswood? He doesn't
even live in India. He's married to a foreign woman."
Kamal was almost shouting.

Papaji said, "Beta, that's no way to talk about your
elder brother. I think it would give him some interest in
coming back to India, that's all."

"Give him some interest! Just give away the largest
piece of property we have left. For what? So that some
childless mame can live in it long-distance from Toronto? What about my son"—he paused to let the words
sink in—"your grandson?"

Papaji sidestepped the last question. "Beta, we did him a great wrong."

"You did. Mumji did. I didn't."

"That's not true. It was your fault." Papaji's fist thudded to the tablecloth; china clinked.

Kamal hissed, "It was an innocent mistake. I pay for it every day." Chaya knew this to be true. He pays for it and she pays for it.

"So does he," said his father, the shame of tainted blood-purity thickening his voice. "He ended up marrying a mame."

Forehead pressed to warm teak, Chaya listened. It is, she thought, a good thing to be an adjustable woman. An innocent motorcycle ride through the Shimla hills and you can end up married to a different man.

They were sitting on the veranda before the rickshaw circle in white cane chairs, barely-sipped tea resting on a cane coffee table, the mountain slope they had descended towering before them.

"You know, you're sitting in my grandfather's chair."

"I am?"

"Yes. He would sit in that chair and tell me how the British Raj brought so many good things to India. Railroads and the telegraph, for instance. We would argue for hours."

"Who won?"

"I did, I suppose. I was raised on history books written by Indians, and I knew all those railroads led nowhere we Indians wanted to go. Later, when he was gone and the arguments lay in the past, I saw educated people agree to dictatorship, censorship and propaganda so the trains he so admired would run on time."

"Aren't you glad you protested then?" She'd told his protest story to women friends at work, basking in their admiration of his heroism.

"It was not enough," he said.

"Enough that you had to leave the country."

"My father had enough money to make it possible. There were others for whom it was not possible."

"Does this house make you want to move back to

India?" A question asked in hope of denial; Anyu's voice saying, "This marriage will not work if you have to live in his country."

"Of course it does—but today, there are roadblocks all the way home for us Sikhs. And," he gestured at the remains of the apple orchard, "there's little of our old way of life that I'd want to continue. Can you imagine yourself living here or living with Papaji and all in Delhi?"

Her expression told him no.

"Then I wouldn't be able to move back here." Options that close need no further exploration.

"We could live somewhere." Now she was prepared to be generous, to explore possibilities as long as they would not move into the realm of the probable.

"Not unless we were prepared to live without many things."

"Your family doesn't live without many things," she noted. "Kaluram, on the other hand . . ."

"It's no longer a poor country. It's a country of very rich people and very poor people."

Anyu's voice: "You could never live in India; you are a woman raised in freedom." Freedom to do what, she sometimes wondered. Freedom to satisfy your curiosity if you have any, perhaps. She remembered the photograph and handed it to Arvind. "That's me with Chaya." Arvind examined the photograph, looking at himself as though looking at someone he used to know well.

Janet said, "She doesn't like me, I can tell."

"Chaya? Chaya likes everyone."

"She seems to like you very much." A question, a challenge.

He laid the photograph down before him, a poker player showing his hand.

"We were engaged for a year."

"You've never told me that." She made her voice expressionless. The voice she used at work, discussing exotic peoples' lives, other peoples' exotic history, in other times. Only this was her history, hers and his, and words that should have been said to her years before. Why did she care now, except that Chaya held his arm and smiled only when he was in the room?

"It was not I who engaged us," he said.

Knollswood sighed at her back. Not his choice, so he can't be held responsible. Not his choice. She, Janet, is. She, Janet alone, is.

"Why were you not married to her, then?" Why come halfway around the world to Janet instead?

He cupped the steaming glass in his brown palms. "I really never found out."

"Never found out!"

"No. I assumed she and Kamal fell in love. I was away at McGill at the time and I got a letter from Mumji simply telling me Chaya would be marrying Kamal instead." An engineer's matter-of-fact voice.

"And you never asked why?"

"I thought Kamal should have told me why."

"And he never did?" Now she was indignant for him. "Never."

"And Chaya? You never asked Chaya?"

"No. They were married by the time I received the letter. And," his hand reached for hers, "I had met you by then."

She was still adjusting to him. A new picture of him. A new picture of Chaya. She stared at the photograph a long, long moment. The pines unfurled and retreated and unfurled again, bucking the familiar pull of the azure sky.

Slowly, with care, she placed her hand in his. Nothing must spoil this visit.

Arvind gave Kaluram a hundred-rupee tip for a daughter's wedding and they made their way back to Woodville. He taught her to climb, lifting her weight from one haunch to the other with the bobbing gait of the leathery-skinned Pahari men who stared at her whiteness as they passed.

"The National Museum of Modern Art? I'll come with you, it wouldn't look nice for you to go alone." Mumji smiled her engaging smile.

Arvind and Janet were back in the furnace of Delhi. There were only a few days left before their return and many relatives to meet. Even the Taj Mahal would have to await their next visit.

Papaji had taken little interest in her thoughts about the trip to Shimla: Did she enjoy it? It was beautiful—mostly beautiful. That's good.

Arvind spent a long time in Papaji's office sanctum the day after they returned to Delhi. That evening, he pulled Janet into their room and closed the door.

"Would you believe it—he wanted to make me a gift of Knollswood." His voice wavered a little: he had been recognized as the eldest son, singled out for a blessing, acknowledged, included. Why had Papaji not spoken to them both together? It probably hadn't occurred to him to acknowledge her presence.

"What did you say?"

Arvind said, "I considered it, of course. And I thanked him."

"And?"

"And I said no."

"Because of me?"

"No—or not only because of you. Many reasons. Large presents carry large price tags. I'd have to fit in here again. I'd have to define achievement as Kamal does, by the extent of Papaji's or Mumji's approval. And going to Knollswood made me realize Anyu is right, there's no return to the past, so you might as well live where you are."

"I'm relieved, you know."

"I know."

But Janet's relief was short-lived; Papaji assumed it had been Janet's influence that caused his son to reject his munificent gift.

"How is Miss Janet?" he would say at breakfast.

"Fine, thank you," Janet would respond.

"And how is Mr. Henpecked Husband today?"

"Fine." Arvind's matter-of-factness was a match for him. It might even have been funny if Papaji hadn't looked so hurt all the time. Janet decided to ignore it; nothing must spoil this visit.

Kamal avoided everyone as usual. "I have to manage the workmen," he said. "They're repairing the tenants' hot-water hamam."

"I can help," said Arvind the engineer.

"And soil your hands?" said Kamal mockingly.

Not once had Janet managed to talk to Chaya or Mumji alone—always there were people and more people. She had not, she realized, learned to ignore the servants as they did.

Now she had asked to visit the National Museum of Modern Art for the chance to ask Mumji the questions that suspended her in that moment on the veranda at Knollswood. Since Shimla, Janet had watched Chaya closely. Would the Arvind she knew today have been happy with so passive a woman? Never an opinion, never any talk. Spoken at but mostly ignored. Rewarded with jewellry and sweetness for that silent, respectful obedience. And always that beautiful, ephemeral, meaningless smile. Then too, perhaps Arvind would have been different today if he'd married Chaya.

Was it her imagination, or did the rest of the family, especially that drink-guzzling, smiling Doctor-sahib, speak in Punjabi far more than they had when she and Arvind first arrived? Anyu's words about freedom came back—now Janet longed to keep a door closed, to take a walk by herself without company, to touch Arvind spontaneously in public. He was her lifeline to pleasant, clean, safe, perhaps even boring Canada.

At the National Museum of Modern Art, Mumji followed as Janet asked for a plan at the information desk. Five clerks at the desk launched into oral directions and then one of them thought to ask what she would like to see. Janet said she would like to know what artifacts and paintings were on display. The conversation began to circle the domed red sandstone lobby without hope of resolution till Mumji took off her sunglasses and intervened. "Thank you *so* much," she said in Hindi, folding her hands with her usual charm.

"Don't ask them, they don't know *anything*," she said as Janet followed the click of her tiny high heels through the red sandstone archways.

"Then why are they there?"

"They have to be somewhere," Mumji said with serene logic.

They wandered through empty rooms of mostly unla-

belled artifacts, and Mumji was a useless tour guide.
"Very rare. Thanjavur, I believe." She squinted at a
group of paintings.

Janet corrected her automatically. "Gujerat. Eighteenth
century."

Mumji frowned. Unaware of any offence, Janet
plunged further; air that smells of old secrets should be
filtered clean, washed and sanitized.

"How come . . ." she blurted, voice amplified in the
high-ceilinged stillness. "How come Chaya married
Kamal when she was engaged to Arvind?"

Mumji put on her reading glasses and peered through
a glass case for a while. When she answered, her voice
did not echo like Janet's. "She had to marry Kamal. He
had compromised her reputation."

That matter-of-factness, so like Arvind's.

Janet told herself to be delicate, sensitive to her
mother-in-law's culture. "Did they . . . sleep together?"

"I don't know," said Mumji. "Of course he said not."

There were many layers of Mumji's artifice that Janet
should have peeled away gently, so gently, but her time
in India was running out. "Then what did he *do* to her?"

No answer. Mumji delved into her purse. Janet placed
a hand on her arm. No sunglasses, she wanted to see
Mumji's eyes.

A look at Janet's set face and Mumji resumed. "After
she was engaged to Arvind, she lived with her father,
waiting for him to finish his studies in Canada and return. Kamal . . . Kamal took her for a ride on his motorcycle and they went for a picnic alone. . . . I have only
myself to blame for permitting it."

"And?" Janet wanted to shout, but that would dismay
Mumji further.

Janet could hear the vroom of a motorcycle, with a
young Kamal, not a brooding, caged Kamal but a laughing, clowning Kamal lifting a soft-bearded chin to the
Shimla wind. And Chaya seated behind him in a salwar
kameez, her chunni furling and unfurling like the pines.
A Chaya laughing and chattering and dreaming of living
with joy.

"And they had a flat tire, he said, somewhere way

above Shimla. I believed him, but the damage was done. She had spent the night *alone* with a man she was not promised to, *and it was my younger son.* Now . . ." Mumji was cloaking herself again in fragile gentility, "do you understand?"

"No." Janet wanted more. More. She could see Chaya look at Kamal as the motorcycle choked to a stop. She could imagine them beginning the unchaperoned walk to find a village, down past one precipitous khud, then another. Darkness before them turning the peace of the mountains to malevolence. Narrow roads to be hair-pinned up on one side and descended on the other. Chasms where a woman's reputation could free-fall to ruin.

Mumji continued, "Her father had given her to me for my son and I had betrayed their trust. I had to hon-our our pledge to take her, but . . ."

Gave her. Took her. As though Chaya were a thing. Janet told herself it was just Mumji's use of English. Oh Lord, now Mumji was in tears . . . how embarrassing.

"I could not give her to Arvind because . . ." Mumji's voice sank as though the pictures on the wall might hear, "because what if Kamal had lied?"

"Didn't you believe him?" Janet was aghast.

"I believed him, my love believed him. But my duty to Arvind was clear."

"So you wrote to Arvind and told him Chaya would marry Kamal."

"Yes."

"But Chaya loved Arvind, didn't she? I can still feel it."

"Love, shove. I gave her to Kamal and she was pro-tected, not ruined nor cast out. She has been treated well, like a daughter. She has been blessed with a son; what more could she ask for? After all, I chose her because I saw from the start she would be an adjustable woman."

Soon, Mumji recovered her agreeable composure and her sunglasses. Janet followed her in silence through the pale green rooms past somnolent security men.

Mumji asked, her bright, persuasive coaxing brooking no denial, "Wear a sari to please Papaji tonight?"

Janet smiled. It couldn't do any harm. There were only a few days left, and then she would return to her work at the Royal Ontario Museum and resume her contemplation of the exotic at a safe distance.

As they drove past ice cream carts at India Gate, Mumji said, "Please, you mustn't tell Arvind. Don't let anything like this spoil your visit."

The stands at the Polo Grounds were almost deserted except for relatives of a few polo players, loyal despite the heat. A bugle sounded the final chukker of the exhibition match and the players lined up for the throw-in. Kamal's team wore blue and gold. "Sikh colours," remarked Arvind. He was impatient today, as though he wanted to be somewhere else.

He would recite poverty statistics tonight, thought Janet. But she wouldn't let him spoil things right now. Because this is it, she thought. This is India. Pageantry and colour. She could say she had been to Arvind's country now, say, his brother plays polo, and watch her women-friends' eyes widen. She brought the camera up to her face.

"You need a telephoto lens," said Arvind. "You'll just get a lot of the field and a few clouds of dust in place of the players."

He was probably right, but she felt a little deflated. Always so realistic. Mirages reflected the players in the distance; they were knights in armour, a few of them turbaned instead of helmeted, but knights in armour nevertheless. A whistle from the umpire and Janet glanced at Arvind.

"Kamal hit the ball in front of a pony's legs in that ride-off," he said. "It'll be a sixty-yard penalty shot."

The players rose in their stirrups at the canter, horses reined in and snorting, as they moved across the field to the opposing team's goal. A helmeted player steadied his horse for the hit. His mallet made a perfect arc, lofting the ball to the mouth of the waiting goal. There was a flurry of hooves, a wild swiping of sticks and the sound of swearing within the mêlée. Then a flag went up, just in time for the call of the bugle.

The hot smell of horse sweat and manure assailed Janet and Arvind as they walked over to Kamal's string. He'd dismounted and his last pony was still heaving, stirrups thrown over the top of the saddle.

"Well played," said Arvind.

"We didn't win." Kamal peeled his shirt over his head and handed it to a waiting groom.

"Get together. Let me take a picture," Janet said.

"Some other time, Janet," said Arvind.

"Let her," said Kamal. "Let her take her pictures and move on."

"Smile," said Janet.

"Just one chota peg and then I must be getting back."

Doctor-sahib smiled his very-wide smile at Mumji, and Chaya rose to offer him the decanter. In her father's home, she was never allowed to pour whisky for men, but times had changed and Doctor-sahib was just like family. He should be, Mumji said daily; he had done so much for them. Still, Chaya couldn't bring herself to touch his sweaty hand; she kept her sari from touching the arm of his safari-suit jacket as she poured the duty-free whisky.

When his glass was replenished, he launched into a story he would rather have told with Arvind present, but Arvind had taken Janet for her never-ending shopping. It was the story of the night he sat with Mumji when Arvind had the mumps and a hundred-and-four-degree temperature.

"I stayed with your Mumji all night. I didn't leave Arvind's bedside once." No one who heard the story ever asked Doctor-sahib what medicines had worked or how his presence had cured Arvind of anything. It was enough that he'd been there, warding off disease with the alphabet talismans he wrote after his name. Even so, Chaya rather liked this story. Now Mumji's soft voice said in her ear, "Get Doctor-sahib some ice, Chaya."

Chaya went to the door to call for ice. When she returned, Doctor-sahib had begun his most favourite story. This wasn't one Chaya liked at all, but one that Doctor-sahib told often.

"Ten years ago your Mumji brought you to me, remember. So beautiful, so sick you were shaking and trembling like a leetle tulsi leaf."

Chaya nodded. Yes, she remembered.

Doctor-sahib wagged a plump finger at her. "It was just after your first wedding night. And you were screaming and shouting and crying like a madwoman."

Mumji shook her head left to right, left to right. "It was so bad we had to wrap her in a blanket so the neighbours wouldn't hear her screaming. If we had still been living in Shimla it wouldn't have been so bad, but here the houses are so close together every vendor in the street could hear her cries."

The cook sent the dishwasher boy in with the ice and Doctor-sahib swirled the honey-coloured bitterness about in his glass. "The monsoon had come so you all had returned to the plains for Kamal's wedding. The afternoon rain was so strong I remember the roads were steaming *pfffft*. The rain made everything green," cloying approval reached out as though threatening to embrace her, "and blessed you and Kamal with fertility."

She moved to sit down next to Mumji. Mumji stroked her arm gently. "My sweet daughter, how you frightened me then. I told Papaji, no matter what the expense, we must take her to Doctor-sahib this minute."

"So there I was in my office just bringing out my instruments for the day, and all of a sudden your Mumji was before me. 'Save my little Chaya!'"

Chaya looked at the floor, her face flushed. Doctor-sahib leaned forward, Mumji's best whisky glass held up to the light.

"I took you into my office and ..." a dramatic pause, "we had just one little talk and I saved you, because I knew you were a reasonable girl." Now a note of magnanimous triumph. "This whole family was saved from dishonour."

This was Mumji's signal to proffer the decanter. But Doctor-sahib said, No no. He must really be going. At the door, he placed two fingers under Chaya's chin and came close, exuding garlic and his pungent male odour. "Now you see, I was right—everything has turned out for the best."

But Chaya didn't remember any little talk. Chaya only remembered how Doctor-sahib had ripped the blanket from her shoulders and slapped her cheeks, shocking her into a state of whimpering docility.

The way Chaya remembered it, Doctor-sahib had lifted her into a chair and commanded she open the jaws she'd clenched tight since her body had been taken by Kamal. Then he had taken a clamp from the table and, holding her head in the crook of his arm, locked its steel coldness over her tongue.

The way she remembered it, he had stood behind her and twisted her tongue back in her throat until her whole body arched backwards and up and her screams were the terrified screams of a woman betrayed.

And then she remembered his narrowed dark eyes an inch from her own and his so-reasonable voice. "If you bring shame to this family, if your Mumji has to bring you to my office like this one more time, I will tear your tongue out and send it to your father."

And the so-reasonable voice went on, the pain increasing with each word till she thought he had decided to turn threat into action. "Your Mumji is a santini. You understand? A saint! She could have thrown you out when you and Kamal spent the night on that hill above Shimla. But she didn't. She loves you like a daughter—see, she even takes you to the doctor when you have a tantrum. Just remember that."

And then, when there were no screams left in her body, the merciful loosening of the clamp on her tongue till she could open her streaming eyes.

And later Mumji, entering the room. "Doctor-sahib, will she be all right?"

Doctor-sahib, returning the clamp to the white-clothed table. "Nothing to worry, dear lady. You have a very pretty little daughter-in-law. We just had a nice little talk. She was frightened that she would not be worthy of such a loving family. I told her she should be grateful—she is such a lucky girl, she has such a wonderful mother-in-law, such a handsome husband. I see so many women every day who are not so lucky."

Afterwards, Chaya didn't make a sound for three

whole days. Mumji had never needed to take her back to Doctor-sahib's office.

"Where would you like me to put these?" Chaya pointed to a pile of export-reject dresses Janet had bought at the shops on Janpath.

"Oh, shove them in somewhere, I don't care."

Really, Chaya was very little use, not much good at packing and incapable of making the simplest decisions. This woman who so nearly married her husband had a studied ineffectual quality to her incompetence. There were moments when the slight jingle of her jewelry was all that betrayed her presence.

Janet gave up and cleared a space on the bed. "Tell you what. Why don't you sit here and talk to me while I pack. Tell me about yourself."

Chaya sat down, confusion in her face.

"What is there to tell?"

"Tell me about you and Arvind, for instance." There, she had asked it, almost commanded it.

"There is nothing to tell." An automated voice.

"You were engaged to him before, weren't you?" A cross-examining barrister with a reluctant witness.

"Yes. I was engaged to Arvind but Mumji decided I should marry Kamal."

"Did that bother you?" Perhaps a psychiatrist's style might produce results.

"It was Mumji's right."

"But Chaya, what about you? If someone decided such an important matter for me, I would feel terrible. I would feel violated. I would feel angry."

Chaya asked, "What should I have done?"

She was being asked what answer she wanted Chaya to give. Tell her what to say and Chaya would say it. Harmony is the mask that covers the absence of song.

What did she want Chaya to say—that Arvind was her one true love? That she still loved him? Where would that leave Janet? And what right did she, Janet, have to tell Chaya she should be angry about any of the past? Anyu would say, "Anger is useful only when life can be otherwise."

"I'm sorry, Chaya." A weight in her voice.

Chaya nodded.

"I am sorry for you, too," she said.

"Sorry for me?"

"Yes, sorry for you, for you have given Arvind no children." Here lay the true test of womanhood for Chaya, the fulfillment of being, the source, however short in duration, of a pure and devoted love.

"I . . ." Janet began. It would be easy now to retreat into privacy—but her questions had allowed Chaya no such right and she could no longer lay claim to it for herself. She could talk about fulfillment in a life without children, tell Chaya there were other ways to know love, other ways of seeing joy, other ways to satisfy dreams of what might have been, but Chaya would never believe her.

Whenever she'd been confused as a child, Anyu had said, "Perhaps the truth would be a good start," so Janet said now, "It is Arvind who cannot have children."

Chaya gave her an uncomprehending stare.

"He had the mumps when he was a teenager, and now he cannot have children."

Chaya said, "You're lying."

"I'm not lying." Janet was indignant.

Chaya took a long, deep breath. Then she raised her childlike hands over her ears. "I'm not listening anymore. You're a very bad wife to say such terrible things about him."

"Chaya, it's true. Ask Arvind."

Chaya lowered her hands and looked at her sister-in-law. Then she began to rock herself forward and back, forward and back, and soon Janet realized she was laughing. Laughing! Laughing at her? At Arvind? At their pain?

"What is it, Chaya? Why are you laughing?" To be angry at Chaya would be like being angry at a child. She knelt on the floor before Chaya, taking her by the shoulders, shaking her gently.

Chaya stopped rocking. For the first time, Janet saw passion in the flare of her nostrils.

"I'm laughing at all of it. All of it. All of it. At Kamal who was worried about our son's inheritance, at Mumji who wants you to bear Arvind's children. At Papaji, who wanted his eldest son to come back to India. And . . ." dark eyes a few inches from Janet's own, "at myself for wanting all these years a man who could not have given me my child."

Janet drew back.

"Are you saying a man who cannot produce children is not worth marrying?"

"Perhaps," Chaya whispered, "not even worth loving."

Her eyes closed again. The rocking motion began again, this time from side to side as though Chaya were holding a baby. After a few moments, Chaya's eyes opened and she said, "I laughed at you, too, you know."

"I know. Why?"

"Because," said Chaya, as though pity were a prelude to friendship, "you will have to learn how to be an adjustable woman."

Janet returned to her packing, her movements swift and urgent. Nothing, but nothing, must spoil this visit.

RUSKIN BOND

Ruskin Bond was born in 1934 in Kasauli, in what was then the Punjab Province of India. His parents were first-generation British immigrants, and his father served in the RAF during World War II. After his parents divorced and his mother married a Punjabi-Hindu, Bond spent his childhood in various locations in the Himalayas, which he came to love. The social life in the hill stations of the Himalayan foothills became a prime source of inspiration in his later writing. He was sent to England for his education and began his writing career there. His first novel, *The Room on the Roof,* was published when he was twenty-one. In 1957, the novel won the John Llewellyn Rhys prize for a Commonwealth writer under thirty. It was later adapted as a film series by the BBC. In 1953, he published a sequel, *Vagrants in the Valley*. A later novel, *A Flight of Pigeons* (1980), was made into the highly acclaimed Merchant-Ivory film *Junoon*.

In 1992, he received the Sahitya Akademi Award for English writing in India for *Our Trees Still Grow in Dehra*. He was also the recipient of Padma Shri, one of the most prestigious awards in India, for his contributions to children's literature. Rich descriptions of the flora and fauna of the Himalayas abound in the more than one hundred short stories, essays, and novels, and more than thirty children's books that he has written over almost five decades. He lives in Mussoorie, India.

My Father's Trees in Dehra

Our trees still grow in Dehra. This is one part of the world where trees are a match for man. An old pipal may be cut down to make way for a new building; two pipal trees will sprout from the walls of the building. In Dehra the air is moist, the soil hospitable to seeds and probing roots. The valley of Dehra Dun lies between the first range of the Himalayas and the smaller but older Siwalik range. Dehra is an old town, but it was not in the reign of Rajput princes or Mughal kings that it really grew and flourished; it acquired a certain size and importance with the coming of British and Anglo-Indian settlers. The English have an affinity with trees, and in the rolling hills of Dehra they discovered a retreat which, in spite of snakes and mosquitoes, reminded them, just a little bit, of England's green and pleasant land.

The mountains to the north are austere and inhospitable; the plains to the south are flat, dry and dusty. But Dehra is green. I look out of the train window at daybreak to see the sal and shisham trees sweep by majestically, while trailing vines and great clumps of bamboo give the forest a darkness and density which add to its mystery. There are still a few tigers in these forests; only a few, and perhaps they will survive, to stalk the spotted deer and drink at forest pools.

I grew up in Dehra. My grandfather built a bungalow on the outskirts of the town at the turn of the century. The house was sold a few years after independence. No one knows me now in Dehra, for it is over twenty years since I left the place, and my boyhood friends are scattered and lost. And although the India of Kim is no more, and the Grand Trunk Road is now a procession of trucks instead of a slow-moving caravan of horses and camels, India is still a country in which people are easily lost and quickly forgotten.

From the station I can take either a taxi or a snappy little scooter-rickshaw (Dehra had neither before 1950), but, because I am on an unashamedly sentimental pilgrimage, I take a tonga, drawn by a lean, listless pony, and driven by a tubercular old Muslim in a shabby green waistcoat. Only two or three tongas stand outside the station. There were always twenty or thirty here in the nineteen-forties when I came home from boarding-school to be met at the station by my grandfather; but the days of the tonga are nearly over, and in many ways this is a good thing, because most tonga ponies are over-worked and underfed. Its wheels squeaking from lack of oil and its seat slipping out from under me, the tonga drags me through the bazaars of Dehra. A couple of miles at this slow, funereal pace makes me impatient to use my own legs, and I dismiss the tonga when we get to the small Dilaram Bazaar.

It is a good place from which to start walking.

The Dilaram Bazaar has not changed very much. The shops are run by a new generation of bakers, barbers and banias, but professions have not changed. The cob-blers belong to the lower castes, the bakers are Muslims, the tailors are Sikhs. Boys still fly kites from the flat rooftops, and women wash clothes on the canal steps. The canal comes down from Rajpur and goes underground here, to emerge about a mile away.

I have to walk only a furlong to reach my grand-father's house. The road is lined with eucalyptus, jaca-randa and laburnum trees. In the compounds there are small groves of mangoes, lichis and papayas. The poin-settia thrusts its scarlet leaves over garden walls. Every veranda has its bougainvillaea creeper, every garden its bed of marigolds. Potted palms, those symbols of Victorian snobbery, are popular with Indian house-wives. There are a few houses, but most of the bunga-lows were built by "old India hands" on their retirement from the army, the police or the railways. Most of the present owners are Indian businessmen or government officials.

I am standing outside my grandfather's house. The wall has been raised, and the wicket-gate has disap-peared; I cannot get a clear view of the house and gar-den. The name-plate identifies the owner as Major

General Saigal; the house has had more than one owner since my grandparents sold it in 1949.

On the other side of the road there is an orchard of lichi trees. This is not the season for fruit, and there is no one looking after the garden. By taking a little path that goes through the orchard, I reach higher ground and gain a better view of our old house.

Grandfather built the house with granite rocks taken from the foothills. It shows no sign of age. The lawn has disappeared; but the big jackfruit tree, giving shade to the side veranda, is still there. In this tree I spent my afternoons, absorbed in my *Magnet*s, *Champion*s and *Hotspur*s, while sticky mango juice trickled down my chin. (One could not eat the jackfruit unless it was cooked into a vegetable curry.) There was a hole in the bole of the tree in which I kept my pocket-knife, top, catapult and any badges or buttons that could be saved from my father's RAF tunics when he came home on leave. There was also an Iron Cross, a relic of the First World War, given to me by my grandfather. I have managed to keep the Iron Cross; but what did I do with my top and catapult? Memory fails me. Possibly they are still in the hole in the jackfruit tree; I must have forgotten to collect them when we went away after my father's death. I am seized by a whimsical urge to walk in at the gate, climb into the branches of the jackfruit tree, and recover my lost possessions. What would the present owner, the Major General (retired), have to say if I politely asked permission to look for a catapult left behind more than twenty years ago?

An old man is coming down the path through the lichi trees. He is not a Major General but a poor street vendor. He carries a small tin trunk on his head, and walks very slowly. When he sees me he stops and asks me if I will buy something. I can think of nothing I need, but the old man looks so tired, so very old, that I am afraid he will collapse if he moves any further along the path without resting. So I ask him to show me his wares. He cannot get the box off his head by himself, but together we manage to set it down in the shade, and the old man insists on spreading its entire contents on the grass; bangles, combs, shoelaces, safety-pins, cheap stationery, buttons, pomades, elastic and scores of other household necessities.

When I refuse buttons because there is no one to sew them on for me, he plies me with safety-pins. I say no; but as he moves from one article to another, his querulous, persuasive voice slowly wears down my resistance, and I end up by buying envelopes, a letter pad (pink roses on bright blue paper), a one-rupee fountain pen guaranteed to leak and several yards of elastic. I have no idea what I will do with the elastic, but the old man convinces me that I cannot live without it.

Exhausted by the effort of selling me a lot of things I obviously do not want, he closes his eyes and leans back against the trunk of a lichi tree. For a moment I feel rather nervous. Is he going to die sitting here beside me? He sinks to his haunches and puts his chin on his hands. He only wants to talk.

"I am very tired, *hazoor*," he says. "Please do not mind if I sit here for a while."

"Rest for as long as you like," I say. "That's a heavy load you've been carrying."

He comes to life at the chance of a conversation and says, "When I was a young man, it was nothing. I could carry my box up from Rajpur to Mussoorie by the bridle-path—seven steep miles! But now I find it difficult to cover the distance from the station to the Dilaram Bazaar."

"Naturally. You are quite old."

"I am seventy, sahib."

"You look very fit for your age." I say this to please him; he looks frail and brittle. "Isn't there someone to help you?" I ask.

"I had a servant boy last month, but he stole my earnings and ran off to Delhi. I wish my son was alive—he would not have permitted me to work like a mule for a living—but he was killed in the riots in forty-seven."

"Have you no other relatives?"

"I have outlived them all. That is the curse of a

healthy life. Your friends, your loved ones, all go before you, and at the end you are left alone. But I must go too, before long. The road to the bazaar seems to grow longer every day. The stones are harder. The sun is hotter in the summer, and the wind much colder in the winter. Even some of the trees that were there in my youth have grown old and have died. I have outlived the trees."

He has outlived the trees. He is like an old tree himself, gnarled and twisted. I have the feeling that if he falls asleep in the orchard, he will strike root here, sending out crooked branches. I can imagine a small bent tree wearing a black waistcoat; a living scarecrow.

He closes his eyes again, but goes on talking.

"The English memsahibs would buy great quantities of elastic. Today it is ribbons and bangles for the girls, and combs for the boys. But I do not make much money. Not because I cannot walk very far. How many houses do I reach in a day? Ten, fifteen. But twenty years ago I could visit more than fifty houses. *That* makes a difference."

"Have you always been here?"

"Most of my life, *hazoor*. I was here before they built the motor road to Mussoorie. I was here when the sahibs had their own carriages and ponies and the memsahibs their own rickshaws. I was here before there were any cinemas. I was here when the Prince of Wales came to Dehra Dun. . . . Oh, I have been here a long time, *hazoor*. I was here when that house was built," he says pointing with his chin towards my grandfather's house. "Fifty, sixty years ago it must have been. I cannot remember exactly. What is ten years when you have lived seventy? But it was a tall, red-bearded sahib who built that house. He kept many creatures as pets. A *kachwa* (turtle) was one of them. And there was a python, which crawled into my box one day and gave me a terrible fright. The sahib used to keep it hanging from his shoulders, like a garland. His wife, the *burra-mem*, always bought a lot from me—lots of elastic. And there were sons, one a teacher, another in the Air Force, and there were always children in the house. Beautiful children. But they went away many years ago. Everyone has gone away."

I do not tell him that I am one of the "beautiful children." I doubt if he will believe me. His memories are of another age, another place, and for him there are no strong bridges into the present.

"But others have come," I say.

"True, and that is as it should be. That is not my complaint. My complaint—should God be listening—is that I have been left behind."

He gets slowly to his feet and stands over his shabby tin box, gazing down at it with a mixture of disdain and affection. I help him to lift and balance it on the flattened cloth on his head. He does not have the energy to turn and make a salutation of any kind; but, setting his sights on the distant hills, he walks down the path with steps that are shaky and slow but still wonderfully straight.

I wonder how much longer he will live. Perhaps a year or two, perhaps a week, perhaps an hour. It will be an end of living, but it will not be death. He is too old for death; he can only sleep; he can only fall gently, like an old, crumpled brown leaf.

I leave the orchard. The bend in the road hides my grandfather's house. I reach the canal again. It emerges from under a small culvert, where ferns and maidenhair grow in the shade. The water, coming from a stream in the foothills, rushes along with a familiar sound; it does not lose its momentum until the canal has left the gently sloping streets of the town.

There are new buildings on this road, but the small police station is housed in the same old limewashed bungalow. A couple of off-duty policemen, partly uniformed but with their pyjamas on, stroll hand in hand on the grass verge. Holding hands (with persons of the same sex of course) is common practice in northern India, and denotes no special relationship.

I cannot forget this little police station. Nothing very exciting ever happened in its vicinity until, in 1947, communal riots broke out in Dehra. Then, bodies were regularly fished out of the canal and dumped on a growing pile in the station compound. I was only a boy, but when I looked over the wall at that pile of corpses, there was no one who paid any attention to me. They were too busy to send me away. At the same time they knew that I was perfectly safe. While Hindus and Muslims were at each other's throats, a white boy could walk the streets in safety. No one was any longer interested in the Europeans.

The people of Dehra are not violent by nature, and the town has no history of communal discord. But when refugees from the partitioned Punjab poured into Dehra in their thousands, the atmosphere became charged with tension. These refugees, many of them Sikhs, had lost their homes and livelihoods; many had seen their loved ones butchered. They were in a fierce and vengeful frame of mind. The calm, sleepy atmosphere of Dehra was shattered during two months of looting and murder. Those Muslims who could get away, fled. The poorer members of the community remained in a refugee camp until the holocaust was over; then they returned to their former occupations, frightened and deeply mistrustful. The old boxman was one of them.

I cross the canal and take the road that will lead me to the river-bed. This was one of my father's favourite walks. He, too, was a walking man. Often, when he was home on leave, he would say, "Ruskin, let's go for a walk," and we would slip off together and walk down to the river-bed or into the sugar-cane fields or across the railway lines and into the jungle.

On one of these walks (this was before Independence), I remember him saying, "After the war is over, we'll be going to England. Would you like that?"

"I don't know," I said. "Can't we stay in India?"

"It won't be ours any more."

"Has it always been ours?" I asked.

"For a long time," he said, "over two hundred years. But we have to give it back now."

"Give it back to whom?" I asked. I was only nine.

"To the Indians," said my father.

The only Indians I had known till then were my ayah

and the cook and the gardener and their children, and I could not imagine them wanting to be rid of us. The only other Indian who came to the house was Dr. Ghose, and it was frequently said of him that he was more English than the English. I could understand my father better when he said, "After the war, there'll be a job for me in England. There'll be nothing for me here."

The war had at first been a distant event; but somehow it kept coming closer. My aunt, who lived in London with her two children, was killed with them during an air-raid; then my father's younger brother died of dysentery on the long walk out from Burma. Both these tragic events depressed my father. Never in good health (he had been prone to attacks of malaria), he looked more worn and wasted every time he came home. His personal life was far from being happy, as he and my mother had separated, she to marry again. I think he looked forward a great deal to the days he spent with me; far more than I could have realized at the time. I was someone to come back to; someone for whom things could be planned; someone who could learn from him.

Dehra suited him. He was always happy when he was among trees, and this happiness communicated itself to me. I felt like drawing close to him. I remember sitting beside him on the veranda steps when I noticed the tendril of a creeping vine that was trailing near my feet. As we sat there, doing nothing in particular—in the best gardens, time has no meaning—I found that the tendril was moving almost imperceptibly away from me and towards my father. Twenty minutes later it had crossed the veranda steps and was touching his feet. This, in India, is the sweetest of salutations.

There is probably a scientific explanation for the plant's behaviour—something to do with the light and warmth on the veranda steps—but I like to think that its movements were motivated simply by an affection for my father. Sometimes, when I sat alone beneath a tree, I felt a little lonely or lost. As soon as my father rejoined me, the atmosphere lightened, the tree itself became more friendly.

Most of the fruit trees round the house were planted

by Father; but he was not content with planting trees in the garden. On rainy days we would walk beyond the river-bed, armed with cuttings and saplings, and then we would amble through the jungle, planting flowering shrubs between the sal and shisham trees.

"But no one ever comes here," I protested the first time. "Who is going to see them?"

"Some day," he said, "*someone* may come this way. . . . If people keep cutting trees, instead of planting them, there'll soon be no forests left at all, and the world will be just one vast desert."

The prospect of a world without trees became a sort of nightmare for me (and one reason why I shall never want to live on a treeless moon), and I assisted my father in his tree-planting with great enthusiasm.

"One day the trees will move again," he said. "They've been standing still for thousands of years. There was a time when they could walk about like people, but someone cast a spell on them and rooted them to one place. But they're always trying to move—see how they reach out with their arms!"

We found an island, a small rocky island in the middle of a dry river-bed. It was one of those river-beds, so common in the foot-hills, which are completely dry in the summer but flooded during the monsoon rains. The rains had just begun, and the stream could still be crossed on foot, when we set out with a number of tamarind, laburnum and coral-tree saplings and cuttings. We spent the day planting them on the island, then ate our lunch there, in the shelter of a wild plum.

My father went away soon after that tree-planting. Three months later, in Calcutta, he died.

I was sent to boarding-school. My grandparents sold the house and left Dehra. After school, I went to England. The years passed, my grandparents died, and when I returned to India I was the only member of the family in the country.

And now I am in Dehra again, on the road to the river-bed.

The houses with their trim gardens are soon behind me, and I am walking through fields of flowering mustard, which make a carpet of yellow blossom stretching away towards the jungle and the foothills.

The river-bed is dry at this time of the year. A herd of skinny cattle graze on the short brown grass at the edge of the jungle. The sal trees have been thinned out. Could our trees have survived? Will our island be there, or has some flash flood during a heavy monsoon washed it away completely?

As I look across the dry water-course, my eye is caught by the spectacular red plumes of the coral blossom. In contrast with the dry, rocky river-bed, the little island is a green oasis. I walk across to the trees and notice that a number of parrots have come to live in them. A koel challenges me with a rising *who-are-you, who-are-you*. . . .

But the trees seem to know me. They whisper among themselves and beckon me nearer. And looking around, I find that other trees and wild plants and grasses have sprung up under the protection of the trees we planted.

They have multiplied. They are moving. In this small forgotten corner of the world, my father's dreams are coming true, and the trees are moving again.

VIKRAM CHANDRA

Vikram Chandra was born in New Delhi in 1961, the son of an executive father and a screenwriter mother. After attending St. Xavier's College in Mumbai, he transferred to Pomona College in Claremont, California, earning a BA in English. He left a film studies program at Columbia University to work on his first novel, Red Earth and Pouring Rain. At Columbia, he had encountered the autobiography of Colonel James "Sikander" Skinner, a legendary nineteenth-century soldier born to an Indian mother and a British father, whose story became the basis for the novel. Published in 1995, it won the Commonwealth Writers Prize for Best First Book and the David Higham Prize for fiction.

In 1997, Chandra published the short story collection Love and Longing in Bombay, containing the story "Dharma," which first appeared in the Paris Review, where it was awarded the annual Discovery Prize. It was also included in Year's Best Fantasy and Horror (1998). His most recent novel, Sacred Games, highly anticipated and the subject of bidding wars among publishers, was published in India by Penguin India in 2006 and by HarperCollins in the U.S. in 2007.

Currently, Chandra divides his time between Mumbai and Berkeley, California, where he teaches creative writing at the University. Speaking of his students' uneasiness about the concept of "patterns" in creative work, he has said in an interview with Bonnie Azan Powell, "The challenge is to do something within that pattern that's original, that's pleasing, and has a sense of the expected—but that blows our mind with the surprise that it holds within itself."

Dharma

Considering the length of Subramaniam's service, it was remarkable that he still came to the Fisherman's Rest. When I started going there, he had been retired for six years from the Ministry of Defense, after a run of forty-one years that had left him a joint-secretary. I was young, and I had just started working at a software company which had its air-conditioned and very streamlined head offices just off the Fountain, and I must confess the first time I heard him speak it was to chastise me. He had been introduced to me at a table on the balcony, sitting with three other older men, and my friend Ramani, who had taken me there, told me that they had been coming there for as long as they had worked and longer. Subramaniam had white hair, he was thin, and in the falling dusk he looked very small to me, the kind of man who would while away the endless boredom of his life in a bar off Sasoon Dock, and so I shaped him up in my mind, and weighed him and dropped him.

I should have noticed then that the waiters brought his drinks to him without being asked, and that the others talked around his silence but always with their faces turned towards him, but I was holding forth on the miserable state of computers in Bombay. The bar was on the second floor of an old house, looking towards the sea, and you wouldn't have known it was there, there was certainly no sign, and it couldn't be seen from the street. There were old trophy fish, half a century old at least, strung along the walls, and on the door to the bathroom there was a picture of a hill stream cut from a magazine, British by the look of it. When the wind came in from the sea it fluttered old flowered curtains and a 1971 calendar, and I was restless already, but I owed at least a drink to the courtesy of my friend Ramani, who understood my loneliness in Bombay and was maybe trying to mix me in with the right circle. So I watched a navy ship, a frigate maybe, wheel into the sun, sipped my drink (despite everything, I noticed, a perfect gin sling), and listened to them talk.

Ramani had been to Bandra that day, and he was telling them about a bungalow on the seafront. It was one of those old three-storied houses with balconies that ran all the way around, set in the middle of a garden filled with palms and fish ponds. It sat stubbornly in the middle of towering apartment buildings, and it had been empty as far back as anyone could remember, and so of course the story that explained this waste of golden real estate was one of ghosts and screams in the night.

"They say it's unsellable," said Ramani. "They say a Gujarati *seth* bought it and died within the month. Nobody'll buy it. Bad place."

"What nonsense," I said. "These are all family property disputes. The cases drag on for years and years in courts, and the houses lie vacant because no one will let anyone else live in them." I spoke at length then, about superstition and ignorance and the state of our benighted nation, in which educated men and women believed in banshees and ghouls. "Even in the information age we will never be free," I said. I went on, and I was particularly witty and sharp, I thought. I vanquished every argument with efficiency and dispatch.

After a while my glass was empty and I stopped to look for the bearer. In the pause the waves gathered against the rocks below, and then Subramaniam spoke. He had a small whispery voice, a departmental voice, I thought, it was full of intrigues and secrets and nuances. "I knew a man once who met a ghost," he said. I still had my body turned around in the seat, but the rest of them turned to him expectantly. He said, "Some people meet their ghosts, and some don't. But we're all haunted by them." Now I turned, too, and he was looking straight at me, and his white hair stood clearly against the extravagant red of the sunset behind him, but his eyes were shadowed and hidden. "Listen," he said.

On the day that Major General Jago Antia turned fifty, his missing leg began to ache. He had been told by the doctors about phantom pain, but the leg had been gone for twenty years without a twinge, and so when he felt a twisting ache two inches under his plastic knee, he stumbled not out of agony but surprise. It was only a little stumble, but the officers who surrounded him turned away out of sympathy, because he was Jago Antia, and he never stumbled. The younger lieutenants flushed with emotion, because they knew for certain that Jago Antia was invincible, and this little lapse, and the way he recovered himself, how he came back to his ram-rod straightness, this reminded them of the metallic density of his discipline, which you could see in his grey eyes. He was famous for his stare, for the cold blackness of his anger, for his tactical skill and his ability to read ground, his whole career from the gold medal at Kharak-vasla to the combat and medals in Leh and NEFA. He was famous for all this, but the leg was the center of the legend, and there was something terrible about it, about the story, and so it was never talked about. He drove himself across jungle terrain and shamed men twenty years younger, and it was as if the leg had never been lost. This is why his politeness, his fastidiousness, the delicate way he handled his fork and knife, his slow smile, all these Jago quirks were imitated by even the cadets at the Academy: they wished for his certainty, and believed that his loneliness was the mark of his genius.

So when he left the *bara khana* his men looked after him with reverence, and curiously the lapse made them believe in his strength all the more. They had done the party to mark an obscure regimental battle day from half a century before, because he would never have allowed a celebration for himself. After he left they lolled on sofas, sipping from their drinks, and told stories about him. His name was Jehangir Antia, but for thirty years, in their stories, he had been Jago Antia. Some of them didn't know his real name.

Meanwhile, Jago Antia lay on his bed under a mos-quito net, his arms flat by his sides, his one leg out as if at attention, the other standing by the bed, and waited for his dream to take him. Every night he thought of falling endlessly through the night, slipping through the cold air, and then somewhere it became a dream, and he was asleep, still falling. He had been doing it for as long as he could remember, long before para school and long before the drop at Sylhet, towards the hostile guns and the treacherous ground. It had been with him from long ago, this leap, and he knew where it took him, but this night a pain grew in that part of him that he no longer had, and he tried to fight it away, imagining the rush of air against his neck, the flapping of his clothes, the complete darkness, but it was no use. He was still awake. When he raised his left hand and uncovered the luminous dial it was oh-four-hundred, and then he gave up and strapped his leg on. He went into the study and spread out some maps and began to work on operational orders. The contour maps were covered with markers, and his mind moved easily among the mountains, seeing the units, the routes of supply, the staging areas. They were fighting an insurgency, and he knew of course that he was doing good work, that his concentration was keen, but he knew he would be tired the next day, and this annoyed him. When he found himself kneading his plastic shin with one hand, he was so angry that he went out on the porch and puffed out a hundred quick push-ups, and in the morning his puzzled *sahayak* found him striding up and down the garden walk as the sun came up behind a gaunt ridge.

"What are you doing out here?" Thapa said. Jago Antia had never married. They had known each other for three decades, since Jago Antia had been a captain, and they had long ago discarded the formalities of master and batman.

"Couldn't sleep, Thapa. Don't know what it was."

Thapa raised an eyebrow. "Eat well then."

"Right. Ten minutes?"

Thapa turned smartly and strode off. He was a small, round man, not fat but bulging everywhere with the compact muscles of the mountains.

"Thapa?" Jago Antia called.

"Yes."

"Nothing." He had for a moment wanted to say something about the pain, but then the habit of a lifetime asserted itself, and he threw back his shoulders and shook his head. Thapa waited for a moment and then walked into the house. Now Jago Antia looked up at the razor edge of the ridge far above, and he could see, if he turned his head to one side, a line of tiny figures walking down it. They would be woodcutters, and perhaps some of the men he was fighting. They were committed, hardy, and well trained. He watched them. He was better. The sun was high now, and Jago Antia went to his work.

The pain didn't go away, and Jago Antia couldn't sleep. Sometimes he was sure he was in his dream, and he was grateful for the velocity of the fall, and he could feel the cold on his face, the dark, but then he would sense something, a tiny glowing pinpoint that spun and grew and finally became a bright hurling maelstrom that wrenched him back into wakefulness. Against this he had no defense: no matter how tired he made himself, how much he exhausted his body, he could not make his mind insensible to his phantom pain, and so his discipline, honed over the years, was made useless. Finally he conquered his shame, and asked—in the strictest confidence—an Army Medical Corps colonel for medication, and got, along with a very puzzled stare, a bottle full of yellow pills, which he felt in his pocket all day, against his chest. But at night these pills too proved no match for the ferocity of the pain, which by now Jago Antia imagined as a beast of some sort, a low growling animal that camouflaged itself until he was almost at rest and then came rushing out to worry at his flesh, or at the memory of his flesh. It was not that Jago Antia minded the defeat, because he had learnt to accept defeat and casualties and loss, but it was that he had once defeated this flesh, it was he who had swung the *kukri,* but it had come back now and surprised him. He felt outflanked, and this infuriated him, and further, there was nothing he could do about it, there was nothing to do anything about. So his work suffered, and he felt the surprise of those around him. It shamed him more than anything else that they were not disappointed but sympathetic. They brought him tea without being asked, he noticed that his aides spoke amongst themselves in whispers, his headquarters ran—if it was possible—even more efficiently than before, with the gleam of spit and polish about it. But now he was tired, and when he looked at the maps he felt the effort he had to make to grasp the flow of the battle—not the facts, which were important, though finally trivial—but the thrust and the energy of the struggle, the movement of the initiative, the flux and ebb of the chaotic thing. One afternoon he sat in his office, the pain a constant hum just below his attention, and the rain beat down in gusts against the windows, and the gleam of lightning startled him into realizing that his jaw was slack, that he had been staring aimlessly out of the window at the green side of the mountain, that he had become the sort of commander he despised, a man who because of his rank allowed himself to become careless. He knew he would soon make the sort of mistake that would get some of his boys killed, and that was unacceptable: without hesitation he called the AMC colonel and asked to be relieved of his command for medical reasons.

The train ride to Bombay from Calcutta was two days long, and there was a kind of relief in the long rhythms of the wheels, in the lonely clanging of the tracks at night. Jago Antia sat next to a window in a first class compartment and watched the landscape change, taken back somehow to a fifth-grade classroom and lessons on the crops of the Deccan. Thapa had taken a week's leave to go to his family in Darjeeling and was to join up in Bombay later. Jago Antia was used to solitude, but the relief from immediate responsibility brought with it a rush of memory, and he found the unbidden recall of images from the past annoying, because it all seemed so useless. He tried to take up the time usefully by reading NATO journals, but even under the hard edge of his concentration the pain throbbed in time with the wheels, and he found himself remembering an afternoon at school when they had run out of history class to watch two fighter planes fly low over the city. By the time the train pulled into Bombay Central, he felt as if he were covered not only with sweat and grit, but also with an oily film of recollection, and he marched through the crowd towards the taxi stand, eager for a shower.

The house stood in a square plot on prime residential land in Khar, surrounded by new, extravagant constructions coloured the pink and green of new money. But it was mostly dark brown, stained by decades of sea air and monsoon rains, and in the late-afternoon sun it seemed to gather the light about it as it sat surrounded by trees and untidy bushes. There was, in its three stories, in the elegant arches on the balconies, and in the rows of shuttered windows, something rich and dense and heavy, like the smell of gun oil on an old hunting rifle, and the taxi driver sighed, "They don't build them like that anymore."

"No, they're draughty and take a fortune to keep up," said Jago Antia curtly as he handed him the money. It was true. Amir Khan the housekeeper was waving slowly from the porch. He was very old, with a thin neck and a white beard that gave him the appearance of a heron, and by the time he was halfway down the flight of stairs Jago Antia had the bags out of the car and up to the house. Inside, with Amir Khan puffing behind him, he paused to let his eyes take to the darkness, but it felt as if he were pushing his way through something substantial and insidious, more clear than fog but as inescapable. It was still much as he had left it many years ago to go to the Academy. There were the Victorian couches covered with faded flower prints, the gold-rimmed paintings on the wall of his grandparents and uncles. He noticed suddenly how quiet it was, as if the street and the city outside had vanished.

"I'll take these bags upstairs," he said.

"Can't," Amir Khan said. "It's been closed up for years. All just sheets on the furniture. Even your parents slept in the old study. They moved a bed into it."

Jago Antia shrugged. It was more convenient on the ground floor in any case. "It's all right. It's just for a few days. I have some work here. I'll see Todywalla too."

"What about?"

"Well, I want to sell the house."

"You want to sell the house?"

"Yes."

Amir Khan shuffled away to the kitchen, and Jago Antia heard him knocking about with cups and saucers. He had no intention of using the house again, and he saw no other alternative. His parents were dead, gone one after another in a year. He had been a distant son, meeting them on leave in Delhi and Lucknow while they were on vacation. Wherever they had met, far away from Bombay, he had always seen the old disappointment and weariness in their eyes. Now it was over, and he wanted not to think about the house anymore.

"Good, sell this house." It was Amir Khan with a cup of tea. "Sell it."

"I will."

"Sell it."

Jago Antia noticed that Amir Khan's hands were shaking, and he remembered suddenly an afternoon in the garden when he had made him throw ball after ball to his off side, and his own attempts at elegant square cuts, and the sun high overhead through the palm trees.

"We'll do something for you," said Jago Antia. "Don't worry."

"Sell it," Amir Khan said. "I'm tired of it."

Jago Antia tried to dream of falling, but his ache stayed with him, and besides the gusts of water against the windows were loud and unceasing. It had begun to rain with nightfall, and now the white illumination of lightning threw the whole room into sharp relief. He was thinking about the Academy, about how he had been named Jago, two weeks after his arrival. His roommate had found him at five o'clock on a Saturday morning doing push-ups on the gravel outside their room, and rubbing his eyes he had said, "Antia, you're an enthusiast." He had never known where the nickname Jago came from, but after the second week nobody except his parents had called him Jehangir again. When he had won the gold medal for best cadet even the major-general who was commandant of the Academy had said to him at the reviewing stand, "Good show, Jago." He had been marked for advancement early, and he had never betrayed his promise. He was thinking of this, and the wind flapped the curtains above him, and when he first heard the voice far away he thought it was a trick of the air, but then he heard it again. It was muffled by distance and the rain but he heard it clearly. He could not make out what it was saying. He was alert instantly and strapped on his leg. Even though he knew it was probably Amir Khan talking to himself, flicking away with a duster in the imagined light of some long-gone day, he moved cautiously, back against the wall. At the bottom of the hallway he paused, and heard it again, small but distinct, above him. He found the staircase and went up, his thighs tense, moving in a fluid half-squat. Now he was truly watchful, because the voice was too young to be Amir Khan. On the first landing, near an open door, he sensed a rush of motion on the balcony that ran around the outside of the house; he came to the corner, feeling his way with his hands. Everything in the darkness appeared as shades, blackness and deeper blackness. He darted a look around the corner and the balcony was empty, he was sure of it. He came around the corner, back against the wall. Then he heard the movement again, not distinct footsteps but the swish of feet on the ground, one after another. He froze. Whatever it was, it was coming towards him. His eyes ached in the darkness, but he could see nothing. Then the white blaze of lightning swept across the lawn, throwing the filigreed ironwork of the railing sharply on the wall, across Jago Antia's belly, and in the long light he saw on the floor the clearly outlined shape of shoes, one after another, the patches of water a sharp black in the light, and as he watched another footprint appeared on the tile, and then another, coming towards him. Before it was dark again he was halfway down the stairs. He stopped, alone with the beating of his heart. He forced himself to stand up straight, to look carefully about and above the staircase for dead ground and lines of fire. He had learnt long ago that professionalism was a much better way to defeat fear than self-castigation and shame, and now he applied himself to the problem. The only possible conclusion was that it had been a trick of the light on the water, and so he was able to move up the staircase, smooth and graceful once again. But on the landing a breath of air curled around his ankle like a flow of cool liquid, and he began to shiver. It was a freezing chill that spread up his thighs and into his groin, and it caught him so suddenly that he let his teeth chatter for a moment. Then he bit down, but despite his straining he could hardly take a step before he stopped again. It was so cold that his fingers ached. His eyes filled with moisture and suddenly the dark was full of soft shadows. Again he heard the voice, far away, melancholy and low. With a groan he collapsed against the banister and slid down the stairs, all the way to the bottom, his leg rattling on the steps. Through the night he tried it again and again, and once he made it to the middle of the landing, but the fear took the strength from his hips, so that he had to crawl on hands and knees to the descent. At dawn he sat shaken and weak on the first step, his arm around the comforting curve of the thick round post.

Finally it was the shock in Thapa's eyes that raised Jago Antia from the stupor he had fallen into. For three days he had been pacing, unshaven and unwashed, at the bottom of the stairs, watching the light make golden shapes in the air. Now Thapa had walked through the front door, and it was his face, slack, and the fact that he forgot to salute that conveyed to Jago Antia how changed he was, how shocking he was.

"It's all right," Jago Antia said. "I'm all right."

Thapa still had his bag in his right hand and an umbrella in the left, and he said nothing. Jago Antia remembered then a story that was a part of his own legend: he had once reduced a lieutenant to tears because of a tea stain on his shirt. It was quite true.

"Put out a change of clothes," he said. "And close your mouth."

The water in the shower drummed against Jago Antia's head and cleared it. He saw the insanity of what had gone on for three days, and he was sure it was exhaustion. There was nothing there, and the important thing was to get to the hospital, and then to sell the house. He ate breakfast eagerly, and felt almost relaxed. Then Amir Khan walked in with a glass of milk on a tray. For three days he had been bringing milk instead of tea, and now when Jago Antia told him to take it back to the kitchen, he said, "Baba, you have to drink it. Mummy said so. You know you're not allowed to drink tea." And he shuffled away, walking through a suddenly revived age when Jehangir Antia was a boy in knickers, agile and confident on two sunburnt legs. For a moment Jago Antia felt time slipping around him like a dark wave, but then he shook away the feeling and stood up.

"Call a taxi," he said to Thapa.

The doctors at Jaslok were crisp and confident in their poking and prodding, and the hum of machinery comforted him. But Todywalla, sitting in his disorderly office, said bluntly, "Sell that house? Na, impossible. There's something in it."

"Oh don't be ridiculous," said Jago Antia vehemently. "That's absurd."

Todywalla looked keenly at him. Todywalla was a toothless old man with a round black cap squarely on the middle of his head. "Ah," he said. "So you've heard it too."

"I haven't heard a damn thing," Jago Antia said. "Be rational."

"You may be a rationalist," Todywalla said. "But I sell houses in Bombay." He sipped tea noisily from a chipped cup. "There's something in that house."

When the taxi pulled through the gate Thapa was standing in the street outside, talking to a vegetable seller and two other men. As Jago Antia pulled off his shoes in the living room, Thapa came in and went to the kitchen. He came back a few minutes later with a glass of water.

"Tomorrow I will find my cousin at the bank at Nariman Point," he said. "And we will get somebody to come to this house. We shouldn't sleep here."

"What do you mean, somebody?"

"Somebody who can clean it up." Thapa's round face

was tight, and there were white crescents around his temples. "Somebody who knows."

"Knows what exactly? What are you talking about?"

Thapa nodded towards the gate. "No one on this street will come near this place after dark. Everyone knows. They were telling me not to stay here."

"Nonsense."

"We can't fight this, *saab*," Thapa said. After a pause: "Not even you."

Jago Antia stood erect. "I will sleep tonight quietly and so will you. No more of this foolishness." He marched into the study and lay on the bed, loosening his body bit by bit, and under the surface of his concentration the leg throbbed evenly. The night came on and passed. He thought finally that nothing would happen, and there was a grey outside the window, but then he heard again the incessant calling. He took a deep breath, and walked into the drawing room. Thapa was standing by the door, his whole body straining away from the stairs. Jago Antia took two steps forward. "Come on," he said. His voice rustled across the room, and both of them jerked. He read the white tightness of terror around Thapa's mouth, and as he had done many times before, he led by example. He felt his legs move far away, towards the stairs, and he did not look behind him to see if Thapa was following. He knew the same pride and shame which was taking him up the stairs would bring Thapa: as long as each saw himself in the other's eyes he would not let the other down. He had tested this in front of machine guns and found it to be true. So now they moved, Thapa a little behind and flanking, up the stairs. This time he came up to the landing and was able to move out, through the door, onto the balcony. He was moving, moving. But then the voice came around a corner and he stood still, feeling a rush in his veins. It was amazing, he found himself thinking, how localized it was. He could tell from moment to moment where it was on the balcony. It was not a trick of the wind, not a hallucination. Thapa was still against the wall, his palms against it, his mouth working back and forth, looking exactly where Jago Antia was. It came closer, and now Jago Antia was able to hear what it was saying: "Where shall I go?" The question was asked with a sob in it, like a tearing hiccup, so close that Jago Antia heard it shake the small frame that asked it. He felt a sound in his own throat, a moan, something like pain, sympathy. Then he felt the thing pause, and though there was nothing but the air he felt it coming at him, first hesitating, then faster, asking again, where shall I go, where, and he backed away from it, fast, tripping over his heels, and he felt the railing of the balcony on his thighs, hard, and then he was falling.

The night was dark below. They plummeted headfirst from the belly of the plane into the cool pit at a thousand feet, and Jago Antia relished the leap into reality. They had been training long enough, and now he did not turn his head to see if the stick was tight because he knew his men and their skill. The chute popped with a flap, and after the jerk he flew the sky with his legs easy in the harness. The only feature he could see was the silver curve of the river far below, and then quite suddenly the dark mass of trees and the swathe of fields. There were no lights in the city of Sylhet, but he knew it was there, to the east, and he knew the men who were in it, defending against him, and he saw the problem clearly and the movements across the terrain below.

Then he was rolling across the ground, and the chute was off. Around him was the controlled confusion of a nighttime drop, and swiftly out of that formed the shape of his battalion. He had the command group around him, and in a few minutes they were racing towards their first objectives. Now he was sweating freely, and the weight of his pistol swung against his hip. He could smell the cardamom seeds his radioman was chewing. In the first grey, to the east, the harsh tearing noise of LMG fire flung the birds out of the trees. *Delta Bravo I have contact over.* As Jago Antia thumbed the mouthpiece, his radioman smiled at him, nineteen and glowing in the dawn. *Delta Bravo, bunkers, platoon strength, I am going in now.* Alpha Company had engaged.

As the day came they moved into the burning city,

and the buildings were torn by explosions and the shriek
of rockets skimming low over the streets and ringing off
the walls. Now the noise echoed and boomed, and it was
difficult to tell where it was coming from, but Jago Antia
still saw it all forming on his map, which was stained
black now with sweat here and there, and dust, and the
plaster knocked from the walls by bullets. He was icy
now, his mind holding it all, and as an excited captain
reported to him he listened silently, and there was the
flat crack of a grenade, not far off, and the captain
flinched, then blushed as he saw that Jago Antia was
calm as if he were walking down a golf course in Well-
ington, not a street shining with glass, thousands of
shards sharp as death, no, he was meditative and easy.
So the captain went back to his boys with something of
Jago Antia's slow watchfulness in his walk, and he put
away his nervousness and smiled at them, and they nodded, crouched behind cracked walls, sure of each other
and Jago Antia.

Now in the morning the guns echoed over the city,
and a plummy BBC voice sounded over a Bush radio in
the remnants of a tailor's shop: "Elements of the Indian
Para Brigade are said to be in the outskirts of Sylhet.
Pakistani troops are dug in . . ." Jago Antia was looking
at the rounded curves of the radio on the tailor's shelf,
at the strange white knobs and the dial from decades
ago, at the deep brown wood, and a shiver came from
low on his back into his heart, a whisper of something
so tiny that he could not name it, and yet it broke his
concentration and took him away from his body and this
room and its drapes of cloth to somewhere else, a flickering vision of a room, curtains blowing in a gusting
wind, a feeling of confusion, he shook his head and swal-
lowed. He curled the knob with the back of his hand so
that it snapped the voice off and broke with a crack.
Outside he could feel the fight approaching a crisis, the
keen whiplash of the carbines and the rattle of the sub-
machine guns and the heavier Pakistani fire, cresting and
falling like waves but always higher, it was likely the
deciding movement. He had learnt the waiting that was
the hardest part of commanding, and now the reports

came quickly, and he felt the battle forming to a cre-
scendo; he had a reserve, sixty men, and he knew now
where he was going to put them. They trotted down the
street to the east and paused on a dusty street corner
(the relentless braying scream of an LMG near by), and
Jung the radioman pointed to a house at the end of the
street, a white three-storied house with a decorative vine
running down the front in concrete, now chipped and
holed. "Tall enough," Jago Antia said: he wanted a vantage point to see the city laid out for him. He started
off confidently across the street, and then all the sound
in the world vanished, leaving a smooth silence, he had
no recollection of being thrown, but now he was falling
through the air, down, he felt distinctly the impact of
the ground, but again there was nothing, no sound.

After a while he was able to see the men above him
as he was lifted, their lips moving serenely even though
their faces were twisted with emotion, they appeared
curved and bent inwards against a spherical sky. He shut
and opened his eyes several times, searching for connec-
tions that seemed severed. They carried him into a
house. Then he was slowly able to hear again, and with
the sound he began to feel the pain. His ears hurt
sharply and deep inside his head, in a place in which he
had never felt pain before. But he strained and finally
he was able to find, inside, some part of himself, and his
body jerked, and they held him still. His jaw cracked,
and he said: "What?"

It was a mine on the corner, they told him. Now he
was fighting it, he was using his mind, he felt his strength
coming back, he could find his hands, and he pushed
against the bed and sat up. A fiercely moustached
nursing-assistant pushed at his shoulders, but he struck
the hands away and took a deep breath. Then he saw
his leg. Below his right knee the flesh was white and
twisted away from the bone. Below the ankle was a
shapeless bulk of matter, and the nursing-assistant was
looking for the artery, but as Jago Antia watched the
black blood seeped out onto the floor. Outside, the firing
was ceaseless now, and Jago Antia was looking at his
leg, and he realized that he no longer knew where his boys

were. The confusion came and howled around his head, and for a moment he was lost. "Cut it off," he said then. "Off."

But, said the nursing-assistant, holding up the useless bandages, but I have nothing, and Jago Antia felt his head swim on an endless swell of pain, it took him up and away and he could no longer see, and it left him breathless and full of loss. "No time. Cut it off now," he said, but the nursing-assistant was dabbing with the bandages. Jago Antia said to Jung: "You do it, now. Quickly." They were all staring at him, and he knew he could not make them cut him. "Give me your *kukri*," he said to Jung. The boy hesitated, but then the blade came out of its scabbard with a hiss that Jago Antia heard despite the ceaseless roar outside. He steadied himself and gripped it with both hands and shut his eyes for a moment, and there was impossibly the sound of the sea inside him, a sob rising in his throat, he opened his eyes and fought it, pulled against it with his shoulders as he raised the *kukri* above his head, against darkness and mad sorrow, and then he brought the blade down below his knee. What surprised him was the crunch it made against the bone. In four strokes he was through. Each was easier. "Now," he said, and the nursing-assistant tied it off. Jago Antia waved off the morphine, and he saw that Jung the radioman was crying. On the radio Jago Antia's voice was steady. He took his reports, and then he sent his reserve in. They heard his voice across Sylhet. "Now then," he said. "Finish it."

The room that Jago Antia woke up in had a cracked white ceiling, and for a long time he did not know where he was, in Sylhet (he could feel an ache under his right knee), in the house of his childhood after a fall from the balcony, or in some other room, unknown: everything seemed to be thrown together in his eyes without shape or distinction, and from moment to moment he forgot the flow of time, and found himself talking to Amir Khan about cricket, and then suddenly it was evening. Finally he was able to sit up in bed, and a doctor fussed about him: there were no injuries, the ground was soft from the rain, his paratrooper's reflexes had turned him in the air and rolled him on the ground, but he was bruised, and a concussion could not be ruled out. He was to stay in bed and rest. When the doctor left Thapa brought in a plate of rice and *dal,* and stood at the foot of the bed with his arms behind him. "I will talk to my cousin tonight."

Jago Antia nodded. There was nothing to say. But when the exorcist came two days later he was not the slavering tribal magician that Jago Antia was expecting, but a sales manager from a large electronics company. Without haste and without stopping he put his briefcase down, stripped off his black pants and white shirt and blue tie, and bathed under the tap in the middle of the garden. Then he put on a white *dhoti* and daubed his forehead with a white powder, and meanwhile Thapa was preparing a *thali* with little mounds of rice and various kinds of coloured paste and a small *diya,* with the wick floating in the oil. Then the man took the *thali* from Thapa and walked slowly into the house, and as he came closer Jago Antia saw that he was in his late forties, that he was heavyset, that he was neither ugly nor handsome. "My name is Thakker," he said to Jago Antia before he sat cross-legged in the middle of the living room, in front of the stairs, and lit the *diya.* It was evening now, and the flame was tiny and flickering in the enormous darkness of the room.

As Thakker began to chant and throw fistfuls of rice from his *thali* into the room Jago Antia felt all the old irritation return, and he was disgusted with himself for letting this insanity gather around him. He walked out into the garden and stood with the grass rustling against his pants. There was a huge bank of clouds on the horizon, mass upon mass of dark heads piled up thousands of feet high, and as he watched a silver dart of lightning flickered noiselessly, and then another. Now his back began to ache slightly, and he shook his head slowly, overwhelmed by the certainty that he no longer knew anything. He turned around and looked up the path, into the house, and through the twilight he could see the tiny gleam of Thakker's *diya,* and as he watched Thakker lifted the *thali* and walked slowly towards the stairs, into the shadow, so that finally it seemed that the flame was rising up the stairs. Then Thapa came out, and they stood in the garden together, and the breeze from the sea was full of the promise of rain. They waited as night fell, and sometimes they heard Thakker's voice, lifted high and chanting, and then, very faint, that other voice, blown away by the gusts of wind. Finally—Jago Antia did not know what time it was—Thakker came down the stairs, carrying the *thali,* but the *diya* was blown out. They walked up to meet him on the patio, under the faint light of a single bulb.

"It is very strong," he said.

"What is it?" said Jago Antia angrily.

Thakker shrugged. "It is most unmovable." His face was drawn and pale. "It is a child. It is looking for something. Most terrible. Very strong."

"Well, get it out."

"I cannot. Nobody can move a child."

Jago Antia felt a rush of panic, like a steady pressure against his chest.

Thapa said, "What can we do?"

Thakker walked past them, down the stairs, and then he turned and looked up at them. "Do you know who it is?" Jago Antia said nothing, his lips held tightly together to stop them from trembling. "It is most powerful because it is a child and because it is helpless and because it is alone. Only one who knows it and who is from its family can help it. Such a person must go up there naked and alone. Remember, alone and naked, and ask it what it seeks." Thakker wiped away the white powder from his forehead slowly, and then he turned and walked away. It was now drizzling, fat drops that fell out of the sky insistently.

Out of the darkness Thakker called. "You must go." Then a pause in which Jago Antia could hear, somewhere, rushing water. "Help him."

At the bottom of the stairs Jago Antia felt his loneliness like a bitterness in his nostrils, like a stench. Thapa watched from the door, remote already, and there seemed to be nothing in the world but the shadows ahead, the creaking of the old house, the wind in the balconies. As Jago Antia walked slowly up the stairs, unbuttoning his shirt, his pulse was rushing in his head, each beat like an explosion, not out of fear anymore but from a kind of anticipation, because now he knew who it was, who waited for him. On the landing he kicked off his shoes and unbuckled his belt, and whispered, "What can you want from me? I was a child too." He walked slowly around the balcony, and the rain dashed against his shoulders and rolled down his back. He came to the end of the balcony, at a door with bevelled glass, and he peered through it, and he could dimly make out the ornate curves of his mother's dressing table, the huge mirror, and beyond that the bed now covered with sheets, he stood with his face against the cool pane. He shut his eyes. Somewhere deep came the poisonous seep of memory, he felt it in his stomach like a living stream, and his mother was looking at him, her eyes unfocussed in a kind of daze. She was a very beautiful woman, and she was sitting in front of her mirror now as she always did, but her hair was untidy, and she was wearing a white sari. He was sitting on the edge of her bed, his feet stuck out, and he was looking at his black shoes and white socks, and he was trying to be very still because he did not know what was going to happen next. He was dressed up, and the house was full of people, but it was very quiet and the only sounds were the pigeons on the balcony. He was afraid to move, and after a while he began to count his breaths, in and out. Then his father came in, he stood next to his mother, put a hand on her shoulder, and they looked at each other for a long time, and he wanted to say that they looked like their picture on the mantelpiece, only older and in white, but he knew he couldn't so he kept himself still and waited. Then his father said to his mother, come, and they rose and he walked behind them a little. She was leaning on his father, and they came down the stairs and everyone watched them. Downstairs he saw his uncles and aunts and other people he didn't know, and in the middle of the room there was a couch and on it lay his brother

Sohrab. Sohrab had been laid out and draped in a white sheet. There was a kind of oil lamp with a wick burning near Sohrab's head, and a man was whispering a prayer into his ear. There was a smell of sandalwood in the air. Then his mother said, "Soli, Soli," and his father turned his face away, and a breath passed through the room, and he saw many people crying. That was what they always called Sohrab. He was Soli, and that was how Jehangir always thought of him. His mother was kneeling next to Soli, and his father too, and he was alone, and he didn't know what to do, but he stood straight up, and he kept his hands by his sides. Then two men came forward, and they covered Soli's face, and then other people lifted him up, and they took him through the door, and for a long time he could see them walking through the garden towards the gate. His mother was sitting on the sofa with her sisters, and after a while he turned around and walked up the stairs, and above there was nobody, and he walked through the rooms and around the balcony, and after a while he thought he was waiting for something to happen, but it never did.

Jago Antia's forehead trembled against the glass and now he turned and walked down the corridor that ran around the house, through darkness and sudden light, and he walked by a playroom, and then his father's study, and as he walked he felt that it was walking beside him, in front of him, around him. He heard the voice asking its question, but his own desperate question seemed to twist in his throat and come out only as a sound, a sort of sob of anger. It went into the room that had been his room and Soli's room, and he stopped at the door, his chest shaking, looking at the floor where they had wrestled each other, the bureau between the beds on which they had stacked their books and their toys. The door creaked open under his hand, and inside he sat on this bed, in the middle, where he used to, and they were listening to the Binaca Geet Mala on the radio, Soli loved his radio and the Binaca Geet Mala. He was lying on the bed in his red pyjamas and the song went *Maine shayad tumhe pahale bhi kahin dekha hai*, Soli sang along with it, Jehangir was not allowed to touch the radio, but when Soli was away he sometimes played with the knobs, and once he switched it on and heard a hiss and a voice far away speaking angrily in a language he didn't understand, it scared him and he ran away from it, and Soli found his radio on, and then there was a fight. Jehangir lost the fight, but Soli always won, even with the other boys on the street, he was fearless, and he jumped over walls, and he led them all, and at cricket he was always the captain of one side, and sometimes in the evenings, still in his barrister's clothes, their father watched their games in the garden, and he said that Soli had a lovely style. When he said this the first time Jehangir raised his head and blinked because he understood instantly what his father meant, he had known it all along but now he knew the words for it, and he said it to himself sometimes under his breath, a lovely style, a lovely style. Now Soli raised himself up in bed on an elbow, and Amir Khan brought in two glasses of milk on a tray, and then their mother came in and sat as she did on Soli's bed, and tonight she had *The Illustrated Weekly of India* in her hand, folded open to a tall picture of a man with a moustache and a bat, and she said, "Look at him, he was the Prince." So she told them about Ranjitsinhji, who was really a prince, who went to England where they called him nigger and wog, but he showed them, he was the most beautiful batsman, like a dancer he turned their bouncers to the boundaries with his wrists, he drove with clean elegance, he had good manners, and he said nothing to their insults, and he showed them all he was the best of them all, he was the Prince, he was lovely. After their mother left Soli put *The Illustrated Weekly* in his private drawer, and after that Jehangir would see him take it out and look at it, and sometimes he would let Jehangir look at it, and Jehangir would look at the long face and the pride in the stance and the dark opaque eyes, and he would feel a surge of pride himself, and Soli would have his wiry hand on his shoulder, and they would both say together, Ranjitsinhji, Ranji.

That summer one Sunday afternoon they were dozing in the heat when suddenly Burjor Mama came in and tumbled them both out of bed, roaring what a pair of sleepyhead sissy types, and they laughed with delight because he was their favorite uncle. They knew his arrival meant at least two weeks of unexpected pleasures, excursions to Juhu, sailing trips, films, shows, and sizzling forbidden pavement foods. Their mother came in and hugged him close, and they were embarrassed by her tears, Burjor was her only younger brother and more precious for his profession of soldiering, she was exclaiming now how he was burnt black by the sun, what are they doing to you now, and he was really dark, but Jehangir liked his unceasing whiplike energy and the sharp pointed ends of his handlebar moustache. Barely pausing to thump down his hold-all and his suitcase, he gathered up the whole family, Amir Khan included, and he whisked them off for a drive, and he whistled as he drove. On the way back Jehangir, weighted down with ice cream, fell asleep with his head in his mother's lap, and once for a moment he awoke and saw, close to his face, his mother's hand holding her brother's wrist tenderly and close, her delicate fingers very pale against his skin with the strong corded muscles underneath.

And Jago Antia, walking down the corridor, walking, felt the sticky sleep of childhood and the cozy hum of the car and safety. And then he was at the bottom of a flight of stairs, he knew he had to go up, because it had gone before him, and now he stumbled because the pain came, and it was full of fear, he went up, one two three, and then leaned over, choking. Above him the stairs angled into darkness and the roof he knew so well, and he couldn't move, again he was trembling, and the voice was speaking somewhere ahead, he said, "I don't want to go," but then he heard it again. He knew his hands were shaking, and he said, "All right you bastard, naked, naked," and he tore at the straps, and then the leg rolled down the stairs to the bottom. He went up, hunching, on hands and knees, his lips curled back and breathing in huge gasps.

Burjor Mama bought them a kite. On Monday morning he had to report in Colaba for work, and so Jehangir's mother brought up his pressed uniform and put it on the bed in the guest room. Jehangir lay on the bed next to the uniform and took in its peculiar smell, it was a deep olive green, and the bars on the front were of many colors but mainly red and orange, and above a breast pocket it said, B. MEHTA. Jehangir's mother sat on the bed too and smoothed out the uniform with an open palm, and then Burjor Mama came out of the bathroom in a towel. As he picked up the shirt, Jehangir saw under the *sadra,* under and behind his left arm, a scar shaped like a star, brown and hard against the pale skin. Then Jehangir looked up and he saw his mother's face, tender and proud and a little angry as she looked at Burjor. After breakfast Soli and Jehangir walked with him to the gate, and he said, "See you later, alligators," and in the afternoon they waited on the porch for him, reading comics and sipping at huge glasses of squash. When the taxi stopped at the gate they had run forward, whooping, because even before he was out they had seen the large triangle of the kite, and then they ran up without pause to the roof, Soli holding the kite at the ends, and Jehangir following behind with the roll of string. Jehangir held the roll as Soli spun off the *manjha,* and Soli said, watch your fingers, and Burjor showed them how to tie the kite string, once up, once down, and then they had it up in the air, it was doing spirals and rolls, and Soli said, "*Yaar,* that's a fighting kite!" Nobody was flying to fight with nearby, but when their father came up he laughed and watched them, and when they went down to tea Soli's fingers were cut from the *manjha,* and when Jehangir asked, Burjor Mama said, "It's ground glass on the line."

Now he came up the stairs, his stump bumping on the edges of the stone, and his palm scraped against something metal, but he felt the sting distantly and without interest. The next day Soli lay stretched across the roof, his mouth open. Jago Antia pulled himself up, his arms around a wooden post, and he could see the same two-level roof, Amir Khan's old room to one side, with its sloping roof coming to the green posts holding it up, beyond that the expanse of brick open to the sky, and then a three-foot drop with a metal ladder leading to the lower level of the roof, and beyond that the treetops and the cold stretch of the ocean. He let go of the post and swayed gently in the rain. Soli walked in front of him, his hands looping back the string, sending the kite fluttering strongly through the sky, and Jehangir held the coil and took up the slack. It flew in circles above them. "Let me fly it," Jehangir said. "Let me fly it." But Soli said, "You can't hold this, it'll cut you." "I can hold anything. I can." "You can't, it'll hurt you." "It won't. I won't let it." And Jehangir ran forward, Soli danced away, light and confident, backwards, and then for a moment his face was surprised, and then he was lying below, three feet below on the ground, and the string flew away from him. Jago Antia dropped to his knee, then fell heavily on his side. He pulled himself through the water, to the edge, next to the metal stairs, and he peered down trying to see the bottom but it seemed endless, but he knew it was only three feet below. How can somebody die falling three feet? He heard the voice asking its question, where shall I go, and he roared into the night, "What do you want? What the hell is it you want?" But it wouldn't stop, and Jago Antia knelt on the edge and wept, "What do you want," and finally he said, "Look, look," and he pushed himself up, leaned forward, and let himself go, and he fell: he saw again Soli backing away, Jehangir reaching up trying to take his hand away from the string, Soli holding his hand far up, and Jehangir helpless against his strength. Then Soli smiling, standing, and Jehangir shouting and running forward and jumping, the solid impact of his small body against Soli's legs, Soli's look of surprise, he's falling, reaching wildly, Jehangir's hand under the bottom of Soli's shorts, he holds on and tries, holds and pulls, but then he feels the weight taking him over, and he won't let go, but he hasn't the strength, he's falling with Soli, he feels the impact of the bricks through Soli's body.

When Jago Antia stirred weakly on the roof, when he looked up, it was dawn. He held himself up and said, "Are you still here? Tell me what you want." Then he saw at the parapet, very dim and shifting in the grey light, the shape of a small body, a boy looking down over the edge towards the ocean. As Jago Antia watched, the boy turned slowly, and in the weak light he saw that the boy was wearing a uniform of olive green, and he asked, "Where shall I go?" Jago Antia began to speak, but then his voice caught, because he was remembering his next and seventh birthday, the first party without Soli, and his parents holding him between them, soothing him, saying you must want something, and he looking up at their faces, at the lines in his father's face, the exhaustion in his mother's eyes. Burjor Mama sits on the carpet behind him with head down, and Amir Khan stands behind, and Jehangir shakes his head, nothing. His mother's eyes fill with tears, and she kisses him on the forehead, "Baba, it's all right, let us give you a present," and his heart breaks beneath a surging weight, but he stands up straight, and looking at her and his father, he says, "I want a uniform." So Jago Antia looked at the boy as he came closer, and he saw the small letters above the pocket, J. ANTIA, and the sun came up, and he saw the boy clearly, he saw the enormous dark eyes, and in the eyes he saw his vicious and ravenous strength, his courage and his devotion, his silence and his pain, his whole misshapen and magnificent life, and Jago Antia said, "Jehangir, Jehangir, you're already at home."

Thapa and Amir Khan came up the stairs slowly, and he called out to them, "Come, come. I'm all right." He was sitting cross-legged, watching the sun move in and out of the clouds.

Thapa squatted beside him. "Was it here?"

"He's gone. I saw him, and then he vanished."

"Who?"

Jago Antia shook his head. "Someone I didn't know before."

"What was he doing here then?"

"He was lost." He leaned on both their shoulders, one arm around each, for the descent down the stairs. Somehow, naked and hopping from stair to stair, he was smiling. He knew that nothing had changed. He knew he was still and forever Jago Antia, that for him it was too late for anything but a kind of solitude, that he would give his body to the fire, that in the implacable hills to the north, among the rocks, he and other men and women, each with histories of their own, would find each other for life and for death. And yet he felt free. He sat on the porch, strapping his leg on, and Amir Khan brought out three cups of tea. Thapa wrapped a sheet around Jago Antia, and looking at each other they both laughed. "Thank you," Jago Antia said. Then they drank the tea together.

MANOJ DAS

Manoj Das was born in 1934 in a remote coastal village of Orissa, India. He has written to great acclaim in both Oriya and English, totaling about forty books in English and an equal number in his mother tongue. His first collection of stories in English was published in 1967. Asked why he began writing in English, he responded, "At one stage, I felt inspired to write in English because I was haunted by the feeling that much of the Indian fiction in English that claimed to project the Indian life and situation was not doing justice to its claim. I thought, born in a village just before Independence and hence living through the transition at an impressionable age, I could present through English a chunk of genuine India." Das is considered by many the foremost bilingual writer in India.

Among his most recent publications in English are *Selected Fiction* (2001), *The Escapist* (2001), *The Lady Who Died One and a Half Times and Other Fantasies* (2003), and *Chasing the Rainbow* (2004).

Das is a recipient of numerous honors, including India's most prestigious award for literature, the Saraswati Samman, and his stories have been translated into many languages. In 1963 he joined the Sri Aurobindo Ashram at Pondicherry, where he is a professor of English literature at the International Center of Education.

Miss Moberly's Targets

It was ten minutes to five p.m. and time for Miss Dolly Moberly to feel excited. She paced along the balcony throwing restless glances at the road. Robinson was already there, gazing up with the devotion of a dog.

Robinson, of course, was a dog, as were Mac and Badal who were yet to arrive. They resided in the slum not far from "The Rest." Their owners, if they had any, must be calling them by other names. One day Miss Moberly had thrown a crust of bread to a dog and the crust had smartly landed in its mouth. Delighted, she had forthwith named it Robinson. Thereafter the dog would bound up to her with wagging tail and twinkling eyes whenever she called it by that name.

One evening, while she relaxed in her easy chair on the balcony and enjoyed the dog's vigorous tail-wagging below, she gave some leisurely thought to this question: Why, of so many names, had Robinson come so readily to her tongue? It did not take long for her to remember the bewhiskered Mr. Robinson, her father's chum who sported impressive sideburns, and was secretary of the local Anglo-Indian society. On the outskirts of the town lived another Robinson whose poultry produce was famous as the Sahib's Eggs. Both had departed long since.

From the parapet a middle-aged cat—one which reminded Miss Moberly of a retired magistrate—watched the dog, disgust writ large on its chubby face. Miss Moberly always felt uneasy at the sight of this cat. "The Rest" was a home for the affluent aged. True, most of the inmates had no near enough relatives to care for them, but the organization which ran it was a sound one and from the attendants right up to the health officers and the prefect everybody worked with commendable dedication. For all their goodwill, however, and for the fat chunks they knocked off your bank-deposit month after month (or you could surrender your regular pension to them), they could not provide you with dear ones if you had none—none to visit you and warm you up with a few endearing words.

That did not mean that anyone could play uncle to you. But that was exactly what this cat was doing! It would appear on the threshold of her cabin near midnight and give out a lusty mew which evidently amounted to "How are you?" but which also seemed to contain an arrogant hint that you were bound to be happy under the arrangements and that if you were not, none but yourself was to blame.

Miss Moberly used to answer the cat, "I'm O.K. Thanks." But despite her perfunctory tone, the cat would hop on to her bedside table and cast a piercing look at her before jumping out through the window.

In the beginning Miss Moberly had quietly put up with this offensive behaviour of her nocturnal visitor, although it had not taken her long to find out that the cat had nothing to do with the management of the institution. But the night she, quite by chance, found out that it was a male cat (and realized that all her life she had thought of all cats as belonging to the female sex), she told it straightaway, "Your supervisorship is rather uncalled for. Please leave me alone." She repeated her protest to the cat at its subsequent visits, but in vain.

This struck her as strange, for she was certain that cats had once been much more sensitive and humble. Of course, that was sixty-five years ago. She remembered at least one of her mother's several cats. They had at the time a young tenant on the upper floor of their house. "There you are!" Miss Moberly told herself and grinned. "He was yet another Robinson!" In fact, the only Robinson that had once mattered to her.

Robinson used to return to his apartment in the evening and cook for himself, invariably inviting his landlady's cat to share his supper with him. The pussy would shoot up the stairs at his call and return an hour later, its tail raised in triumph.

After a few months devoted to an exchange of shy smiles with the tenant, Miss Moberly, then a teenager and beautiful, had tied a love letter to the cat's neck just before it was summoned upstairs. The letter was not long, but behind it lay a week's toil over numerous drafts.

When the cat returned, what it carried, tied to its tail instead of neck, was not a reply but the same letter, soiled with butter, jam and curry.

Sixty-five years later Miss Moberly called out from her balcony, "Robinson!"

Robinson wagged its mangy tail and gave out a tender bark.

Once Miss Moberly had realized the significance of the name she had given it she had consciously named the second and the third dogs as Mac and Badal. Mac deceived her, after carrying on an affair with her long enough to make it the talk of the town. It would have been hard to find a dignified match after the scandal and Miss Moberly did not bother to try.

It was a decade later that the millionaire Badal had come forward to propose to her. He was a widower with a clean reputation and, at fifty, had suddenly fallen in love, for the first time, he declared on oath. "What a headlong fall is here, my countrymen!" a professor friend used to tease them with a parody of Shakespeare. "Then, religion, caste and kin sank down slain whilst bloody love flourished over them!"

Badal closed down his business in Saigon but on his way back died in a shipwreck.

Badal, of course, could not be grouped with Robinson and Mac. But no longer did Miss Moberly bear any resentment even against those two. Not that she had ever formally excused them, but God must have. That alone explains her slowly transcending her anguish.

The gallant Badal died while he was at the peak of his happiness. For a long time Miss Moberly loved to imagine that the ship had sunk while Badal was fast asleep, dreaming of her, and the next moment he had found himself in the neighbourhood of God where he still awaited her, sporting the same milky smile under his bushy moustache.

But what about Mac? After he had squeezed out of her all he wanted, he joined a gang of international thugs. Injured in an encounter with the police, he died of gangrene. (Till she tired of the fantasy, Miss Moberly had nursed a faint hope that Mac's last words, soon to be delivered to her, would be: "Dolly dear, I'm sorry, I'm sorry, I'm sorry. . . .")

And Robinson! Perhaps the chap had never been able to love anything better than a cat all his life. Miss Moberly was convinced, though she could not say why, that unheard and unsung, he had died of leukaemia in some mofussil town, and that his skeleton was dangling in the anatomy section of the new medical college attached to the impoverished local hospital.

Miss Moberly stopped pacing to and fro and, leaning on the railing, looked down. At once three tails began wagging and three tongues lolled. Robinson, Mac and Badal.

Miss Moberly disappeared into her room and emerged, chuckling, with a small plastic tray filled with crumbs of cake, bread, and biscuit.

"Would you now set the chairs on the balcony and prepare tea?" she called faintly to her attendant. It was time for her friends to arrive. Mr. Doss was already in the park below, whacking his stick in the air and killing time. That was his virtue. If he arrived even half a minute early, he would kill that half-minute prayerfully looking at his watch, outside the door. "You are almost an Englishman, Mr. Doss!" his boss used to observe when he was in service. Mr. Doss took the tribute as the crowning glory of his life and was never tired of repeating it.

Mrs. Sawoo should be arriving any moment, accompanied or followed by Mr. Jacob. All three, now in their late eighties, were slightly older than Miss Moberly. Her father had been an influential man in the town, with a variety of successes and a couple of titles earned from the British raj. Her acquaintances, naturally, were numerous. But these three were the last surviving members of an inner circle which had sighed at every phase of the tragedy that was her life. They claimed to be younger than she in spirit and had begun to insist that she had lately been prone to mild hallucination and should be careful about it. Mrs. Sawoo, for instance, asserted that it was wrong to imagine that a male cat could

ever talk! Miss Moberly should have quipped that the
cat talked in its own language and not in English. But
the fitting rejoinder always evaded her when needed and
occurred long after she had been snubbed.

All that the three had done for a good many years
now was to sympathize with her. At last the day had
come for them to realize that it was not just sympathy
that was her due; she deserved congratulations too.
Henceforth no one would be able to say that her life
had been nothing if not a calendar of failures. She was
now ready to demonstrate to all concerned her spectacular success in striking her target.

"Dolly darling!"

Doss, Mrs. Sawoo and Jacob entered together and
Mrs. Sawoo gave her a noisy kiss.

Miss Moberly did not neglect to receive them warmly
but she remained thoughtful. She must demonstrate her
feat in an artful manner; nobody should suspect that she
was making a deliberate show of it.

A crumb fell from Mrs. Sawoo's hand. Miss Moberly
stooped to pick it up.

"Sorry, but leave it there, dear," murmured Mrs.
Sawoo.

Miss Moberly smiled and holding the crumb in her
hand long enough to draw everybody's attention to it,
suddenly threw it over the railing. Robinson jumped up
and caught it in its mouth. Mac and Badal, knowing that
their turns were coming, licked their lips and gave out
subdued barks.

"Excellent!" said Jacob and Doss.

"Thank you, but wait and see!" Miss Moberly turned
her chair to face the road and, placing the plastic tray
on her lap, began throwing the crumbs with style and
verve. The dogs romped and hopped, catching the mis-
siles with dexterity.

"Excellent. Wonderful!"

The guests were liberal with their exclamations.

Miss Moberly did not recall at what point she had
stood up. The rhythm of the romping dogs found an
echo in her own motions. She almost danced as she
threw the crumbs.

"Come on, Dolly, enough of it. Drink your tea!" said Mrs. Sawoo in a matronly tone.

The plastic tray had been emptied. Miss Moberly sat down, satisfaction visible as distinctly as a sunrise on her face.

"Hah! You are surprised, aren't you? Believe it or not, rarely do I miss my target. Who could have thought that I would be able to achieve success ninety times out of a hundred," she managed to say between mild gasps, and laughed.

"Why not, Dolly!" Mrs. Sawoo remarked while stirring her tea.

Miss Moberly looked down and waving at the dogs, said, "Still waiting, eh! Disperse, quick! See you tomorrow!"

"It is a regular sport with you, is it, Dolly?" Jacob queried with a chuckle.

"Who could have dreamed that I would be such a success at it!" Miss Moberly trilled bashfully.

"Well, Dolly, is there a cleverer hunter among the beasts than a dog?" said Doss.

"Exactly," elucidated Mrs. Sawoo. "A dog will snap up a crumb even if you throw it with your eyes shut!"

"Do you remember my Alsatian, Don Juan? Once he nabbed a robin from a branch two and half yards above the ground—yes—he did so while I looked on," reminisced Doss, drawing in the air with his stick the location of the bird's perch and the swiftness with which Don Juan had pounced upon its prey.

"And I believe you all remember," he continued, "Sweet Heart, my spaniel during my Delhi days, whose picture had appeared in Vol. 3, No. 7, Page 12, March 1921 number of *Dogs International,* with a feature by Mr. Richard Whites. How Sweet Heart used to fetch the tennis ball with a soft bite!" Doss kept a slice of cake under his own soft bite for a while and then resumed, "I just can't help recalling again and again the observation Mr. Whites had made—that looking at Mr. Doss the ideal doggy and Sweet Heart, his regal spaniel, one would think that Sweet Heart was the master and Mr. Doss was her dog! But I used to protest, 'Such compli-

ments, sir, are not my due!' Mr. Whites would say, 'Mr.
Doss! You were almost an Englishman, except for this
humility of yours.' Ha ha!"

For the next half-hour they remained engrossed in discussing the great dogs they had met. Nobody marked
how dead Miss Moberly's face looked and how awkward
the movement of her limbs had become.

The guests stood up.

"Till next week, Dolly, darling!" said the gentlemen,
and Mrs. Sawoo kissed her goodbye.

Miss Moberly, as lively as an orchestra-conductor only
a little while ago, walked into her room holding on to
the wall and fell sprawled on the bed.

"Despite all your glittering false teeth with which you
smile cleverly, you are a fool, Mrs. Sawoo. And despite
your dyed moustache which you still strive to keep
forked out in your damned desire to look dashing, you
are a snob, Mr. Doss. And, Mr. Jacob, you are a nincom-
poop!" mumbled out Miss Moberly and that gave her
the strength to sit up for a while. She did not know
when sleep overtook her.

As soon as she woke up early in the morning and saw
her supper lying untouched on the table and recollected
the events of the evening, she began taking determined
steps to tide over her anguish. At first she reminded
herself for the thousandth time that it was vain to expect
justice from human beings, including those who had
been near and dear for decades. Then she tried to forget
the matter and, failing, set to analysing the minds of her
three friends. She concluded that since they had fallen
into the habit of sympathizing with her for her missing
the target all her life, they had grown chronically incapable of accepting her success even when it was so glar-
ingly evident.

She was charmed by her own power to delve into the
very crux of the matter and that gave her some peace.

But she soon hit upon the real mischief the deplorable
episode had done. It had bred some misgivings in her
own mind about her capacity and the doubts bred a
deepening sense of frustration. But could she afford to
lose her self-confidence just because of the superficial

observations of a few foolish friends? "No!" she told herself, "No, no, no!"

She must prove, at least to herself, that her achievement was as real as her confidence in herself.

In the evening Miss Moberly stole several peeps into David Dawson's room. The retired brigadier passed his mornings in humming or whistling ancient war tunes and his afternoons in snoozing against a huge pillow.

After strolling for a while along the balcony in front of Dawson's room during which she assessed the brigadier's condition, Miss Moberly stealthily entered the room and came out in a minute. Dawson did not open his eyes.

Back on the balcony she breathed deeply, inhaling a lot of oxygen and courage. She knew under which side of the pillow Dawson kept his pistol. She wavered for a moment and then entered the room again, picked up the weapon, and tiptoed out.

Now she could prove it. The dogs might get the credit in the case of the crumbs. But surely, it could not be the same when it came to receiving a bullet! If she could hit one, it would be entirely due to her accuracy of aim, not the dogs.

Who should it be? Robinson, Mac or Badal? Any would do. Poor Badal! But what business had he to fall in love if he must die in a shipwreck? None of them deserved mercy. She could shoot down any of them. Couldn't she? Of course she could! she assured herself, breathing in deeply several times.

"Damn it! Who the hell took away my pistol? Good God! Dolly, you!" Brigadier Dawson screamed and hobbled towards the door. Miss Moberly stood still, pressing the pistol to her breast, like a child adamant not to part with a toy.

"You meant to commit suicide, Dolly? Yo ho!" the old warrior screamed again, trembling all over.

"Suicide?" cried out Jayshri Mishra, former actress and one-time mistress of a prodigal prince, as she came running, her eyes ignited by the brigadier's exclamation.

"Suicide? Oh no!" shouted in a cracking voice the retired principal Jonathan Jana, who generally kept quiet during the day but at night taught Milton in his sleep.

"Suicide?" shrieked Miss Moberly herself and she broke into wild sobs.

The actress and the principal tried to take hold of Miss Moberly's tiny head. She obliged both, first leaning on the actress's breast and then on the principal's. She also allowed the brigadier, who showed remarkable consideration and patience in relieving her of the weapon, to fondle her.

It was the principal who first echoed her sobs. He was instantly joined by the actress and the brigadier.

Fifteen feet below, Robinson, Mac and Badal yapped politely.

The well-wishers led Miss Moberly to her bed. Jayshri prepared coffee for all. The duty of hurling crumbs at the dogs was discharged by the brigadier. They all sat around Miss Moberly till late in the night, had their supper together, and talked of human goodness and God's kindness and exchanged anecdotes of profound significance.

"Now, go to sleep, sweet child, my very sweet child," said the principal stroking Miss Moberly's head and bidding her an affectionate goodnight.

When the male cat appeared at midnight and put its usual question to Miss Moberly, she did not feel offended at all. She had begun to see a guardian in everyone. "I'm quite all right. Thank you," she told the cat politely and fell asleep.

ANITA DESAI

Born in Mussoorie, India, and educated at Delhi University, Anita Desai is the daughter of a Bengali father and a German mother. The author of eight novels and children's books as well as short stories, she has been described as "one of the most gifted of contemporary Indian writers" (*The New Yorker*) and "a writer's writer" (*The Times Literary Supplement*). Married and the mother of four children, she was a Visiting Fellow at Girton College, Cambridge, and has taught creative writing at Mount Holyoke and Smith colleges. Desai has described her work as an attempt to reveal "the truth that is nine-tenths of the iceberg that lies submerged beneath the one-tenth visible portion we call Reality." *Fire on the Mountain* (1977), perhaps Desai's best-known novel, depicts an elderly widow whose way of life is irrevocably altered with the arrival of her erratic and destructive great-granddaughter. Typically in Desai's fiction, modern family life is filled with discord, and even violence.

Among her early novels are *Cry, the Peacock* (1963), *Voices in the City* (1965), *Bye-Bye, Blackbird* (1968), and *Where Shall We Go This Summer* (1975). Two of her other novels, *Clear Light of Day* (1980) and *In Custody* (1984), were nominated for England's Booker Prize. Desai's recent publications include *Journey to Ithaca* (1995), *Fasting, Feasting* (1999), *Diamond Dust and Other Stories* (2000), and *The Zigzag Way* (2004).

The Farewell Party

Before the party she had made a list, faintheartedly, and marked off the items as they were dealt with, inexorably—cigarettes, soft drinks, ice, *kebabs* and so on. But she had forgotten to provide lights. The party was to be held on the lawn: on these dry summer nights one could plan a lawn party weeks in advance and be certain of fine weather, and she had thought happily of how the roses would be in bloom and of the stars and perhaps even fireflies, so decorative and discreet, all gracefully underlining her unsuspected talent as a hostess. But she had not realized that there would be no moon and therefore it would be very dark on the lawn. All the lights on the veranda, in the portico and indoors were on, like so many lanterns, richly copper and glowing, with extraordinary beauty as though aware that the house would soon be empty and these were the last few days of illumination and family life, but they did very little to light the lawn which was vast, a still lake of inky grass.

Wandering about with a glass in one hand and a plate of cheese biscuits in another, she gave a start now and then to see an acquaintance emerge from the darkness which had the gloss, the sheen, the coolness but not the weight of water, and present her with a face, vague and without outlines but eventually recognizable. "Oh," she cried several times that evening, "I didn't know you had arrived. I've been looking for you," she would add with unaccustomed intimacy (was it because of the gin and lime, her second, or because such warmth could safely be held to lead to nothing now that they were leaving town?). The guest, also having had several drinks between beds of flowering balsam and torenias before launching out onto the lawn, responded with an equal vivacity. Sometimes she had her arm squeezed or a hand slid down the bareness of her back—which was athletic; she had once played tennis, rather well—and once someone said, "I've been hiding in this corner, watching you," while another went so far as to say, "Is it true you are leaving us, Bina? How can you be so cruel?" And if it were a woman guest, the words were that much more effusive. It was all heady, astonishing.

It was astonishing because Bina was a frigid and friendless woman. She was thirty-five. For fifteen years she had been bringing up her children and, in particular, nursing the eldest who was severely spastic. This had involved her deeply in the workings of the local hospital and with its many departments and doctors, but her care for this child was so intense and so desperate that her relationship with them was purely professional. Outside this circle of family and hospital—ringed, as it were, with barbed wire and lit with one single floodlight—Bina had no life. The town had scarcely come to know her, for its life turned in the more jovial circles of mah-jong, bridge, coffee parties, club evenings and, occasionally, a charity show in aid of the Red Cross. For these Bina had a kind of sad contempt and certainly no time. A tall, pale woman, heavy-boned and sallow, she had a certain presence, a certain dignity, and people, having heard of the spastic child, liked and admired her, but she had not thought she had friends. Yet tonight they were coming forth from the darkness in waves that quite overwhelmed.

Now here was Mrs. Ray, the Commissioner's wife, chirping inside a nest of rustling embroidered organza. "Why are you leaving us so soon, Mrs. Raman? You've only been here—two years, is it?"

"Five," exclaimed Bina, widening her eyes, herself surprised at such a length of time. Although time dragged heavily in their household, agonizingly slow, and the five years had been so hard that sometimes, at night, she did not know how she had crawled through the day and if she would crawl through another, her back almost literally broken by the weight of the totally dependent child and of the three smaller ones who seemed perpetually to clamor for their share of attention, which they felt they never got. Yet now these five years had telescoped. They were over. The Raman family was moving and their time here was spent. There had been the hospital, the girls' school, the boys' school, picnics, monsoons, birthday parties and measles. Crushed together into a handful. She gazed down at her hands, tightened around glass and plate. "Time has flown," she murmured incredulously.

"Oh, I wish you were staying, Mrs. Raman," cried the Commissioner's wife and, as she squeezed Bina's arm, her fragrant talcum powder seemed to lift off her chalky shoulders and some of it settled on Bina who sneezed. "It's been so nice to have a family like yours here. It's a small town, so little to do, at least one must have good friends . . ."

Bina blinked at such words of affection from a woman she had met twice, perhaps thrice before. Bina and her husband did not go in for society. The shock of their first child's birth had made them both fanatic parents. But she knew that not everyone considered this vital factor in their lives, and spoke of "social duties" in a somehow reproving tone. The Commissioner's wife had been annoyed, she always felt, by her refusal to help out at the Red Cross fair. The hurt silence with which her refusal had been accepted had implied the importance of these "social duties" of which Bina remained so stubbornly unaware.

However, this one evening, this last party, was certainly given over to their recognition and celebration. "Oh, everyone, everyone is here," rejoiced the Commissioner's wife, her eyes snapping from face to face in that crowded aquarium, and, at a higher pitch, cried "Renu, why weren't you at the mah-jong party this morning?" and moved off into another powdery organza embrace that rose to meet her from the night like a moth and then was submerged again in the shadows of the lawn. Bina gave one of those smiles that easily-frightened people found mocking, a shade too superior, somewhat scornful. Looking down into her glass of gin and lime, she moved on and in a minute found herself brought up short against the quite regal although overweight figure, in raw silk and homespun and the somewhat saturnine air of underpaid culture, of Bose, an employee of the local museum whom she had met once or twice at the art competitions and exhibitions to which she was fond of hauling her children, whether reluctant or enthusiastic, because "it made a change," she said.

"Mrs. Raman," he said in the fruity tones of the culture-bent Bengali, "how we'll miss you at the next children's art competitions. You used to be my chief inspiration—"

"Inspiration?" she laughed, incredulously, spilling some of her drink and proffering the plate of cheese biscuits from which he helped himself, half-bowing as though it were gold she offered, gems.

"Yes, yes, inspiration," he went on, even more fruitily now that his mouth was full. "Think of me—alone, the hapless organizer—surrounded by mammas, by primary school teachers, by three, four, five hundred children. And the judges—they are always the most trouble, those judges. And then I look at you—so cool, controlling your children, handling them so wonderfully and with such superb results—my inspiration!"

She was flustered by this unaccustomed vision of herself and half-turned her face away from Bose the better to contemplate it, but could find no reflection of it in the ghostly white bush of the Queen of the Night, and listened to him murmur on about her unkindness in deserting him in this cultural backwater to that darkest of dooms—guardian of a provincial museum—where he saw no one but school teachers herding children through his halls or, worse, Government officials who periodically and inexplicably stirred to create trouble for him and made their official presences felt amongst the copies of the Ajanta frescoes (in which even the mouldy and peeled-off portions were carefully reproduced) and the cupboards of Indus Valley seals. Murmuring commiseration, she left him to a gloomy young professor of history who was languishing at another of the institutions of provincial backwaters that they so deplored and whose wife was always having a baby, and slipped away, still feeling an unease at Bose's unexpected vision of her which did not tally with the cruder reality, into the less equivocal company provided by a ring of twittering "company wives."

These women she had always encountered in just such

a ring as they formed now, the kind that garden babblers
form under a hedge where they sit gabbling and whirring
with social bitchiness, and she had always stood outside
it, smiling stiffly, not wanting to join and refusing their
effusively nodded invitation. They were the wives of men
who represented various mercantile companies in the
town—Imperial Tobacco, Brooke Bond, Esso and so
on—and although they might seem exactly alike to one
who did not belong to this circle, inside it were subtle
gradations of importance according to the particular
company for which each one's husband worked and of
these only they themselves were initiates. Bina was, however unwillingly, an initiate. Her husband worked for
one of these companies but she had always stiffly refused
to recognize these gradations, or consider them. They
noted the rather set sulkiness of her silence when
amongst them and privately labeled her queer, proud,
boring and difficult. Also, they felt she belonged to their
circle whether she liked it or not.

Now she entered this circle with diffidence, wishing
she had stayed with the more congenial Bose (why
hadn't she? What was it in her that made her retreat
from anything like a friendly approach?) and was taken
aback to find their circle parting to admit her and hear
their cries of welcome and affection that did not, however, lose the stridency and harshness of garden babblers' voices.

"Bina, how do you like the idea of going back to
Bombay?"

"Have you started packing, Bina? Poor you. Oh, are
you having packers over from Delhi? Oh well, then it's
not so bad."

Never had they been so vociferous in her company,
so easy, so warm. They were women to whom the most
awful thing that had ever happened was the screw of a
golden earring disappearing down the bathroom sink or
a mother-in-law's visit or an ayah deserting just before
the arrival of guests: what could they know of Bina's
life, Bina's ordeal? She cast her glance at the drinks they
held—but they were mostly of orange squash. Only the
Esso wife, who participated in amateur dramatics and

ran a boutique and was rather taller and bolder than the rest, held a whisky and soda. So much affection generated by just orange squash? Impossible. Rather tentatively, she offered them the remains of the cheese biscuits, found herself chirping replies, deploring the nuisance of having packing crates all over the house, talking of the flat they would move into in Bombay, and then, sweating unobtrusively with the strain, saw another recognizable fish swim towards her from the edge of the liquescent lawn, and swung away in relief, saying, "Mrs. D'Souza! How late you are, but I'm so glad—" for she really was.

Mrs. D'Souza was her daughter's teacher at the convent school and had clearly never been to a cocktail party before so that all Bina's compassion was aroused by those school-scuffed shoes and her tea-party best— quite apart from the simple truth that she found in her an honest individuality that all those beautifully dressed and poised babblers lacked, being stamped all over by the plain rubber stamps of their husbands' companies— and she hurried off to find Mrs. D'Souza something suitable to drink. "Sherry? Why yes, I think I'll be able to find you some," she said, a bit flabbergasted at such an unexpected fancy of the pepper-haired schoolteacher, "and I'll see if Tara's around—she'll want to see you," she added, vaguely and fraudulently, wondering why she had asked Mrs. D'Souza to a cocktail party, only to see, as she skirted the rose bed, the admirable Bose appear at her side and envelop her in this strange intimacy that marked the whole evening, and went off, lighthearted, towards the table where her husband was trying, with the help of some hired waiters in soggy white uniforms with the name of the restaurant from which they were hired embroidered in red across their pockets, to cope with the flood of drinks this party atmosphere had called for and released.

Harassed, perspiring, his feet burning, Raman was nevertheless pleased to be so obviously employed and be saved the strain of having to converse with his motley assembly of guests: he had no more gift for society than his wife had. Ice cubes were melting on the tablecloth in sopping puddles and he had trouble in keeping track of his bottles: they were, besides the newly bought dozens of beer bottles and Black Knight whisky, the remains of their five years in this town that he now wished to bring to their end—bottles brought by friends from trips abroad, bottles bought cheap through "contacts" in the army or air force, some gems, extravaganzas bought for anniversaries such as a nearly full bottle of Vat 69, a bottle with a bit of crême de menthe growing sticky at the bottom, some brown sherry with a great deal of rusty sediment, a red Golconda wine from Hyderabad, and a bottle of Remy Martin that he was keeping guiltily to himself, pouring small quantities into a whisky glass at his elbow and gulping it down in between mixing some very weird cocktails for his guests. There was no one at the party he liked well enough to share it with. Oh, one of the doctors perhaps, but where were they? Submerged in grass, in dark, in night and chatter, clatter of ice in glass, teeth on biscuit, teeth on teeth. Enamel and gold. Crumbs and dregs. All awash, all soaked in night. Watery sound of speech, liquid sound of drink. Water and ice and night. It occurred to him that everyone had forgotten him, the host, that it was a mistake to have stationed himself amongst the waiters, that he ought to move out, mingle with the guests. But he felt himself drowned, helplessly and quite delightfully, in Remy Martin, in grass, in a border of purple torenias.

Then he was discovered by his son who galloped through the ranks of guests and waiters to fling himself at his father and ask if he could play the new Beatles record, his friends had asked to hear it.

Raman considered, taking the opportunity to pour out and gulp down some more of the precious Remy Martin. "All right," he said, after a judicious minute or two, "but keep it low, everyone won't want to hear it," not adding that he himself didn't, for his taste in music ran to slow and melancholy, folk at its most frivolous. Still, he glanced into the lighted room where his children and the children of neighbours and guests had collected, making themselves tipsy on Fanta and Coca-Cola, the girls giggling in a multicoloured huddle and the boys swaggering around the record-player with a kind of lounging strut, holding bottles in their hands with a sophisticated ease, exactly like experienced cocktail party guests, so that he smiled and wished he had a ticket, a passport that would make it possible to break into that party within a party. It was chillingly obvious to him that he hadn't one. He also saw that a good deal of their riotousness was due to the fact that they were raiding the snack trays that the waiters carried through the room to the lawn, and that they were seeing to it that the trays emerged half-empty. He knew he ought to go in and see about it but he hadn't the heart, or the nerve. He couldn't join that party but he wouldn't wreck it either, so he only caught hold of one of the waiters and suggested that the snack trays be carried out from the kitchen straight onto the lawn, not by way of the drawing room, and led him towards a group that seemed to be without snacks and saw too late that it was a group of the company executives that he loathed most. He half-groaned, then hiccupped at his mistake, but it was too late to alter course now. He told himself that he ought to see to it that the snacks were offered around without snag or error.

Poor Raman was placed in one of the lower ranks of the companies' hierarchy. That is, he did not belong to a British concern, or even to an American-collaboration one, but merely to an Indian one. Oh, a long-established, prosperous and solid one but, still, only Indian. Those cigarettes that he passed around were made by his own company. Somehow it struck a note of bad taste amongst these fastidious men who played golf, danced at the club on Independence Eve and New Year's Eve, invited at least one foreign couple to every party and called their decorative wives "darling" when in public. Poor Raman never had belonged. It was so obvious to everyone, even to himself, as he passed around those awful cigarettes that sold so well in the market. It had been obvious since their first disastrous dinner party for this very ring of jocular gentlemen, five years ago. Nono had cried right through the party, Bina had spent the evening racing upstairs to see to the babies' baths and bedtime and then crawling reluctantly down, the hired cook had got

drunk and stolen two of the chickens so that there was
not enough on the table, no one had relaxed for a minute or enjoyed a second—it had been too sad and har-
rowing even to make a good story or a funny anecdote.
They had all let it sink by mutual consent and the invita-
tions to play a round of golf on Saturday afternoon or
a rubber of bridge on Sunday morning had been issued
and refused with conspiratorial smoothness. Then there
was that distressing hobby of Raman's: his impossibly
long walks on which he picked up bits of wood and took
them home to sandpaper and chisel and then call wood
sculpture. What could one do with a chap who did that?
He himself wasn't sure if he pursued such odd tastes
because he was a social pariah or if he was one on account of this oddity. Not to speak of the spastic child.
Now that didn't even bear thinking of, and so it was no
wonder that Raman swayed towards them so hesitantly,
as though he were wading through water instead of over
clipped grass, and handed his cigarettes around with
such an apologetic air.

But, after all, hesitation and apology proved unnecessary. One of them—was he Polson's Coffee or Brooke
Bond Tea?—clasped Raman about the shoulders as
proper men do on meeting, and hearty voices rose together, congratulating him on his promotion (it wasn't
one, merely a transfer, and they knew it), envying him his
move to the metropolis. They talked as if they had known
each other for years, shared all kinds of public schoolboy
fun. One—was he Voltas or Ciba?—talked of golf matches
at the Willingdon as though he had often played there
with Raman, another spoke of *kebabs* eaten on the roadside after a party as though Raman had been one of the
gang. Amazed and grateful as a schoolboy admitted to
a closed society, Raman nodded and put in a few cautious words, put away his cigarettes, called a waiter to
refill their glasses and broke away before the clock
struck twelve and the golden carriage turned into a
pumpkin, he himself into a mouse. He hated mice.

Walking backwards, he walked straight into the soft
barrier of Miss Dutta's ample back wrapped and bound
in rich Madras silk.

"Sorry, sorry, Miss Dutta. I'm clumsy as a bear," he apologized, but here, too, there was no call for apology for Miss Dutta was obviously delighted at having been bumped into.

"My dear Mr. Raman, what can you expect if you invite the whole town to your party?" she asked in that piercing voice that invariably made her companions drop theirs self-consciously. "You and Bina have been so popular—what are we going to do without you?"

He stood pressing his glass with white-tipped fingers and tried to think what he or Bina had provided her with that she could possibly miss. In any case, Miss Dutta could always manage, and did manage, everything single-handedly. She was the town busybody, secretary and chairman of more committees than he could count: they ranged from the Film Society to the Blood Bank, from the Red Cross to the Friends of the Museum, for Miss Dutta was nothing if not versatile. "We hardly ever saw you at our film shows of course," her voice rang out, making him glance furtively over his shoulder to see if anyone were listening, "but it was so nice *knowing* you were in town and that I could count on you. So few people here *care,* you know," she went on, and affectionately bumped her comfortable middle-aged body into his as someone squeezed by, making him remember that he had once heard her called a man-eater, and wonder which man she had eaten and even consider, for a moment, if there were not, after all, some charm in those powdered creases of her creamy arms, equaling if not surpassing that of his worn and harassed wife's bony angles. Why did suffering make for angularity? he even asked himself with uncharacteristic unkindness. But when Miss Dutta laid an arm on top of his glass-holding one and raised herself on her toes to bray something into his ear, he loyally decided that he was too accustomed to sharp angles to change them for such unashamed luxuriance, and, contriving to remove her arm by grasping her elbow—how one's fingers sank into the stuff!—he steered her towards his wife who was standing at the table and inefficiently pouring herself another gin and lime.

"This is my third," she confessed hurriedly, "and I can't

tell you how gay it makes me feel. I giggle at everything everyone says."

"Good," he pronounced, feeling inside a warm expansion of relief at seeing her lose, for the moment, her tension and anxiety. "Let's hear you giggle," he said, sloshing some more gin into her glass.

"Look at those children," she exclaimed, and they stood in a bed of balsam, irredeemably crushed, and looked into the lighted drawing room where their daughter was at the moment the cynosure of all juvenile eyes, having thrown herself with abandon into a dance of monkey-like movements. "What is it, Miss Dutta?" the awed mother enquired. "You're more up in the latest fashions than I am—is it the twist, the rock or the jungle?" and all three watched, enthralled, till Tara began to totter and, losing her simian grace, collapsed against some wildly shrieking girlfriends.

A bit embarrassed by their daughter's reckless abandon, the parents discussed with Miss Dutta whose finger, by her own admission, was placed squarely on the pulse of youth, the latest trends in juvenile culture on which Miss Dutta gave a neat sociological discourse (all the neater for having been given earlier that day at the convocation of the Home Science College) and Raman wondered uneasily at this opening of floodgates in his own family—his wife grown giggly with gin, his daughter performing wildly to a Chubby Checkers record—how had it all come about? Was it the darkness all about them, dense as the heavy curtains about a stage, that made them act, for an hour or so, on the tiny lighted stage of brief intimacy with such a lack of inhibition? Was it the drink, so freely sloshing from end to end of the house and lawn on account of his determination to clear out his "cellar" (actually one-half of the sideboard and the top shelf of the wardrobe in his dressing room) and his muddling and mixing them, making up untried and experimental cocktails and lavishly pouring out the whisky without a measure? But these were solid and everyday explanations and there was about this party something out of the ordinary and everyday—at least to the Ramans, normally so austere and unpopular. He knew the real reason too—it was all because the party had been labelled a "farewell party," everyone knew it was the last one, that the Ramans were leaving and they would not meet up again. There was about it exactly that kind of sentimental euphoria that is generated at a shipboard party, the one given on the last night before the end of the voyage. Everyone draws together with an intimacy, a lack of inhibition not displayed or guessed at before, knowing this is the last time, tomorrow they will be dispersed, it will be over. They will not meet, be reminded of it or be required to repeat it.

As if to underline this new and Cinderella's ball–like atmosphere of friendliness and gaiety, three pairs of neighbours now swept in (and three kochias lay down and died under their feet, to the gardener's rage and sorrow): the couple who lived to the Ramans' left, the couple who lived to their right, and the couple from across the road, all crying, "So sorry to be late, but you know what a long way we had to come," making everyone laugh identically at the identical joke. Despite the disparity in their looks and ages—one couple was very young, another middle-aged, the third grandparents—they were, in a sense, as alike as the company executives and their wives, for they too bore a label if a less alarming one: Neighbours, it said. Because they were neighbours, and although they had never been more than nodded to over the hedge, waved to in passing cars or spoken to about anything other than their children, dogs, flowers and gardens, their talk had a vivid immediacy that went straight to the heart.

"Diamond's going to miss you so—he'll be heartbroken," moaned the grandparents who lived alone in their spotless house with a black Labrador who had made a habit of visiting the Ramans whenever he wanted young company, a romp on the lawn or an illicit biscuit.

"I don't know what my son will do without Diamond," reciprocated Bina with her new and sympathetic warmth. "He'll force me to get a dog of his own, I know, and how will I ever keep one in a flat in Bombay?"

"When are you going to throw out those rascals?" demanded a father of Raman, pointing at the juvenile revelers indoors. "My boy has an exam tomorrow, you know, but he said he couldn't be bothered about it—he had to go to the Ramans' farewell party."

One mother confided to Bina, winning her heart forever, "Now that you are leaving, I can talk to you about it at last: did you know my Vinod is sweet on your Tara? Last night when I was putting him to bed, he said 'Mama, when I grow up I will marry Tara. I will sit on a white horse and wear a turban and carry a sword in my belt and I will go and marry Tara.' What shall we do about that, eh? Only a ten-year difference in age, isn't there—or twelve?" and both women rocked with laughter.

The party had reached its crest, like a festive ship, loud and illuminated for that last party before the journey's end, perched on the dizzy top of the dark wave. It could do nothing now but descend and dissolve. As if by simultaneous and unanimous consent, the guests began to leave (in the wake of the Commissioner and his wife who left first, like royalty) streaming towards the drive where cars stood bumper to bumper—more than had visited the Ramans' house in the previous five years put together. The light in the portico fell on Bina's pride and joy, a Chinese orange tree, lighting its miniature globes of fruit like golden lanterns. There was a babble, an uproar of leavetaking (the smaller children, already in pyjamas, watched open-mouthed from a dark window upstairs). Esso and Caltex left together, arms about each other and smoking cigars, like figures in a comic act. Miss Dutta held firmly to Bose's arm as they dipped, bowed, swayed and tripped on their way out. Bina was clasped, kissed—earrings grazed her cheek, talcum powder tickled her nose. Raman had his back slapped till he thrummed and vibrated like a beaten gong.

It seemed as if Bina and Raman were to be left alone at last, left to pack up and leave—now the good-byes had been said, there was nothing else they could possibly do—but no, out popped the good doctors from the hospital who had held themselves back in the darkest corners of the party, and made themselves inconspicuous throughout the party, and now, in the manner in which they clasped the host by the shoulders and the hostess by her hands, and said, "Ah *now* we have a chance to be with you at last, now we can begin *our* party," revealed that although this was the first time they had come to the Ramans' house on any but professional visits, they were not merely friends—they were almost a part of that self-defensive family, the closest to them in sympathy. Raman and Bina both felt a warm, moist expansion of tenderness inside themselves, the tenderness they had till today restricted to the limits of their family, no farther, as though they feared it had not an unlimited capacity. Now its close horizons stepped backwards, with some surprise.

And it was as the doctors said—the party now truly began. Cane chairs were dragged out of the veranda onto the lawn, placed in a ring next to the flowering Queen of the Night which shook out flounces and frills of white scent with every rustle of night breeze. Bina could give in now to her two most urgent needs and dash indoors to smear her mosquito-bitten arms and feet with Citronella and fetch Nono to sit on her lap, to let Nono have a share, too, in the party. The good doctors and their wives leant forward and gave Nono the attention that made the parents' throats tighten with gratitude. Raman insisted on their each having a glass of Remy Martin—they must finish it tonight, he said, and would not let the waiters clear away the ice or glasses yet. So they sat on the veranda steps, smoking and yawning.

Now it turned out that Dr. Bannerji's wife, the lady in the Dacca sari and the steel-rimmed spectacles, had studied in Shantiniketan, and she sang, at her husband's and his colleagues' urging, Tagore's sweetest, saddest songs. When she sang, in heartbroken tones that seemed to come from some distance away, from the damp corners of the darkness where the fireflies flitted,

> *"Father, the boat is carrying me away,*
> *Father, it is carrying me away from home,"*

the eyes of her listeners, sitting tensely in that grassy, inky dark, glazed with tears that were compounded equally of drink, relief and regret.

KIRAN DESAI

Kiran Desai was born in New Delhi, India, in 1971 and lived there until she was fourteen. She lived with her mother in London for a year and then moved to the U.S., where she studied creative writing at Bennington College, Hollins University, and Columbia University. Her first novel, *Hullaballoo in the Guava Orchard* (1998), is a comic tale about a postal clerk in a provincial Indian town who becomes a local celebrity until his profitable situation is imperiled by an attack of langur monkeys. The novel won the Betty Trask Award, given by the Society of Authors for the best new novels written by citizens of the Commonwealth of Nations under the age of thirty-five. Her second novel, *The Inheritance of Loss* (2006), is set in a small Himalayan town against the background of a Nepalese uprising; a parallel story follows the adventures of a young man who pursues the American dream. It won both the Man Booker Prize and the National Book Critics Circle Fiction Award. Of the novel, a *New York Times* reviewer has written, "In scene after scene . . . a boardinghouse in England, derelict bungalows in Kalimpong, immigrant-packed basements in New York—Desai's novel seems lit by a moral intelligence at once fierce and tender."

Kiran Desai is the daughter of the well-respected novelist and short story writer Anita Desai.

Excerpt from

The Inheritance of Loss

Biju had started his second year in America at Pinoc-
chio's Italian Restaurant, stirring vats of spluttering
Bolognese, as over a speaker an opera singer sang of
love and murder, revenge and heartbreak.

"He smells," said the owner's wife. "I think I'm aller-
gic to his hair oil." She had hoped for men from the
poorer parts of Europe—Bulgarians perhaps, or Czecho-
slovakians. At least they might have something in common with them like religion and skin color, grandfathers
who ate cured sausages and looked like them too, but
they weren't coming in numbers great enough or they
weren't coming desperate enough, she wasn't sure. . . .

The owner bought soap and toothpaste, toothbrush,
shampoo plus conditioner, Q-tips, nail clippers, and most
important of all, deodorant, and told Biju he'd picked
up some things he might need.

They stood there embarrassed by the intimacy of the
products that lay between them.

He tried another tactic: "What do they think of the
pope in India?"

By showing his respect for Biju's mind he would raise
Biju's self-respect, for the boy was clearly lacking in
that department.

"You've tried," his wife said, comforting him a few
days later when they couldn't detect any difference in
Biju. "You even *bought* the soap," she said.

Biju approached Tom & Tomoko's—"No jobs."
    McSweeney's Pub—"Not hiring."
    Freddy's Wok—"Can you ride a bicycle?"
    Yes, he could.

Szechuan wings and French fries, just $3.00. Fried rice
$1.35 and $1.00 for pan-fried dumplings fat and tight as
babies—slice them open and flood your plate with a run

of luscious oil. In this country poor people eat like kings! General Tso's chicken, emperor's pork, and Biju on a bicycle with the delivery bag on his handlebars, a tremulous figure between heaving buses, regurgitating taxis—what growls, what sounds of flatulence came from this traffic. Biju pounded at the pedals, heckled by taxi drivers direct from Punjab—a man is not a caged thing, a man is wild *wild* and he must drive as such, in a bucking yodeling taxi. They harassed Biju with such blows from their horns as could split the world into whey and solids: paaaaaawww!

One evening, Biju was sent to deliver hot-and-sour soups and egg foo yong to three Indian girls, students, new additions to the neighborhood in an apartment just opened under reviewed city laws to raised rents. Banners reading "Antigentrification Day" had been hauled up over the street by the longtime residents for a festival earlier in the afternoon when they had played music, grilled hot dogs in the street, and sold all their gritty junk. One day the Indian girls hoped to be gentry, but right now, despite being unwelcome in the neighborhood, they were in the student stage of vehemently siding with the poor people who wished them gone.

The girl who answered the buzzer smiled, shiny teeth, shiny eyes through shiny glasses. She took the bag and went to collect the money. It was suffused with Indian femininity in there, abundant amounts of sweet newly washed hair, gold strung Kolhapuri slippers lying about. Heavyweight accounting books sat on the table along with a chunky Ganesh brought all the way from home despite its weight, for interior decoration plus luck in money and exams.

"Well," one of them continued with the conversation Biju had interrupted, discussing a fourth Indian girl not present, "why doesn't she just go for an Indian boy then, who'll understand all that temper tantrum stuff?"

"She won't look at an Indian boy, she doesn't want a nice Indian boy who's grown up chatting with his aunties in the kitchen."

"What does she want then?"

"She wants the Marlboro man with a Ph.D."

They had a self-righteousness common to many Indian women of the English-speaking upper-educated, went out to mimosa brunches, ate their Dadi's roti with adept fingers, donned a sari or smacked on elastic shorts for aerobics, could say *"Namaste,* Kusum Aunti, *aayiye, baethiye, khayiye!"* as easily as "Shit!" They took to short hair quickly, were eager for Western-style romance, and happy for a traditional ceremony with lots of jewelry: green set (meaning emerald), red set (meaning ruby), white set (meaning diamond). They considered themselves uniquely positioned to lecture everyone on a variety of topics: accounting professors on accounting, Vermonters on the fall foliage, Indians on America, Americans on India, Indians on India, Americans on America. They were poised; they were impressive; in the United States, where luckily it was still assumed that Indian women were downtrodden, they were lauded as extraordinary—which had the unfortunate result of making them even more of what they already were.

Fortune cookies, they checked, chili sauce, soy sauce, duck sauce, chopsticks, napkins, plastic spoons knives forks.

"Dhanyawad. Shukria. Thank you. Extra tip. You should buy topi-muffler-gloves to be ready for the winter."

The shiny-eyed girl said it many ways so that the meaning might be conveyed from every angle—that he might comprehend their friendliness completely in this meeting between Indians abroad of different classes and languages, rich and poor, north and south, top caste bottom caste.

Standing at that threshold, Biju felt a mixture of emotions: hunger, respect, loathing. He mounted the bicycle he had rested against the railings and was about to go on, but something made him stop and draw back. It was a ground-floor apartment with black security bars, and he put two fingers to his lips and whistled into the window at the girls dunking their spoons into the plastic containers where the brown liquid and foggy bits of egg looked horrible against the plastic, *twe tweeeeee twhoo,* and before he saw their response, he pedaled as fast as he could into the scowling howling traffic down Broadway, and as he pedaled, he sang loudly, *"O, yeh ladki zara si deewani lagti hai. . . ."*

Old songs, best songs.

But then, in a week, five people called up Freddy's Wok to complain that the food was cold. It had turned to winter.

The shadows drew in close, the night chomped more than its share of hours. Biju smelled the first of the snow and found it had the same pricking, difficult smell that existed inside the freezer; he felt the Thermocol scrunch of it underfoot. On the Hudson, the ice cracked loudly into pieces, and within the contours of this gray, broken river it seemed as if the city's inhabitants were being provided with a glimpse of something far and forlorn that they might use to consider their own loneliness.

Biju put a padding of newspapers down his shirt—leftover copies from kind Mr. Iype the newsagent—and sometimes he took the scallion pancakes and inserted them below the paper, inspired by the memory of an uncle who used to go out to the fields in winter with his lunchtime *parathas* down his vest. But even this did not seem to help, and once, on his bicycle, he began to weep from the cold, and the weeping unpicked a deeper vein of grief—such a terrible groan issued from between the whimpers that he was shocked his sadness had such depth.

When he returned home to the basement of a building at the bottom of Harlem, he fell straight into sleep.

The building belonged to an invisible management company that listed its address as One and a Quarter Street and owned tenements all over the neighborhood, the superintendent supplementing his income by illegally renting out basement quarters by the week, by the month, and even by the day, to fellow illegals. He spoke about as much English as Biju did, so between Spanish, Hindi, and wild mime, Jacinto's gold tooth flashing in

the late evening sun, they had settled the terms of rental.
Biju joined a shifting population of men camping out
near the fuse box, behind the boiler, in the cubby holes,
and in odd-shaped corners that once were pantries,
maids' rooms, laundry rooms, and storage rooms at the
bottom of what had been a single-family home, the entrance still adorned with a scrap of colored mosaic in
the shape of a star. The men shared a yellow toilet; the
sink was a tin laundry trough. There was one fuse box
for the whole building, and if anyone turned on too
many appliances or lights, *PHUT,* the entire electricity
went, and the residents screamed to nobody, since there
was nobody, of course, to hear them.

Biju had been nervous there from his very first day.
"Howdy," a man on the steps of his new abode said,
holding out his hand and nodding, "my name's Joey, and
I just had me some WHEES-KAY!" Power and hiss.
This was the local homeless man at the edge of his hunting and gathering territory, which he sometimes marked
by peeing a bright arc right across the road. He wintered
here on a subway grate in a giant plastic-bag igloo that
sagged, then blew taut with stale air each time a train
passed. Biju had taken the sticky hand offered, the man
had held tight, and Biju had broken free and run, a
cackle of laughter following him.

"The food is cold," the customers complained. "Soup
arrived cold! Again! The rice is cold each and every
time."

"I'm also cold," Biju said losing his temper.

"Pedal faster," said the owner.

"I cannot."

It was a little after one a.m. when he left Freddy's Wok
for the last time, the street lamps were haloes of light
filled with starry scraps of frozen vapor, and he trudged
between snow mountains adorned with empty take-out
containers and solidified dog pee in surprised yellow.
The streets were empty but for the homeless man who
stood looking at an invisible watch on his wrist while
talking into a dead pay phone. "Five! Four! Three!

Two! One—TAKEOFF!!" he shouted, and then he hung up the phone and ran holding onto his hat as if it might get blown off by the rocket he had just launched into space.

Biju turned in mechanically at the sixth somber house with its tombstone facade, past the metal cans against which he could hear the unmistakable sound of rat claws, and went down the flight of steps to the basement.

"I am very tired," he said out loud.

A man near him was frying in bed, turning this way, that way. Someone else was grinding his teeth.

By the time he had found employment again, at a bakery on Broadway and LaSalle, he had used up all the money in the savings envelope in his sock.

It was spring, the ice was melting, the freed piss was flowing. All over, in city cafés and bistros, they took advantage of this delicate nutty sliver between the winter, cold as hell, and summer, hot as hell, and dined al fresco on the narrow pavement under the cherry blossoms. Women in baby-doll dresses, ribbons, and bows that didn't coincide with their personalities indulged themselves with the first fiddleheads of the season, and the fragrance of expensive cooking mingled with the eructation of taxis and the lascivious subway breath that went up the skirts of the spring-clad girls making them wonder if *this* was how Marilyn Monroe felt—somehow not, somehow not. . . .

The mayor found a rat in Gracie Mansion.

And Biju, at the Queen of Tarts bakery, met Saeed Saeed, who would become the man he admired most in the United States of America.

"I am from Zanzibar, *not* Tanzania," he said, introducing himself.

Biju knew neither one nor the other. "Where is that?"

"Don't you know?? Zanzibar full of Indians, man! My grandmother—she is Indian!"

In Stone Town they ate samosas and *chapatis, jalebis,* pilau rice. . . . Saeed Saeed could sing like Amitabh Bachhan and Hema Malini. He sang, *"Mera joota hai japani. . . ."* and *"Bombay se aaya mera dost—Oi!"* He could gesture with his arms out and wiggle his hips, as could Kavafya from Kazakhstan and Omar from Malaysia, and together they assailed Biju with thrilling dance numbers. Biju felt so proud of his country's movies he almost fainted.

SHASHI DESHPANDE

The daughter of Shriranga, a well-known Kannada dramatist and Sanskrit scholar, Shashi Deshpande was born in 1938 in Dharwar, India, and educated in Bombay and Bangalore, where she earned degrees in economics and law. A course in journalism turned her in the direction of a writing career, and she worked for a time as a journalist.

Her literary career began in earnest in 1971 with the publication of *The Legacy*, a volume of short stories, followed by five additional story collections. Her first novel, *The Dark Holds No Terror*, was published in 1980 and won the Sahitya Akademi Award for fiction. Since then she has written seven additional novels. A writer of exceptional versatility, she has also published a collection of essays entitled *Writing from the Margins* (2006), two short crime novels, *If I Die Today* (1982) and *Come Up and Be Dead* (1985), and four books for children. In addition, she has authored the script and screenplay for a full-length Hindi feature film *Drishti*.

She lives in Bangalore with her husband.

A Day Like Any Other

"**Y**ou know how it is," the voice went on with a note of sly triumph in it, "I thought everyone would say, 'Why should I tell her?' And that is why the wife is always the last to know."

And also because you trust your husband. Or you did. Until a voice, thin and sharp like a knife, came and ripped into your trust.

"But you know me. I believe in being frank. It's the kindest thing, after all. Better to know the truth always. Don't you agree?"

"Yes," she said sourly.

For the first time, her distaste, her dislike, came through sharply. And communicated itself across the table. So that the face changed, malice breaking through the veneer of sympathetic concern, and became one with the voice.

"Actually, I wouldn't have spoken myself, if it had been just once. But when it happened twice—I saw them together twice, you know. I felt it was only right you should know."

"You did right." She spoke in a dead monotone. Twice . . . what is twice in a man's lifetime?

"Of course," the voice went on, placating now, "it may not be his fault, really. Your husband's, I mean. Men are simple."

The words were said, not with contempt, but with bitterness. Why was she bitter? Was it the coffee?

"More sugar in your coffee?" she asked, the solicitous hostess now.

"No, thanks. Never more than half a spoon. Only way to keep your figure."

Yes, keep your figure, but at what cost? Shadows in your eyes, shadows under them. Oh, take some more sugar and keep your bitterness from spilling over me.

"What was I saying? Yes, about your husband. I mean, he may have been trapped by that girl, you know. I know how these girls are. Specially the working ones. Bold. Too bold."

Bold? And if they weren't . . . ? You and I can stay safe and snug in the warm cocoon of our homes. We can afford not to be bold. Can they?

"And it isn't just that . . ." the voice went on impatiently, pushing away the coffee cup.

"A biscuit?"

"No, thanks. I never eat anything before lunch."

Perhaps we need a new maxim. A breakfast a day keeps the bitterness away. And suddenly she was ashamed of herself for the rancour she bore her guest. And it's

not her I hate, really. It's myself. I shouldn't listen to
her. I should tell her to go away. But I want to listen.
Like the book I had to read when I was a girl just because they said "don't."

"It's not just that they're bold. I can forgive them that.
But, they're shameless as well. This girl now—the way
she was dressed when I saw her . . ."

"How does she look?" The question slipped out of
her mouth and the next minute she regretted it. But it
could not be retrieved. And the reply came with an alac-
rity that showed how welcome her question was.

"She's quite tall, came up to his ears . . ."

I come up to his shoulders.

"And quite dark really . . ."

I've been always called fair.

"And funnily enough, no makeup. Not much, that
is."

I don't use it either.

"And that day she was wearing a sari, starting from
here"—the hand dropped to below the waist, nearly to
the hips—"and a sleeveless blouse, with the neck coming
down to here"—the hand rose and dropped again—
"showing everything she had. Not that she had much to
show. A skinny wretch. Looked better in the T-shirt and
slacks I saw her in the next time."

T-shirt and slacks. And a tiny waist, perhaps, accentu-
ated by a broad belt. Firm small breasts showing up
clearly under the T-shirt. Flat hips so that from behind
she would look like a boy, except that she was unmistakably a girl. And I . . .

She thought of the number of times she had told herself she would diet. And pushed away the butter, the
ghee, the sugar. And then, bubbling with laughter, suc-
cumbed to it after all. I can never wear anything but a
sari. And be thankful it hides so many faults. But I can
still take pleasure in the sight of a youthful, slim body.
And if he does so too . . . ?

"I remember when I saw them at the movies that day,
for a minute I thought you were with him. I almost got
up to speak to you. Then I saw him smiling, and I wondered. No man smiles at his wife like that!"

And what do you know about how he looks at me and smiles at me? And what do you know about him and me anyway? What do you know about any man except that husband of yours whom you hate so much that it overflows on to all other men, all husbands . . .

"And she too, she was looking up at him and smiling. They looked very happy together," the voice ended acidly.

And for the first time, anger pierced her like a steel splinter, opening her skin, her whole body to pain. And hatred. Of this woman who could talk of anyone's happiness that way. But she had to hide her feelings. She would not reveal any of them to this woman.

"Oh, I don't believe it's anything serious," she said, making a great effort to speak lightly. "After all, a man needs some fun, some entertainment. And he can't go alone. You know I don't go out much. I'm really tied down to the house since Asha's birth. No reason for him to stay in all the time with me."

"Yes, that's how it is. You stay at home and sacrifice yourself to the kids. And he goes out and has a gay time."

The discontented droop of the mouth. The petulant scowl on the face. The face of a woman cheated of all joy, all happiness. Will I look like that some time? But who can cheat me out of what I alone can create for myself?

"Life is never fair to women." The voice seemed to be coining a slogan in the battle against men.

"Isn't it?" she asked wonderingly, as if she had never heard the phrase before.

"No, it isn't. You sacrifice yourself, your whole life, you give it all to your husband and children . . ."

Sacrifice? What have I sacrificed? I always wanted to marry, to have children. I have what I want. A life without all this makes no sense. I enjoy this. What then have I sacrificed?

". . . and in the end you're left with nothing."

Nothing? I still have my life. It is my own. No one has taken it away from me.

"Look at you, now. Absolutely no fault of yours at all."

"I don't know." She had to say this. "Can anyone ever be faultless?"

He isn't a brute. A man like many others. So much of good. So much of bad. So much of neither.

"You have no pride," the voice said scornfully and angrily. She seemed disappointed. What had she expected?

"You will let a man deceive you, cheat you, and you will keep quiet because you don't want to risk your security. Your comfortable life."

The voice was truly like a knife. But wasn't the truth always sharp-edged? Was she afraid to face the facts because she was worried about her comfort and security? So many years together, and she thought they had built something between them. And now the voice made it all seem an illusion. The only truths were concern about oneself. Comfort. Security. She suddenly felt as if she had stepped into a pool of filth.

"You don't know," she said stonily. "You don't understand. You have done your duty in telling me. Now, please go."

Years to create. Minutes to destroy. But her face . . . I am destroying her illusions about herself. She truly thought she was doing me a kindness.

"I appreciate your telling me this very much," she said more gently. "I agree it's better to know the truth."

The truth . . . can anyone ever know it?

"But I'm terribly confused, I don't know what to think."

"You poor girl. I really feel very sorry for you. And those three little ones of yours. But it's always like that. You have children and lose your youth and looks. And . . ."

The minute she was alone she rushed to the mirror. She stared at herself dispassionately. This face, this body . . . is that all I mean when I say "I"? Is that all he says when he says "my wife"? The thing we have built between us—and we have built it, no bitch can change that fact—does it all depend on this face, this body? Love, she thought, I wish I knew what it meant.

Rustling noises from the crib, emphasized by the absolute quiet of the house, warned her that it was time to get the next feed ready. The other two would soon be back from the nursery. She had to set their lunch on the table. She could not weigh up her life now. She had to just go on living it.

It was only later, after she had fed and changed the baby and given the two boys their lunch, that she picked up the phone.

"He's not in the room, I'm sorry. He's in a conference. Can I take a message? May I know who's calling, please?"

All the stock phrases, but they were said as if they really meant something. The voice was not dead, but alive, with a lilt of enjoyment in it. She's smiling, she thought, and if I could see her I would smile too. Because it would be that kind of a smile, one you have to respond to.

"Will you please tell him his wife called? And ask him to call me back when he's free."

"Oh . . . !" The voice faltered. She imagined the smile, the efficiency, being wiped off it, leaving behind only a young and confused girl. "Yes, I'll do that, certainly."

She put down the phone and thought—Now what? Do I compete? Do I rush and change from this old cotton into something nice, comb my disheveled plait into a slick hairdo, and make something special for tea? Hug him when he comes, fuss over him, encourage him to talk about himself and say "I love you" ten times? All the magic formulas trotted out innumerable times by women's magazines as the sure way to win back your husband.

"You have no pride." She remembered the words. On the contrary, I have too much of it. It's no use. I cannot change. I will always be like this, careless, a little untidy, incapable of socializing, of dissembling. And it's not only "I cannot." I will not change, either. He will have to take me as I am. And so, I will do none of those things, but go on with my every day work.

And so she slept a little, read, played with the children, fed them again, washed the boys and sent them out to play. And then the key turned in the lock, and there was his usual whistle to let her know he was home. And the morning became a fantasy. This was the only reality, this home they had made together, the life they lived together. Girl? She laughed. What girl?

"How was your day?" he asked, vigorously scrubbing his face with soap.

"Oh, a day like any other," she said, stacking the children's dirty plates and milk mugs in the sink. "Want some tea?"

"No, I've had it. Where are the children?"

"Gone down to play. Baby is in the bedroom."

He went out to the girl and she could hear her crowing with delight as her father picked her up and began tickling her. The servant girl came into the kitchen and began washing up. She went into the bedroom and sat down to brush her hair. She was still doing this, slowly, reflectively, when he came in, the child in his arms, and asked her, "Did you ring me up today?"

"Yes, I did."

"I'm sorry I didn't ring you back. I was all tied up. What was it? Anything important?"

This was part of the normal pattern of their lives. Little questions that needed no answers, trivial talk, small silences. All meaningless, insignificant in themselves, but, she suddenly realized now, for them a way of communicating with each other, an assurance that they were in contact after so many hours apart. No, she could not go on with it. She could not participate in this usual ritual. It would be like deceiving him, making him believe that it was indeed, for her, a day like any other. It would be like stalking an innocent, unknowing animal and she went rigid with self-hatred at the thought of doing it.

Here goes, she said to herself, and then, without hesitation, she told him all that she had heard in the morning. He had no face for deception. His face revealed the truth to her at once, as if she had, with her words, peeled a mask off his face. He looked confused, frightened, even contrite, like his own son caught in a wrongdoing.

"Who told you?" he asked her foolishly.

She told him, again just the facts, neither abuses, accusations, nor tears. Not a trace of anger. Her stolidity seemed to bewilder him. He stared at her in silence, like an actor on the stage who hasn't got his cue. What do I do? she thought wildly. Shall I burst into tears to help him out of this? But there was nothing she could do, nothing she could say.

It was her silence which frightened him, she thought. He felt her withdrawal from him. And, as if that terrified him, words poured out of him.

Explanations, justifications, accusations of himself. And then promises. He threw promises recklessly at her, promising her a lifetime of fidelity, of loyalty, but not, she noticed, love. The word was not said. And she understood that. For if he had ever loved her before, he loved her still. And then he said it. "She means nothing to me, nothing at all. The children and you—this is my real life. You mean everything to me."

And again she knew it was true. But she felt a pang of pity for that girl, discarded so easily, forgotten so fast. So young, she thought, so sure of herself and her attractions—how will she bear this? If I ring up tomorrow, will I hear that lilt in her voice? Or, will it leave her forever?

That evening his mood was one of gentle exhilaration. He was like a man who has narrowly escaped some danger. He was absorbed in the children, but again and again she could feel his glance flit to her, trying to catch her eye, trying to weave, across the children, a magic web between them that excluded everyone else. He will make love to me tonight, she told herself with the first flash of anger against him, and that shadow will come between us. I can't bear it.

But surprisingly, there was no shadow between them. It was as if that girl was an illusion, a phantasm of her mind that he dispelled by the ardour of his lovemaking. Afterwards he lay on his side as usual, his face pillowed on one palm. And she, as usual too, lay awake, listening to the silence in the house, her ears keyed up for a cry, a whimper, a call. A night like any other to end a day like any other. But something in her fiercely refuted the idea. It could never be a day like any other. Something strange, something terrible had happened to her that day. And it had nothing to do with the fact that she had come to know of her husband's pleasure in a young woman, not even in the fact that he had so strongly reaffirmed his feelings for her. No, it was something else. She groped for it, feeling she was trembling on the verge of some discovery.

And then, as she lay, gathering into herself all the threads of her day, as she always did, she knew. She had not been shattered by what she had heard that day. *My life is my own,* she had said the words in the morning. Now the words, the thought, grew in her, filling her with a rare and fearful happiness, a feeling of being suspended in space and time all by herself. *My life is my own . . .* she said the words to herself again, knowing how true they were, knowing she had discovered the only thing that would make life bearable. In her excitement, a laugh escaped her. He heard her in his sleep and turned towards her. He said her name questioningly, and when she did not respond, fearfully. He put his hand to her face, her cheeks, doubtfully, and found to his surprise that they were dry.

CHITRA BANERJEE DIVAKARUNI

Born in Calcutta in 1957, Chitra Banerjee Divakaruni was raised a devout Hindu and earned a bachelor's degree from the University of Calcutta. In 1976, she came to the United States and was awarded a master's degree at Wright State University and a PhD from the University of California at Berkeley in 1995. She has taught creative writing at Foothill College in Los Altos Hills, California, and now teaches in the University of Houston Creative Writing Program.

Her first published works were books of poetry, *Dark Like the River* (1987), *The Reason for Nasturtiums* (1990), and *Black Candle* (1991). After enrolling in a fiction-writing class, she published *Arranged Marriage: Stories* (1995), which won three awards. She published her first novel, *The Mistress of Spices,* in 1997, followed by a second novel, *Sister of My Heart,* in 1998. The former was made into a film in 2005, and the latter into a television series in Tamil. She is also in the process of writing a juvenile fantasy series, *The Brotherhood of the Conch,* set, like her adult fiction, in India.

In addition to her writing, Divakaruni is cofounder and former president of Maitri, a helpline for South Asian women who are dealing with abuse.

The Forgotten Children

Through the years of my childhood when there wasn't much else to hold on to, I had a fantasy. Those rum-scented evenings when Father's slurred yells slammed into the peeling walls of wherever we were living at the moment, I would lie wedged behind a sofa or under a bed, and close my eyes and slide into it. Sometimes my brother lay there also, curled tight against me, sucking his thumb, although Mother had told him he was too old to be doing that. The knobs of his spine would push into my chest; his heart would thud against my palm like the hooves of a runaway horse—like my own heart, so that after a while I couldn't tell the two apart. Maybe that's how he, too, became part of the fantasy.

Our family moved a lot those days, flurried migrations that took us from rooming house to dingier rooming house as my father lost one job after another. He always managed to find a new one because he was a skilled machinist—perhaps that was part of his trouble, knowing that he would. But each job was a little worse than the previous one, a small movement down the spiral that our life had turned into. We never spoke of it—we were not a family much given to discussion. But we saw it in our mother's face, the way she sometimes broke off in the middle of a sentence and stared out the window, forgetting that my brother and I were waiting.

We children learned some skills of our own as we traveled through the small hot factory towns of north India that after a while blurred into a single oily smell, a grimy dust that stung the nostrils. We knew how to be almost invisible as we sat on the last bench in class, not knowing the answers because we had missed the previous lessons or didn't have the books. Or as we sat in the far corner of the canteen at lunchtime because we didn't want anyone to see the rolled brown rutis Mother packed for us in old paper. We looked longingly—but sidewise, so no one would guess—at the starched uniforms of the others, their tiffin boxes filled with sandwiches made from store-bought bread so white it dazzled the eye. Each time they laughed, we flinched, pulling the edge of a skirt over a bruised thigh, a shirtsleeve over discolored finger marks left on a forearm. Were they talking about us—how Mother had asked the sabji-wallah for credit, how Father had to be helped home from the toddy shop last payday? How long before they learned of the noises that sometimes exploded from our flat at night? We learned to arrange our hair so that the pink ridges of a forehead scar would hardly show. To look casually into the middle distance, as though we didn't notice the curious eyes. To not think of the futile, scattered trailings we had left behind: a book of fairy tales, a stray yellow dog we used to feed, a mango tree perfect for climbing, the few friendships formed before we knew better.

We. That was how I thought of my brother in those days, as though he were as much a part of me as my arm or leg. Indispensable, to be protected instinctively, like one shields the face from a blow, but not something one thinks about. It never occurred to me as he followed me around in silence (he was not a talkative boy) that he might feel differently about our life—that knotted, misshapen thing, like a fracture healed wrong—which I accepted because it was what I'd always known. Perhaps that was my first mistake.

The year I was eleven and my brother eight, we ended up in Duligarh, an Assam oil town as sagging and discolored as a cardboard box left to rot in the rain. It was a town of many toddy shops, all of which my father would soon discover. A town where credit was difficult to get, where from the first people looked at us with faces like closed fists. I didn't blame them. We were a far cry from the model families displayed on the family-planning posters the municipal office had put up all over town.

One of these posters was pasted on the back wall of our school. I remember it perfectly from all the afternoons I stood there looking up until my neck ached. My fantasy fed on that poster through those sweat-studded afternoons, spreading its insidious roots, leading me to my other errors.

In the poster, a young couple held hands and smiled into each other's eyes while a boy and girl played tag around them. The man carried a shiny leather briefcase. The woman's gold chain sparkled in the sun, and the edge of her pink sari lifted in the breeze. The children wore real leather Bata shoes, the kind I'd seen in the store window in Lal Bahadur Market, spit-shined to a mirror polish. *We Two, Our Two,* declared the poster, as though it were the mantra for a happy life. *We Two, Our Two.* Where then had our parents gone wrong?

Sometimes I stood watching until the sky changed to the dull yellow of late afternoon and my brother tugged at my arm in exasperation. Let's go, Didi, I'm hungry. Why do you like to waste your time staring at that silly picture? He wanted, instead, to be shaking down ripe guavas from the trees on the edge of the orchard across the street. People shouldn't plant their trees along the public road if they don't want anyone to pick the fruit, he said, thrusting out his chin, when I protested.

Sometimes we missed the bus because of that poster and had to walk home, trudging through the heat, our clothes sticking to our skin, our books getting heavier, all the way past the edge of town. Walking through the bazaar I would feel the shopkeepers' unsmiling eyes on us, a lanky girl with hair pulled back in two tight, careful braids, a juice-stained boy with his wrists sticking out of a shirt he'd outgrown, striding impatiently ahead of his sister. Did they connect us with our parents—that woman who came down to the bazaar at the end of the day, moving among the dull-scaled fish and shriveled beans, her beautiful face like a parched oleander, that man who held his body with brilliant belligerence like a boxer who knew that the key to his survival was to trust no one? Did they compare us to the family on the poster?

In Assam we lived in an old British bungalow which we children loved. It was the first real house we'd lived in, a long, low structure built for some forgotten purpose outside of town. It was inconveniently far from everything (it took Father an hour to bike to the factory where he tested drilling equipment), but the rent was cheap and there were no prying neighbors. If it was lonely for Mother all day when we were gone, she didn't complain. Perhaps she was glad to have the time to herself. Only occasionally would she grumble that the house was falling apart on us.

And it was. Perhaps in sympathy with some other, unvisible disintegration, flakes of falling plaster coated everything like giant dandruff. The windows would not shut properly, so that malevolent-looking insects with burnished stings wandered in at will. The roof leaked and when it rained, which was often, we had to make our way around strategically placed buckets.

But we children thought it was perfect—the wooden porch where we played marbles, the claw-footed bathtub where Mother would pour steaming water for our baths, the spear-shaped grilles at the windows that made us feel as if we were living in a medieval fortress.

Best of all we loved the servant's quarter, a small cottage set far back into the bamboo grove that grew behind the house. My brother and I were the first to discover it. When we told Mother, she gave an unusually bitter laugh. A servant's quarter for us! she said, the corners of her mouth turning downward. What a joke! For a while she kept asking Father to see if he could rent it out to one of the factory watchmen. But nothing ever came of that. Perhaps we were too far from the factory. Perhaps Father, who wasn't the type to go around asking, never mentioned it to anyone. My brother believed it was because he and I had prayed so hard for it to stay empty.

The cottage was dim and cool even in the brassy Assam afternoons because it sat under a huge tree of a kind I'd never seen before, with large round leaves like upturned palms. Spiderwebs hung from its ceilings, intelligently angled to enmesh intruders, and in the far room we discovered a trapdoor that blended almost perfectly into the wooden flooring. Underneath was a small space with a packed dirt floor, just right for a make-believe prison or an underground cave. We told no one of it, and never used it ourselves. It was enough to know it was there. Instead, we dusted off a rope cot that was in the corner and dragged it over the trapdoor to hide it. Then we smuggled an old sheet from the house. In the afternoons when we got back from school we lay on the cot in the half-dark and I told my brother stories.

That was when I told my brother about the fantasy. For a long time I'd kept it to myself, knowing instinctively that it was not for sharing. But something about the cottage made me feel weightless and uncatchable, as though I were a dust mote tumbling in lazy light. When I looked up from the cot, the leaves made a canopy of hands, holding off the rest of my life. I'd thought my pragmatic brother would laugh at the fantasy. But from the beginning it was his favorite, the final story I had to tell before we returned to the house to help Mother with chores.

Here is the fantasy:

My parents are moving again. They climb into a battered three-wheeler loaded down with bundles and boxes. But we are not with them because they have forgotten us. From behind the bamboo grove we watch as the three-wheeler lurches to a start, as it becomes smaller and smaller and finally disappears. We emerge from the fronds cautiously. Yes, they're really gone. For a moment we are stunned. Then we grab each other and spin until the world is an ecstatic whirl.

The fantasy is not without its problems. The most important one is our mother. Just before she gets into the three-wheeler she looks around uncertainly, the way an animal might, scenting something amiss in the air. (I do not tell my brother this, but I know he sees it, too.) I would like to include her in the fantasy. To have her see a flicker of white—my brother's shirt—in the bamboo. She would walk into the grove to explore and never return to my father. But I know it cannot be. Their lives are tangled together beyond my powers of extrication. So, sadly, I let her go.

We live in the servant's quarter. By now the bamboo has grown so thick that no one remembers the existence of the cottage. I cook and clean and teach my brother everything I learned at school. He catches fish for us in the stream behind the cottage, lots of fish, and we sell some of it in the bazaar and buy rice, salt, shoes. We begin to look like the children in the family-planning poster.

You think I'll be able to catch that many? my brother always asks at this point, not totally convinced of his angling skills.

Of course, I reply.

In our fantasy, no one drags us over the cracked driveway so that its exposed brick scours our backs. In the dark garage, no one lights a match and brings it so close that we can feel the heat of it on our eyelids. In our fantasy, entire sections of words have disappeared from the dictionary: *fear, fracture, furious, fatal, father.*

We keep on living like this.

What about when we get old? my brother asks.

We don't, I say. But he is not satisfied. So I have to devise an end for the fantasy.

One winter it snows and snows.

Snow? asks my brother. He has never seen any. Nor have I, but in my geography book I've come across pictures of the silvered peaks of the Himalayas. I explain it to him.

One winter it snows and snows. The snow drifts in through the windows and doors. It falls on the bed where the brother and sister are sleeping side by side.

Like this? My brother slips his hand into mine and lays his head on my shoulder. A pale scar whose origin I cannot remember slants across his cheekbone.

Yes, I say.

The snow forms a thick white quilt that covers the brother and sister. It doesn't hurt. They never wake up. They sleep like this forever.

Sleep forever, repeats my brother consideringly as we walk back to the house through the humid afternoon.

Things were disappearing from the house. At first it was food, little items that Mother wouldn't have noticed if money hadn't been so tight—a small box of biscuits, a half-empty packet of sugar. Then it was clothes—an old shirt of my brother's, my green kameez with the frayed collar. A moth-eaten blanket that Mother was intending to throw away as soon as we could afford a new one.

Did you take it for a game? she asked when I came into the kitchen for a snack after school.

No, I didn't, I said, glad not to have to lie. I was afraid she might follow up with questions I'd have more

difficulty sidestepping. But she shook her head in a pre-
occupied way and started kneading dough for rutis.

I can't figure it out, she said. It's not as though we
have a servant who might be stealing. And now the level
in the rice bin seems to be dropping.

Spirits, that's what it is, declared Lakshmi-aunty, the
old woman who sold spices down in the bazaar, when
Mother mentioned it to her the next day. Spirits. People
say a saheb lived in that house a long time ago—a smug-
gler, they say he was—came to a bad end. Hanged himself from the living room rafters. Here, take this mustard
seed and burn it in an iron pot while chanting the name
of Rama. That should make the spirit go away.

The next afternoon when we returned from school,
Mother did as Lakshmi-aunty had instructed. We helped
her with the homemade exorcism, chanting and sneezing
as the acrid smoke rose from the pot and the mustard
seeds began to sputter. We said nothing to Father.

For a while after that, there were no more disappear-
ances. By the time they started again, Mother had worse
problems to worry about.

Father had fallen foul of the foreman. It wasn't unexpected. At each of his jobs he found someone to hate,
someone who, he believed, was out to get him. (Why
does he always have to fight with people? my brother
asked once. Mother sighed and said he always was a free
spirit, he never did take kindly to being ordered around.)
It was only a matter of time before the chance remark
exploded into a fistfight or worse. In the last town he'd
gashed an overseer's arm with a broken bottle, and the
police had taken him away for a while. Then we would
be packing again, looking up railway timetables, deciding
what to leave behind.

At dinner Father ate sullenly, muttering curses at the
foreman, not noticing what kind of food Mother put in
front of him. He held tightly to the neck of a bottle,
raised it to his mouth in one glinting arc. Mother would
rub his arm, a gesture which sometimes calmed him.
From the table in the corner where we did our home-

work, we could see the muscles of her back through the thin fabric of her blouse, bunched with tension. Just try to avoid him, please, she'd whisper. Why don't you ask for a transfer to another shift? Think of the children— they're just beginning to settle down, to catch up in school. Times are so bad, what if you don't find another job. You're not getting any younger either. . . .

Some nights he would merely shake his head and say, You're right, Mother, that whoremonger isn't worth the spit out of my mouth. Or he would swat her entreating hands away, growling, Leave me alone, woman, don't interfere in things you know nothing about. But there were those other nights. Bitch, we'd hear him bellow, and we'd melt into the moldy shadows under the porch. Here I am, killing myself to feed all of you, and all you do is nag at me. Sound of a slap, a pan clanking onto the floor, spilling the dal that was to have been our lunch tomorrow. A breathless grunt. We knew how it felt, that fist slammed into the side of the head, turning everything black for a moment. The kick against the ribs that left you knotted and gasping on the floor. And the pain. We knew about pain. How it rose like a wall of water and crashed over you. We gripped each other's hands, afraid even to sob, hating ourselves for not trying to stop him. We held our breath and plunged into our other fantasy, the one we shared without ever having spoken it, where our father was dead, dead, dead.

I never asked Mother why she didn't leave him, though I often wondered. Why didn't she run away with us to her parents' village? She sometimes described it wistfully as a peaceful cluster of huts under emerald co- conut trees filled with singing birds. (I didn't know then that she had eloped with Father and, in the traditional Indian scheme of things, had shut that door behind her- self forever.) Was it that she feared Father was just too powerful? That wherever we went, he would smell us out, like the ogre in a fairy tale?

No. There was something else, which I couldn't quite put into words. It had to do with my father's broad shoulders, the muscles that rippled along his arms like playful snakes when he swung us up. The way he could make us feel safe even when we were high in the air. The way he could make us forget. Maybe it was the sun woven into his thick black hair, the fresh smell of ritha in it on holidays after Mother had washed it for him. He'd burst into snatches of song (he had once taken lessons, Mother said), his voice rising as unhesitant as light—*Mehbooba, Mehbooba, my dearest darling*—until it came up against the words he had forgotten. Then he'd throw himself at Mother's feet like a hero out of a Hindi movie, arms flung out, until she couldn't stop herself from laughing. Or he would come home with a package tied with the flat red string used by sari shops. He would gather her to him and thrust it into her hands. And while her trembling fingers tugged at the knots and a blush rose up from her throat (my mother was unusually fair, with skin that bruised easily), he would drop a kiss on the top of her head or play with the ends of her long braid.

Once when I woke late at night and went to the kitchen for a tumbler of water, I found them sitting at the table, their backs toward me. Perhaps it was one of those times when the electric company had cut off our power because we couldn't pay, for there was a small kerosene lamp on the table between them.

Shanti, my father was saying in a small, choked voice, I've only made you unhappy. Sometimes I wish we'd never met. Or that I were dead. On the wall his shadow hunkered, anguished, against her slim silhouette. My very own Beauty and the Beast. Mother put her hand over his mouth, and her voice, too, was choked. Hush, Swapan (it was the first time I heard her call him by his name), don't say that. How could I live on without you?

I tried to back away silently, but Father saw me. I couldn't breathe. He would be furious now. I'd spoiled it all. But he held out an arm, and when I edged over, he sat me on his lap and stroked my hair. His hand was awkward with the unaccustomed motion and his calluses caught in my hair, but I didn't want him to stop. Mother leaned her head against his shoulder. The planes of her face were angular and lovely in the flickering light. Her eyes were tightly shut, as though in prayer. I breathed in their blended odor—his Teen Patti tobacco, her sweet Neem soap—and in that way I came to know something of love, how complex it is, how filled with the need to believe.

We came home from school and the black trunk was in our bedroom. Its lid was open and some of our clothes had already been thrown inside. They formed small wadded lumps at the bottom of the box. When I looked at them, I wanted to cry.

We went to find Mother, who was in the kitchen emptying the rickety wire cabinet where she kept the spices.

We're leaving day after tomorrow, she said. She didn't offer any explanation and we didn't ask. There were new lines at the corners of her eyes and mouth, as though someone had lifted the skin off her face, crumpled it, and then replaced it carelessly. We went back to our room, and I emptied out the trunk to pack it right, shoes and books at the bottom, clothes on top, folded into neat squares, like I knew from all those other times.

Come and help me, I said to my brother, but he lay on his mattress and stared at the cracks in the ceiling until it grew dark and the cicadas outside started their buzzing. He spoke only once, when I tried to pack his clothes. Don't touch my things, he said. His voice was decisive in its viciousness, like a grownup's.

When I woke in the morning, he was gone.

Where is he? Father yelled again. Spittle from his mouth struck my cheek and I flinched, though I tried not to.

Leave the poor girl alone. Mother's voice rose up from behind, startling me with its brittle, unusual loudness. Her hair, come undone from its neat knot, hung wild about her face, and her sari was splotched with mud from the ditch behind the house where she'd been searching, calling my brother's name. There was an unmoored look in her eyes. She's been telling you all day that she doesn't know. Why don't you bike down instead to the bus station in the bazaar and ask if anyone saw him?

I drew in a sharp breath and stiffened in readiness,

but perhaps Father was as taken aback as I was. He got on his cycle and left.

Once my father's silhouette, wavery black against the setting sun, disappeared around the bend, Mother slumped down on the kitchen floor. She did this jerkily, in stages, as if a series of springs inside her were snapping, one by one. Surrounded by the cheap aluminum pots and chipped dishes that summarized her life, she put her face in her hands and began to cry. It was a sound like cloth tearing. Not even the time when she had to go to the clinic to have her arm set had she cried like this. I went and put my arms around her. My chest felt as though it was tearing, too. I almost told her then.

Mother looked up as though she could sense my thoughts. She wasn't crying anymore.

You know where he is, don't you, she said. She caught me by the elbows. Please tell me, please. Her voice sounded as though it were pushing its way past something that had broken and stuck in her throat. I promise I won't let your father do anything to him.

I bit down on my lips because I didn't want to hurt her further. But I couldn't stop myself. You always did before, I said. What's so different about this time?

Something passed over Mother's face. Was it sorrow, or a cloud of shame? She took a deep breath, as though preparing for an underwater journey, then cupped my face in her hands. Her nails were broken and dirt-caked, but her fingers were long and cool. I'll protect my baby, she said quietly. I swear it on my dead mother's soul.

I believed her then, although she hadn't answered my question. Perhaps it was because she wasn't a woman who promised lightly. Or because her face was so like my brother's with those same straight eyebrows, the same scattering of moles across the cheekbones. The face I loved most in all the world, after his. Or because finally, with the tarry night pressing itself down on us, I accepted what I'd always known in some vanquished part of myself: Fantasies can't really come true.

He was where I thought he would be, huddled against the far corner of the crawl space my parents had missed in their perfunctory search of the servant's quarter. (They hadn't believed he would choose such an obvious place, so close to home, to hide in.) When I pushed away the cot and lifted the trapdoor, his eyes glinted, feral, in the beam from Mother's flashlight. There were crumbs around his mouth from the biscuits he'd been eating. Around his shoulders was bunched the old blanket he'd secreted away a long time back, believing in imagination. I reached down to help him up, but he shrank from me, his face heavy with hate.

Mother carried my brother all the way back to the house, although he was really too heavy for her, holding him close to her chest as one would an infant. She asked me to walk ahead with the flashlight, so I didn't hear what she was murmuring to him, but by the time they were in the kitchen, he had stopped struggling. He even managed a small smile when Mother fixed us mashed rice and bananas with hot milk and sugar, which used to be his favorite meal when he was little.

We had just started eating when we heard Father. He made his way up the porch slowly and noisily, and once it sounded like he bumped into the wall. We froze, my brother and I at the table, the food halfway to our mouths, Mother at the counter where she had been chopping bananas. Then he was in the kitchen, the kicked-open door banging against the wall, the hulk of his shadow falling on the table between my brother and me. His huge voice filled me, the echoes booming outward until I thought I would split open.

I remember the rest only in fragments, black-and-white frames that appear even now without warning, branding themselves across my vision, forcing me to abandon whatever I'm doing. I'm going to kill you today, you little shit-eater. Heavy clunk of a belt being unbuckled. My brother runs for my mother. She must have thrust him behind her, because he's gone and instead I see her hands, the fingers stiffly splayed, pushing against Father's chest. Her mouth's open, she's shouting something, she's on the floor. The belt moves through the air in a perfect, lazy arc. Now it's a cobra, striking, the metal fang gashing my brother's cheek just under his left eye, gouging out a piece of flesh, the blood exploding from what is left. A thin scream that goes on and on. Mother you promised you promised you . . . She pushes me out of her way, grasps the edge of the counter to pull herself up. Her hand closes around the knife. And now the voice is screaming again. I listen. I have no control over the voice, which I recognize vaguely as my own. Father turns. The belt buckle catches mother's wrist. A crack, as of a stick snapping. I hear the knife clatter down, each metallic unit of sound clear and disparate. A sound, half whinny, half gasp, reeling back into itself. They must both be on the floor, grappling for it.

But I can't tell what's going on back there because I've turned to watch my brother, who is running, who has made it through the door and past the porch and out to the bamboo grove. The sheltering dark gathers him in—elbows and knees, hands, the back of his head. Only his shirt glows in the moonlight like the snow we had imagined together, then disappears as he steps into shadow, then glows more palely farther ahead. There are fireflies everywhere tonight, pinpoints of light blurring into a luminous ooze. Perhaps to disappear is the next best thing to being forgotten. Am I crying from happiness because he has escaped, if only for now? Or is it regret at that thin scream (my final error?) which shot from my mouth like an arrow of blood? Is it because I know I cannot join him? That in a moment I (my mother's daughter, bound after all by her genes of mistimed loyalties) must turn toward whatever is behind me, wheezing wetly, trying to get to its feet? All I know is that this is how I will remember my brother: a patch of dwindling white (melting, melting) as the bamboos shiver close. As the fireflies hover above him with their frail, fitful light.

AMITAV GHOSH

Amitav Ghosh was born in 1956 in Calcutta and was educated at St. Stephen's College, Delhi, Delhi University, and Oxford University, where he earned a PhD in 1982 in social anthropology. In 1999 he joined the faculty of Queens College of the City University of New York. He has also been a visiting professor at Harvard University since 2005.

Ghosh's latest work of fiction, *Sea of Poppies*, was published in 2008. His other novels include *The Circle of Reason* (1986); *The Shadow Lines* (1990), which won the Sahitya Akademi Award, India's most prestigious literary award; *The Calcutta Chromosome* (1995), winner of the Arthur C. Clarke Award in 1997; *The Glass Palace* (2000); and *The Hungry Tide* (2004).

Ghosh was described by the *New York Times* reviewer Pankaj Mishra as one of the few postcolonial writers "to have expressed in his work a developing awareness of the aspirations, defeats, and disappointments of colonized peoples as they figure out their place in the world." He received the Padma Shri from the Indian Government in 2007.

Currently, Ghosh lives with his wife, an author and editor, and their children in New York and teaches at Columbia University.

Excerpt from
The Shadow Lines

In 1962, the year I turned ten, my grandmother retired, upon reaching the age of sixty. She had taught in a girls' high school since 1936. When she'd first joined, the school had had only fifty pupils and the premises had consisted of two sheds with tin roofs. During the monsoons she had often had to teach standing in ankle-deep water—once, or so she claimed, it had been so bad that a girl had actually managed to spear a fish with a compass during a geometry lesson. But over the next two decades the school had grown into a successful institution and had acquired a big building near Deshapriya Park. For the last six years before she retired, my grandmother had been its headmistress.

She had been looking forward to her retirement although she'd grown very attached to the school in the twenty-seven years she had spent there. But she no longer had the stomach for staff-room intrigues and battles with the board, she would tell my parents; she was growing old, she had earned her rest. And besides, my father's career was going well, so she had no real worries left.

There was a farewell ceremony on her last day at school, to which my parents and I were invited. It was a touching ceremony in a solemn kind of way. The Calcutta Corporation sent a representative and so did the Congress and the CPI. There were many speeches and my grandmother was garlanded by a girl from every class. Then the head girl, a particular favourite of hers, unveiled the farewell present the girls had bought for her by subscription. It was a large marble model of the Taj Mahal; it had a bulb inside and could be lit up like a table lamp. My grandmother made a speech too, but she couldn't finish it properly, for she began to cry before she got to the end of it and had to stop to wipe away her tears. I turned away when she began dabbing at her eyes with a huge green handkerchief, and discovered, to my surprise, that many of the girls sitting around me were wiping their eyes too. I was very jealous, I remember. I had always taken it for granted that it was my own special right to love her; I did not know how to cope with the discovery that my right had been infringed by a whole school.

Later we were served a meal in the staff room. The teachers had decided to give her a surprise.

When she was headmistress my grandmother had decided once that every girl who opted for home science
ought to be taught how to cook at least one dish that
was a speciality of some part of the country other than
her own. It would be a good way, she thought, of teaching them about the diversity and vastness of the country.
As a farewell surprise, the home science department had
arranged for us to sample the results of my grandmother's initiative.

After we had been led into the staff room the girls
came in, one by one, bearing dishes on trays. My grandmother was delighted; she understood at once what was
in store for us. She had taken so keen an interest in
this project that she knew each girl's speciality by heart.
There's Ranjana (or Matangini), she would say, clapping
her hands as they entered the room—Ranjana's doing
Kerala, so avyal is what you'll get. Or: That's Sunayana,
she's our Tamil for this term, wait till you taste her up-
pama, you'll want to be Tamil yourself. But then, in
her mounting excitement, she began to make mistakes.
There's a nice Gujarati mutton korma for you, she said,
and then, leaping to her feet, she cried: Ah, there's my
dear dahi-bara, you wait and see what a plump and juicy
Punjabi she is!

As it happened, the girl who had made the dahi-baras
was unusually fat. She burst into tears, dropped her plate
of dahi-baras with a loud splash on the Sanskrit teacher's
silk sari and ran out of the room.

We ate the rest of our meal in silence.

That was the only false note, however, and afterwards,
since there would not have been room for the Taj Mahal
in a taxi, the headmistress lent us one of the school's
buses to go home in. The whole school lined up to wave
as we steamed out through the gates. My grandmother
waved back, tears streaming down her cheeks.

I remember very well the first day of her retirement.
She spent the morning clearing away all the old files and
papers that had accumulated in her room over the years.
In the evening, we were invited to have a look. It was
transformed. The files and papers were gone and the
room was bathed in the gentle white glow of the Taj

Mahal. She was very happy that night. At dinner, smiling her real smile, warm and impish, not the tight-lipped headmistress's smile that we had grown accustomed to, she told us funny stories about her early days in the school.

But her happiness did not last very long.

One afternoon, a few days later, I came home from school and found that both she and my mother had locked themselves into their rooms. That night I over-heard my mother complaining tearfully to my father that she'd been nagged all day long—about her cooking, her clothes, the way she kept the house. My grandmother had never paid any attention to these matters before.

Soon she began to worry about other things too.

One afternoon my friend Montu and I were walking back together from Gole Park, where the school bus had dropped us, when he stopped dead on the street and pointed up at our flat. Look! he cried, There's a man with a turban in your grandmother's room!

Montu was my best friend at that time. He and his family lived in the building next to ours, but our flats were so close we could talk to each other from our respective balconies. His name wasn't really Montu. It was Mansoor and he was from Lucknow. But he had grown up in Calcutta—his father was a teacher in the Ballygunge Science College—and when they'd moved to Gole Park from Park Circus, someone had shortened his name to Montu. There was very little we did not know about each other's families. He knew perfectly well that it was quite unprecedented for my grandmother to let any man into her room, let alone a stranger in a turban.

Liar! I said. But when I looked up, I saw he was right: there was an unmistakably turbaned head framed in my grandmother's window.

I sprinted down the street and up the stairs, jammed my finger into our doorbell and kept it there till my mother opened the door.

Who's that in Tha'mma's room? I whispered breathlessly. She raised a finger to her lips and gave me a warning tap on the shoulder, but ignoring her, I ran straight into my grandmother's room.

She was sitting on a chair in front of the open window with her head wrapped in a wet sari.

Speechless, I withdrew backwards, step by step, and fled to look for my mother.

What's Tha'mma doing? What's happened to her head?

My mother made me sit down and explained carefully that my grandmother had started on a course of Ayurvedic treatment and that the doctor had given her various herbal oils, with instructions to keep her head tied up all morning.

But why? I asked. What's happened to her head?

My mother frowned at me sternly.

Tha'mma thinks she's going bald, she said.

Then her composure dissolved and she began to laugh. She had to hold a pillow over her face so that my grandmother would not hear her.

I did not go out to our balcony that evening; I didn't see how I could begin to explain to Montu that my grandmother had tied up her head because she was afraid of going bald.

Fortunately she did not persist with that treatment for very long. Her vanity was not really strong enough to keep her sitting in a chair for hours on end with a wet sari wrapped around her head. And in any case she had a full head of thick silver hair.

Instead she took to visiting her school again. She would leave in the afternoon and come back a couple of hours later, bursting with the horror stories she had heard in the staff room: how the new headmistress was planning to dig up the rose beds she had planted, in order, if you please, to lay down a basketball court; how the wretched woman had insulted poor Mrs. So-and-so in a staff council meeting and so on. After a dozen or so of these visits the new headmistress rang my father at his office and told him that if he could not think of some way of keeping his mother away from the school she would instruct the chowkidars not to let her in the next time she came.

I do not know what my father said to her, but she did not go back again till Founder's Day.

After that, for a few weeks, she spent all her time alone in her room. Once I pushed open her door and saw her sitting by the window staring blankly at her cupped hands. I shut the door quickly. I knew what she had in her hands. Time—great livid gouts of it; I could smell it stinking.

We left her to herself for a while and soon she began to spend more time with us. She would sit with us in the evenings with a book or a half-finished letter on her knees and talk about our relatives or my father's work or my homework much as she used to before—but even I could tell that she was merely making an effort now; it was plain that she no longer cared.

I was puzzled and worried by the change in her and in my own way I began to make an effort to combat it. I had always resented the tyranny she had exercised over everything to do with my schoolwork, but now, of my own accord, I began to ask her for help with my homework. And on those occasions when I could persuade her to sit with me at my desk as she used to before, I found myself devising small ruses—like spilling ink on my textbooks—to keep her attention from straying. Sometimes my ploys would work and she would jerk herself out of her trance and rap me on my knuckles with the thin edge of a ruler. But then, soon, her mind would wander off again and I would sit doodling in my exercise book while she gazed out of the window. But for all that, her eyes had lost none of their glitter nor her walk its old rhythm or energy.

There's something stirring in her head, my mother whispered to me one day, watching her with narrowed eyes. I can tell from the look on her face. We have to be careful.

1962 was an exciting year for us. A couple of months after my grandmother retired my father became General Manager of his firm. The appointment was unexpected because there were many older and more experienced executives in the firm. It was a promotion such as he had not dared dream of. But my grandmother, who had always been very quick to tell our relatives about every small sign of success in my father's career, seemed hardly to notice this unforeseen and spectacular advancement. I heard her making a couple of calls once, but that was all. I remembered clearly how she had spent hours ringing everyone she knew when he'd been promoted from the position of Assistant Manager, Personnel, to Manager, Marketing, and I could not help noticing how brief her calls were this time.

Soon after my father's promotion we moved to a new house on Southern Avenue, opposite the lake. To me, after our cramped little flat in Gole Park, our new house seemed immense: it seemed to have more space than we could possibly use—rooms upstairs, rooms downstairs, verandas, a garden as well as a roof big enough to play cricket on. Best of all, as far as I was concerned, I still had Montu and my other friends close at hand because our new house was only a few minutes' walk from Gole Park.

I took it upon myself to introduce my grandmother to the house. I led her around it several times pointing out hidden lofts and unexpected doors and passageways. She made a few approbatory noises, but since they all sounded the same I knew soon enough that she was only pretending to be interested for my sake.

As we settled into our new house, it gradually became evident that the balances within our family had subtly but irrevocably shifted. In our old flat my grandmother had always been careful to maintain a titular control over the running of our household: now she didn't seem to care any more. It was to my mother that I had to go now when I was hungry and wanted the keys to the cupboard in which the dalmuth was kept, or when I wanted money to buy peanuts at the lake.

My grandmother's enveloping, placental presence was slowly withdrawing from the rest of the house and concentrating itself within the four walls of her room.

She had the best room in the house. It was very large and its walls were lined with tall shuttered windows. The few bits of furniture she had collected over the years seemed to be adrift in the vast spaces of that room, like leaves in a lake. I still occasionally took my homework to her. Usually when I went into her room, I would find her sitting in an armchair beside an open window—a shrunken, fragile little figure, gazing out across the lake. I would pull up a chair and sit beside her, scratching noisily in my exercise book to attract her attention.

One evening, when she seemed particularly distracted, I threw my exercise book down in frustration and cried: Tha'mma, why do you always stare out of the window like that? Don't you like this house?

She glanced at me in surprise and patted my shoulder. It's a nice house, she said, smiling. It's a nice house for a child, like you.

But then a frown appeared on her forehead and she bit her lip and said: But you know, it's very different from the house Maya and I grew up in.

How? I asked.

And so, over months of such evenings, she told me about the house she had grown up in—in Dhaka.

It was a very odd house. It had evolved slowly, growing like a honeycomb, with every generation of Boses adding layers and extensions, until it was like a huge, lopsided step-pyramid, inhabited by so many branches of the family that even the most knowledgeable amongst them had become a little confused about their relationships.

Their own part of the house was quite large, and in my grandmother's earliest memory it was very crowded. Theirs was a big joint family then, with everyone living and eating together: her grandparents, her parents, she and Mayadebi, her Jethamoshai—her father's elder brother—and his family, which included three cousins of roughly her own age, as well as a couple of spinster aunts. She remembered her grandfather, although she had only been six when he died: a thin, stern-looking man with a frown etched permanently into his forehead. In his presence everyone, including her father and Jethamoshai, spoke in whispers, with their heads down and their eyes fixed firmly on the floor. But when he left the house for the district courts, where he practised as an advocate, the house would erupt with the noisy games of the five cousins. Every evening the five children would be led by their mothers into his study, where they would each have to recite their alphabets—Bengali first and then English—with their hands held out, palm downwards, and he would rap them on the knuckles with the handle of his umbrella every time they made a mistake. If they cried they were rapped on their shins.

Still, terrifying though he was, he did manage to keep the house together. After he died, Jethamoshai, as the eldest son, tried hard to step into his place, but without success. He was an odd man, Jethamoshai; in some ways he was an oddly lovable man, but in others he was even more frightening than his father. He was thinner, for one, cadaverous in fact, and he had very bright, piercing eyes, set deep in the hollows of his long, gaunt face. But he had odd "notions"—he liked to eat standing up, for instance, because he thought it was better for the digestion: no animal has a better digestive system than the cow, he used to say, and look at them, they eat standing up. He was undeniably eccentric, and the children found it hard to take him altogether seriously. For example, after his father died, he insisted that the children recite the alphabet every evening to him too, while he sat exactly as his father had, with the handle of his umbrella poised over their knuckles. But although he looked every bit as stern as his father, he had an odd trick of blowing through his lips, exactly like a tired tonga-horse, when he was listening. So, often, either she or Mayadebi would burst into laughter, halfway through their recitation. This would infuriate him and he would begin to pound out a drum roll of raps on their knuckles, whereupon they would begin to scream their lungs out, and then he would lose his temper altogether and start kicking them in the shins. The children usually enjoyed this production hugely because Jethamoshai wasn't really strong enough to hurt them, and besides his face became very funny when he was really angry. But of course their mother would be furious: she didn't understand that he didn't mean badly—it was just that he had no control over his temper at all. Often, after he had lost his temper, he would secretly buy the children halwa and shandesh as a kind of apology. But their mother didn't know this, and within a month or so of her father-in-law's death she was no longer on speaking terms with Jethamoshai and his wife and family.

It did not take long for the quarrels to get worse. The two women began to suspect each other of favouring their own children above the rest, of purloining the best little tidbits of food for them from the common larder and so on. In the privacy of their rooms they would both berate their husbands, calling them unmanly and incapable of protecting the interests of their own children. Soon the two brothers were quarrelling too. And since they were both lawyers their quarrels took a peculiarly vicious, legalistic form, in which very little was actually said. Instead, they would send each other notes on legal stationery. My grandmother, since she was the elder, would always have to carry these, and she came to dread those missions for she would have to wait beside Jethamoshai's chair while he read them over and over again until the veins in his forehead began to throb with anger.

Those were terrible days for the children—spent cowering in the background, listening, while their mothers quarrelled in whispers behind locked doors or lay crying in their bedrooms. When the cousins played now, it had to be in secret so that their parents would not see them together.

Soon things came to such a pass that they decided to divide the house with a wooden partition wall: there was no other alternative. But the building of the wall proved to be far from easy because the two brothers, insisting on their rights with a lawyerlike precision, demanded that the division be exact down to the minutest detail. When the wall was eventually built, they found that it had ploughed right through a couple of doorways so that no one could get through them any more; it had also gone through a lavatory, bisecting an old commode. The brothers even partitioned their father's old nameplate. It was divided down the middle by a thin white line, and their names were inscribed on the two halves—of necessity in letters so tiny that nobody could read them.

They sprang from notoriously litigious stock.

They had all longed for the house to be divided when

the quarrels were at their worst, but once it had actually happened and each family had moved into their own part of it, instead of the peace they had so much looked forward to, they found that a strange, eerie silence had descended on the house. It was never the same again after that; the life went out of it. It was worse for my grandmother than Mayadebi, for she could remember a time when it had been otherwise. She would often look across at her cousins on the other side and wonder about them, but so much bitterness lay between the two families now that she could not bring herself to actually speak to them.

In later years it always made my grandmother a little nervous when she heard people saying: We're like brothers. What does that mean? she would ask hurriedly. Does that mean you're friends? As for herself, having learnt the meaning of brotherhood very early, she had not dared to take the risk of providing my father with one.

And yet, those very women, my grandmother's mother and her aunt, the accumulated spleen of whose quarrels had probably shortened their lives by several years, became close, though silent, allies when it came to the business of their daughters' marriages. For example, their aunt played a central role in arranging Mayadebi's marriage to the Shaheb. It was she who first learnt of it when old Mr. Justice Datta-Chaudhuri came to Dhaka on tour with his son (then an eminently eligible stripling of eighteen), and since she had already married off her own daughters, she made sure that the old judge got to hear of Mayadebi (whose beauty was already famous in the city). Once that had been accomplished the rest was easy, for their horoscopes, as well as every other circumstance, were eminently well suited. The pact was quickly sealed, and within six months Mayadebi was married. When she left, their mother gave her strict instructions not to forget to send her aunt half a dozen saris from Calcutta.

But here, at home in Dhaka, they never so much as exchanged a single word across that wall.

As for my grandmother, she had been married off four

years before Mayadebi. My grandfather was an engineer with the railways, in Burma; my grandmother spent the first twelve years of her married life in a succession of railway colonies in towns with fairy-tale names like Moulmein and Mandalay. But later, all she remembered of them was hospitals and railway stations and Bengali societies: to her, nothing else in that enchanted pagoda-land had seemed real enough to remember.

My father was born in Mandalay, in 1925. My grand-mother used to take him back to Dhaka every year for a couple of months to stay with her parents. Their part of the house was much emptier now because her cousins (of whom there were three, two boys and a girl) had scattered to various parts of the subcontinent. After Mayadebi got married and went to live in Calcutta, only those four elderly people—her uncle, aunt and her parents—were left in the house. They had very little to quarrel about now, but the passage of time had in no way diminished that ancient bitterness. My grandmother did what she could to make them forget the past, but they had grown so thoroughly into the habits engendered by decades of hostility that none of them wanted to venture out into the limbo of reconciliation. They liked the wall now; it had become a part of them.

GITHA HARIHARAN

Githa Hariharan was born in 1954 in Coimbatore, Tamilnadu, and grew up in Bombay and in Manila. She was educated in these two cities and in the United States. She was a staff writer for WNET Channel 13 in New York and also worked in Bombay, Madras, and New Delhi as an editor, first for a publishing house and then freelance.

Hariharan's published work includes novels, short stories, children's stories, essays, newspaper articles, and columns. Her first novel, *The Thousand Faces of Night* (1992), won the Commonwealth Writers Prize for Best First Book. Her other novels include *The Ghosts of Vasu Master* (1994); *When Dreams Travel* (1999); *In Times of Siege* (2003); and *Fugitive Histories* (2009). Hariharan says of her writing, "All my novels and stories look at power politics in some way or the other. Fiction has a thousand ways of giving us a new take on the dynamics of power relations."

She has been visiting professor or writer-in-residence at several universities in the United States, Britain, and India. She currently lives in New Delhi with her husband and two sons.

Field Trip

It took Krishna only a week in the village to find out. Village boys were stupid. He was also scared of them.

They knew so little, they made him laugh. They had never seen an aquarium or a planetarium. Their English—what little they knew of it—was really hilarious. If his best friends in Bombay, Vivek and Suresh, were here with him, how they would have laughed together!

But it was the village boys who laughed at him. He, who had won a school quiz last year, and who wanted to be an astronaut or at least a space scientist, couldn't swim. He couldn't climb a tree without feeling dizzy.

"Sissy!" they taunted. "Little girl, where's your skirt? Go help your aunt in the kitchen!"

Once, unable to bear their stupid, grinning, mocking faces, he had rushed at them blindly. "You ignorant idiots," he yelled. "You don't know anything."

But there were six of them. The biggest, Mani, was a grimy thirteen-year-old whose nose still ran. He snatched Krishna's spectacles off his nose in one quick movement.

"That's not fair," shouted Krishna, groping toward the six laughing bodies that now surrounded him on all sides.

"Not fair! Not fair!" they chanted, their grins turning into something blurred and menacing.

Krishna shut his eyes. Through the noise, the heat of the afternoon sun, his sweat, and the tears of anger just behind his closed eyelids, he heard a bellowing voice. A strong, decisive voice, a voice used to giving orders. Sundaram Mama could never have been called a sissy. He could never have been mistaken for a girl. Not if he had fifty louts on his trail.

"Who's making that noise?" the voice bellowed again.

Like magic, as if Krishna had wished them away, the boys vanished. He was alone. He had been saved. He walked slowly across the yard and picked up his glasses where Mani had dropped them in a panic. They were not broken, but the lenses were cloudy and smudged with dirt. There was a small, slimy patch on the frame that was thick and grey, like Mani's snot.

The sun shone brightly, as it had every day since Krishna had come to the village for his summer holiday. He was on his way to the village tank with Sundaram Mama.

Sundaram Mama had not asked him about the afternoon. Krishna had cleaned his glasses twice, thrice, with soap and water. He had spent the rest of the day in the

house, leafing through the stamp collection he had
brought with him from Bombay. But somehow the fifty-
four colourful pages of shiny, plastic-covered stamps did
not give him the thrill of possession they usually did. He
shut the album listlessly and went looking for his aunt.

Parvati Mami hummed to herself as she worked, and
he usually enjoyed telling her about his school, his
friends Suresh and Vivek, Bombay, the skyscraper he
lived in, and what he had seen on television.

"Is that so," she would say, always prepared to be
impressed. She would stop what she was doing and gape
at him, her mouth open in a little O. She looked, he
thought, like a surprised fish.

Usually he felt like giggling when she did that, and he
also felt like hugging her. But today he kept hearing
Mani's voice—"Sissy! Girl!"—and looking into Parvati
Mami's passive, all-believing face, he felt an ache begin
to creep up his neck to his forehead.

Then Sundaram Mama came back early from the
fields. "Come on," he said to Krishna. "Let's go to the
village tank. I'll teach you how to swim." He held in
his hands a pair of coconut husks, scooped out like two
little boats. A hole had been pierced in each so that it
could be tied with rope to Krishna's arm.

There was no one at the tank when they got there,
and Krishna was so relieved that he forgot his fear of
the water. He could learn in secret, without Sundaram's
friends shouting their cheerful, man-to-man advice at
him.

They were just like the rest of them. "Look at your
uncle," the old men in the village liked to tell Krishna.
"His brothers know nothing of their family lands. But
he—that Sundaram—is one of us. The oil lamp is still
lit every evening in your old ancestral house."

"He knows the old ways," they said, their heads nodding in a chorus of approval.

The husks floated like a dream. The taunts that
Krishna had heard in the last few weeks receded like
distant memories. The echoes that had tormented his
ears—"You're a girl! Be a man!"—were almost forgotten.

He found that his arms worked well together. They moved one after the other, in brisk, purposeful strokes. His legs learnt to hit the water, keeping time with the movement of his arms. A few afternoons later, he threw away the coconut husks. Sundaram Mama yelled his approval. He was a simple farmer, Mama said, so he always spoke as if he was shouting across the fields. And Krishna swam, clumsy at first, but soon with swift and aggressive strokes.

I've done it, I've done it, he thought, as he shook the water off his face and his feet searched for the gritty bottom of the tank. They found it, and the moment he was upright again he felt something thin and snaky entangling itself around his right ankle.

Krishna froze. He peered down at the murky water, but all he could see through the dirt, without his glasses, was a hazy rippling of water. Then the thing moved. He could feel it wriggling up his leg, cold, clammy, clinging.

"Mama," he screamed, "a snake! There's a snake on my leg!" At his very first scream, Sundaram Mama was swimming towards him, his dark muscular arms and legs breaking wave-like swells of water before them.

Mama's head emerged from the water and looked at his face for an instant. Then the head disappeared under the water. And in what seemed a painfully long moment to Krishna, Mama was up again, the green snake in his hands. He looked at Krishna's pale, frightened face and burst into laughter. "It's a weed, you silly boy," he spluttered. "Don't you see those hyacinths and weeds choking up the corners of the tank?"

Krishna looked at the snake-like weed in dismay. He wished it was real and that he had been bitten. Or that he had saved Mama from a snake. Or Mani. Then they would never laugh at him again.

Sundaram Mama had laughed at him, but he didn't say a word about it to anyone else. Saved again. Krishna glowed with pride every time someone in the village said he looked like Sundaram.

As the bullock cart jolted its way down the dirt track, Krishna felt the excitement in his stomach heaving up to his mouth. He held on to Sundaram Mama's shirt sleeve as if it was a charm.

I am ten and a half years old, said Krishna to himself, over and over again. I am not a sissy from the big city. And he forced himself to look at the green stretches of fields they bumped past, breathing in great big lungfuls of dusty air. He stole a look at the big, dark man who sat next to him, frowning at the fields of sugarcane on either side.

Sundaram Mama was no ordinary village-uncle. The villagers called him Big Master; his house was the Big House. Sundaram, Krishna had heard a hundred times, had stayed behind and nurtured the family fields while the other brothers had each gone his own way. But to Krishna, Sundaram was not just one of the village pillars. He was something more—a strong-armed, honour-bound man, like a hero.

When they reached the small farmhouse that stood on a clearing walled in on all sides by tall sugarcane plants, it was late afternoon.

They were met, it seemed to Krishna, by a horde of smiling, waving farmhands. Then Karuppayya, who lived in the small, pucca farmhouse, waved the rest of them away.

Karuppayya was a huge, jet-black, shiny-skinned man. He looked after the sugarcane fields for Sundaram Mama who was too busy with his paddy fields near the village. Karuppayya, Krishna had heard, was like Sundaram's right arm. Karuppayya's teeth shone like polished white tiles when he beamed at Krishna. "The little master!" he cried with pleasure. He lifted him off the cart as if Krishna was a baby.

Karuppayya's wife and sister-in-law stood at the doorstep, smiling. It was clear that they were expected. The porch was washed and decorated with floral kolams. A few rickety cane chairs had been arranged in the centre for the visitors.

Krishna sat cross-legged on a little wooden stool, in the thatched hut which was the bathroom. Through the gaps in the thin, rustling walls, he felt a soft, cool breeze, and saw the narrow shafts of light deepening into a misty blue-grey.

He squinted at the walls, pretending his naked body was not his own. Vengamma bent over him, rubbing warm oil into his dry, dust-choked skin. Vengamma was Karuppayya's sister-in-law. She had waved aside Krishna's protests that he could bathe himself. He had turned to Sundaram Mama, helpless, but this time Mama too had not saved him. He had laughed and said, "What? You want to spend a night in the fields without a good oil bath first?" Karuppayya had roared with laughter, as if he had not heard a better joke before. Vengamma had giggled, and led Krishna to the bath-hut.

She was massaging his scalp now, with brisk, firm strokes. Krishna could smell the sharp, warm sesame oil, mixed with the jasmine and sweat smell of Vengamma. Her tight choli, a shiny, smooth pink, was a few inches from his face. Two large wet patches made her underarms a deeper pink. Above her choli, below the face he could not see, her long, slender neck ended in a surprisingly fleshy but firm expanse of bare brown skin.

Krishna closed his eyes. The smell, the oil being worked into every pore of his skin, the small, windowless bathroom, and the nearness of something soft, alien and insistent gave him an empty, throbbing sensation in the pit of his stomach. It was like the time he had looked out of the twelfth-floor balcony in Bombay. Or the time he had sat by the seashore during high tide, and the waves had come rolling up, one after the other, one bigger than the other, teasing, frightening, inviting, swallowing. He had stood hypnotized at the spot, overcome by the desire to jump, but he had been too afraid.

After the village noises he had got used to, Krishna felt the strange quietness of the farmhouse stretch like a long night before him. Sundaram Mama and he had been given a room of their own—they even had two small wooden cots—but Mama had not yet come to bed.

The petromax lamp on the floor hissed and sizzled as if the flame would burst out of its glass prison any minute. The shadows on the walls were unnaturally long and

menacing. They trembled, or they shifted abruptly, so
that one merged with the other, like the disjointed fragments of a nightmare.

Krishna heard the sound of bottles and glasses in the
front room. A low voice and silence again. Then a soft
giggle that dissolved into a moan. Vengamma's breasts
were full and round in her tight, shiny, pink choli. Her
hips swelled softly in her coarse sari, which was as green
as the sugarcane fields. She was a woman, like Parvati
Mami. A girl. Krishna tossed and turned in the unfamiliar bed, wishing the morning would come. He couldn't
wait to get back to the village. He couldn't wait to get
back to Bombay. To Vivek and Suresh, with whom he
could be an astronaut again. Or a space scientist.

The next morning they were back in the bumpy bullock
cart. This time Krishna, an experienced traveller in villages, sat facing the opening at the back, his arms full
of sugarcane. His eyes were red and they stung, as if it
was he, not Sundaram Mama, who had not slept at all
the night before.

They had all gathered to see them off. Karuppayya,
his wife and children, even Vengamma. Krishna couldn't
bring himself to look at her, but she had come running
forward and thrust a pile of cut sugarcane in his arms.
"For the little master," she said. "I know he has a sweet
tooth, just like our Big Master here." They had all
laughed with her. Even Sundaram Mama had smiled graciously, like a man used to tokens of gratitude.

They were silent on their journey homeward. The sun
shone on the endless stretches of sugarcane the cart
bumped past. The dust flew in fine sprays and tickled
Krishna's nostrils. As they left the fields behind, and the
cart began to jolt up and down, up and down, in a faster,
more regular rhythm, Sundaram Mama cleared his
throat.

"Krishna," he said, his bellowing voice dropping to a
low, velvety pitch. "Maybe you will also become a Big
Master one day. I work hard, and these peasants who
opened their doors to us last night respect me. They
need me. Not everyone can understand that, you see."

As if he had spoken to himself, Sundaram fell back into silence, looking thoughtfully at the road before them. Krishna too was silent. He felt the dust in his nose and mouth choking him.

He wiped his nose on his sleeve, in an abrupt gesture of impatience, and put a small stick of sugarcane in his mouth. Its skin was hard, but his teeth pulled at it ferociously till it peeled off. Then the crisp sweetness inside trickled into his mouth like a warm, mysterious secret.

He chewed and chewed on the cane, and by the time he spat out the dry, stringy stick, he felt far far away. He saw before him, not the dark and bewildering figure of his uncle, but himself, alone. For a minute he felt naked and frightened, as he had when Vengamma bathed him. But when he saw the village at a distance, coming toward them with every jolt, his lips stopped trembling. He sat still for a moment, as if in preparation. Then his mouth hardened and set, and his eyes became cool and intense behind his thick spectacles, a little like his childhood hero.

RUTH PRAWER JHABVALA

Born in Cologne, Germany, in 1927 to Polish-Jewish parents Ruth Prawer Jhabvala emigrated to England in 1939. After earning an MA at Queen Mary College of London University, she married C. S. H. Jhabvala, an Indian architect, and moved with him to Delhi. An insider by virtue of her decades of living in India yet an outsider by virtue of her Western youth and education, she frequently depicts characters torn between their desire for modern Western comfort and the spiritual consolation of Hinduism and traditional Indian family relationships and cultural values.

In analyzing one of Jhabvala's recurring subjects, the experience of Westerners in India, S. M. Mollinger has observed that the novelist "uses India as a catalyst, as an outrageous force that elicits unexpected, frequently frightening, reactions from its visitors." Among her many honors, Jhabvala has been awarded a Booker Prize, a Neil Gunn International Fellowship, a Guggenheim Fellowship, and a MacArthur Foundation Award.

A prolific novelist and story writer, she has also had a successful career as a screenwriter. Among the more than twenty screenplays she has authored or coauthored are *Shakespeare Wallah, The Europeans, The Golden Bowl, A Room with a View, Howards End, Mr. and Mrs. Bridge,* and *The Remains of the Day.* Among her best-known novels are *Esmond in India* (1958), *A Backward Place* (1965), *Heat and Dust* (1976), *In Search of Love and Beauty* (1983), and *Shards of Memory* (1995).

Her short story collections include *Like Birds, Like Fishes* (1964), *How I Became a Holy Mother and Other Stories* (1976), *Out of India* (1986), and *My Nine Lives* (2004).

Two More Under the Indian Sun

$\mathcal{E}$lizabeth had gone to spend the afternoon with Margaret. They were both English, but Margaret was a much older woman and they were also very different in character. But they were both in love with India, and it was this fact that drew them together. They sat on the veranda, and Margaret wrote letters and Elizabeth addressed the envelopes. Margaret always had letters to write; she led a busy life and was involved with several organizations of a charitable or spiritual nature. Her interests were centered in such matters, and Elizabeth was glad to be allowed to help her.

There were usually guests staying in Margaret's house. Sometimes they were complete strangers to her when they first arrived, but they tended to stay weeks, even months, at a time—holy men from the Himalayas, village welfare workers, organizers of conferences on spiritual welfare. She had one constant visitor throughout the winter, an elderly government officer who, on his retirement from service, had taken to a spiritual life and gone to live in the mountains at Almora. He did not, however, very much care for the winter cold up there, so at that season he came down to Delhi to stay with Margaret, who was always pleased to have him. He had a soothing effect on her—indeed, on anyone with whom he came into contact, for he had cast anger and all other bitter passions out of his heart and was consequently always smiling and serene. Everyone affectionately called him Babaji.

He sat now with the two ladies on the veranda, gently rocking himself to and fro in a rocking chair, enjoying the winter sunshine and the flowers in the garden and everything about him. His companions, however, were less serene. Margaret, in fact, was beginning to get angry with Elizabeth. This happened quite frequently, for Margaret tended to be quickly irritated, and especially with a meek and conciliatory person like Elizabeth.

"It's very selfish of you," Margaret said now.

Elizabeth flinched. Like many very unselfish people, she was always accusing herself of undue selfishness, so that whenever this accusation was made by someone else it touched her closely. But because it was not in her power to do what Margaret wanted, she compressed her lips and kept silent. She was pale with this effort at obstinacy.

"It's your duty to go," Margaret said. "I don't have much time for people who shirk their duty."

"I'm sorry, Margaret," Elizabeth said, utterly miserable, utterly ashamed. The worst of it, almost, was that she really wanted to go; there was nothing she would have enjoyed more. What she was required to do was take a party of little Tibetan orphans on a holiday treat to Agra and show them the Taj Mahal. Elizabeth loved children, she loved little trips and treats, and she loved the Taj Mahal. But she couldn't go, nor could she say why.

Of course Margaret very easily guessed why, and it irritated her more than ever. To challenge her friend, she said bluntly, "Your Raju can do without you for those few days. Good heavens, you're not a honeymoon couple, are you? You've been married long enough. Five years."

"Four," Elizabeth said in a humble voice.

"Four, then. I can hardly be expected to keep count of each wonderful day. Do you want me to speak to him?"

"Oh no."

"I will, you know. It's nothing to me. I won't mince my words." She gave a short, harsh laugh, challenging anyone to stop her from speaking out when occasion demanded. Indeed, at the thought of anyone doing so, her face grew red under her crop of gray hair, and a pulse throbbed in visible anger in her tough, tanned neck.

Elizabeth glanced imploringly toward Babaji. But he was rocking and smiling and looking with tender love at two birds pecking at something on the lawn.

"There are times when I can't help feeling you're afraid of him," Margaret said. She ignored Elizabeth's little disclaiming cry of horror. "There's no trust between you, no understanding. And married life is nothing if it's not based on the twin rocks of trust and understanding."

Babaji liked this phrase so much that he repeated it to himself several times, his lips moving soundlessly and his head nodding with approval.

"In everything I did," Margaret said, "Arthur was with me. He had complete faith in me. And in those days— Well." She chuckled. "A wife like me wasn't altogether a joke."

Her late husband had been a high-up British official, and in those British days he and Margaret had been expected to conform to some very strict social rules. But the idea of Margaret conforming to any rules, let alone those! Her friends nowadays often had a good laugh at it with her, and she had many stories to tell of how she had shocked and defied her fellow countrymen.

"It was people like you," Babaji said, "who first extended the hand of friendship to us."

"It wasn't a question of friendship, Babaji. It was a question of love."

"Ah!" he exclaimed.

"As soon as I came here—and I was only a chit of a girl, Arthur and I had been married just two months— yes, as soon as I set foot on Indian soil, I knew this was the place I belonged. It's funny, isn't it? I don't suppose there's any rational explanation for it. But then, when was India ever the place for rational explanations."

Babaji said with gentle certainty, "In your last birth, you were one of us. You were an Indian."

"Yes, lots of people have told me that. Mind you, in the beginning it was quite a job to make them see it. Naturally, they were suspicious—can you blame them? It wasn't like today. I envy you girls married to Indians. You have a very easy time of it."

Elizabeth thought of the first time she had been taken to stay with Raju's family. She had met and married Raju in England, where he had gone for a year on a Commonwealth scholarship, and then had returned with him to Delhi; so it was some time before she met his family, who lived about two hundred miles out of Delhi, on the outskirts of a small town called Ankhpur. They all lived together in an ugly brick house, which was divided into two parts—one for the men of the family, the other for the women. Elizabeth, of course, had stayed in the women's quarters. She couldn't speak any Hindi and they spoke very little English, but they had not had much trouble communicating with her. They managed to make it clear at once that they thought her too ugly and too old for Raju (who was indeed some five years her junior), but also that they did not hold this against her and were ready to accept her, with all her shortcomings, as the will of God. They got a lot of amusement out of her, and she enjoyed being with them. They dressed and undressed her in new saris, and she smiled good-naturedly while they stood around her clapping their hands in wonder and doubling up with laughter. Various fertility ceremonies had been performed over her, and before she left she had been given her share of the family jewelry.

"Elizabeth," Margaret said, "if you're going to be so slow, I'd rather do them myself."

"Just these two left," Elizabeth said, bending more eagerly over the envelopes she was addressing.

"For all your marriage," Margaret said, "sometimes I wonder how much you do understand about this country. You live such a closed-in life."

"I'll just take these inside," Elizabeth said, picking up the envelopes and letters. She wanted to get away, not because she minded being told about her own wrong way of life but because she was afraid Margaret might start talking about Raju again.

It was cold inside, away from the sun. Margaret's house was old and massive, with thick stone walls, skylights instead of windows, and immensely high ceilings. It was designed to keep out the heat in summer, but it also sealed in the cold in winter and became like some cavernous underground fortress frozen through with the cold of earth and stone. A stale smell of rice, curry, and mango chutney was chilled into the air. Elizabeth put the letters on Margaret's work table, which was in the drawing room. Besides the drawing room, there was a dining room, but every other room was a bedroom, each with its dressing room and bathroom attached. Sometimes Margaret had to put as many as three or four visitors into each bedroom, and on one occasion—this was when she had helped to organize a conference on Meditation as the Modern Curative—the drawing and dining rooms too had been converted into dormitories, with string cots and bedrolls laid out end to end. Margaret was not only an energetic and active person involved in many causes but she was also the soul of generosity, ever ready to throw open her house to any friend or acquaintance in need of shelter. She had thrown it open to Elizabeth and Raju three years ago, when they had had to vacate their rooms almost overnight because the landlord said he needed the accommodation for his relatives. Margaret had given them a whole suite—a bedroom and dressing room and bathroom—to themselves and they had had all their meals with her in the big dining room, where the table was always ready laid with white crockery plates, face down so as not to catch the dust, and a thick white tablecloth that got rather stained toward the end of the week. At first, Raju had been very grateful and had praised their hostess to the skies for her kind and generous character. But as the weeks wore on, and every day, day after day, two or three times a day, they sat with Margaret and whatever other guests she had around the table, eating alternately lentils and rice or string beans with boiled potatoes and beetroot salad, with Margaret always in her chair at the head of the table talking inexhaustibly about her activities and ideas—about Indian spirituality and the Mutiny and village uplift and the industrial revolution—Raju, who had a lot of ideas of his own and rather liked to talk, began to get restive. "But Madam, Madam," he would frequently say, half rising in his chair in his impatience to interrupt her, only to have to sit down again, unsatisfied, and continue with his dinner, because Margaret was too busy with her own ideas to have time to take in his.

Once he could not restrain himself. Margaret was talk-

ing about—Elizabeth had even forgotten what it was—
was it the first Indian National Congress? At any rate,
she said something that stirred Raju to such disagreement that this time he did not restrict himself to the
hesitant appeal of "Madam" but said out loud for everyone to hear, "Nonsense, she is only talking nonsense."
There was a moment's silence; then Margaret, sensible
woman that she was, shut her eyes as a sign that she would
not hear and would not see, and, repeating the sentence
he had interrupted more firmly than before, continued
her discourse on an even keel. It was the other two or
three people sitting with them around the table—a Bud-
dhist monk with a large shaved skull, a welfare worker,
and a disciple of the Gandhian way of life wearing nothing but the homespun loincloth in which the Mahatma
himself had always been so simply clad—it was they who
had looked at Raju, and very, very gently one of them
had clicked his tongue.

Raju had felt angry and humiliated, and afterward,
when they were alone in their bedroom, he had quar-
reled about it with Elizabeth. In his excitement, he
raised his voice higher than he would have if he had
remembered that they were in someone else's house,
and the noise of this must have disturbed Margaret, who
suddenly stood in the doorway, looking at them. Unfor-
tunately, it was just at the moment when Raju, in his
anger and frustration, was pulling his wife's hair, and
they both stood frozen in this attitude and stared back at
Margaret. The next instant, of course, they had collected
themselves, and Raju let go of Elizabeth's hair, and she
pretended as best she could that all that was happening
was that he was helping her comb it. But such a feeble
subterfuge would not do before Margaret's penetrating
eye, which she kept fixed on Raju, in total silence, for
two disconcerting minutes; then she said, "We don't
treat English girls that way," and withdrew, leaving the
door open behind her as a warning that they were under
observation. Raju shut it with a vicious kick. If they had
had anywhere to go, he would have moved out that
instant.

Raju never came to see Margaret now. He was a

proud person, who would never forget anything he considered a slight to his honor. Elizabeth always came on her own, as she had done today, to visit her friend. She sighed now as she arranged the letters on Margaret's work table; she was sad that this difference had arisen between her husband and her only friend, but she knew that there was nothing she could do about it. Raju was very obstinate. She shivered and rubbed the tops of her arms, goose-pimpled with the cold in that high, bleak room, and returned quickly to the veranda, which was flooded and warm with afternoon sun.

Babaji and Margaret were having a discussion on the relative merits of the three ways toward realization. They spoke of the way of knowledge, the way of action, and that of love. Margaret maintained that it was a matter of temperament, and that while she could appreciate the beauty of the other two ways, for herself there was no path nor could there ever be but that of action. It was her nature.

"Of course it is," Babaji said. "And God bless you for it."

"Arthur used to tease me. He'd say, 'Margaret was born to right all the wrongs of the world in one go.' But I can't help it. It's not in me to sit still when I see things to be done."

"Babaji," said Elizabeth, laughing, "once I saw her—it was during the monsoon, and the river had flooded and the people on the bank were being evacuated. But it wasn't being done quickly enough for Margaret! She waded into the water and came back with someone's tin trunk on her head. All the people shouted, 'Memsahib, Memsahib! What are you doing?' but she didn't take a bit of notice. She waded right back in again and came out with two rolls of bedding, one under each arm."

Elizabeth went pink with laughter, and with pleasure and pride, at recalling this incident. Margaret pretended to be angry and gave her a playful slap, but she could not help smiling, while Babaji clasped his hands in joy and opened his mouth wide in silent, ecstatic laughter.

Margaret shook her head with a last fond smile. "Yes,

but I've got into the most dreadful scrapes with this nature of mine. If I'd been born with an ounce more patience, I'd have been a pleasanter person to deal with and life could have been a lot smoother all round. Don't you think so?"

She looked at Elizabeth, who said, "I love you just the way you are."

But a moment later, Elizabeth wished she had not said this. "Yes," Margaret took her up, "that's the trouble with you. You love everybody just the way they are." Of course she was referring to Raju. Elizabeth twisted her hands in her lap. These hands were large and bony and usually red, although she was otherwise a pale and rather frail person.

The more anyone twisted and squirmed, the less inclined was Margaret to let them off the hook. Not because this afforded her any pleasure but because she felt that facts of character must be faced just as resolutely as any other kinds of fact. "Don't think you're doing anyone a favor," she said, "by being so indulgent toward their faults. Quite on the contrary. And especially in marriage," she went on unwaveringly. "It's not mutual pampering that makes a marriage but mutual trust."

"Trust and understanding," Babaji said.

Elizabeth knew that there was not much of these in her marriage. She wasn't even sure how much Raju earned in his job at the municipality (he was an engineer in the sanitation department), and there was one drawer in their bedroom whose contents she didn't know, for he always kept it locked and the key with him.

"I'll lend you a wonderful book," Margaret said. "It's called *Truth in the Mind,* and it's full of the most astounding insight. It's by this marvelous man who founded an ashram in Shropshire. Shafi!" she called suddenly for the servant, but of course he couldn't hear, because the servants' quarters were right at the back, and the old man now spent most of his time there, sitting on a bed and having his legs massaged by a granddaughter.

"I'll call him," Elizabeth said, and got up eagerly.

She went back into the stone-cold house and out again

at the other end. Here were the kitchen and the crowded servant quarters. Margaret could never bear to dismiss anyone, and even the servants who were no longer in her employ continued to enjoy her hospitality. Each servant had a great number of dependents, so this part of the house was a little colony of its own, with a throng of people outside the rows of peeling hutments, chatting or sleeping or quarreling or squatting on the ground to cook their meals and wash their children. Margaret enjoyed coming out there, mostly to advise and scold—but Elizabeth felt shy, and she kept her eyes lowered.

"Shafi," she said, "Memsahib is calling you."

The old man mumbled furiously. He did not like to have his rest disturbed and he did not like Elizabeth. In fact, he did not like any of the visitors. He was the oldest servant in the house—so old that he had been Arthur's bearer when Arthur was still a bachelor and serving in the districts, almost forty years ago.

Still grumbling, he followed Elizabeth back to the veranda.

"Tea, Shafi!" Margaret called out cheerfully when she saw them coming.

"Not time for tea yet," he said.

She laughed. She loved it when her servants answered her back; she felt it showed a sense of ease and equality and family irritability, which was only another side of family devotion. "What a cross old man you are," she said. "And just look at you—how dirty."

He looked down at himself. He was indeed very dirty. He was unshaven and unwashed, and from beneath the rusty remains of what had once been a uniform coat there peeped out a ragged assortment of gray vests and torn pullovers into which he had bundled himself for the winter.

"It's hard to believe," Margaret said, "that this old scarecrow is a terrible, terrible snob. You know why he doesn't like you, Elizabeth? Because you're married to an Indian."

Elizabeth smiled and blushed. She admired Margaret's forthrightness.

"He thinks you've let down the side. He's got very

firm principles. As a matter of fact, he thinks I've let down the side too. All his life he's longed to work for a real memsahib, the sort that entertains other memsahibs to tea. Never forgave Arthur for bringing home little Margaret."

The old man's face began working strangely. His mouth and stubbled cheeks twitched, and then sounds started coming that rose and fell—now distinct, now only a mutter and a drone—like waves of the sea. He spoke partly in English and partly in Hindi, and it was some time before it could be made out that he was telling some story of the old days—a party at the Gymkhana Club for which he had been hired as an additional waiter. The sahib who had given the party, a Major Waterford, had paid him not only his wages but also a tip of two rupees. He elaborated on this for some time, dwelling on the virtues of Major Waterford and also of Mrs. Waterford, a very fine lady who had made her servants wear white gloves when they served at table.

"Very grand," said Margaret with an easy laugh. "You run along now and get our tea."

"There was a little Missie sahib too. She had two ayahs, and every year they were given four saris and one shawl for the winter."

"Tea, Shafi," Margaret said more firmly, so that the old man, who knew every inflection in his mistress's voice, saw it was time to be off.

"Arthur and I've spoiled him outrageously," Margaret said. "We spoiled all our servants."

"God will reward you," said Babaji.

"We could never think of them as servants, really. They were more our friends. I've learned such a lot from Indian servants. They're usually rogues, but underneath all that they have beautiful characters. They're very religious, and they have a lot of philosophy—you'd be surprised. We've had some fascinating conversations. You ought to keep a servant, Elizabeth—I've told you so often." When she saw Elizabeth was about to answer something, she said, "And don't say you can't afford it. Your Raju earns enough, I'm sure, and they're very cheap."

"We don't need one," Elizabeth said apologetically. There were just the two of them, and they lived in two small rooms. Sometimes Raju also took it into his head that they needed a servant, and once he had even gone to the extent of hiring an undernourished little boy from the hills. On the second day, however, the boy was discovered rifling the pockets of Raju's trousers while their owner was having his bath, so he was dismissed on the spot. To Elizabeth's relief, no attempt at replacing him was ever made.

"If you had one you could get around a bit more," Margaret said. "Instead of always having to dance attendance on your husband's mealtimes. I suppose that's why you don't want to take those poor little children to Agra?"

"It's not that I don't want to," Elizabeth said hopelessly.

"Quite apart from anything else, you ought to be longing to get around and see the country. What do you know, what will you ever know, if you stay in one place all the time?"

"One day you will come and visit me in Almora," Babaji said.

"Oh, Babaji, I'd love to!" Elizabeth exclaimed.

"Beautiful," he said, spreading his hands to describe it all. "The mountains, trees, clouds . . ." Words failed him, and he could only spread his hands farther and smile into the distance, as if he saw a beautiful vision there.

Elizabeth smiled with him. She saw it too, although she had never been there: the mighty mountains, the grandeur and the peace, the abode of Shiva where he sat with the rivers flowing from his hair. She longed to go, and to so many other places she had heard and read about. But the only place away from Delhi where she had ever been was Ankhpur, to stay with Raju's family.

Margaret began to tell about all the places she had been to. She and Arthur had been posted from district to district, in many different parts of the country, but even that hadn't been enough for her. She had to see everything. She had no fears about traveling on her own, and had spent weeks tramping around in the mountains, with a shawl thrown over her shoulders and a stick held firmly in her hand. She had traveled many miles by any mode of transport available—train, bus, cycle, rickshaw, or even bullock cart—in order to see some little-known and almost inaccessible temple or cave or tomb. Once she had sprained her ankle and lain all alone for a week in a derelict rest house, deserted except for one decrepit old watchman, who had shared his meals with her.

"That's the way to get to know the country," she declared. Her cheeks were flushed with the pleasure of remembering everything she had done.

Elizabeth agreed with her. Yet although she herself had done none of these things, she did not feel that she was on that account cut off from all knowledge. There was much to be learned from living with Raju's family in Ankhpur, much to be learned from Raju himself. Yes, he was her India! She felt like laughing when this thought came to her. But it was true.

"Your trouble is," Margaret suddenly said, "you let Raju bully you. He's got something of that in his character—don't contradict. I've studied him. If you were to stand up to him more firmly, you'd both be happier."

Again Elizabeth wanted to laugh. She thought of the nice times she and Raju often had together. He had invented a game of cricket that they could play in their bedroom between the steel almirah and the opposite wall. They played it with a rubber ball and a hairbrush, and three steps made a run. Raju's favorite trick was to hit the ball under the bed, and while she lay flat on the floor groping for it he made run after run, exhorting her with mocking cries of "Hurry up! Where is it? Can't you find it?" His eyes glittered with the pleasure of winning; his shirt was off, and drops of perspiration trickled down his smooth, dark chest.

"You should want to do something for those poor children!" Margaret shouted.

"I do want to. You know I do."

"I don't know anything of the sort. All I see is you leading an utterly useless, selfish life. I'm disappointed in you, Elizabeth. When I first met you, I had such high hopes of you. I thought, Ah, here at last is a serious person. But you're not serious at all. You're as frivolous as any of those girls that come here and spend their days playing mah-jongg."

Elizabeth was ashamed. The worst of it was she really had once been a serious person. She had been a school-teacher in England, and devoted to her work and her children, on whom she had spent far more time and care than was necessary in the line of duty. And, over and above that, she had put in several evenings a week visiting old people who had no one to look after them. But all that had come to an end once she met Raju.

"It's criminal to be in India and not be committed," Margaret went on. "There isn't much any single person can do, of course, but to do nothing at all—no, I wouldn't be able to sleep at nights."

And Elizabeth slept not only well but happily, bliss-fully! Sometimes she turned on the light just for the pleasure of looking at Raju lying beside her. He slept like a child, with the pillow bundled under his cheek and his mouth slightly open, as if he were smiling.

"But what are you laughing at!" Margaret shouted.

"I'm not, Margaret." She hastily composed her face. She hadn't been aware of it, but probably she had been smiling at the image of Raju asleep.

Margaret abruptly pushed back her chair. Her face was red and her hair disheveled, as if she had been in a fight. Elizabeth half rose in her chair, aghast at whatever it was she had done and eager to undo it.

"Don't follow me," Margaret said. "If you do, I know I'm going to behave badly and I'll feel terrible afterward. You can stay here or you can go home, but *don't fol-low me.*"

She went inside the house, and the screen door banged after her. Elizabeth sank down into her chair and looked helplessly at Babaji.

He had remained as serene as ever. Gently he rocked himself in his chair. The winter afternoon was drawing to its close, and the sun, caught between two trees, was beginning to contract into one concentrated area of gold.

Though the light was failing, the garden remained bright and gay with all its marigolds, its phlox, its pansies, and its sweet peas. Babaji enjoyed it all. He sat wrapped in his woolen shawl, with his feet warm in thick knitted socks and sandals.

"She is a hot-tempered lady," he said, smiling and forgiving. "But good, good."

"Oh, I know," Elizabeth said. "She's an angel. I feel so bad that I should have upset her. Do you think I ought to go after her?"

"A heart of gold," said Babaji.

"I know it." Elizabeth bit her lip in vexation at herself.

Shafi came out with the tea tray. Elizabeth removed some books to clear the little table for him, and Babaji said, "Ah," in pleasurable anticipation. But Shafi did not put the tray down.

"Where is she?" he said.

"It's all right, Shafi. She's just coming. Put it down, please."

The old man nodded and smiled in a cunning, superior way. He clutched his tray more tightly and turned back into the house. He had difficulty in walking, not only because he was old and infirm but also because the shoes he wore were too big for him and had no laces.

"Shafi!" Elizabeth called after him. "Babaji wants his tea!" But he did not even turn around. He walked straight up to Margaret's bedroom and kicked the door and shouted, "I've brought it!"

Elizabeth hurried after him. She felt nervous about going into Margaret's bedroom after having been so explicitly forbidden to follow her. But Margaret only looked up briefly from where she was sitting on her bed, reading a letter, and said, "Oh, it's you," and "Shut the door." When he had put down the tea, Shafi went out again and the two of them were left alone.

Margaret's bedroom was quite different from the rest of the house. The other rooms were all bare and cold, with a minimum of furniture standing around on the stone floors; there were a few isolated pictures hung up

here and there on the whitewashed walls, but nothing
more intimate than portraits of Mahatma Gandhi and
Sri Ramakrishna and a photograph of the inmates of
Mother Teresa's Home. But Margaret's room was
crammed with a lot of comfortable, solid old furniture,
dominated by the big double bed in the center, which
was covered with a white bedcover and a mosquito curtain on the top like a canopy. A log fire burned in the
grate, and there were photographs everywhere—family
photos of Arthur and Margaret, of Margaret as a little
girl, and of her parents and her sister and her school
and her friends. The stale smell of food pervading the
rest of the house stopped short of this room, which was
scented very pleasantly by woodsmoke and lavender
water. There was an umbrella stand that held several
alpenstocks, a tennis racket, and a hockey stick.

"It's from my sister," Margaret said, indicating the
letter she was reading. "She lives out in the country and
they've been snowed under again. She's got a pub."

"How lovely."

"Yes, it's a lovely place. She's always wanted me to
come and run it with her. But I couldn't live in England
anymore, I couldn't bear it."

"Yes, I know what you mean."

"What do you know? You've only been here a few
years. Pour the tea, there's a dear."

"Babaji was wanting a cup."

"To hell with Babaji."

She took off her sandals and lay down on the bed,
leaning against some fat pillows that she had propped
against the headboard. Elizabeth had noticed before that
Margaret was always more relaxed in her own room than
anywhere else. Not all her visitors were allowed into this
room—in fact, only a chosen few. Strangely enough,
Raju had been one of these when he and Elizabeth had
stayed in the house. But he had never properly appreciated the privilege; either he sat on the edge of a chair
and made signs to Elizabeth to go or he wandered rest-
lessly around the room looking at all the photographs
or taking out the tennis racquet and executing imaginary
services with it; till Margaret told him to sit down and

not make them all nervous, and then he looked sulky
and made even more overt signs to Elizabeth.

"I brought my sister out here once," Margaret said.
"But she couldn't stand it. Couldn't stand anything—the
climate, the water, the food. Everything made her ill.
There are people like that. Of course, I'm just the opposite. You like it here too, don't you?"

"Very, very much."

"Yes, I can see you're happy."

Margaret looked at her so keenly that Elizabeth tried
to turn away her face slightly. She did not want anyone
to see too much of her tremendous happiness. She felt
somewhat ashamed of herself for having it—not only
because she knew she didn't deserve it but also because
she did not consider herself quite the right person to
have it. She had been over thirty when she met Raju
and had not expected much more out of life than had
up till then been given to her.

Margaret lit a cigarette. She never smoked except in
her own room. She puffed slowly, luxuriously. Suddenly
she said, "He doesn't like me, does he?"

"Who?"

" 'Who?' " she repeated impatiently. "Your Raju, of
course."

Elizabeth flushed with embarrassment. "How you talk,
Margaret," she murmured deprecatingly, not knowing
what else to say.

"I know he doesn't," Margaret said. "I can always
tell."

She sounded so sad that Elizabeth wished she could
lie to her and say that no, Raju loved her just as everyone else did. But she could not bring herself to it. She
thought of the way he usually spoke of Margaret. He
called her by rude names and made coarse jokes about
her, at which he laughed like a schoolboy and tried to
make Elizabeth laugh with him; and the terrible thing
was sometimes she did laugh, not because she wanted
to or because what he said amused her but because it
was he who urged her to, and she always found it difficult to refuse him anything. Now when she thought of

this compliant laughter of hers she was filled with anguish, and she began unconsciously to wring her hands, the way she always did at such secretly appalling moments.

But Margaret was having thoughts of her own, and was smiling to herself. She said, "You know what was my happiest time of all in India? About ten years ago, when I went to stay in Swami Vishwananda's ashram."

Elizabeth was intensely relieved at the change of subject, though somewhat puzzled by its abruptness.

"We bathed in the river and we walked in the mountains. It was a time of such freedom, such joy. I've never felt like that before or since. I didn't have a care in the world and I felt so—light. I can't describe it—as if my feet didn't touch the ground."

"Yes, yes!" Elizabeth said eagerly, for she thought she recognized the feeling.

"In the evening we all sat with Swamiji. We talked about everything under the sun. He laughed and joked with us, and sometimes he sang. I don't know what happened to me when he sang. The tears came pouring down my face, but I was so happy I thought my heart would melt away."

"Yes," Elizabeth said again.

"That's him over there." She nodded toward a small framed photograph on the dressing table. Elizabeth picked it up. He did not look different from the rest of India's holy men—naked to the waist, with long hair and burning eyes.

"Not that you can tell much from a photo," Margaret said. She held out her hand for it, and then she looked at it herself, with a very young expression on her face. "He was such fun to be with, always full of jokes and games. When I was with him, I used to feel—I don't know—like a flower or a bird." She laughed gaily, and Elizabeth with her.

"Does Raju make you feel like that?"

Elizabeth stopped laughing and looked down into her lap. She tried to make her face very serious so as not to give herself away.

"Indian men have such marvelous eyes," Margaret

said. "When they look at you, you can't help feeling all young and nice. But of course your Raju thinks I'm just a fat, ugly old memsahib."

"Margaret, Margaret!"

Margaret stubbed out her cigarette and, propelling herself with her heavy legs, swung down from the bed. "And there's poor old Babaji waiting for his tea."

She poured it for him and went out with the cup. Elizabeth went after her. Babaji was just as they had left him, except that now the sun, melting away between the trees behind him, was even more intensely gold and provided a heavenly background, as if to a saint in a picture, as he sat there at peace in his rocking chair.

Margaret fussed over him. She stirred his tea and she arranged his shawl more securely over his shoulders. Then she said, "I've got an idea, Babaji." She hooked her foot around a stool and drew it close to his chair and sank down on it, one hand laid on his knee. "You and I'll take those children up to Agra. Would you like that? A little trip?" She looked up into his face and was eager and bright. "We'll have a grand time. We'll hire a bus and we'll have singing and games all the way. You'll love it." She squeezed his knee in anticipatory joy, and he smiled at her and his thin old hand came down on the top of her head in a gesture of affection or blessing.

GINU KAMANI

Ginu Kamani was born in Bombay in 1962 and moved to the United States fourteen years later. She graduated from the University of Colorado, Boulder, in 1987 with an MA in creative writing. After returning to Bombay for three years to work in film production, she came back to the U.S. to pursue writing full time.

Now an essayist and fiction writer, Kamani authored *Junglee Girl* in 1995; it is a collection of short stories exploring sexuality, sensuality, and power in women's lives. She has published fiction and essays in various anthologies, literary journals, newspapers, and magazines; generally, her essays and talks deal with gender and sexual self knowledge and the dual identities within hyphenated American subcultures. Kamani is also a filmmaker and has coauthored the play *The Cure* with Joel Barraquiel-Tan. She has been a Writing Fellow with the Sundance Institute and has taught creative writing at Mills College in Oakland, California, where she has also been Writer in Residence.

Publishers Weekly has called Kamani "a savvy, gifted writer." Filmmaker Pratibha Parmar said of her work, "Ginu Kamani's stories are tinged with humor and are often disturbing in their exploration of taboo passions and desires. Kamani is an original storyteller who tells from "inside" the culture, claiming a rightful space for Indian women to define themselves."

This Anju

These three sons of mine all insist on choosing their own brides. Who am I to say no to them? It's best if they don't involve me in such matters. I'm of a different generation, baba; who can tell which girls are good or bad for them? All I know is who will make a wife and who won't. And this Anju, I can tell you, doesn't know the first thing about being a wife. In all my years I have never met such an aggravating woman! She's put such funny ideas about marriage into *my* Sanjay's head. She thinks she has the answer to everything, but let's just see how long this Miss Know-it-all will stay so bold.

I had nothing to do with this Anju's meeting my Sanjay. I call him *my* Sanjay, because clearly he takes after me. Sanjay is a lovely boy, so talented; he's everybody's darling. He has so many friends you can't even count them. And on top of that he's just so handsome, like a film star! Right from his school days, so many girls have been running after him, literally hundreds of them. Who can blame them? Naturally, this Anju would feel attracted to him too.

Sanjay is my oldest, and his two younger brothers are complete copycats. But it's just not the same, because they take more after their papa, Dev. Anil and Tarun are very shy with girls, and even with me, their own mother! So naturally I'm concerned about how they will get married, no? Still, if I mention any nice girl, the two younger ones go on and on like parrots about choosing their own girlfriends. It's one thing if you know how to, like Sanjay. Of course some people call him a Romeo and all, but really they're just jealous.

"How can you let him run around like that? What if he gets some girl into trouble? What about your family name?" They keep asking all this rubbish as though Sanjay is my daughter! God has given me three healthy sons, no, so can't I have some fun in this life?

My Sanjay is an artist, I don't care what people say. There is a reason for the way he is, wandering around

Bombay, staying out all night. I never ask where he goes or what he does; why should I meddle? In his college days we heard that he was sleeping with foreign hippie girls in some cockroach-y hotel in Colaba, even paying them money. Why would I believe such stories? Why would Sanjay need to sleep around like that? He had all these girls from good families chasing after him.

Not that a traditional girl would have done for this mad boy of ours! His head is full of jazz-shazz and he's all the time playing drums in the air and singing pa-pa-pa-pa-dhish-dhish and there's that ring in the top of his ear and he doesn't wear any underwear and god knows what all he's been smoking all these years. In a way he must have been lonely, because of course the girls of Sanjay's age all got married right after college. So when he met Anju, at first I was very happy that at least she was a decent girl of good family. The only reason she was single was because she had been studying all these years in the States. At least, that's what I thought until I got to know her better. Sometimes I think she must be just pretending to be Indian, an impostor. I realize that she's become Americanized after all the years away, but then she should at least talk like one, or dye her hair blond or wear some funny clothes, so that we can all see clearly that she is one of them and not one of us.

The truth is, I have always wanted to know everything about my Sanjay's life, but you know how it is, after they get older, children like to keep their secrets. So I arranged this special plan: every time Sanjay needed money, he would come to me, and no matter how much he asked for, I gave it to him, as long as he told me honestly what it was for. In this way I learned about all kinds of new things, like discos and cocaine and jam sessions and big-big parties and sometimes he told me about girls he wanted to buy little gifts for. In my hum-drum life, it was nice to hear of such excitement from my son.

That was how I first heard about this Anju. She had asked Sanjay to buy a small Walkman-type recording machine, so the two of them could carry it everywhere and talk. I remember thinking to myself, this is very odd.

What is she up to? Is she going to blackmail my Sanjay? Maybe he shouldn't say anything into a recording machine. What if something happens? Dev would never forgive me. I kept asking Sanjay to bring her to the house, and he said, "I will, I will," but weeks went by and there was no sign of her.

I asked Sanjay to tell me a little bit, what he likes about her and so on. He told me, "She knows me so well, it's as though she can read my mind. She is so honest; I've never met anyone like her." And to prove it, he showed me some letters she had written to him. Horrible things! Terrible, thick letters, full of millions of words all pointing to Sanjay saying *You you you!* Poor fellow. I mean, why did she have to write such letters where everything was spelled out in detail? Why not just say a few words in private?

My poor son. He was excited to share with me. I read one page of one letter and let me tell you I got very scared. I thought to myself, Oh baba, I can't read this hot knife of a letter that she is sticking inside my Sanjay, twisting it this way and that. She wrote the letters so that all their problems were out in the open where they could be looked at. *But everybody else can look at them too, no?* Shameless girl, listing all his faults like a shopping list.

I tell you, the *nerve* of the girl! When she finally came to the house, I was so upset, I barely said a word. But she, upstart, she talked the whole time! She said she had come to me for help. She said that Sanjay had some problems with trusting women. Imagine! And did she stop to ask them how he managed to trust his mother? On and on she went: How could she get Sanjay to trust in her? Couldn't I possibly help her? Yakety-yakety-yak.

Did she really think I could take sides against my son? Could I really teach him to trust a woman who is nothing like his mother? Even Dev knows I can never go against my boys. But what to do, I talked to her a little bit. I told her all the usual things a mother can say: men are different; it is a woman's duty to take care of her man; with a little compromise, a woman can find the strength to make things work.

But it wasn't my advice that she wanted, oh no. She wanted me to *talk* to Sanjay. She wanted me to answer some of his questions about *me,* his mother. That was her plan to get him to trust her. In this way, the blame was to be shifted to me! I felt like vomiting, just exactly. What could I possibly say to Sanjay? Not even one word.

I tell you, I felt blamed by her. I just couldn't relax with her in the room. She came during lunch, and I swear I lost my appetite. Halfway through her speech, I just stopped listening and sang songs in my head. I held my breath till my ears started ringing, and then I truly couldn't hear a single word she was saying. *I, me, want, I, me, want.* I swear, she knew only those three words! I got fed up. I thought, my god, Sanjay is involved with a lunatic.

What is this thing all the time of doing what you want and being what you want and finding yourself and losing yourself? There's no right person or wrong person, you know, there's only right attitude and wrong attitude. These Indian girls, they go to America and come back absolutely brainless. They think they know everything. They think they can understand everything. As though such a thing is possible.

Sanjay's daddy, Dev, was the first to say out loud that she's not very friendly, that she doesn't stop for chitchat. There's nothing wrong, I mean, some people just are that way. But once, just for the sake of asking, I asked Sanjay if she was angry at us or what. After all how much effort can it take to say a simple "Hello auntie, hello uncle." But Sanjay didn't like my asking, and he said, "Ma, come on, she always greets you. Don't dig where there are no crabs. She's not like you. When she has something to say, she says it."

They say modern girls are like that, a little on the cold side.

I tried, you know, I tried to be friendly. I told this Anju that sometimes my Sanjay gets nervous and it's very difficult for anyone to take care of him. The things he does! All day without food, only lemon water. Taking one-one puffs from cigarettes then throwing them out. Running up and down the hill till his feet are bleeding.

Talking, talking, talking with somebody, anybody. It's like a fit comes over him. In front of the whole world he punishes himself, in front of the whole world he asks forgiveness, like a beggar-sadhu. It breaks my heart. I can't bear it, baba, to see him suffering this way, but nothing helps him in these moods.

In this way I thought I might scare her a little bit, but right from the start, Anju handled him. When he got into these funny moods, straightaway she would start lecturing him, *la-la-la-la-la,* for hours. I've never seen any woman so cold! She was like ice, that girl. She spent hours and hours discussing with him. From outside the door I could only hear Sanjay sobbing pitifully, god, it broke my heart when he was that way, and her half-angry, half-laughing voice, asking him why, why he's always hurting himself, and herself . . . all this-self and that-self. I know for a fact that Sanjay's problems are neverending. He's always been that way. But she knew how to wear him down, till his nervousness was all sucked out of him, till he was completely defeated, with not a word left to say. Anju, cool as a cucumber, would end by telling Sanjay that he could easily fix his life . . . if he wanted.

As though Sanjay doesn't want to be happy! As though any of us chooses to be unhappy! Why would she talk that way if she really loved my Sanjay?

In this way the time passed. Everything would go well for days or even weeks, until Sanjay had another break-down. Then he would lock himself in his room, and if I tried to talk to him, he would scream and shout for me to leave him alone. As though it was my fault! Sooner or later, Anju would come, and the two of them would disappear for hours. He would come back looking like all the blood had been sucked out of him. And she would be looking all happy and satisfied.

I told Dev, "These two have some funny relationship, baba!" It was clear that she was manipulating him some-how, because *he* was always crying, and *she* was always scolding. You check with any woman, and it's always the opposite, like with Dev and me. No matter how many tantrums my Sanjay had, that girl always stayed by his side. Long after my ears closed up from the anger and shouting and cursing that flew out of his body, she stood by him, talking, talking, talking. Nothing scared her, nothing made her go away.

The two of them started spending all their time together. They were inseparable. I thought to myself, be honest and admit that Anju is the be-all and end-all of Sanjay's life. They might get married, and you'll have her as your daughter-in-law! Then what? Better get to know her before she takes over your life.

So I observed this Anju seriously for some time. Quite a lovely girl, very attractive, laughing and joking all the time, and of course her family name speaks for itself. Very clever, with her M.A. from America and all that, and good with money. But in some ways, just like a man. Never wearing a sari, no makeup, no jewelry except earrings, sitting with her legs wide open, taking drinks, talking all big-big talk. Not for one second will she discuss the price of fruits and vegetables or those new actresses on my favorite TV program. Not even a flicker of interest in going with me to the vault to see what jewelry I have set aside for Sanjay's wife-to-be.

All that I could have lived with, but the worst thing was the way Sanjay's two copycat brothers became exactly like her pets, like her stupid faithful puppy dogs. They wouldn't hear a word against her. I tell you, when all three sons stick together like thieves, it's impossible to knock any sense into them. Any chance I had of convincing Anju that Sanjay was wrong for her was completely destroyed once those two younger boys started meddling, waiting on her hand and foot, buying her flowers and what all other junk. That was the end of that! This Anju was thrilled at having her own fan club, and the four of them became inseparable. So much attention cannot be good for a woman, and sure enough, this Anju turned all my sons against me.

She has never tried to understand me. For all her babble about knowing and understanding and this-ing and that-ing, she was too selfish, really, to waste time on anyone but her Sanjay. I mean, Sanjay was put on this earth by his mother and father. She said, "When I marry,

I will be marrying only my one man, not his entire family." The cheek of her! Thank god I only have sons, baba. I don't think I could survive having an unfeeling daughter like her.

I tell you, I got so tired of her meddling and fiddling, so fed up with her coming and going that every time she came near me I got a splitting headache. Why should I have to suffer like this in my own home? So I told Sanjay to stop bringing her to the house; I would welcome her back to my house when she became humble enough to marry my son, devoted enough to be my daughter-in-law, and genius enough to shut her mouth forever.

So now she's left. Just as suddenly as she came, she's gone away. After spending all that time with Sanjay, spoiling and pampering him, turning him into *her* Sanjay, she's left. Two years of putting up with her strange behavior, and just when I am hoping that I can return to having a peaceful relationship with my Sanjay again, he turns around and blames *me* for having ruined his relationship with her! The things he said, I thought I had died and gone to hell. The words are sticking in my throat. He called me a miser, a liar, a coward, a traitor. He said that I have such a jealous nature that Anju was afraid of marrying into the family. He said that . . . oh dear god, he said that if only he were a motherless orphan, then everything would have turned out fine. That's just exactly what he said. A *motherless orphan* . . .

What could I say? I just wanted to run to my room and cry. But he stood there waiting for an answer! I told him that this Anju had turned his head completely around so that now he was talking to me in exactly that horrible *you-you-you* way that she always talked. He said, "Your problem is you just cannot tolerate honesty. She's put my head on straight, and for the first time in my life, I have the courage to ask you who you are and what you want. I need to clear up our relationship. Can you handle that?" he shouted. "Can you do that for me?" I covered my ears, baba, I couldn't listen to her voice coming out of my Sanjay's mouth. I said, "You cannot force me to do such things, I am your *mother*!"

And he said, "All right, my mother, I can't live in the same house as you anymore. Consider me dead." And he left.

And then would you believe *more* trouble? I was cleaning out the desk of Sanjay's younger brother and I found pictures of this Anju. At first I thought, how sweet, Anil is keeping them as a memento, but then I thought, why aren't these in frames on *top* of his desk, why hidden away? When I asked Anil, he was so angry with me, so angry, I can't tell you. He said that I had no right to be fiddling with his personal possessions, he said that if he ever met a girl he liked, he would never bring her to the house to meet his jealous mother, he said that he was sick to death of me and was moving out of the house.

So now, can you believe it, *two* of my sons hate me! What kind of crazy world do we live in? At least my youngest son is still with me. But the truth is that he doesn't talk very much, so god knows what is going on inside his head. Dev says it's all my fault, that I've always tried to control our boys and make them feel sorry for me. I don't know what to think. Of course I'm lonely and of course I want my sons to love me, but how can that be a fault?

What is a mother to do, I ask you.

My own sons, behaving like this with me!

Ohhhh . . . I tell you, my heart is completely broken. I can't make head or tail of it.

There's a curse on this house, and it's all because of this Anju.

So many weeks alone in the house, without my two big boys. Yesterday I spent the whole day writing letters. I wrote a long letter to Sanjay, who is living in that cockroach-y hotel in Colaba, poor boy. He refuses to come home; he says he wants space. Space! In that filthy broken-down hotel? He's living like a beggar. I also wrote a long letter to Anil, who at least has rented a room at the Club, where they change the bed sheets every day. I wrote them both long stories of their childhood, about how they used to love me like crazy, how they always cried for me when I went away from home, how they wouldn't fall asleep unless they were lying right next to me. I reminded them both about their duty toward their younger brother, who was still impressionable, and to their old mother, who was still waiting for her sons to bring happiness into her life.

That was yesterday.

Today I'm writing a different letter, a kind of letter I have never written before and will never, god willing, write again. Every five minutes I feel like crying, so I stop, otherwise the tears will make the ink run.

I'm writing a long letter to Anju, begging her to come back and marry my Sanjay. I am telling her that I just cannot bear to be separated from my sons like this, that nothing is worth this kind of pain. I am assuring her that Sanjay and I are alike, so if he can stand to talk to her and cry in her arms and be happy with her, then maybe I can learn a little of the same. I'm telling her that Anil will be a devoted brother-in-law and will soon find the courage to find a decent girl to take his name. And I'm crying to her to forget my meddling, that I'm a confused old woman who wants only to see her sons settled and happy.

And lastly, I am buying that recording machine she always wanted, small enough to carry in her purse. She and Sanjay can spend their whole lives filling up cassettes with their misery, the way other people fill up albums with smiling photographs. And then when they're old and all their precious cassettes are broken and useless, then perhaps they will bend a little and open their hearts and allow my old voice to join in with their own.

JHUMPA LAHIRI

Jhumpa Lahiri, born in London in 1967, the daughter of Indian immigrants, came to the U.S. when she was three and considers herself an American. She grew up in Kingston, Rhode Island, where her father worked as a librarian at the University. The main character in her short story "The Third and Final Continent" is based on her father. Her family often returned to Calcutta with her in order to maintain their Bengali culture. Conflict between immigrant parents and first-generation children born in America became a major theme of her work. A *New York Times* reviewer has suggested that her work possesses "the elegiac and haunting power of tragedy."

Lahiri graduated from Barnard College and received several master's degrees and a PhD from Boston University. Her first short story collection, *Interpreter of Maladies* (1999), begun while she was in graduate school, won the Pulitzer Prize for Fiction in 2000. *The Namesake*, her first novel, was published to wide acclaim and made into a film in 2006. Her most recent work, a collection of short stories, *Unaccustomed Earth*, became a *New York Times* #1 bestseller immediately after its release.

Lahiri currently lives with her husband and two children in Brooklyn, New York.

The Third and Final Continent

I left India in 1964 with a certificate in commerce and the equivalent, in those days, of ten dollars to my name. For three weeks I sailed on the SS *Roma*, an Italian cargo vessel, in a third-class cabin next to the ship's engine, across the Arabian Sea, the Red Sea, the Mediterranean, and finally to England. I lived in north London, in Finsbury Park, in a house occupied entirely by penniless Bengali bachelors like myself, at least a dozen and sometimes more, all struggling to educate and establish ourselves abroad.

I attended lectures at LSE and worked at the university library to get by. We lived three or four to a room, shared a single, icy toilet, and took turns cooking pots of egg curry, which we ate with our hands on a table covered with newspapers. Apart from our jobs we had few responsibilities. On weekends we lounged barefoot in drawstring pajamas, drinking tea and smoking Rothmans, or set out to watch cricket at Lord's. Some weekends the house was crammed with still more Bengalis, to whom we had introduced ourselves at the greengrocer, or on the Tube, and we made yet more egg curry, and played Mukhesh on a Grundig reel-to-reel, and soaked our dirty dishes in the bathtub. Every now and then someone in the house moved out, to live with a woman whom his family back in Calcutta had determined he was to wed. In 1969, when I was thirty-six years old, my own marriage was arranged. Around the same time I was offered a full-time job in America, in the processing department of a library at MIT. The salary was generous enough to support a wife, and I was honored to be hired by a world-famous university, and so I obtained a sixth-preference green card, and prepared to travel farther still.

By now I had enough money to go by plane. I flew first to Calcutta, to attend my wedding, and a week later I flew to Boston, to begin my new job. During the flight I read *The Student Guide to North America,* a paperback volume that I'd bought before leaving London, for seven shillings six pence on Tottenham Court Road, for although I was no longer a student I was on a budget all the same. I learned that Americans drove on the right side of the road, not the left, and that they called a lift an elevator and an engaged phone busy. "The pace of life in North America is different from Britain as you will soon discover," the guidebook informed me. "Everybody feels he must get to the top. Don't expect an English cup of tea." As the plane began its descent over Boston Harbor, the pilot announced the weather and time, and that President Nixon had declared a national holiday: two American men had landed on the moon. Several passengers cheered. "God bless America!" one of them hollered. Across the aisle, I saw a woman praying.

I spent my first night at the YMCA in Central Square, Cambridge, an inexpensive accommodation recommended by my guidebook. It was walking distance from MIT, and steps from the post office and a supermarket called Purity Supreme. The room contained a cot, a desk, and a small wooden cross on one wall. A sign on the door said cooking was strictly forbidden. A bare window overlooked Massachusetts Avenue, a major thoroughfare with traffic in both directions. Car horns, shrill and prolonged, blared one after another. Flashing sirens heralded endless emergencies, and a fleet of buses rumbled past, their doors opening and closing with a powerful hiss, throughout the night. The noise was constantly distracting, at times suffocating. I felt it deep in my ribs, just as I had felt the furious drone of the engine on the SS *Roma*. But there was no ship's deck to escape to, no glittering ocean to thrill my soul, no breeze to cool my face, no one to talk to. I was too tired to pace the gloomy corridors of the YMCA in my drawstring pajamas. Instead I sat at the desk and stared out the window, at the city hall of Cambridge and a row of small shops. In the morning I reported to my job at the Dewey Library, a beige fortlike building by Memorial Drive. I also opened a bank account, rented a post office box, and bought a plastic bowl and a spoon at Woolworth's, a store whose name I recognized from London. I went to Purity Supreme, wandering up and down the aisles, converting ounces to grams and comparing prices to things in England. In the end I bought a small carton of milk and a box of cornflakes. This was my first meal in America. I ate it at my desk. I preferred it to hamburgers or hot dogs, the only alternative I could afford in the coffee shops on Massachusetts Avenue, and, besides, at the time I had yet to consume any beef. Even the simple chore of buying milk was new to me; in London we'd had bottles delivered each morning to our door.

In a week I had adjusted, more or less. I ate cornflakes and milk, morning and night, and bought some bananas for variety, slicing them into the bowl with the edge of my spoon. In addition I bought tea bags and a flask, which the salesman in Woolworth's referred to as a thermos (a flask, he informed me, was used to store whiskey, another thing I had never consumed). For the price of one cup of tea at a coffee shop, I filled the flask with boiling water on my way to work each morning, and brewed the four cups I drank in the course of a day. I bought a larger carton of milk, and learned to leave it on the shaded part of the windowsill, as I had seen another resident at the YMCA do. To pass the time in the evenings I read the *Boston Globe* downstairs, in a spacious room with stained-glass windows. I read every article and advertisement, so that I would grow familiar with things, and when my eyes grew tired I slept. Only I did not sleep well. Each night I had to keep the window wide open; it was the only source of air in the stifling room, and the noise was intolerable. I would lie on the cot with my fingers pressed into my ears, but when I drifted off to sleep my hands fell away, and the noise of the traffic would wake me up again. Pigeon feathers drifted onto the windowsill, and one evening, when I poured milk over my cornflakes, I saw that it had soured. Nevertheless I resolved to stay at the YMCA for six weeks, until my wife's passport and green card were ready. Once she arrived I would have to rent a proper apartment, and from time to time I studied the classified section of the newspaper, or stopped in at the housing office at MIT during my lunch break, to see what was available in my price range. It was in this manner that I discovered a room for immediate occupancy, in a house on a quiet street, the listing said, for eight dollars per week. I copied the number into my guidebook and dialed from a pay telephone, sorting through the coins with which I was still unfamiliar, smaller and lighter than shillings, heavier and brighter than *paisas*.

"Who is speaking?" a woman demanded. Her voice was cold and clamorous.

"Yes, good afternoon, madame. I am calling about the room for rent."

"Harvard or Tech?"

"I beg your pardon?"

"Are you from Harvard or Tech?"

Gathering that Tech referred to the Massachusetts Institute of Technology, I replied, "I work at Dewey Library," adding tentatively, "at Tech."

"I only rent rooms to boys from Harvard or Tech!"

"Yes, madame."

I was given an address and an appointment for seven o'clock that evening. Thirty minutes before the hour I set out, my guidebook in my pocket, my breath fresh with Listerine. I turned down a street shaded with trees, perpendicular to Massachusetts Avenue. Stray blades of grass poked between the cracks of the footpath. In spite of the heat I wore a coat and a tie, regarding the event as I would any other interview; I had never lived in the home of a person who was not Indian. The house, surrounded by a chain-link fence, was off-white with dark brown trim. Unlike the stucco row house I'd lived in in London, this house, fully detached, was covered with wooden shingles, with a tangle of forsythia bushes plastered against the front and sides. When I pressed the calling bell, the woman with whom I had spoken on the phone hollered from what seemed to be just the other side of the door, "One minute, please!"

Several minutes later the door was opened by a tiny, extremely old woman. A mass of snowy hair was arranged like a small sack on top of her head. As I stepped into the house she sat down on a wooden bench positioned at the bottom of a narrow carpeted staircase. Once she was settled on the bench, in a small pool of light, she peered up at me with undivided attention. She wore a long black skirt that spread like a stiff tent to the floor, and a starched white shirt edged with ruffles

at the throat and cuffs. Her hands, folded together in
her lap, had long pallid fingers, with swollen knuckles
and tough yellow nails. Age had battered her features
so that she almost resembled a man, with sharp,
shrunken eyes and prominent creases on either side of
her nose. Her lips, chapped and faded, had nearly disappeared, and her eyebrows were missing altogether.
Nevertheless she looked fierce.

"Lock up!" she commanded. She shouted even though
I stood only a few feet away. "Fasten the chain and
firmly press that button on the knob! This is the first
thing you shall do when you enter, is that clear?"

I locked the door as directed and examined the house.
Next to the bench on which the woman sat was a small
round table, its legs fully concealed, much like the woman's, by a skirt of lace. The table held a lamp, a transis-
tor radio, a leather change purse with a silver clasp, and
a telephone. A thick wooden cane coated with a layer
of dust was propped against one side. There was a parlor
to my right, lined with bookcases and filled with shabby
claw-footed furniture. In the corner of the parlor I saw
a grand piano with its top down, piled with papers. The
piano's bench was missing; it seemed to be the one on
which the woman was sitting. Somewhere in the house
a clock chimed seven times.

"You're punctual!" the woman proclaimed. "I expect
you shall be so with the rent!"

"I have a letter, madame." In my jacket pocket was
a letter confirming my employment from MIT, which I
had brought along to prove that I was indeed from Tech.

She stared at the letter, then handed it back to me
carefully, gripping it with her fingers as if it were a dinner plate heaped with food instead of a sheet of paper.
She did not wear glasses, and I wondered if she'd read
a word of it. "The last boy was always late! Still owes
me eight dollars! Harvard boys aren't what they used to
be! Only Harvard and Tech in this house! How's Tech,
boy?"

"It is very well."

"You checked the lock?"

"Yes, madame."

She slapped the space beside her on the bench with one hand, and told me to sit down. For a moment she was silent. Then she intoned, as if she alone possessed this knowledge:

"There is an American flag on the moon!"

"Yes, madame." Until then I had not thought very much about the moon shot. It was in the newspaper, of course, article upon article. The astronauts had landed on the shores of the Sea of Tranquillity, I had read, traveling farther than anyone in the history of civilization. For a few hours they explored the moon's surface. They gathered rocks in their pockets, described their surroundings (a magnificent desolation, according to one astronaut), spoke by phone to the president, and planted a flag in lunar soil. The voyage was hailed as man's most awesome achievement. I had seen full-page photographs in the *Globe,* of the astronauts in their inflated costumes, and read about what certain people in Boston had been doing at the exact moment the astronauts landed, on a Sunday afternoon. A man said that he was operating a swan boat with a radio pressed to his ear; a woman had been baking rolls for her grandchildren.

The woman bellowed, "A flag on the moon, boy! I heard it on the radio! Isn't that splendid?"

"Yes, madame."

But she was not satisfied with my reply. Instead she commanded, "Say 'splendid'!"

I was both baffled and somewhat insulted by the request. It reminded me of the way I was taught multiplication tables as a child, repeating after the master, sitting cross-legged, without shoes or pencils, on the floor of my one-room Tollygunge school. It also reminded me of my wedding, when I had repeated endless Sanskrit verses after the priest, verses I barely understood, which joined me to my wife. I said nothing.

"Say 'splendid'!" the woman bellowed once again.

"Splendid," I murmured. I had to repeat the word a second time at the top of my lungs, so she could hear. I am soft-spoken by nature and was especially reluctant to raise my voice to an elderly woman whom I had met only moments ago, but she did not appear to be of-

fended. If anything the reply pleased her because her
next command was:

"Go see the room!"

I rose from the bench and mounted the narrow carpeted staircase. There were five doors, two on either side
of an equally narrow hallway, and one at the opposite
end. Only one door was partly open. The room contained a twin bed under a sloping ceiling, a brown oval
rug, a basin with an exposed pipe, and a chest of drawers. One door, painted white, led to a closet, another to
a toilet and a tub. The walls were covered with gray and
ivory striped paper. The window was open; net curtains
stirred in the breeze. I lifted them away and inspected
the view: a small back yard, with a few fruit trees and
an empty clothesline. I was satisfied. From the bottom
of the stairs I heard the woman demand, "What is
your decision?"

When I returned to the foyer and told her, she picked
up the leather change purse on the table, opened the
clasp, fished about with her fingers, and produced a key
on a thin wire hoop. She informed me that there was a
kitchen at the back of the house, accessible through the
parlor. I was welcome to use the stove as long as I left
it as I found it. Sheets and towels were provided, but
keeping them clean was my own responsibility. The rent
was due Friday mornings on the ledge above the piano
keys. "And no lady visitors!"

"I am a married man, madame." It was the first time
I had announced this fact to anyone.

But she had not heard. "No lady visitors!" she insisted. She introduced herself as Mrs. Croft.

My wife's name was Mala. The marriage had been arranged by my older brother and his wife. I regarded the
proposition with neither objection nor enthusiasm. It was
a duty expected of me, as it was expected of every man.
She was the daughter of a schoolteacher in Beleghata. I
was told that she could cook, knit, embroider, sketch
landscapes, and recite poems by Tagore, but these tal-
ents could not make up for the fact that she did not
possess a fair complexion, and so a string of men had

rejected her to her face. She was twenty-seven, an age when her parents had begun to fear that she would never marry, and so they were willing to ship their only child halfway across the world in order to save her from spinsterhood.

For five nights we shared a bed. Each of those nights, after applying cold cream and braiding her hair, which she tied up at the end with a black cotton string, she turned from me and wept; she missed her parents. Although I would be leaving the country in a few days, custom dictated that she was now a part of my household, and for the next six weeks she was to live with my brother and his wife, cooking, cleaning, serving tea and sweets to guests. I did nothing to console her. I lay on my own side of the bed, reading my guidebook by flashlight and anticipating my journey. At times I thought of the tiny room on the other side of the wall which had belonged to my mother. Now the room was practically empty; the wooden pallet on which she'd once slept was piled with trunks and old bedding. Nearly six years ago, before leaving for London, I had watched her die on that bed, had found her playing with her excrement in her final days. Before we cremated her I had cleaned each of her fingernails with a hairpin, and then, because my brother could not bear it, I had assumed the role of eldest son, and had touched the flame to her temple, to release her tormented soul to heaven.

The next morning I moved into the room in Mrs. Croft's house. When I unlocked the door I saw that she was sitting on the piano bench, on the same side as the previous evening. She wore the same black skirt, the same starched white blouse, and had her hands folded together the same way in her lap. She looked so much the same that I wondered if she'd spent the whole night on the bench. I put my suitcase upstairs, filled my flask with boiling water in the kitchen, and headed off to work. That evening when I came home from the university, she was still there.

"Sit down, boy!" She slapped the space beside her.

I perched beside her on the bench. I had a bag of

groceries with me—more milk, more cornflakes, and more bananas, for my inspection of the kitchen earlier in the day had revealed no spare pots, pans, or cooking utensils. There were only two saucepans in the refrigerator, both containing some orange broth, and a copper kettle on the stove.

"Good evening, madame."

She asked me if I had checked the lock. I told her I had.

For a moment she was silent. Then suddenly she declared, with the equal measures of disbelief and delight as the night before, "There's an American flag on the moon, boy!"

"Yes, madame."

"A flag on the moon! Isn't that splendid?"

I nodded, dreading what I knew was coming. "Yes, madame."

"Say 'splendid'!"

This time I paused, looking to either side in case anyone were there to overhear me, though I knew perfectly well that the house was empty. I felt like an idiot. But it was a small enough thing to ask. "Splendid!" I cried out.

Within days it became our routine. In the mornings when I left for the library Mrs. Croft was either hidden away in her bedroom, on the other side of the staircase, or she was sitting on the bench, oblivious to my presence, listening to the news or classical music on the radio. But each evening when I returned the same thing happened: she slapped the bench, ordered me to sit down, declared that there was a flag on the moon, and declared that it was splendid. I said it was splendid, too, and then we sat in silence. As awkward as it was, and as endless as it felt to me then, the nightly encounter lasted only about ten minutes; inevitably she would drift off to sleep, her head falling abruptly toward her chest, leaving me free to retire to my room. By then, of course, there was no flag on the moon. The astronauts, I had read in the paper, had taken it down before flying back to Earth. But I did not have the heart to tell her.

*   *   *

Friday morning, when my first week's rent was due, I went to the piano in the parlor to place my money on the ledge. The piano keys were dull and discolored. When I pressed one, it made no sound at all. I had put eight one-dollar bills in an envelope and written Mrs. Croft's name on the front of it. I was not in the habit of leaving money unmarked and unattended. From where I stood I could see the profile of her tent-shaped skirt. She was sitting on the bench, listening to the radio. It seemed unnecessary to make her get up and walk all the way to the piano. I never saw her walking about, and assumed, from the cane always propped against the round table at her side, that she did so with difficulty. When I approached the bench she peered up at me and demanded:

"What is your business?"

"The rent, madame."

"On the ledge above the piano keys!"

"I have it here." I extended the envelope toward her, but her fingers, folded together in her lap, did not budge. I bowed slightly and lowered the envelope, so that it hovered just above her hands. After a moment she accepted, and nodded her head.

That night when I came home, she did not slap the bench, but out of habit I sat beside her as usual. She asked me if I had checked the lock, but she mentioned nothing about the flag on the moon. Instead she said:

"It was very kind of you!"

"I beg your pardon, madame?"

"Very kind of you!"

She was still holding the envelope in her hands.

On Sunday there was a knock on my door. An elderly woman introduced herself: she was Mrs. Croft's daughter, Helen. She walked into the room and looked at each of the walls as if for signs of change, glancing at the shirts that hung in the closet, the neckties draped over the doorknob, the box of cornflakes on the chest of drawers, the dirty bowl and spoon in the basin. She was short and thick-waisted, with cropped silver hair and bright pink lipstick. She wore a sleeveless summer dress, a row of white plastic beads, and spectacles on a chain that hung like a swing against her chest. The backs of her legs were mapped with dark blue veins, and her upper arms sagged like the flesh of a roasted eggplant. She told me she lived in Arlington, a town farther up Massachusetts Avenue. "I come once a week to bring Mother groceries. Has she sent you packing yet?"

"It is very well, madame."

"Some of the boys run screaming. But I think she likes you. You're the first boarder she's ever referred to as a gentleman."

"Not at all, madame."

She looked at me, noticing my bare feet (I still felt strange wearing shoes indoors, and always removed them before entering my room). "Are you new to Boston?"

"New to America, madame."

"From?" She raised her eyebrows.

"I am from Calcutta, India."

"Is that right? We had a Brazilian fellow, about a year ago. You'll find Cambridge a very international city."

I nodded, and began to wonder how long our conversation would last. But at that moment we heard Mrs. Croft's electrifying voice rising up the stairs. When we stepped into the hallway we heard her hollering:

"You are to come downstairs immediately!"

"What is it?" Helen hollered back.

"Immediately!"

I put on my shoes at once. Helen sighed.

We walked down the staircase. It was too narrow for us to descend side by side, so I followed Helen, who seemed to be in no hurry, and complained at one point that she had a bad knee. "Have you been walking without your cane?" Helen called out. "You know you're not supposed to walk without that cane." She paused, resting her hand on the banister, and looked back at me. "She slips sometimes."

For the first time Mrs. Croft seemed vulnerable. I pictured her on the floor in front of the bench, flat on her back, staring at the ceiling, her feet pointing in opposite directions. But when we reached the bottom of the staircase she was sitting there as usual, her hands folded together in her lap. Two grocery bags were at her feet. When we stood before her she did not slap the bench, or ask us to sit down. She glared.

"What is it, Mother?"

"It's improper!"

"What's improper?"

"It is improper for a lady and gentleman who are not married to one another to hold a private conversation without a chaperone!"

Helen said she was sixty-eight years old, old enough to be my mother, but Mrs. Croft insisted that Helen and I speak to each other downstairs, in the parlor. She added that it was also improper for a lady of Helen's station to reveal her age, and to wear a dress so high above the ankle.

"For your information, Mother, it's 1969. What would you do if you actually left the house one day and saw a girl in a miniskirt?"

Mrs. Croft sniffed. "I'd have her arrested."

Helen shook her head and picked up one of the grocery bags. I picked up the other one, and followed her through the parlor and into the kitchen. The bags were filled with cans of soup, which Helen opened up one by one with a few cranks of a can opener. She tossed the old soup in the saucepans into the sink, rinsed the pans under the tap, filled them with soup from the newly opened cans, and put them back in the refrigerator. "A few years ago she could still open the cans herself," Helen said. "She hates that I do it for her now. But the piano killed her hands." She put on her spectacles, glanced at the cupboards, and spotted my tea bags. "Shall we have a cup?"

I filled the kettle on the stove. "I beg your pardon, madame. The piano?"

"She used to give lessons. For forty years. It was how she raised us after my father died." Helen put her hands on her hips, staring at the open refrigerator. She reached into the back, pulled out a wrapped stick of butter, frowned, and tossed it into the garbage. "That ought to do it," she said, and put the unopened cans of soup in the cupboard. I sat at the table and watched as Helen washed the dirty dishes, tied up the garbage bag, watered a spider plant over the sink, and poured boiling water into two cups. She handed one to me without milk, the string of the tea bag trailing over the side, and sat down at the table.

"Excuse me, madame, but is it enough?"

Helen took a sip of her tea. Her lipstick left a smiling pink stain on the inside rim of the cup. "Is what enough?"

"The soup in the pans. Is it enough food for Mrs. Croft?"

"She won't eat anything else. She stopped eating solids after she turned one hundred. That was, let's see, three years ago."

I was mortified. I had assumed Mrs. Croft was in her eighties, perhaps as old as ninety. I had never known a person who had lived for over a century. That this person was a widow who lived alone mortified me further still. It was widowhood that had driven my own mother insane. My father, who worked as a clerk at the General Post Office of Calcutta, died of encephalitis when I was sixteen. My mother refused to adjust to life without him; instead she sank deeper into a world of darkness from which neither I, nor my brother, nor concerned relatives, nor psychiatric clinics on Rashbihari Avenue could save her. What pained me most was to see her so unguarded, to hear her burp after meals or expel gas in front of company without the slightest embarrassment. After my father's death my brother abandoned his schooling and began to work in the jute mill he would eventually manage, in order to keep the household running. And so it was my job to sit by my mother's feet and study for my exams as she counted and recounted the bracelets on her arm as if they were the beads of an abacus. We tried to keep an eye on her. Once she had wandered half naked to the tram depot before we were able to bring her inside again.

"I am happy to warm Mrs. Croft's soup in the evenings," I suggested, removing the tea bag from my cup and squeezing out the liquor. "It is no trouble."

Helen looked at her watch, stood up, and poured the

rest of her tea into the sink. "I wouldn't if I were you. That's the sort of thing that would kill her altogether."

That evening, when Helen had gone back to Arlington and Mrs. Croft and I were alone again, I began to worry. Now that I knew how very old she was, I worried that something would happen to her in the middle of the night, or when I was out during the day. As vigorous as her voice was, and imperious as she seemed, I knew that even a scratch or a cough could kill a person that old; each day she lived, I knew, was something of a miracle. Although Helen had seemed friendly enough, a small part of me worried that she might accuse me of negligence if anything were to happen. Helen didn't seem worried. She came and went, bringing soup for Mrs. Croft, one Sunday after the next.

In this manner the six weeks of that summer passed. I came home each evening, after my hours at the library, and spent a few minutes on the piano bench with Mrs. Croft. I gave her a bit of my company, and assured her that I had checked the lock, and told her that the flag on the moon was splendid. Some evenings I sat beside her long after she had drifted off to sleep, still in awe of how many years she had spent on this earth. At times I tried to picture the world she had been born into, in 1866—a world, I imagined, filled with women in long black skirts, and chaste conversations in the parlor. Now, when I looked at her hands with their swollen knuckles folded together in her lap, I imagined them smooth and slim, striking the piano keys. At times I came downstairs before going to sleep, to make sure she was sitting upright on the bench, or was safe in her bedroom. On Fridays I made sure to put the rent in her hands. There was nothing I could do for her beyond these simple gestures. I was not her son, and apart from those eight dollars, I owed her nothing.

At the end of August, Mala's passport and green card were ready. I received a telegram with her flight information; my brother's house in Calcutta had no telephone. Around that time I also received a letter from her, written only a few days after we had parted. There was no salutation; addressing me by name would have assumed an intimacy we had not yet discovered. It contained only a few lines. "I write in English in preparation for the journey. Here I am very much lonely. Is it very cold there. Is there snow. Yours, Mala."

I was not touched by her words. We had spent only a handful of days in each other's company. And yet we were bound together; for six weeks she had worn an iron bangle on her wrist, and applied vermilion powder to the part in her hair, to signify to the world that she was a bride. In those six weeks I regarded her arrival as I would the arrival of a coming month, or season—something inevitable, but meaningless at the time. So little did I know her that, while details of her face sometimes rose to my memory, I could not conjure up the whole of it.

A few days after receiving the letter, as I was walking to work in the morning, I saw an Indian woman on the other side of Massachusetts Avenue, wearing a sari with its free end nearly dragging on the footpath, and pushing a child in a stroller. An American woman with a small black dog on a leash was walking to one side of her. Suddenly the dog began barking. From the other side of the street I watched as the Indian woman, startled, stopped in her path, at which point the dog leapt up and seized the end of the sari between its teeth. The American woman scolded the dog, appeared to apologize, and walked quickly away, leaving the Indian woman to fix her sari in the middle of the footpath, and quiet her crying child. She did not see me standing there, and eventually she continued on her way. Such a mishap, I realized that morning, would soon be my concern. It was my duty to take care of Mala, to welcome her and protect her. I would have to buy her her first pair of snow boots, her first winter coat. I would have to tell her which streets to avoid, which way the traffic came, tell her to wear her sari so that the free end did not drag on the footpath. A five-mile separation from her parents, I recalled with some irritation, had caused her to weep.

Unlike Mala, I was used to it all by then: used to

cornflakes and milk, used to Helen's visits, used to sitting on the bench with Mrs. Croft. The only thing I was not used to was Mala. Nevertheless I did what I had to do. I went to the housing office at MIT and found a furnished apartment a few blocks away, with a double bed and a private kitchen and bath, for forty dollars a week. One last Friday I handed Mrs. Croft eight one-dollar bills in an envelope, brought my suitcase downstairs, and informed her that I was moving. She put my key into her change purse. The last thing she asked me to do was hand her the cane propped against the table, so that she could walk to the door and lock it behind me. "Goodbye, then," she said, and retreated back into the house. I did not expect any display of emotion, but I was disappointed all the same. I was only a boarder, a man who paid her a bit of money and passed in and out of her home for six weeks. Compared to a century, it was no time at all.

At the airport I recognized Mala immediately. The free end of her sari did not drag on the floor, but was draped in a sign of bridal modesty over her head, just as it had draped my mother until the day my father died. Her thin brown arms were stacked with gold bracelets, a small red circle was painted on her forehead, and the edges of her feet were tinted with a decorative red dye. I did not embrace her, or kiss her, or take her hand. Instead I asked her, speaking Bengali for the first time in America, if she was hungry.

She hesitated, then nodded yes.

I told her I had prepared some egg curry at home. "What did they give you to eat on the plane?"

"I didn't eat."

"All the way from Calcutta?"

"The menu said oxtail soup."

"But surely there were other items."

"The thought of eating an ox's tail made me lose my appetite."

When we arrived home, Mala opened up one of her suitcases, and presented me with two pullover sweaters, both made with bright blue wool, which she had knitted

in the course of our separation, one with a V neck, the
other covered with cables. I tried them on; both were
tight under the arms. She had also brought me two new
pairs of drawstring pajamas, a letter from my brother,
and a packet of loose Darjeeling tea. I had no present
for her apart from the egg curry. We sat at a bare table,
each of us staring at our plates. We ate with our hands,
another thing I had not yet done in America.

"The house is nice," she said. "Also the egg curry."
With her left hand she held the end of her sari to her
chest, so it would not slip off her head.

"I don't know many recipes."

She nodded, peeling the skin off each of her potatoes
before eating them. At one point the sari slipped to her
shoulders. She readjusted it at once.

"There is no need to cover your head," I said. "I don't
mind. It doesn't matter here."

She kept it covered anyway.

I waited to get used to her, to her presence at my
side, at my table and in my bed, but a week later we
were still strangers. I still was not used to coming home
to an apartment that smelled of steamed rice, and finding
that the basin in the bathroom was always wiped clean,
our two toothbrushes lying side by side, a cake of Pears
soap from India resting in the soap dish. I was not used
to the fragrance of the coconut oil she rubbed every
other night into her scalp, or the delicate sound her
bracelets made as she moved about the apartment. In
the mornings she was always awake before I was. The
first morning when I came into the kitchen she had
heated up the leftovers and set a plate with a spoonful
of salt on its edge on the table, assuming I would eat
rice for breakfast, as most Bengali husbands did. I told
her cereal would do, and the next morning when I came
into the kitchen she had already poured the cornflakes
into my bowl. One morning she walked with me down
Massachusetts Avenue to MIT, where I gave her a short
tour of the campus. On the way we stopped at a hard-
ware store and I made a copy of the key, so that she
could let herself into the apartment. The next morning

before I left for work she asked me for a few dollars. I parted with them reluctantly, but I knew that this, too, was now normal. When I came home from work there was a potato peeler in the kitchen drawer, and a table-cloth on the table, and chicken curry made with fresh garlic and ginger on the stove. We did not have a television in those days. After dinner I read the newspaper, while Mala sat at the kitchen table, working on a cardigan for herself with more of the bright blue wool, or writing letters home.

At the end of our first week, on Friday, I suggested going out. Mala set down her knitting and disappeared into the bathroom. When she emerged I regretted the suggestion; she had put on a clean silk sari and extra bracelets, and coiled her hair with a flattering side part on top of her head. She was prepared as if for a party, or at the very least for the cinema, but I had no such destination in mind. The evening air was balmy. We walked several blocks down Massachusetts Avenue, looking into the windows of restaurants and shops. Then, without thinking, I led her down the quiet street where for so many nights I had walked alone.

"This is where I lived before you came," I said, stopping at Mrs. Croft's chain-link fence.

"In such a big house?"

"I had a small room upstairs. At the back."

"Who else lives there?"

"A very old woman."

"With her family?"

"Alone."

"But who takes care of her?"

I opened the gate. "For the most part she takes care of herself."

I wondered if Mrs. Croft would remember me; I wondered if she had a new boarder to sit with her on the bench each evening. When I pressed the bell I expected the same long wait as that day of our first meeting, when I did not have a key. But this time the door was opened almost immediately, by Helen. Mrs. Croft was not sitting on the bench. The bench was gone.

"Hello there," Helen said, smiling with her bright pink lips at Mala. "Mother's in the parlor. Will you be visiting awhile?"

"As you wish, madame."

"Then I think I'll run to the store, if you don't mind. She had a little accident. We can't leave her alone these days, not even for a minute."

I locked the door after Helen and walked into the parlor. Mrs. Croft was lying flat on her back, her head on a peach-colored cushion, a thin white quilt spread over her body. Her hands were folded together on top of her chest. When she saw me she pointed at the sofa, and told me to sit down. I took my place as directed, but Mala wandered over to the piano and sat on the bench, which was now positioned where it belonged.

"I broke my hip!" Mrs. Croft announced, as if no time had passed.

"Oh dear, madame."

"I fell off the bench!"

"I am so sorry, madame."

"It was the middle of the night! Do you know what I did, boy?"

I shook my head.

"I called the police!"

She stared up at the ceiling and grinned sedately, exposing a crowded row of long gray teeth. Not one was missing. "What do you say to that, boy?"

As stunned as I was, I knew what I had to say. With no hesitation at all, I cried out, "Splendid!"

Mala laughed then. Her voice was full of kindness, her eyes bright with amusement. I had never heard her laugh before, and it was loud enough so that Mrs. Croft had heard, too. She turned to Mala and glared.

"Who is she, boy?"

"She is my wife, madame."

Mrs. Croft pressed her head at an angle against the cushion to get a better look. "Can you play the piano?"

"No, madame," Mala replied.

"Then stand up!"

Mala rose to her feet, adjusting the end of her sari over her head and holding it to her chest, and, for the first time since her arrival, I felt sympathy. I remembered my first days in London, learning how to take the Tube to Russell Square, riding an escalator for the first time, being unable to understand that when the man cried "piper" it meant "paper," being unable to decipher, for a whole year, that the conductor said "mind the gap" as the train pulled away from each station. Like me, Mala had traveled far from home, not knowing where she was going, or what she would find, for no reason other than to be my wife. As strange as it seemed, I knew in my heart that one day her death would affect me, and stranger still, that mine would affect her. I wanted somehow to explain this to Mrs. Croft, who was still scrutinizing Mala from top to toe with what seemed to be placid disdain. I wondered if Mrs. Croft had ever seen a woman in a sari, with a dot painted on her forehead and bracelets stacked on her wrists. I wondered what she would object to. I wondered if she could see the red dye still vivid on Mala's feet, all but obscured by the bottom edge of her sari. At last Mrs. Croft declared, with the equal measures of disbelief and delight I knew well:

"She is a perfect lady!"

Now it was I who laughed. I did so quietly, and Mrs. Croft did not hear me. But Mala had heard, and, for the first time, we looked at each other and smiled.

I like to think of that moment in Mrs. Croft's parlor as the moment when the distance between Mala and me began to lessen. Although we were not yet fully in love, I like to think of the months that followed as a honeymoon of sorts. Together we explored the city and met other Bengalis, some of whom are still friends today. We discovered that a man named Bill sold fresh fish on Prospect Street, and that a shop in Harvard Square called Cardullo's sold bay leaves and cloves. In the evenings we walked to the Charles River to watch sailboats drift across the water, or had ice cream cones in Harvard Yard. We bought an Instamatic camera with which to document our life together, and I took pictures of her posing in front of the Prudential building, so that she could send them to her parents. At night we kissed, shy at first but quickly bold, and discovered pleasure and solace in each other's arms. I told her about my voyage on the SS *Roma,* and about Finsbury Park and the YMCA, and my evenings on the bench with Mrs. Croft. When I told her stories about my mother, she wept. It was Mala who consoled me when, reading the *Globe* one evening, I came across Mrs. Croft's obituary. I had not thought of her in several months—by then those six weeks of the summer were already a remote interlude in my past—but when I learned of her death I was stricken, so much so that when Mala looked up from her knitting she found me staring at the wall, the newspaper neglected in my lap, unable to speak. Mrs. Croft's was the first death I mourned in America, for hers was the first life I had admired; she had left this world at last, ancient and alone, never to return.

As for me, I have not strayed much farther. Mala and I live in a town about twenty miles from Boston, on a tree-lined street much like Mrs. Croft's, in a house we own, with a garden that saves us from buying tomatoes in summer, and room for guests. We are American citizens now, so that we can collect social security when it is time. Though we visit Calcutta every few years, and bring back more drawstring pajamas and Darjeeling tea, we have decided to grow old here. I work in a small college library. We have a son who attends Harvard University. Mala no longer drapes the end of her sari over her head, or weeps at night for her parents, but occasionally she weeps for our son. So we drive to Cambridge to visit him, or bring him home for a weekend, so that he can eat rice with us with his hands, and speak in Bengali, things we sometimes worry he will no longer do after we die.

Whenever we make that drive, I always make it a point to take Massachusetts Avenue, in spite of the traffic. I barely recognize the buildings now, but each time I am there I return instantly to those six weeks as if they were only the other day, and I slow down and point to Mrs. Croft's street, saying to my son, here was my first home in America, where I lived with a woman who was

103. "Remember?" Mala says, and smiles, amazed, as I am, that there was ever a time that we were strangers. My son always expresses his astonishment, not at Mrs. Croft's age, but at how little I paid in rent, a fact nearly as inconceivable to him as a flag on the moon was to a woman born in 1866. In my son's eyes I see the ambition that had first hurled me across the world. In a few years he will graduate and pave his way, alone and unprotected. But I remind myself that he has a father who is still living, a mother who is happy and strong. Whenever he is discouraged, I tell him that if I can survive on three continents, then there is no obstacle he cannot conquer. While the astronauts, heroes forever, spent mere hours on the moon, I have remained in this new world for nearly thirty years. I know that my achievement is quite ordinary. I am not the only man to seek his fortune far from home, and certainly I am not the first. Still, there are times I am bewildered by each mile I have traveled, each meal I have eaten, each person I have known, each room in which I have slept. As ordinary as it all appears, there are times when it is beyond my imagination.

SAADAT HASAN MANTO

Saadat Hasan Manto was born in 1912 into a Muslim family in the Indian State of Punjab. After a generally unsuccessful career as a student, he turned to writing and published his first collection of short stories, *Atish Pare*, in 1936. The next year he traveled to Bombay to edit *Musawwir*, a monthly film magazine, and between his reviews and short stories he became something of a celebrity.

Apprehensive about his family's situation after the partition of India, in 1948 Manto moved with his wife and children from present-day India to the newly created Muslim-majority nation of Pakistan. Some of his best work was written in the last seven years of his life, years of tremendous emotional and financial turmoil. During his career, he was tried six times for obscenity.

A very prolific writer, over a twenty-year period Manto produced twenty-two short story collections, a novel, five collections of radio plays, three collections of essays, two volumes of personal reminiscences, and numerous film scripts. His best-known work, *Toba Tek Singh*, was published in 1953. He died in Lahore in 1955.

Khalid Hasan, translator of Manto's work, has observed, "No one has written about the holocaust of Partition with greater power than Manto. What distinguishes his writing from that of others ·was his deep humanism and his refusal to treat people as Hindu or Muslim or Sikh. To him they are all human beings. What he finds incomprehensible is why they turned on each other with such savagery at a time which should have been their greatest moment of joy: independence from alien rule."

The Assignment

Beginning with isolated incidents of stabbing, it had now developed into full-scale communal violence, with no holds barred. Even home-made bombs were being used.

The general view in Amritsar was that the riots could not last long. They were seen as no more than a manifestation of temporarily inflamed political passions which were bound to cool down before long. After all, these were not the first communal riots the city had known. There had been so many of them in the past. They never lasted long. The pattern was familiar. Two weeks or so of unrest and then business as usual. On the basis of experience, therefore, the people were quite justified in believing that the current troubles would also run their course in a few days. But this did not happen. They not only continued, but grew in intensity.

Muslims living in Hindu localities began to leave for safer places, and Hindus in Muslim majority areas followed suit. However, everyone saw these adjustments as strictly temporary. The atmosphere would soon be clear of this communal madness, they told themselves.

Retired judge Mian Abdul Hai was absolutely confident that things would return to normal soon, which was why he wasn't worried. He had two children, a boy of eleven and a girl of seventeen. In addition, there was an old servant who was now pushing seventy. It was a small family. When the troubles started, Mian sahib, being an extra cautious man, had stocked up on food . . . just in case. So on one count, at least, there were no worries.

His daughter, Sughra, was less sure of things. They lived in a three-storey house with a view of almost the entire city. Sughra could not help noticing that, whenever she went on the roof, there were fires raging everywhere. In the beginning, she could hear fire engines rushing past, their bells ringing, but this had now stopped. There were too many fires in too many places.

The nights had become particularly frightening. The

sky was always lit by conflagrations like giants spitting
out flames. Then there were the slogans which rent the
air with terrifying frequency—"Allaho Akbar," "Har
Har Mahadev."

Sughra never expressed her fears to her father, because he had declared confidently that there was no
cause for anxiety. Everything was going to be fine. Since
he was generally always right, she had initially felt
reassured.

However, when the power and water supplies were
suddenly cut off, she expressed her unease to her father
and suggested apologetically that, for a few days at least,
they should move to Sharifpura, a Muslim locality,
where many of the old residents had already moved to.
Mian sahib was adamant. "You're imagining things.
Everything is going to be normal very soon."

He was wrong. Things went from bad to worse. Before
long there was not a single Muslim family to be found
in Mian Abdul Hai's locality. Then one day Mian sahib
suffered a stroke and was laid up. His son, Basharat,
who used to spend most of his time playing self-devised
games, now stayed glued to his father's bed.

All the shops in the area had been permanently
boarded up. Dr. Ghulam Hussain's dispensary had been
shut for weeks and Sughra had noticed from the rooftop
one day that the adjoining clinic of Dr. Goranditta Mal
was also closed. Mian sahib's condition was getting
worse day by day. Sughra was almost at her wits' end.
One day she took Basharat aside and said to him,
"You've got to do something. I know it's not safe to go
out, but we must get some help. Our father is very ill."

The boy went, but came back almost immediately. His
face was pale with fear. He had seen a blood-drenched
body lying in the street and a group of wild-looking men
looting shops. Sughra took the terrified boy in her arms
and said a silent prayer, thanking God for his safe return. However, she could not bear her father's suffering.
His left side was now completely lifeless. His speech had
been impaired and he mostly communicated through
gestures, all designed to reassure Sughra that soon all
would be well.

It was the month of Ramadan and only two days to Id. Mian sahib was quite confident that the troubles would be over by then. He was again wrong. A canopy of smoke hung over the city, with fires burning everywhere. At night the silence was shattered by deafening explosions. Sughra and Basharat hadn't slept for days.

Sughra in any case couldn't because of her father's deteriorating condition. Helplessly, she would look at him, then at her young, frightened brother and the seventy-year-old servant Akbar, who was useless for all practical purposes. He mostly kept to his bed, coughing and fighting for breath. One day Sughra told him angrily, "What good are you? Do you realize how ill Mian sahib is? Perhaps you are too lazy to want to help, pretending that you are suffering from acute asthma. There was a time when servants used to sacrifice their lives for their masters."

Sughra felt very bad afterwards. She had been unnecessarily harsh on the old man. In the evening, when she took his food to him in his small room, he was not there. Basharat looked for him all over the house, but he was nowhere to be found. The front door was unlatched. He was gone, perhaps to get some help for Mian sahib. Sughra prayed for his return, but two days passed and he hadn't come back.

It was evening and the festival of Id was now only a day away. She remembered the excitement which used to grip the family on this occasion. She remembered standing on the rooftop, peering into the sky, looking for the Id moon and praying for the clouds to clear. But how different everything was today. The sky was covered in smoke and on distant roofs one could see people looking upwards. Were they trying to catch sight of the new moon or were they watching the fires, she wondered.

She looked up and saw the thin sliver of the moon peeping through a small patch in the sky. She raised her hands in prayer, begging God to make her father well. Basharat, however, was upset that there would be no Id this year.

The night hadn't yet fallen. Sughra had moved her father's bed out of the room on to the veranda. She was sprinkling water on the floor to make it cool. Mian sahib was lying there quietly looking with vacant eyes at the sky where she had seen the moon. Sughra came and sat next to him. He motioned her to get closer. Then he raised his right arm slowly and put it on her head. Tears began to run from Sughra's eyes. Even Mian sahib looked moved. Then with great difficulty he said to her, "God is merciful. All will be well."

Suddenly there was a knock on the door. Sughra's heart began to beat violently. She looked at Basharat, whose face had turned white like a sheet of paper. There was another knock. Mian sahib gestured to Sughra to answer it. It must be old Akbar who had come back, she thought. She said to Basharat, "Answer the door. I'm sure it's Akbar." Her father shook his head, as if to signal disagreement.

"Then who can it be?" Sughra asked him.

Mian Abdul Hai tried to speak, but before he could do so Basharat came running in. He was breathless. Taking Sughra aside, he whispered, "It's a Sikh."

Sughra screamed, "A Sikh! What does he want?"

"He wants me to open the door."

Sughra took Basharat in her arms and went and sat on her father's bed, looking at him desolately.

On Mian Abdul Hai's thin, lifeless lips, a faint smile appeared. "Go and open the door. It is Gurmukh Singh."

"No, it's someone else," Basharat said.

Mian sahib turned to Sughra. "Open the door. It's him."

Sughra rose. She knew Gurmukh Singh. Her father had once done him a favour. He had been involved in a false legal suit and Mian sahib had acquitted him. That was a long time ago, but every year, on the occasion of Id, he would come all the way from his village with a bag of sawwaiyaan. Mian sahib had told him several times, "Sardar sahib, you really are too kind. You shouldn't inconvenience yourself every year." But Gurmukh Singh would always reply, "Mian sahib, God has given you everything. This is only a small gift which I bring every year in humble acknowledgement of the kindness you did me once. Even a hundred generations of mine would not be able to repay your favour. May God keep you happy."

Sughra was reassured. Why hadn't she thought of it in the first place? But why had Basharat said it was someone else? After all, he knew Gurmukh Singh's face from his annual visit.

Sughra went to the front door. There was another knock. Her heart missed a beat. "Who is it?" she asked in a faint voice.

Basharat whispered to her to look through a small hole in the door.

It wasn't Gurmukh Singh, who was a very old man. This was a young fellow. He knocked again. He was holding a bag in his hand of the same kind Gurmukh Singh used to bring.

"Who are you?" she asked, a little more confident now.

"I am Sardar Gurmukh Singh's son Santokh."

Sughra's fear had suddenly gone. "What brings you here today?" she asked politely.

"Where is Judge sahib?" he asked.

"He is not well," Sughra answered.

"Oh, I'm sorry," Santokh Singh said. Then he shifted his bag from one hand to the other. "Here is some saw-waiyaan." Then after a pause, "Sardarji is dead."

"Dead!"

"Yes, a month ago, but one of the last things he said to me was, 'For the last ten years, on the occasion of Id, I have always taken my small gift to Judge sahib. After I am gone, it will become your duty.' I gave him my word that I would not fail him. I am here today to honour the promise made to my father on his death-bed."

Sughra was so moved that tears came to her eyes. She opened the door a little. The young man pushed the bag towards her. "May God rest his soul," she said.

"Is Judge sahib not well?" he asked.

"No."

"What's wrong?"

"He had a stroke."

"Had my father been alive, it would have grieved him

deeply. He never forgot Judge sahib's kindness until his last breath. He used to say, 'He is not a man, but a god.' May God keep him under his care. Please convey my respects to him."

He left before Sughra could make up her mind whether or not to ask him to get a doctor.

As Santokh Singh turned the corner, four men, their faces covered with their turbans, moved towards him. Two of them held burning oil torches; the others carried cans of kerosene oil and explosives. One of them asked Santokh, "Sardarji, have you completed your assignment?"

The young man nodded.

"Should we then proceed with ours?" he asked.

"If you like," he replied and walked away.

ROHINTON MISTRY

Rohinton Mistry was born in 1952 in Mumbai, India, where he belonged to the Parsi Zoroastrian religious minority. He immigrated to Canada in 1975 after receiving an undergraduate degree in mathematics and economics from Bombay University.

While he was a part-time student at the University of Toronto in 1983, earning degrees in English and philosophy and working at a bank, his short story "One Sunday" won the Hart House literary prize, the first of numerous awards he has received for his work.

He is the author of the short story collection *Tales from Firozsha Baag* (1987) (also published as *Swimming Lessons and Other Stories from Firozsha Baag*), and the novels *Such a Long Journey* (1991), *A Fine Balance* (1995), and *Family Matters* (2002), all three of which were short-listed for the Booker Prize. Most recently he published *The Scream* (2008), a limited-edition single-story volume illustrated by Canadian artist Tony Urquhart. According to Canadian reviewer Jennifer Takhar, Mistry's work deals with the "double displacement" of Parsis in contemporary India and "the resilience of the individual and that of the community in a world without a shred of pity."

In 2002 Mistry canceled his U.S. book tour for *Family Matters* because he and his wife were targeted by security agents at every airport he visited, apparently because Mistry appeared to be Muslim. In a statement Mistry's publisher described the author's humiliation as "unbearable."

One Sunday

ajamai was getting ready to lock up her flat in Firozsha Baag and take the train to spend the day with
her sister's family in Bandra.

She bustled her bulk around, turning the keys in the
padlocks of her seventeen cupboards, then tugged at
each to ensure the levers had tumbled properly. Soon,
she was breathless with excitement and exertion.

Her breathlessness reminded her of the operation she
had had three years ago to remove fat tissue from the
abdomen and breasts. The specialist had told her, "You
will not notice any great difference in the mirror. But
you will appreciate the results when you are over sixty.
It will keep you from sagging."

Here she was at fifty-five, and would soon know the
truth of his words if merciful God kept her alive for five
more years. Najamai did not question the ways of merciful God, even though her Soli was taken away the very
year after first Dolly and then Vera went abroad for
higher studies.

Today would be the first Sunday that the flat would
be empty for the whole day. "In a way it is good," she
reflected, "that Tehmina next door and the Boyces
downstairs use my fridge as much as they do. Anyone
who has evil intentions about my empty flat will think
twice when he sees the coming-going of neighbours."

Temporarily reconciled towards the neighbours whom
she otherwise regarded as nuisances, Najamai set off.
She nodded at the boys playing in the compound. Outside, it did not feel as hot, for there was a gentle breeze.
She felt at peace with the world. It was a twenty-minute
walk, and there would be plenty of time to catch the
ten-fifteen express. She would arrive at her sister's well
before lunch-time.

At eleven-thirty Tehmina cautiously opened her door
and peered out. She made certain that the hallway was
free of the risk of any confrontation with a Boyce on

the way to Najamai's fridge. "It is shameful the way those people misuse the poor lady's goodness," thought Tehmina. "All Najamai said when she bought the fridge was to please feel free to use it. It was only out of courtesy. Now those Boyces behave as if they have a share in the ownership of the fridge."

She shuffled out in slippers and duster-coat, clutching one empty glass and the keys to Najamai's flat. She reeked of cloves, lodged in her mouth for two reasons: it kept away her attacks of nausea and alleviated her chronic toothaches.

Cursing the poor visibility in the hallway, Tehmina, circumspect, moved on. Even on the sunniest of days, the hallway persisted in a state of half-light. She fumbled with the locks, wishing her cataracts would hurry and ripen for removal.

Inside at last, she swung open the fridge door to luxuriate in the delicious rush of cold air. A curious-looking package wrapped in plastic caught her eye; she squeezed it, sniffed at it, decided against undoing it. The freezer section was almost bare; the Boyces' weekly packets of beef had not yet arrived.

Tehmina placed two ice-cubes in the empty glass she had brought along—the midday drink of chilled lemonade was as dear to her as the evening Scotch and soda—and proceeded to lock up the place. But she was startled in her battle with Najamai's locks and bolts by footsteps behind her.

"Francis!"

Francis did odd jobs. Not just for Tehmina and Najamai in C Block, but for anyone in Firozsha Baag who required his services. This was his sole means of livelihood ever since he had been laid off or dismissed, it was never certain which, from the furniture store across the road where he used to be a delivery boy. The awning of that store still provided the only roof he had ever known. Strangely, the store owner did not mind, and it was a convenient location—all that Tehmina or Najamai or any of the other neighbours had to do was lean out of their verandas and wave or clap hands and he would come.

Grinning away as usual, Francis approached Tehmina.

"Stop staring, you idiot," started Tehmina, "and check if this door is properly locked."

"Yes, *bai.* But when will Najamai return? She said she would give me some work today."

"Never. Could not be for today. She won't be back till very late. You must have made a mistake." With a loud suck she moved the cloves to the other cheek and continued, "So many times I've told you to open your ears and listen properly when people tell you things. But no. You never listen."

Francis grinned again and shrugged his shoulders. In order to humour Tehmina he replied, "Sorry, *bai,* it is my mistake." He stood only about five feet two but possessed strength which was out of all proportion to his light build. Once, in Tehmina's kitchen during a cleaning spree he had picked up the stone slab used for grinding spices. It weighed at least fifty pounds, and it was the way in which he lifted it, between thumb and fingertips, that amazed Tehmina. Later, she had reported the incident to Najamai. The two women had marvelled at his strength, giggling at Tehmina's speculation that he must be built like a bull.

As humbly as possible Francis now asked, "Do you have any work for me today?"

"No. And I do not' like it, you skulking here in the hallway. When there is work we will call you. Now go away."

Francis left. Tehmina could be offensive, but he needed the few paise the neighbours graciously let him earn and the leftovers Najamai allowed him whenever there were any. So he returned to the shade of the furniture store awning.

While Tehmina was chilling her lemonade with Najamai's ice, downstairs, Silloo Boyce cleaned and portioned the beef into seven equal packets. She disliked being obligated to Najamai for the fridge, though it was a great convenience. "Besides," she argued with herself, "we do enough to pay her back, every night she borrows the newspaper. And every morning I receive her milk and bread so she does not have to wake up early. Madam will not even come down, my sons must carry it upstairs." Thus she mused and reasoned each Sunday, as she readied the meat in plastic bags which her son Kersi later stacked in Najamai's freezer.

Right now, Kersi was busy repairing his cricket bat. The cord around the handle had come unwound and had gathered in a black cluster at its base, leaving more than half the length of the handle naked. It looked like a clump of pubic hair, Kersi thought, as he untangled the cord and began gluing it back around the handle.

The bat was a size four, much too small for him, and he did not play a lot of cricket any more. But for some reason he continued to care for it. The willow still possessed spring enough to send a ball to the boundary line, in glaring contrast to his brother Percy's bat. The latter was in sad shape. The blade was dry and cracked in places; the handle, its rubber grip and cord having come off long ago, had split; and the joint where the blade met the handle was undone. But Percy did not care. He never had really cared for cricket, except during that one year when the Australian team was visiting, when he had spent whole days glued to the radio, listening to the commentary. Now it was aeroplanes all the time, model kits over which he spent hours, and Biggles books in which he buried himself.

But Kersi had wanted to play serious cricket ever since primary school. In the fifth standard he was finally chosen for the class team. On the eve of the match, however, the captain contracted mumps, and the vice-captain took over, promptly relegating Kersi to the extras and moving up his own crony. That was the end of serious cricket for Kersi. For a short while, his father used to take him and his Firozsha Baag friends to play at the Marine Drive *maidaan* on Sunday mornings. And nowadays, they played a little in the compound. But it was not the same. Besides, they were interrupted all the time by people like that mean old Rustomji in A Block. Of all the neighbours who yelled and scolded, Rustomji-the-curmudgeon did the loudest and the most. He always threatened to confiscate their bat and ball if they didn't stop immediately.

Kersi now used his bat mainly for killing rats. Rat poison and a variety of traps were also employed with unflagging vigilance. But most of the rat population, with some rodent sixth sense, circumnavigated the traps. Kersi's bat remained indispensable.

His mother was quite proud of his skill, and once she had bragged about it to Najamai upstairs: "So young, and yet so brave, the way he runs after the ugly things. And he never misses." This was a mistake, because Kersi was promptly summoned the next time Najamai spied a rat in her flat. It had fled into the daughters' room and Kersi rushed in after it. Vera had just finished her bath and was not dressed. She screamed, first when she saw the rat, and again, when Kersi entered after it. He found it hard to keep his eyes on the rat—it escaped easily. Soon after, Vera had gone abroad for higher studies, following her sister Dolly's example.

The first time that Kersi successfully used his bat against a rat, it had been quite messy. Perhaps it was the thrill of the chase, or his rage against the invader, or just an ignorance about the fragility of that creature of fur and bone. The bat had come down with such vehemence that the rat was badly squashed. A dark red stain had oozed across the floor, almost making him sick. He discovered how sticky that red smear was only when he tried to wipe it off with an old newspaper.

The beef was now ready for the freezer. With seven packets of meat, and Najamai's latchkeys in his pocket, Kersi plodded upstairs.

When Najamai's daughters had gone abroad, they took with them the youthful sensuality that once filled the flat, and which could drive Kersi giddy with excitement on a day like this, with no one home, and all before him the prospect of exploring Vera and Dolly's bedroom, examining their undies that invariably lay scattered around, running his hands through lacy frilly things, rubbing himself with these and, on one occasion, barely rescuing them from a sticky end. Now, exploration would yield nothing but Najamai's huge underclothes. Kersi could not think of them as bras and panties—their vastness forfeited the right to these dainty names.

Feeling sadness, loss, betrayal, he descended the stairs lifelessly. Each wooden step, with the passage of years and the weight of tenants, was worn to concavity, and he felt just as worn. Not so long ago, he was able to counter spells of low spirits and gloominess by turning to his Enid Blyton books. A few minutes was all it took before he was sharing the adventures of the Famous Five or the Secret Seven, an idyllic existence in a small English village, where he would play with dogs, ride horses in the meadows, climb hills, hike through the countryside, or, if the season was right, build a snowman and have a snowball fight.

But lately, this had refused to work, and he got rid of the books. Percy had made fun of him for clinging to such silly and childish fantasy, inviting him to share, instead, the experience of aerial warfare with Biggles and his men in the RAF.

Everything in Firozsha Baag was so dull since Pesi *paadmaroo* had been sent away to boarding school. And all because of that sissy Jehangir, the Bulsara Bookworm.

Francis was back in the hallway, and was disappointed when Kersi did not notice him. Kersi usually stopped to chat; he got on well with all the servants in the building, especially Francis. Kersi's father had taught him to play cricket but Francis had instructed him in kite-flying. With a kite and string bought with fifty paise earned for carrying Najamai's quota of rice and sugar from the rationing depot, and with the air of a mentor, he had taught Kersi everything he knew about kites.

But the time they spent together was anathema to Kersi's parents. They looked distastefully on the growing friendship, and all the neighbours agreed it was not proper for a Parsi boy to consort in this way with a man who was really no better than a homeless beggar, who would starve were it not for their thoughtfulness in providing him with odd jobs. No good would come of it, they said.

Much to their chagrin, however, when the kite-flying season of high winds had passed, Kersi and Francis started spinning tops and shooting marbles. These, too, were activities considered inappropriate for a Parsi boy.

At six-thirty, Tehmina went to Najamai's flat for ice. This was the hour of the most precious of all ice-cubes—she'd just poured herself two fingers of Scotch.

A red glow from the Ambica Saris neon display outside Firozsha Baag floated eerily over the compound wall. Though the street lamps had now come on, they hardly illuminated the hallway, and tonight's full moon was no help either. Tehmina cursed the locks eluding her efforts. But as she continued the unequal struggle by twilight, her armpits soaked with sweat, she admitted that life before the fridge had been even tougher.

In those days she had to venture beyond the compound of Firozsha Baag and buy ice from the Irani Restaurant in Tar Gully. It was not the money she minded but the tedium of it all. Besides, the residents of Tar Gully amused themselves by spitting from their tenement windows on all comers who were better-heeled than they. In impoverished Tar Gully she was certainly considered better-heeled, and many well-aimed globs had found their mark. On such evenings Tehmina, in tears, would return to her flat and rush to take a bath, cursing those satanic animals and fiends of Tar Gully. Meanwhile, the ice she had purchased would sit melting to a sliver.

As the door finally unlocked, Tehmina spied a figure at the far end of the darkened hallway. Heart racing a little, she wondered who it might be, and called out as authoritatively as she could, "*Kaun hai?* What do you want?"

The answer came: "*Bai*, it's only Francis."

The familiar voice gave her courage. She prepared to scold him. "Did I not tell you this morning not to loiter here? Did I not say we would call if there was work?

Did I not tell you that Najamai would be very late? Tell me then, you rascal, what are you doing here?"

Francis was hungry. He had not eaten for two whole days, and had been hoping to earn something for dinner tonight. Unable to tolerate Tehmina much longer, he replied sullenly, "I came to see if Najamai had arrived," and turned to go.

But Tehmina suddenly changed her mind. "Wait here while I get my ice," she said, realizing that she could use his help to lock the door.

Inside, she decided it was best not to push Francis too far. One never knew when this type of person would turn vicious. If he wanted to, he could knock her down right now, ransack Najamai's flat and disappear completely. She shuddered at these thoughts, then composed herself.

From downstairs came the strains of "The Blue Danube." Tehmina swayed absently. Strauss! The music reminded her of a time when the world was a simpler, better place to live in, when trips to Tar Gully did not involve the risk of spit globs. She reached into the freezer, and "The Blue Danube" concluded. Grudgingly, Tehmina allowed that there was one thing about the Boyces: they had good taste in music. Those senseless and monotonous Hindi film-songs never blared from their flat as they did sometimes from the other blocks of Firozsha Baag.

In control of herself now, she briskly stepped out. "Come on, Francis," she said peremptorily, "help me lock this door. I will tell Najamai that you will be back tomorrow for her work." She held out the ring of keys and Francis, not yet appeased by her half-hearted attempt at pacification, slowly and resentfully reached for them.

Tehmina was thankful at asking him to wait. "If it takes him so long, I could never do it in this darkness," she thought, as he handed back the keys.

Silloo downstairs heard the door slam when Tehmina returned to her own flat. It was time to start dinner. She rose and went to the kitchen.

*   *   *

Najamai stepped off the train and gathered together her belongings: umbrella, purse, shopping bag of leftovers, and cardigan. Sunday night had descended in full upon the station, and the platforms and waiting-rooms were deserted. She debated whether to take the taxi waiting in the night or to walk. The station clock showed nine-thirty. Even if it took her forty minutes to walk instead of the usual twenty, it would still be early enough to stop at the Boyces' before they went to bed. Besides, the walk would be healthy and help digest her sister's *pupeta-noo-gose* and *dhandar-paatyo*. With any luck, to-night would be a night unencumbered by the pressure of gas upon her gut.

The moon was full, the night was cool, and Najamai enjoyed her little walk. She neared Firozsha Baag and glanced quickly at the menacing mouth of Tar Gully. In there, streetlights were few, and sections of it had no lights at all. Najamai wondered if she would be able to spot any of the pimps and prostitutes who were said to visit here after dark even though Tar Gully was not a red-light district. But it looked deserted.

She was glad when the walk was over. Breathing a little rapidly, she rang the Boyce doorbell.

"Hullo, hullo—just wanted to pick up today's paper. Only if you've finished with it."

"Oh yes," said Silloo, "I made everyone read it early."

"This is very sweet of you," said Najamai, raising her arm so Silloo could tuck the paper under it. Then, as Silloo reached for the flashlight, she protested: "No no, the stairs won't be dark, there's a full moon."

Lighting Najamai's way up the stairs at night was one of the many things Silloo did for her neighbour. She knew that if Najamai ever stumbled in the dark and fell down the stairs, her broken bones would be a problem for the Boyces. It was simpler to shine the flashlight and see her safely to the landing.

"Good-night," said Najamai and started up. Silloo waited. Like a spotlight in some grotesque cabaret, the torch picked up the arduous swaying of Najamai's buttocks. She reached the top of the stairs, breathless, thanked Silloo and disappeared.

Silloo restored the flashlight to its niche by the door. The sounds of Najamai's preparation for bed and sleep now started to drip downstairs, as relentlessly as a leaky tap. A cupboard slammed . . . the easy chair in the bedroom, next to the window by day, was dragged to the bedside . . . footsteps led to the extremities of the flat . . . after a suitable interval, the flush . . . then the sound of water again, not torrential this time but steady, gentle, from a faucet . . . footsteps again . . .

The flow of familiar sounds was torn out of sequence by Najamai's frantic cries.

"Help! Help! Oh quickly! Thief!"

Kersi and his mother were the first to reach the door. They were outside in time to see Francis disappear in the direction of Tar Gully. Najamai, puffing, stood at the top of the stairs. "He was hiding behind the kitchen door," she gasped. "The front door—Tehmina as usual—"

Silloo was overcome by furious indignation. "I don't know why, with her bad eyes, that woman must fumble and mess with your keys. What did he steal?"

"I must check my cupboards," Najamai panted. "That rascal of a loafer will have run far already."

Tehmina now shuffled out, still clad in the duster-coat, anxiously sucking cloves and looking very guilty. She had heard everything from behind her door but asked anyway, "What happened? Who was screaming?"

The senseless fluster irritated Kersi. He went indoors. Confused by what had happened, he sat on his bed and cracked the fingers of both hands. Each finger twice, expertly, once at the knuckle, then at the joint closest to the nail. He could also crack his toes—each toe just once, though—but he did not feel like it right now. Don't crack your fingers, they used to tell him, your hands will become fat and ugly. For a while then he had cracked his knuckles more fervently than ever, hoping they would swell into fists the size of a face. Such fists would be useful to scare someone off in a fight. But the hands had remained quite normal.

Kersi picked up his bat. The cord had set firmly around the handle and the glue was dry; the rubber grip could go back on. There was a trick to fitting it right; if not done correctly, the grip would not cover the entire handle, but hang over the tip, like uncircumcised foreskin. He rolled down the cylindrical rubber tube onto itself, down to a rubber ring. Then he slipped the ring over the handle and unrolled it. A condom was probably put on the same way, he thought; someone had showed him those things at school, only this looked like one with the tip lopped off. Just as in that joke about a book called *The Unwanted Child* by F. L. Burst.

He posed before the mirror and flourished the bat. Satisfied with his repair work, he sat down again. He felt angry and betrayed at the thought of Francis vanishing into Tar Gully. His anger, coupled with the emptiness of this Sunday which, like a promise unfulfilled, had primed him many hours ago, now made him succumb to the flush of heroics starting to sweep through him. He glanced at himself in the mirror again and went outside with the bat.

A small crowd of C Block neighbours and their servants had gathered around Najamai, Silloo, and Tehmina. "I'm going to find him," Kersi announced grimly to this group.

"What rubbish are you talking?" his mother exclaimed. "In Tar Gully, alone at night?"

"Oh what a brave boy!" cried Najamai. "But maybe we should call the police."

Tehmina, by this time, was muttering non sequiturs about ice-cubes and Scotch and soda. Kersi repeated: "I'm going to find him."

This time Silloo said, "Your brother must go with you. Alone you'll be no match for that rascal. Percy! Bring the other bat and go with Kersi."

Obediently, Percy joined his brother and they set off in the direction of Tar Gully. Their mother shouted instructions after them: "Be careful for God's sake! Stay together and don't go too far if you cannot find him."

In Tar Gully the two drew a few curious glances as they strode along with cricket bats. But the hour was late and there were not many people around. Those who were, waited only for the final *Matka* draw to decide their financial destinies. Some of these men now hooted at Kersi and Percy. "Parsi *bawaji*! Cricket at night? Parsi *bawaji*! What will you hit, boundary or sixer?"

"Just ignore the bloody *ghatis*," said Percy softly. It was good advice; the two walked on as if it were a well-rehearsed plan, Percy dragging his bat behind him. Kersi carried his over the right shoulder to keep the puddles created by the overflowing gutters of Tar Gully from wetting it.

"It's funny," he thought, "just this morning I did not see any gutter spilling over when I went to the *bunya* for salt." Now they were all in full spate. The gutters of Tar Gully were notorious for their erratic habits and their stench, although the latter was never noticed by the denizens.

The *bunya*'s shop was closed for regular business but a small window was still open. The *bunya*, in his nocturnal role of bookie, was accepting last-minute *Matka* bets. Midnight was the deadline, when the winning numbers would be drawn from the earthen vessel that gave the game its name.

There was still no sign of Francis. Kersi and Percy approached the first of the tenements, with the familiar cow tethered out in front—it was the only one in this neighbourhood. Each morning, accompanied by the owner's comely daughter and a basket of cut green grass, it made the round of these streets. People would reverently feed the cow, buying grass at twenty-five paise a mouthful. When the basket was empty the cow would be led back to Tar Gully.

Kersi remembered one early morning when the daughter was milking the cow and a young man was standing behind her seated figure. He was bending over the girl, squeezing her breasts with both hands, while she did her best to work the cow's swollen udder. Neither of them had noticed Kersi as he'd hurried past. Now, as Kersi recalled the scene, he thought of Najamai's daughters, the rat in the bedroom, Vera's near-nude body, his dispossessed fantasy, and once again felt cheated, betrayed.

It was Percy who first spotted Francis and pointed him out to Kersi. It was also Percy who yelled *"Chor! Chor! Stop him!"* and galvanized the waiting *Matka* patrons into action.

Francis never had a chance. Three men in the distance heard the uproar and tripped him as he ran past. Without delay they started to punch him. One tried out a clumsy version of a dropkick but it did not work so well, and he diligently resumed with his fists. Then the others arrived and joined in the pounding.

The ritualistic cry of *"Chor! Chor!"* had rendered Francis into fair game in Tar Gully. But Kersi was horrified. This was not the way he had wanted it to end when he'd emerged with his bat. He watched in terror as Francis was slapped and kicked, had his arms twisted and his hair pulled, and was abused and spat upon. He looked away when their eyes met.

Then Percy shouted: "Stop! No more beating! We must take the thief back to the *bai* from whom he stole. She will decide!"

The notion of delivering the criminal to the scene of his crime and to his victim, like something out of a Hindi movie, appealed to this crowd. Kersi managed to shake off his numbness. Following Percy's example, he grabbed Francis by the arm and collar, signifying that this was their captive, no longer to be bashed around.

In this manner they led Francis back to Firozsha Baag—past the tethered cow, past the *bunya*'s shop, past the overflowing gutters of Tar Gully. Every once in a while someone would punch Francis in the small of his back or on his head. But Percy would remind the crowd of the *bai* who had been robbed, whereupon the procession would resume in an orderly way.

A crowd was waiting outside C Block. More neighbours had gathered, including the solitary Muslim tenant in Firozsha Baag, from the ground floor of B Block, and his Muslim servant. Both had a long-standing grudge against Francis over some incident with a prostitute, and were pleased at his predicament.

Francis was brought before Najamai. He was in tears

and his knees kept buckling. "Why, Francis?" asked Najamai. "Why?"

Suddenly, a neighbour stepped out of the crowd and slapped him hard across the face: "You *budmaash*! You have no shame? Eating her food, earning money from her, then stealing from her, you rascal?"

At the slap, the gathering started to move in for a fresh round of thrashing. But Najamai screamed and the crowd froze. Francis threw himself at her feet, weeping. "*Bai*," he begged, "you hit me, you kick me, do whatever you want to me. But please don't let them, please!"

While he knelt before her, the Muslim servant saw his chance and moved swiftly. He swung his leg and kicked Francis powerfully in the ribs before the others could pull him away. Francis yelped like a dog and keeled over.

Najamai was formally expressing her gratitude to Silloo. "How brave your two sons are. If they had not gone after that rogue I would never have seen my eighty rupees again. Say thanks to Percy and Kersi, God bless them, such fine boys." Both of them pointedly ignored Tehmina who, by this time, had been established as the minor villain in the piece, for putting temptation in Francis's path.

Meanwhile, the crowd had dispersed. Tehmina was chatting with the Muslim neighbour. Having few friends in this building, he was endeavouring to ingratiate himself with her while she was still vulnerable, and before she recovered from C Block's excommunication. By the light of the full moon he sympathized with her version of the episode.

"Najamai knows my eyes are useless till these cataracts are removed. Yet she wants me to keep her keys, look after her flat." The cloves ventured to her lips, agitated, but she expertly sucked them back to the safety of her cheeks. "How was I to know what Francis would do? If only I could have seen his eyes. It is always so dark in that hallway." And the Muslim neighbour shook his head slowly, making clucking sounds with his tongue to show he understood perfectly.

*　　*　　*

Back in her flat, Najamai chuckled as she pictured the two boys returning with Francis. "How silly they looked. Going after poor Francis with their big bats! As if he would ever have hurt them. Wonder what the police will do to him now." She went into the kitchen, sniffing. A smell of ammonia was in the air and a pool of yellowish liquid stood where Francis had been hiding behind the kitchen door. She bent down, puzzled, and sniffed again, then realized he must have lost control of his bladder when she screamed.

She mopped and cleaned up, planning to tell Silloo tomorrow of her discovery. She would also have to ask her to find someone to bring the rations next week. Maybe it was time to overcome her aversion to full-time servants and hire one who would live here, and cook and clean, and look after the flat. Someone who would also provide company for her, sometimes it felt so lonely being alone in the flat.

Najamai finished in the kitchen. She went to the bedroom, lowered her weight into the easy chair and picked up the Boyces' Sunday paper.

Kersi was in the bathroom. He felt like throwing up, but returned to the bedroom after retching without success. He sat on the bed and picked up his bat. He ripped off the rubber grip and slowly, meditatively, started to tear the freshly glued cord from around the handle, bit by bit, circle by circle.

Soon, the cord lay on the floor in a black tangled heap, and the handle looked bald, exposed, defenceless. Never before had Kersi seen his cricket bat in this flayed and naked state. He stood up, grasped the handle with both hands, rested the blade at an angle to the floor, then smashed his foot down upon it. There was a loud crack as the handle snapped.

BHARATI MUKHERJEE

A writer of Bengali-Indian origin, Bharati Mukherjee was born in 1940 in Calcutta. As a young child she traveled to England, returning to India after Independence in the early fifties with a developing command of English. By the time she was ten, she had written numerous short stories and knew she wanted to become a writer. She earned a BA from the University of Calcutta in 1959 and an MA from the University of Baroba, India. Mukherjee attended the Iowa Writers Conference where she received an MFA and earned a PhD from the University of Iowa in 1969. She married the Canadian writer Clark Blaise and lived and taught in Canada, eventually returning to the U.S. In 1989, she settled at the University of California, Berkeley.

Her novels include *The Tiger's Daughter* (1971), *Wife* (1975), *Jasmine* (1989), *The Holder of the World* (1993), *Leave It to Me* (1997), *Desirable Daughters* (2002), and *Tree Bride* (2004). She has published two collections of short stories, *Darkness* (1985) and *The Middleman and Other Stories* (1988). The latter won the National Book Critics Circle Award for best fiction.

According to her biographer, Fakrul Alam, Mukherjee's writing has explored the phases of her own life: her exile from India, her life as an Indian expatriate in Canada, and currently her life in the U.S. as an immigrant in a country of immigrants.

A Wife's Story

Imre says forget it, but I'm going to write David Mamet. So Patels are hard to sell real estate to. You buy them a beer, whisper Glengarry Glen Ross, and they smell swamp instead of sun and surf. They work hard, eat cheap, live ten to a room, stash their savings under futons in Queens, and before you know it they own half of Hoboken. You say, where's the sweet gullibility that made this nation great?

Polish jokes, Patel jokes: that's not why I want to write Mamet.

Seen their women?

Everybody laughs. Imre laughs. The dozing fat man with the Barnes & Noble sack between his legs, the woman next to him, the usher, everybody. The theater isn't so dark that they can't see me. In my red silk sari I'm conspicuous. Plump, gold paisleys sparkle on my chest.

The actor is just warming up. *Seen their women?* He plays a salesman, he's had a bad day and now he's in a Chinese restaurant trying to loosen up. His face is pink. His wool-blend slacks are creased at the crotch. We bought our tickets at half-price, we're sitting in the front row, but at the edge, and we see things we shouldn't be seeing. At least I do, or think I do. Spittle, actors goosing each other, little winks, streaks of makeup.

Maybe they're improvising dialogue too. Maybe Mamet's provided them with insult kits, Thursdays for Chinese, Wednesdays for Hispanics, today for Indians. Maybe they get together before curtain time, see an Indian woman settling in the front row off to the side, and say to each other: "Hey, forget Friday. Let's get *her* today. See if she cries. See if she walks out." Maybe, like the salesmen they play, they have a little bet on.

Maybe I shouldn't feel betrayed.

Their women, he goes again. *They look like they've just been fucked by a dead cat.*

The fat man hoots so hard he nudges my elbow off our shared armrest.

"Imre. I'm going home." But Imre's hunched so far forward he doesn't hear. English isn't his best language. A refugee from Budapest, he has to listen hard. "I didn't pay eighteen dollars to be insulted."

I don't hate Mamet. It's the tyranny of the American dream that scares me. First, you don't exist. Then you're invisible. Then you're funny. Then you're disgusting. Insult, my American friends will tell me, is a kind of acceptance. No instant dignity here. A play like this, back home, would cause riots. Communal, racist, and antisocial. The actors wouldn't make it off stage. This play, and all these awful feelings, would be safely locked up.

I long, at times, for clear-cut answers. Offer me instant dignity, today, and I'll take it.

"What?" Imre moves toward me without taking his eyes off the actor. "Come again?"

Tears come. I want to stand, scream, make an awful scene. I long for ugly, nasty rage.

The actor is ranting, flinging spittle. *Give me a chance. I'm not finished, I can get back on the board. I tell that asshole, give me a real lead. And what does that asshole give me? Patels. Nothing but Patels.*

This time Imre works an arm around my shoulders "Panna, what is Patel? Why are you taking it all so personally?"

I shrink from his touch, but I don't walk out. Expensive girls' schools in Lausanne and Bombay have trained me to behave well. My manners are exquisite, my feelings are delicate, my gestures refined, my moods undetectable. They have seen me through riots, uprooting, separation, my son's death.

"I'm not taking it personally."

The fat man looks at us. The woman looks too, and shushes.

I stare back at the two of them. Then I stare, mean and cool, at the man's elbow. Under the bright blue polyester Hawaiian shirt sleeve, the elbow looks soft and runny. "Excuse me," I say. My voice has the effortless meanness of well-bred displaced Third World women, though my rhetoric has been learned elsewhere. "You're exploiting my space."

Startled, the man snatches his arm away from me. He cradles it against his breast. By the time he's ready with comebacks, I've turned my back on him. I've probably ruined the first act for him. I know I've ruined it for Imre.

It's not my fault; it's the *situation.* Old colonies wear

down. Patels—the new pioneers—have to be suspicious. Idi Amin's lesson is permanent. AT&T wires move good advice from continent to continent. Keep all assets liquid. Get into 7-11s, get out of condos and motels. I know how both sides feel, that's the trouble. The Patel sniffing out scams, the sad salesmen on the stage: postcolonialism has made me their referee. It's hate I long for; simple, brutish, partisan hate.

After the show Imre and I make our way toward Broadway. Sometimes he holds my hand; it doesn't mean anything more than that crazies and drunks are crouched in doorways. Imre's been here over two years, but he's stayed very old-world, very courtly, openly protective of women. I met him in a seminar on special ed. last semester. His wife is a nurse somewhere in the Hungarian countryside. There are two sons, and miles of petitions for their emigration. My husband manages a mill two hundred miles north of Bombay. There are no children.

"You make things tough on yourself," Imre says. He assumed Patel was a Jewish name or maybe Hispanic; everything makes equal sense to him. He found the play tasteless, he worried about the effect of vulgar language on my sensitive ears. "You have to let go a bit." And as though to show me how to let go, he breaks away from me, bounds ahead with his head ducked tight, then dances on amazingly jerky legs. He's a Magyar, he often tells me, and deep down, he's an Asian too. I catch glimpses of it, knife-blade Attila cheekbones, despite the blondish hair. In his faded jeans and leather jacket, he's a rock video star. I watch MTV for hours in the apartment when Charity's working the evening shift at Macy's. I listen to WPLJ on Charity's earphones. Why should I be ashamed? Television in India is so uplifting.

Imre stops as suddenly as he'd started. People walk around us. The summer sidewalk is full of theatergoers in seersucker suits; Imre's year-round jacket is out of place. European. Cops in twos and threes huddle, lightly tap their thighs with nightsticks and smile at me with benevolence. I want to wink at them, get us all in trouble, tell them the crazy dancing man is from the Warsaw

Pact. I'm too shy to break into dance on Broadway. So
I hug Imre instead.

The hug takes him by surprise. He wants me to let
go, but he doesn't really expect me to let go. He stag-
gers, though I weigh no more than 104 pounds, and with
him, I pitch forward slightly. Then he catches me, and
we walk arm in arm to the bus stop. My husband would
never dance or hug a woman on Broadway. Nor would
my brothers. They aren't stuffy people, but they went to
Anglican boarding schools and they have a well-
developed sense of what's silly.

"Imre." I squeeze his big, rough hand. "I'm sorry I
ruined the evening for you."

"You did nothing of the kind." He sounds tired.
"Let's not wait for the bus. Let's splurge and take a
cab instead."

Imre always has unexpected funds. The Network, he
calls it, Class of '56.

In the back of the cab, without even trying, I feel light,
almost free. Memories of Indian destitutes mix with the
hordes of New York street people, and they float free,
like astronauts, inside my head. I've made it. I'm making
something of my life. I've left home, my husband, to get
a Ph.D. in special ed. I have a multiple-entry visa and a
small scholarship for two years. After that, we'll see. My
mother was beaten by her mother-in-law, my grandmother, when she'd registered for French lessons at the
Alliance Française. My grandmother, the eldest daughter
of a rich zamindar, was illiterate.

Imre and the cabdriver talk away in Russian. I keep
my eyes closed. That way I can feel the floaters better.
I'll write Mamet tonight. I feel strong, reckless. Maybe
I'll write Steven Spielberg too; tell him that Indians don't
eat monkey brains.

We've made it. Patels must have made it. Mamet,
Spielberg: they're not condescending to us. Maybe
they're a little bit afraid.

Charity Chin, my roommate, is sitting on the floor drinking Chablis out of a plastic wineglass. She is five foot
six, three inches taller than me, but weighs a kilo and a

half less than I do. She is a "hands" model. Orientals are supposed to have a monopoly in the hands-modelling business, she says. She had her eyes fixed eight or nine months ago and out of gratitude sleeps with her plastic surgeon every third Wednesday.

"Oh, good," Charity says. "I'm glad you're back early. I need to talk."

She's been writing checks. MCI, Con Ed, Bonwit Teller. Envelopes, already stamped and sealed, form a pyramid between her shapely, knee-socked legs. The checkbook's cover is brown plastic, grained to look like cowhide. Each time Charity flips back the cover, white geese fly over sky-colored checks. She makes good money, but she's extravagant. The difference adds up to this shared, rent-controlled Chelsea one-bedroom.

"All right. Talk."

When I first moved in, she was seeing an analyst. Now she sees a nutritionist.

"Eric called. From Oregon."

"What did he want?"

"He wants me to pay half the rent on his loft for last spring. He asked me to move back, remember? He *begged* me."

Eric is Charity's estranged husband.

"What does your nutritionist say?" Eric now wears a red jumpsuit and tills the soil in Rajneeshpuram.

"You think Phil's a creep too, don't you? What else can he be when creeps are all I attract?"

Phil is a flutist with thinning hair. He's very touchy on the subject of *flautists* versus *flutists*. He's touchy on every subject, from music to books to foods to clothes. He teaches at a small college upstate, and Charity bought a used blue Datsun ("Nissan," Phil insists) last month so she could spend weekends with him. She returns every Sunday night, exhausted and exasperated. Phil and I don't have much to say to each other—he's the only musician I know; the men in my family are lawyers, engineers, or in business—but I like him. Around me, he loosens up. When he visits, he bakes us loaves of pumpernickel bread. He waxes our kitchen floor. Like many men in this country, he seems to me a displaced child, or even a woman, looking for something that passed him by, or for something that he can never have. If he thinks I'm not looking, he sneaks his hands under Charity's sweater, but there isn't too much there. Here, she's a model with high ambitions. In India, she'd be a flat-chested old maid.

I'm shy in front of the lovers. A darkness comes over me when I see them horsing around.

"It isn't the money," Charity says. Oh? I think. "He says he still loves me. Then he turns around and asks me for five hundred."

What's so strange about that, I want to ask. She still loves Eric, and Eric, red jumpsuit and all, is smart enough to know it. Love is a commodity, hoarded like any other. Mamet knows. But I say, "I'm not the person to ask about love." Charity knows that mine was a traditional Hindu marriage. My parents, with the help of a marriage broker, who was my mother's cousin, picked out a groom. All I had to do was get to know his taste in food.

It'll be a long evening, I'm afraid. Charity likes to confess. I unpleat my silk sari—it no longer looks too showy—wrap it in muslin cloth and put it away in a dresser drawer. Saris are hard to have laundered in Manhattan, though there's a good man in Jackson Heights. My next step will be to brew us a pot of chrysanthemum tea. It's a very special tea from the mainland. Charity's uncle gave it to us. I like him. He's a humpbacked, awkward, terrified man. He runs a gift store on Mott Street, and though he doesn't speak much English, he seems to have done well. Once upon a time he worked for the railways in Chengdu, Szechwan Province, and during the Wuchang Uprising, he was shot at. When I'm down, when I'm lonely for my husband, when I think of our son, or when I need to be held, I think of Charity's uncle. If I hadn't left home, I'd never have heard of the Wuchang Uprising. I've broadened my horizons.

Very late that night my husband calls me from Ahmadabad, a town of textile mills north of Bombay. My husband is a vice president at Lakshmi Cotton Mills. Lakshmi is the goddess of wealth, but LCM (Priv.), Ltd., is doing poorly. Lockouts, strikes, rock-throwings. My husband lives on digitalis, which he calls the food for our *yuga* of discontent.

"We had a bad mishap at the mill today." Then he says nothing for seconds.

The operator comes on. "Do you have the right party, sir? We're trying to reach Mrs. Butt."

"Bhatt," I insist. "*B* for Bombay, *H* for Haryana, *A* for Ahmadabad, double *T* for Tamil Nadu." It's a litany. "This is she."

"One of our lorries was firebombed today. Resulting in three deaths. The driver, old Karamchand, and his two children."

I know how my husband's eyes look this minute, how the eye rims sag and the yellow corneas shine and bulge with pain. He is not an emotional man—the Ahmadabad Institute of Management has trained him to cut losses, to look on the bright side of economic catastrophes— but tonight he's feeling low. I try to remember a driver named Karamchand, but can't. That part of my life is over, the way *trucks* have replaced *lorries* in my vocabu-lary, the way Charity Chin and her lurid love life have replaced inherited notions of marital duty. Tomorrow he'll come out of it. Soon he'll be eating again. He'll sleep like a baby. He's been trained to believe in turn-overs. Every morning he rubs his scalp with cantharidine oil so his hair will grow back again.

"It could be your car next." Affection, love. Who can tell the difference in a traditional marriage in which a wife still doesn't call her husband by his first name?

"No. They know I'm a flunky, just like them. Well paid, maybe. No need for undue anxiety, please."

Then his voice breaks. He says he needs me, he misses me, he wants me to come to him damp from my evening shower, smelling of sandalwood soap, my braid decor-ated with jasmines.

"I need you too."

"Not to worry, please," he says. "I am coming in a fortnight's time. I have already made arrangements."

Outside my window, fire trucks whine, up Eighth Avenue. I wonder if he can hear them, what he thinks of a life like mine, led amid disorder.

"I am thinking it'll be like a honeymoon. More or less."

When I was in college, waiting to be married, I imagined honeymoons were only for the more fashionable girls, the girls who came from slightly racy families, smoked Sobranies in the dorm lavatories and put up posters of Kabir Bedi, who was supposed to have made it as a big star in the West. My husband wants us to go to Niagara. I'm not to worry about foreign exchange. He's arranged for extra dollars through the Gujarati Network, with a cousin in San Jose. And he's bought four hundred more on the black market. "Tell me you need me. Panna, please tell me again."

I change out of the cotton pants and shirt I've been wearing all day and put on a sari to meet my husband at JFK. I don't forget the jewelry; the marriage necklace of *mangalsutra*, gold drop earrings, heavy gold bangles. I don't wear them every day. In this borough of vice and greed, who knows when, or whom, desire will overwhelm.

My husband spots me in the crowd and waves. He has lost weight, and changed his glasses. The arm, uplifted in a cheery wave, is bony, frail, almost opalescent.

In the Carey Coach, we hold hands. He strokes my fingers one by one. "How come you aren't wearing my mother's ring?"

"Because muggers know about Indian women," I say. They know with us it's 24-karat. His mother's ring is showy, in ghastly taste anywhere but India: a blood-red Burma ruby set in a gold frame of floral sprays. My mother-in-law got her guru to bless the ring before I left for the States.

He looks disconcerted. He's used to a different role. He's the knowing, suspicious one in the family. He seems to be sulking, and finally he comes out with it. "You've said nothing about my new glasses." I compliment him on the glasses, how chic and Western-executive they make him look. But I can't help the other things, necessities until he learns the ropes. I handle the money, buy the tickets. I don't know if this makes me unhappy.

Charity drives her Nissan upstate, so for two weeks we are to have the apartment to ourselves. This is more privacy than we ever had in India. No parents, no servants, to keep us modest. We play at housekeeping. Imre has lent us a hibachi, and I grill saffron chicken breasts. My husband marvels at the size of the Perdue hens. "They're big like peacocks, no? These Americans, they're really something!" He tries out pizzas, burgers, McNuggets. He chews. He explores. He judges. He loves it all, fears nothing, feels at home in the summer odors, the clutter of Manhattan streets. Since he thinks that the American palate is bland, he carries a bottle of red peppers in his pocket. I wheel a shopping cart down the aisles of the neighborhood Grand Union, and he follows, swiftly, greedily. He picks up hair rinses and high-protein diet powders. There's so much I already take for granted.

One night, Imre stops by. He wants us to go with him to a movie. In his work shirt and red leather tie, he looks arty or strung out. It's only been a week, but I feel as though I am really seeing him for the first time. The yellow hair worn very short at the sides, the wide, narrow lips. He's a good-looking man, but self-conscious, almost arrogant. He's picked the movie we should see. He always tells me what to see, what to read. He buys the *Voice*. He's a natural avant-gardist. For tonight he's chosen *Numéro Deux*.

"Is it a musical?" my husband asks. The Radio City Music Hall is on his list of sights to see. He's read up on the history of the Rockettes. He doesn't catch Imre's sympathetic wink.

Guilt, shame, loyalty. I long to be ungracious, not ingratiate myself with both men.

That night my husband calculates in rupees the money

we've wasted on Godard. "That refugee fellow, Nagy, must have a screw loose in his head. I paid very steep price for dollars on the black market."

Some afternoons we go shopping. Back home we hated shopping, but now it is a lovers' project. My husband's shopping list startles me. I feel I am just getting to know him. Maybe, like Imre, freed from the dignities of old-world culture, he too could get drunk and squirt Cheez Whiz on a guest. I watch him dart into stores in his gleaming leather shoes. Jockey shorts on sale in outdoor bins on Broadway entrance him. White tube socks with different bands of color delight him. He looks for microcassettes, for anything small and electronic and smuggleable. He needs a garment bag. He calls it a "wardrobe," and I have to translate.

"All of New York is having sales, no?"

My heart speeds watching him this happy. It's the third week in August, almost the end of summer, and the city smells ripe, it cannot bear more heat, more money, more energy.

"This is so smashing! The prices are so excellent!" Recklessly, my prudent husband signs away traveller's checks. How he intends to smuggle it all back I don't dare ask. With a microwave, he calculates, we could get rid of our cook.

This has to be love, I think. Charity, Eric, Phil: they may be experts on sex. My husband doesn't chase me around the sofa, but he pushes me down on Charity's battered cushions, and the man who has never entered the kitchen of our Ahmadabad house now comes toward me with a dish tub of steamy water to massage away the pavement heat.

Ten days into his vacation my husband checks out brochures for sightseeing tours. Shortline, Grayline, Crossroads: his new vinyl briefcase is full of schedules and pamphlets. While I make pancakes out of a mix, he comparison-shops. Tour number one costs $10.95 and will give us the World Trade Center, Chinatown, and the United Nations. Tour number three would take us both uptown *and* downtown for $14.95, but my husband

is absolutely sure he doesn't want to see Harlem. We
settle for tour number four: Downtown and the Dame.
It's offered by a new tour company with a small, dirty
office at Eighth and Forty-eighth.

The sidewalk outside the office is colorful with tourists. My husband sends me in to buy the tickets because
he has come to feel Americans don't understand his
accent.

The dark man, Lebanese probably, behind the counter
comes on too friendly. "Come on, doll, make my day!"
He won't say which tour is his. "Number four? Honey,
no! Look, you've wrecked me! Say you'll change your
mind." He takes two twenties and gives back change.
He holds the tickets, forcing me to pull. He leans closer.
"I'm off after lunch."

My husband must have been watching me from the
sidewalk. "What was the chap saying?" he demands. "I
told you not to wear pants. He thinks you are Puerto
Rican. He thinks he can treat you with disrespect."

The bus is crowded and we have to sit across the aisle
from each other. The tour guide begins his patter on
Forty-sixth. He looks like an actor, his hair bleached and
blow-dried. Up close he must look middle-aged, but
from where I sit his skin is smooth and his cheeks
faintly red.

"Welcome to the Big Apple, folks," The guide uses a
microphone. "Big Apple. That's what we native Manhattan degenerates call our city. Today we have guests from
fifteen foreign countries and six states from this U.S. of
A. That makes the Tourist Bureau real happy. And let
me assure you that while we may be the richest city in
the richest country in the world, it's okay to tip your
charming and talented attendant." He laughs. Then he
swings his hip out into the aisle and sings a song.

"And it's mighty fancy on old Delancey Street, you
know. . . ."

My husband looks irritable. The guide is, as expected,
a good singer. "The bloody man should be giving us
histories of buildings we are passing, no?" I pat his hand,
the mood passes. He cranes his neck. Our window seats
have both gone to Japanese. It's the tour of his life.

Next to this, the quick business trips to Manchester and Glasgow pale.

"And tell me what street compares to Mott Street, in July. . . ."

The guide wants applause. He manages a derisive laugh from the Americans up front. He's working the aisles now. "I coulda been somebody, right? I coulda been a star!" Two or three of us smile, those of us who recognize the parody. He catches my smile. The sun is on his harsh, bleached hair. "Right, your highness? Look, we gotta maharani with us! Couldn't I have been a star?"

"Right!" I say, my voice coming out a squeal. I've been trained to adapt; what else can I say?

We drive through traffic past landmark office buildings and churches. The guide flips his hands. "Art Deco," he keeps saying. I hear him confide to one of the Americans: "Beats me. I went to a cheap guide's school." My husband wants to know more about this Art Deco, but the guide sings another song.

"We made a foolish choice," my husband grumbles. "We are sitting in the bus only. We're not going into famous buildings." He scrutinizes the pamphlets in his jacket pocket. I think, at least it's air-conditioned in here. I could sit here in the cool shadows of the city forever.

Only five of us appear to have opted for the Downtown and the Dame tour. The others will ride back uptown past the United Nations after we've been dropped off at the pier for the ferry to the Statue of Liberty.

An elderly European pulls a camera out of his wife's designer tote bag. He takes pictures of the boats in the harbor, the Japanese in kimonos eating popcorn, scavenging pigeons, me. Then, pushing his wife ahead of him, he climbs back on the bus and waves to us. For a second I feel terribly lost. I wish we were on the bus going back to the apartment. I know I'll not be able to describe any of this to Charity, or to Imre. I'm too proud to admit I went on a guided tour.

The view of the city from the Circle Line ferry is seductive, unreal. The skyline wavers out of reach, but never quite vanishes. The summer sun pushes through fluffy clouds and dapples the glass of office towers. My husband looks thrilled, even more than he had on the shopping trips down Broadway. Tourists and dreamers, we have spent our life's savings to see this skyline, this statue.

"Quick, take a picture of me!" my husband yells as he moves toward a gap of railings. A Japanese matron has given up her position in order to change film. "Before the Twin Towers disappear!"

I focus, I wait for a large Oriental family to walk out of my range. My husband holds his pose tight against the railing. He wants to look relaxed, an international businessman at home in all the financial markets.

A bearded man slides across the bench toward me. "Like this," he says and helps me get my husband in focus. "You want me to take the photo for you?" His name, he says, is Goran. He is Goran from Yugoslavia, as though that were enough for tracking him down. Imre from Hungary. Panna from India. He pulls the old Leica out of my hand, signaling the Orientals to beat it, and clicks away. "I'm a photographer," he says. He could have been a camera thief. That's what my husband would have assumed. Somehow, I trusted. "Get you a beer?" he asks.

"I don't. Drink, I mean. Thank you very much." I say those last words very loud, for everyone's benefit. The odd bottles of Soave with Imre don't count.

"Too bad." Goran gives back the camera.

"Take one more!" my husband shouts from the railing. "Just to be sure!"

The island itself disappoints. The Lady has brutal scaffolding holding her in. The museum is closed. The snack bar is dirty and expensive. My husband reads out the prices to me. He orders two french fries and two Cokes. We sit at picnic tables and wait for the ferry to take us back.

"What was that hippie chap saying?"

As if I could say. A day-care center has brought its

kids, at least forty of them, to the island for the day. The kids, all wearing name tags, run around us. I can't help noticing how many are Indian. Even a Patel, probably a Bhatt if I looked hard enough. They toss hamburger bits at pigeons. They kick styrofoam cups. The pigeons are slow, greedy, persistent. I have to shoo one off the table top. I don't think my husband thinks about our son.

"What hippie?"

"The one on the boat. With the beard and the hair."

My husband doesn't look at me. He shakes out his paper napkin and tries to protect his french fries from pigeon feathers.

"Oh, him. He said he was from Dubrovnik." It isn't true, but I don't want trouble.

"What did he say about Dubrovnik?"

I know enough about Dubrovnik to get by. Imre's told me about it. And about Mostar and Zagreb. In Mostar white Muslims sing the call to prayer. I would like to see that before I die: white Muslims. Whole peoples have moved before me; they've adapted. The night Imre told me about Mostar was also the night I saw my first snow in Manhattan. We'd walked down to Chelsea from Columbia. We'd walked and talked and I hadn't felt tired at all.

"You're too innocent," my husband says. He reaches for my hand. "Panna," he cries with pain in his voice, and I am brought back from perfect, floating memories of snow, "I've come to take you back. I have seen how men watch you."

"What?"

"Come back, now. I have tickets. We have all the things we will ever need. I can't live without you."

A little girl with wiry braids kicks a bottle cap at his shoes. The pigeons wheel and scuttle around us. My husband covers his fries with spread-out fingers. "No kicking," he tells the girl. Her name, Beulah, is printed in green ink on a heart-shaped name tag. He forces a smile, and Beulah smiles back. Then she starts to flap her arms. She flaps, she hops. The pigeons go crazy for fries and scraps.

"Special ed. course is two years," I remind him. "I can't go back."

My husband picks up our trays and throws them into the garbage before I can stop him. He's carried disposability a little too far. "We've been taken," he says, moving toward the dock, though the ferry will not arrive for another twenty minutes. "The ferry costs only two dollars round-trip per person. We should have chosen tour number one for $10.95 instead of tour number four for $14.95."

With my Lebanese friend, I think. "But this way we don't have to worry about cabs. The bus will pick us up at the pier and take us back to midtown. Then we can walk home."

"New York is full of cheats and whatnot. Just like Bombay." He is not accusing me of infidelity. I feel dread all the same.

That night, after we've gone to bed, the phone rings. My husband listens, then hands the phone to me. "What is this woman saying?" He turns on the pink Macy's lamp by the bed. "I am not understanding these Negro people's accents."

The operator repeats the message. It's a cable from one of the directors of Lakshmi Cotton Mills. "Massive violent labor confrontation anticipated. Stop. Return posthaste. Stop. Cable flight details. Signed Kantilal Shah."

"It's not your factory," I say. "You're supposed to be on vacation."

"So, you are worrying about me? Yes? You reject my heartfelt wishes but you worry about me?" He pulls me close, slips the straps of my nightdress off my shoulder. "Wait a minute."

I wait, unclothed, for my husband to come back to me. The water is running in the bathroom. In the ten days he has been here he has learned American rites: deodorants, fragrances. Tomorrow morning he'll call Air India; tomorrow evening he'll be on his way back to Bombay. Tonight I should make up to him for my years away, the gutted trucks, the degree I'll never use in

India. I want to pretend with him that nothing has changed.

In the mirror that hangs on the bathroom door, I watch my naked body turn, the breasts, the thighs glow. The body's beauty amazes. I stand here shameless, in ways he has never seen me. I am free, afloat, watching somebody else.

R. K. NARAYAN

Born in 1906 in Madras, India, into a Hindu Brahmin family, Rasipuram Krishnaswami Narayan was sent to live with his grandmother and uncle at the age of two because of his mother's health problems and his father's numerous transfers to different schools as a headmaster. Narayan spoke and studied Tamil (one of the South Indian languages) at home, where his grandmother taught him about music, religion, and Indian mythology and literature. Simultaneously, he was the only Brahmin at the Lutheran mission school, where he studied English and the Christian Bible. He earned an undergraduate degree at Maharaja's College (now the University of Mysore) in 1930. Supported by his family, he began to write, setting his novels and stories in Malgudi, a fictional city in South India. He chronicled the life of Malgudi in extraordinary detail in fourteen novels and numerous stories published over more than six decades. His Malgudi characters range from people at the highest level of the Hindu religion to the middle-class Brahmin caste to which Narayan himself belongs, to the merchants, teachers, shopkeepers, clerks, herdsmen, civil servants, laborers, and beggars, whom he observes with compassion and understanding as well as with a wry sense of the comedy of daily life in India. During a BBC interview with Narayan, William Walsh observed, "Whatever happens in India happens in Malgudi, and whatever happens in Malgudi happens everywhere."

Narayan received numerous awards, including the National Prize of the Indian Literary Academy, the Sahitya Akademi Award for the novel *The Guide,* and the Padma Bhushan. Among his best-known novels are *Swami and Friends: A Novel of Malgudi* (1935), *The English Teacher* (1945), *The Guide* (1958), *The Vendor of Sweets* (1967), *The Painter of Signs* (1976), and *The World of*

Nagaraj (1990). Among his story collections are *Lawley Road: Thirty-Two Short Stories* (1956), *Gods, Demons and Others* (1965), *A Horse and Two Goats* (1970), *Under the Banyan Tree and Other Stories* (1985), and *The World of Malgudi* (2000). Several of Narayan's novels and stories were made into films and television series. He died in 2001.

A Horse and Two Goats

Of the seven hundred thousand villages dotting the map of India, in which the majority of India's five hundred million live, flourish, and die, Kritam was probably the tiniest, indicated on the district survey map by a microscopic dot, the map being meant more for the revenue official out to collect tax than for the guidance of the motorist, who in any case could not hope to reach it since it sprawled far from the highway at the end of a rough track furrowed up by the iron-hooped wheels of bullock carts. But its size did not prevent its giving itself the grandiose name Kritam, which meant in Tamil "coronet" or "crown" on the brow of this subcontinent. The village consisted of fewer than thirty houses, only one of them built with brick and cement. Painted a brilliant yellow and blue all over with gorgeous carvings of gods and gargoyles on its balustrade, it was known as the Big House. The other houses, distributed in four streets, were generally of bamboo thatch, straw, mud, and other unspecified material. Muni's was the last house in the fourth street, beyond which stretched the fields. In his prosperous days, Muni had owned a flock of forty sheep and goats and sallied forth every morning driving the flock to the highway a couple of miles away. There he would sit on the pedestal of a clay statue of a horse while his cattle grazed around. He carried a crook at the end of a bamboo pole and snapped foliage from the avenue trees to feed his flock; he also gathered faggots and dry sticks, bundled them, and carried them home for fuel at sunset.

His wife lit the domestic fire at dawn, boiled water in a mud pot, threw into it a handful of millet flour, added salt, and gave him his first nourishment for the day. When he started out, she would put in his hand a packed lunch, once again the same millet cooked into a little ball, which he could swallow with a raw onion at midday. She was old, but he was older and needed all the attention she could give him in order to be kept alive.

His fortunes had declined gradually, unnoticed. From a flock of forty which he drove into a pen at night, his stock had now come down to two goats, which were not worth the rent of a half rupee a month the Big House charged for the use of the pen in their backyard. And so the two goats were tethered to the trunk of a drumstick tree which grew in front of his hut and from which occasionally Muni could shake down drumsticks. This morning he got six. He carried them in with a sense of triumph. Although no one could say precisely who owned the tree, it was his because he lived in its shadow.

She said, "If you were content with the drumstick leaves alone, I could boil and salt some for you."

"Oh, I am tired of eating those leaves. I have a craving to chew the drumstick out of sauce, I tell you."

"You have only four teeth in your jaw, but your craving is for big things. All right, get the stuff for the sauce, and I will prepare it for you. After all, next year you may not be alive to ask for anything. But first get me all the stuff, including a measure of rice or millet, and I will satisfy your unholy craving. Our store is empty today. Dhall, chili, curry leaves, mustard, coriander, gingelley oil, and one large potato. Go out and get all this." He repeated the list after her in order not to miss any item and walked off to the shop in the third street.

He sat on an upturned packing case below the platform of the shop. The shopman paid no attention to him. Muni kept clearing his throat, coughing, and sneezing until the shopman could not stand it any more and demanded, "What ails you? You will fly off that seat into the gutter if you sneeze so hard, young man." Muni laughed inordinately, in order to please the shopman, at being called "young man." The shopman softened and said, "You have enough of the imp inside to keep a second wife busy, but for the fact the old lady is still alive." Muni laughed appropriately again at this joke. It completely won the shopman over; he liked his sense of humor to be appreciated. Muni engaged his attention in local gossip for a few minutes, which always ended with a reference to the postman's wife, who had eloped to the city some months before.

The shopman felt most pleased to hear the worst of the postman, who had cheated him. Being an itinerant postman, he returned home to Kritam only once in ten days and every time managed to slip away again without passing the shop in the third street. By thus humoring the shopman, Muni could always ask for one or two items of food, promising repayment later. Some days the shopman was in a good mood and gave in, and sometimes he would lose his temper suddenly and bark at Muni for daring to ask for credit. This was such a day, and Muni could not progress beyond two items listed as essential components. The shopman was also displaying a remarkable memory for old facts and figures and took out an oblong ledger to support his observations. Muni felt impelled to rise and flee. But his self-respect kept him in his seat and made him listen to the worst things about himself. The shopman concluded, "If you could find five rupees and a quarter, you will have paid off an ancient debt and then could apply for admission to swarga. How much have you got now?"

"I will pay you everything on the first of the next month."

"As always, and whom do you expect to rob by then?"

Muni felt caught and mumbled, "My daughter has sent word that she will be sending me money."

"Have you a daughter?" sneered the shopman. "And she is sending you money! For what purpose, may I know?"

"Birthday, fiftieth birthday," said Muni quietly.

"Birthday! How old are you?"

Muni repeated weakly, not being sure of it himself, "Fifty." He always calculated his age from the time of the great famine when he stood as high as the parapet around the village well, but who could calculate such things accurately nowadays with so many famines occurring? The shopman felt encouraged when other customers stood around to watch and comment. Muni thought helplessly, My poverty is exposed to everybody. But what can I do?

"More likely you are seventy," said the shopman. "You also forget that you mentioned a birthday five weeks ago when you wanted castor oil for your holy bath."

"Bath! Who can dream of a bath when you have to scratch the tank-bed for a bowl of water? We would all be parched and dead but for the Big House, where they let us take a pot of water from their well." After saying this Muni unobtrusively rose and moved off.

He told his wife, "That scoundrel would not give me anything. So go out and sell the drumsticks for what they are worth."

He flung himself down in a corner to recoup from the fatigue of his visit to the shop. His wife said, "You are getting no sauce today, nor anything else. I can't find anything to give you to eat. Fast till the evening, it'll do you good. Take the goats and be gone now," she cried and added, "Don't come back before the sun is down." He knew that if he obeyed her she would somehow conjure up some food for him in the evening. Only he must be careful not to argue and irritate her. Her temper was undependable in the morning but improved by evening time. She was sure to go out and work—grind corn in the Big House, sweep or scrub somewhere, and earn enough to buy foodstuff and keep a dinner ready for him in the evening.

Unleashing the goats from the drumstick tree, Muni started out, driving them ahead and uttering weird cries from time to time in order to urge them on. He passed through the village with his head bowed in thought. He did not want to look at anyone or be accosted. A couple of cronies lounging in the temple corridor hailed him, but he ignored their call. They had known him in the days of affluence when he lorded over a flock of fleecy sheep, not the miserable gawky goats that he had today. Of course he also used to have a few goats for those who fancied them, but real wealth lay in sheep; they bred fast and people came and bought the fleece in the shearing season; and then that famous butcher from the town came over on the weekly market days bringing him betel leaves, tobacco, and often enough some bhang, which they smoked in a hut in the coconut grove, undisturbed by wives and well-wishers. After a smoke one felt light and elated and inclined to forgive everyone including that brother-in-law of his who had once tried to set fire to his home. But all this seemed like the memories of a previous birth. Some pestilence afflicted his cattle (he could of course guess who had laid his animals under a curse), and even the friendly butcher would not touch one at half the price . . . and now here he was left with the two scraggy creatures. He wished someone would rid him of their company, too. The shopman had said that he was seventy. At seventy, one only waited to be summoned by God. When he was dead what would his wife do? They had lived in each other's company since they were children. He was told on their day of wedding that he was ten years old and she was eight. During the wedding ceremony they had had to recite their respective ages and names. He had thrashed her only a few times in their career, and later she had the upper hand. Progeny, none. Perhaps a large progeny would have brought him the blessing of the gods. Fertility brought merit. People with fourteen sons were always so prosperous and at peace with the world and themselves. He recollected the thrill he had felt when he mentioned a daughter to that shopman; although it was not believed, what if he did not have a daughter?—his cousin in the next village had many daughters, and any one of them was as good as his; he was fond of them all and would buy them sweets if he could afford it. Still, everyone in the village whispered behind their backs that Muni and his wife were a barren couple. He avoided looking at anyone; they all professed to be so high up, and everyone else in the village had more money than he. "I am the poorest fellow in our caste and no wonder that they spurn me, but I won't look at them either," and so he passed on with his eyes downcast along the

edge of the street, and people left him also very much
alone, commenting only to the extent, "Ah, there he
goes with his two goats; if he slits their throats, he may
have more peace of mind." "What has he to worry about
anyway? They live on nothing and have none to worry
about." Thus people commented when he passed
through the village. Only on the outskirts did he lift his
head and look up. He urged and bullied the goats until
they meandered along to the foot of the horse statue on
the edge of the village. He sat on its pedestal for the
rest of the day. The advantage of this was that he could
watch the highway and see the lorries and buses pass
through to the hills, and it gave him a sense of belonging
to a larger world. The pedestal of the statue was broad
enough for him to move around as the sun travelled up
and westward; or he could also crouch under the belly
of the horse, for shade.

The horse was nearly life-size, molded out of clay,
baked, burnt, and brightly colored, and reared its head
proudly, prancing its forelegs in the air and flourishing
its tail in a loop; beside the horse stood a warrior with
scythe-like mustachios, bulging eyes, and aquiline nose.
The old image-makers believed in indicating a man of
strength by bulging out his eyes and sharpening his
moustache tips, and also decorated the man's chest with
beads which looked today like blobs of mud through the
ravages of sun and wind and rain (when it came), but
Muni would insist that he had known the beads to sparkle like the nine gems at one time in his life. The horse
itself was said to have been as white as a dhobi-washed
sheet, and had had on its back a cover of pure brocade
of red and black lace, matching the multicolored sash
around the waist of the warrior. But none in the village
remembered the splendor as no one noticed its existence. Even Muni, who spent all his waking hours at its
foot, never bothered to look up. It was untouched even
by the young vandals of the village who gashed tree
trunks with knives and tried to topple off milestones and
inscribed lewd designs on all walls. This statue had been
closer to the population of the village at one time, when
this spot bordered the village; but when the highway was

laid through (or perhaps when the tank and wells dried up completely here) the village moved a couple of miles inland.

Muni sat at the foot of the statue, watching his two goats graze in the arid soil among the cactus and lantana bushes. He looked at the sun; it was tilted westward no doubt, but it was not the time yet to go back home; if he went too early his wife would have no food for him. Also he must give her time to cool off her temper and feel sympathetic, and then she would scrounge and manage to get some food. He watched the mountain road for a time signal. When the green bus appeared around the bend he could leave, and his wife would feel pleased that he had let the goats feed long enough.

He noticed now a new sort of vehicle coming down at full speed. It looked like both a motor car and a bus. He used to be intrigued by the novelty of such spectacles, but of late work was going on at the source of the river on the mountain and an assortment of people and traffic went past him, and he took it all casually and described to his wife, later in the day, everything he saw. Today, while he observed the yellow vehicle coming down, he was wondering how to describe it later to his wife, when it sputtered and stopped in front of him. A red-faced foreigner, who had been driving it, got down and went round it, stooping, looking, and poking under the vehicle; then he straightened himself up, looked at the dashboard, stared in Muni's direction, and approached him. "Excuse me, is there a gas station nearby, or do I have to wait until another car comes—" He suddenly looked up at the clay horse and cried, "Marvellous," without completing his sentence. Muni felt he should get up and run away, and cursed his age. He could not readily put his limbs into action; some years ago he could outrun a cheetah, as happened once when he went to the forest to cut fuel and it was then that two of his sheep were mauled—a sign that bad times were coming. Though he tried, he could not easily extricate himself from his seat, and then there was also the problem of the goats. He could not leave them behind.

The red-faced man wore khaki clothes—evidently a

policeman or a soldier. Muni said to himself, He will chase or shoot if I start running. Some dogs chase only those who run—O Siva, protect me. I don't know why this man should be after me. Meanwhile the foreigner cried, "Marvellous!" again, nodding his head. He paced around the statue with his eyes fixed on it. Muni sat frozen for a while, and then fidgeted and tried to edge away. Now the other man suddenly pressed his palms together in a salute, smiled, and said, "Namaste! How do you do?"

At which Muni spoke the only English expressions he had learnt, "Yes, no." Having exhausted his English vocabulary, he started in Tamil: "My name is Muni. These two goats are mine, and no one can gainsay it—though our village is full of slanderers these days who will not hesitate to say that what belongs to a man doesn't belong to him." He rolled his eyes and shuddered at the thought of evil-minded men and women peopling his village.

The foreigner faithfully looked in the direction indicated by Muni's fingers, gazed for a while at the two goats and the rocks, and with a puzzled expression took out his silver cigarette case and lit a cigarette. Suddenly remembering the courtesies of the season, he asked, "Do you smoke?" Muni answered "Yes, no." Whereupon the red-faced man took a cigarette and gave it to Muni, who received it with surprise, having had no offer of a smoke from anyone for years now. Those days when he smoked bhang were gone with his sheep and the large-hearted butcher. Nowadays he was not able to find even matches, let alone bhang. (His wife went across and borrowed a fire at dawn from a neighbor.) He had always wanted to smoke a cigarette; only once did the shopman give him one on credit, and he remembered how good it had tasted. The other flicked the lighter open and offered a light to Muni. Muni felt so confused about how to act that he blew on it and put it out. The other, puzzled but undaunted, flourished his lighter, presented it again, and lit Muni's cigarette. Muni drew a deep puff and started coughing; it was racking, no doubt, but extremely pleasant. When his cough subsided he wiped his eyes and took stock of the situation, understanding that the other man was not an Inquisitor of any kind. Yet, in order to make sure, he remained wary. No need to run away from a man who gave him such a potent smoke. His head was reeling from the effect of one of those strong American cigarettes made from roasted tobacco. The man said, "I come from New York," took out a wallet from his hip pocket, and presented his card.

Muni shrank away from the card. Perhaps he was trying to present a warrant and arrest him. Beware of khaki, one part of his mind warned. Take all the cigarettes or bhang or whatever is offered, but don't get caught. Beware of khaki. He wished he weren't seventy as the shopman had said. At seventy one didn't run, but surrendered to whatever came. He could only ward off trouble by talk. So he went on, all in the chaste Tamil for which Kritam was famous. (Even the worst detractors could not deny that the famous poetess Avaiyar was born in this area, although no one could say whether it was in Kritam or Kuppam, the adjoining village.) Out of this heritage the Tamil language gushed through Muni in an unimpeded flow. He said, "Before God, sir, Bhagwan, who sees everything, I tell you, sir, that we know nothing of the case. If the murder was committed, whoever did it will not escape. Bhagwan is all-seeing. Don't ask me about it. I know nothing." A body had been found mutilated and thrown under a tamarind tree at the border between Kritam and Kuppam a few weeks before, giving rise to much gossip and speculation. Muni added an explanation. "Anything is possible there. People over there will stop at nothing." The foreigner nodded his head and listened courteously though he understood nothing.

"I am sure you know when this horse was made," said the red man and smiled ingratiatingly.

Muni reacted to the relaxed atmosphere by smiling himself, and pleaded, "Please go away, sir, I know nothing. I promise we will hold him for you if we see any bad character around, and we will bury him up to his neck in a coconut pit if he tries to escape; but our village has always had a clean record. Must definitely be the other village."

Now the red man implored, "Please, please, I will speak slowly, please try to understand me. Can't you understand even a simple word of English? Everyone in this country seems to know English. I have gotten along with English everywhere in this country, but you don't speak it. Have you any religious or spiritual scruples against English speech?"

Muni made some indistinct sounds in his throat and shook his head. Encouraged, the other went on to explain at length, uttering each syllable with care and deliberation. Presently he sidled over and took a seat beside the old man, explaining, "You see, last August, we probably had the hottest summer in history, and I was working in shirt-sleeves in my office on the fortieth floor of the Empire State Building. We had a power failure one day, you know, and there I was stuck for four hours, no elevator, no air conditioning. All the way in the train I kept thinking, and the minute I reached home in Connecticut, I told my wife, Ruth, 'We will visit India this winter, it's time to look at other civilizations.' Next day she called the travel agent first thing and told him to fix it, and so here I am. Ruth came with me but is staying back at Srinagar, and I am the one doing the rounds and joining her later."

Muni looked reflective at the end of this long oration and said, rather feebly, "Yes, no," as a concession to the other's language, and went on in Tamil, "When I was this high"—he indicated a foot high—"I had heard my uncle say . . ."

No one can tell what he was planning to say, as the other interrupted him at this stage to ask, "Boy, what is the secret of your teeth? How old are you?"

The old man forgot what he had started to say and remarked, "Sometimes we too lose our cattle. Jackals or cheetahs may sometimes carry them off, but sometimes it is just theft from over in the next village, and then we will know who has done it. Our priest at the temple can see in the camphor flame the face of the thief, and when he is caught . . ." He gestured with his hands a perfect mincing of meat.

The American watched his hands intently and said, "I know what you mean. Chop something? Maybe I am holding you up and you want to chop wood? Where is your axe? Hand it to me and show me what to chop. I do enjoy it, you know, just a hobby. We get a lot of driftwood along the backwater near my house, and on Sundays I do nothing but chop wood for the fireplace. I really feel different when I watch the fire in the fireplace, although it may take all the sections of the Sunday *New York Times* to get a fire started." And he smiled at this reference.

Muni felt totally confused but decided the best thing would be to make an attempt to get away from this place. He tried to edge out, saying, "Must go home," and turned to go. The other seized his shoulder and said desperately, "Is there no one, absolutely no one here, to translate for me?" He looked up and down the road, which was deserted in this hot afternoon; a sudden gust of wind churned up the dust and dead leaves on the roadside into a ghostly column and propelled it toward the mountain road. The stranger almost pinioned Muni's back to the statue and asked, "Isn't this statue yours? Why don't you sell it to me?"

The old man now understood the reference to the horse, thought for a second, and said in his own language, "I was an urchin this high when I heard my grandfather explain this horse and warrior, and my grandfather himself was this high when he heard his grandfather, whose grandfather . . ."

The other man interrupted him. "I don't want to seem to have stopped here for nothing. I will offer you a good price for this," he said, indicating the horse. He had concluded without the least doubt that Muni owned this mud horse. Perhaps he guessed by the way he sat on its pedestal, like other souvenir sellers in this country presiding over their wares.

Muni followed the man's eyes and pointing fingers and dimly understood the subject matter and, feeling relieved that the theme of the mutilated body had been aban-

doned at least for the time being, said again, enthusiasti-
cally, "I was this high when my grandfather told me
about this horse and the warrior, and my grandfather
was this high when he himself . . ." and he was getting
into a deeper bog of reminiscence each time he tried to
indicate the antiquity of the statue.

The Tamil that Muni spoke was stimulating even as
pure sound, and the foreigner listened with fascination.
"I wish I had my tape-recorder here," he said, assuming
the pleasantest expression. "Your language sounds wonderful. I get a kick out of every word you utter, here"—
he indicated his ears—"but you don't have to waste your
breath in sales talk. I appreciate the article. You don't
have to explain its points."

"I never went to a school, in those days only Brahmin
went to schools, but we had to go out and work in the
fields morning till night, from sowing to harvest time . . .
and when Pongal came and we had cut the harvest, my
father allowed me to go out and play with others at the
tank, and so I don't know the Parangi language you
speak, even little fellows in your country probably speak
the Parangi language, but here only learned men and
officers know it. We had a postman in our village who
could speak to you boldly in your language, but his wife
ran away with someone and he does not speak to anyone
at all nowadays. Who would if a wife did what she did?
Women must be watched; otherwise they will sell themselves and the home." And he laughed at his own quip.

The foreigner laughed heartily, took out another cigarette, and offered it to Muni, who now smoked with
ease, deciding to stay on if the fellow was going to be
so good as to keep up his cigarette supply. The American now stood up on the pedestal in the attitude of a
demonstrative lecturer and said, running his finger along
some of the carved decorations around the horse's neck,
speaking slowly and uttering his words syllable by syllable, "I could give a sales talk for this better than anyone
else. . . . This is a marvelous combination of yellow and
indigo, though faded now. . . . How do you people of
this country achieve these flaming colors?"

Muni, now assured that the subject was still the horse

and not the dead body, said, "This is our guardian, it means death to our adversaries. At the end of Kali Yuga, this world and all other worlds will be destroyed, and the Redeemer will come in the shape of a horse called Kalki; this horse will come to life and gallop and trample down all bad men." As he spoke of bad men the figures of his shopman and his brother-in-law assumed concrete forms in his mind, and he revelled for a moment in the predicament of the fellow under the horse's hoof: served him right for trying to set fire to his home. . . .

While he was brooding on this pleasant vision, the foreigner utilized the pause to say, "I assure you that this will have the best home in the U.S.A. I'll push away the bookcase, you know I love books and am a member of five book clubs, and the choice and bonus volumes mount up to a pile really in our living room, as high as this horse itself. But they'll have to go. Ruth may disapprove, but I will convince her. The TV may have to be shifted, too. We can't have everything in the living room. Ruth will probably say what about when we have a party? I'm going to keep him right in the middle of the room. I don't see how that can interfere with the party—we'll stand around him and have our drinks."

Muni continued his description of the end of the world. "Our pundit discoursed at the temple once how the oceans are going to close over the earth in a huge wave and swallow us—this horse will grow bigger than the biggest wave and carry on its back only the good people and kick into the floods the evil ones—plenty of them about—" he said reflectively. "Do you know when it is going to happen?" he asked.

The foreigner now understood by the tone of the other that a question was being asked and said, "How am I transporting it? I can push the seat back and make room in the rear. That van can take in an elephant"—waving precisely at the back of the seat.

Muni was still hovering on visions of avatars and said again, "I never missed our pundit's discourses at the temple in those days during every bright half of the month, although he'd go on all night, and he told us that

Vishnu is the highest god. Whenever evil men trouble us, he comes down to save us. He has come many times. The first time he incarnated as a great fish, and lifted the scriptures on his back when the flood and sea waves . . ."

"I am not a millionaire, but a modest businessman. My trade is coffee."

Amidst all this wilderness of obscure sound Muni caught the word "coffee" and said, "If you want to drink 'kapi,' drive further up, in the next town, they have Friday market and there they open 'kapi-otels'—so I learn from passersby. Don't think I wander about. I go nowhere and look for nothing." His thoughts went back to the avatars. "The first avatar was in the shape of a little fish in a bowl of water, but every hour it grew bigger and bigger and became in the end a huge whale which the seas could not contain, and on the back of the whale the holy books were supported, saved, and carried." Once he had launched on the first avatar, it was inevitable that he should go on to the next, a wild boar on whose tusk the earth was lifted when a vicious conqueror of the earth carried it off and hid it at the bottom of the sea. After describing this avatar Muni concluded, "God will always save us whenever we are troubled by evil beings. When we were young we staged at full moon the story of the avatars. That's how I know the stories; we played them all night until the sun rose, and sometimes the European collector would come to watch, bringing his own chair. I had a good voice and so they always taught me songs and gave me the women's roles. I was always Goddess Lakshmi, and they dressed me in a brocade sari, loaned from the Big House . . ."

The foreigner said, "I repeat I am not a millionaire. Ours is a modest business; after all, we can't afford to buy more than sixty minutes of TV time in a month, which works out to two minutes a day, that's all, although in the course of time we'll maybe sponsor a one-hour show regularly if our sales graph continues to go up . . ."

Muni was intoxicated by the memory of his theatrical days and was about to explain how he had painted his face and worn a wig and diamond earrings when the visitor, feeling that he had spent too much time already, said, "Tell me, will you accept a hundred rupees or not for the horse? I'd love to take the whiskered soldier also but no space for him this year. I'll have to cancel my air ticket and take a boat home, I suppose. Ruth can go by air if she likes, but I will go with the horse and keep him in my cabin all the way if necessary." And he smiled at the picture of himself voyaging across the seas hugging this horse. He added, "I will have to pad it with straw so that it doesn't break . . ."

"When we played *Ramayana,* they dressed me as Sita," added Muni. "A teacher came and taught us the songs for the drama and we gave him fifty rupees. He incarnated himself as Rama, and he alone could destroy Ravana, the demon with ten heads who shook all the worlds; do you know the story of *Ramayana*?"

"I have my station wagon as you see. I can push the seat back and take the horse in if you will just lend me a hand with it."

"Do you know *Mahabharata*? Krishna was the eighth avatar of Vishnu, incarnated to help the Five Brothers regain their kingdom. When Krishna was a baby he danced on the thousand-hooded giant serpent and trampled it to death; and then he suckled the breasts of the demoness and left them flat as a disc, though when she came to him her bosoms were large, like mounds of earth on the banks of a dug-up canal." He indicated two mounds with his hands.

The stranger was completely mystified by the gesture. For the first time he said, "I really wonder what you are saying because your answer is crucial. We have come to the point when we should be ready to talk business."

"When the tenth avatar comes, do you know where you and I will be?" asked the old man.

"Lend me a hand and I can lift off the horse from its pedestal after picking out the cement at the joints. We can do anything if we have a basis of understanding."

At this stage the mutual mystification was complete, and there was no need even to carry on a guessing game at the meaning of words. The old man chattered away in a spirit of balancing off the credits and debits of conversational exchange, and said in order to be on the credit side, "Oh, honorable one, I hope God has blessed you with numerous progeny. I say this because you seem to be a good man, willing to stay beside an old man and talk to him, while all day I have none to talk to except when somebody stops by to ask for a piece of tobacco. But I seldom have it, tobacco is not what it used to be at one time, and I have given up chewing. I cannot afford it nowadays." Noting the other's interest in his speech, Muni felt encouraged to ask, "How many children have you?" with appropriate gestures with his hands.

Realizing that a question was being asked, the red man replied, "I said a hundred," which encouraged Muni to go into details. "How many of your children are boys and how many girls? Where are they? Is your daughter married? Is it difficult to find a son-in-law in your country also?"

In answer to these questions the red man dashed his hand into his pocket and brought forth his wallet in order to take immediate advantage of the bearish trend in the market. He flourished a hundred-rupee currency note and said, "Well, this is what I meant."

The old man now realized that some financial element was entering their talk. He peered closely at the currency note, the like of which he had never seen in his life; he knew the five and ten by their colors although always in other people's hands, while his own earning at any time was in coppers and nickels. What was this man flourishing the note for? Perhaps asking for change. He laughed to himself at the notion of anyone coming to him for changing a thousand- or ten-thousand-rupee note. He said with a grin, "Ask our village headman, who is also a moneylender; he can change even a lakh of rupees in gold sovereigns if you prefer it that way; he thinks nobody knows, but dig the floor of his puja room and your head will reel at the sight of the hoard. The man disguises himself in rags just to mislead the public. Talk to the headman yourself because he goes mad at the sight of me. Someone took away his pumpkins with the creeper and he, for some reason, thinks it was me and my goats . . . that's why I never let my goats be seen anywhere near the farms." His eyes travelled to his goats nosing about, attempting to wrest nutrition from minute greenery peeping out of rock and dry earth.

The foreigner followed his look and decided that it would be a sound policy to show an interest in the old man's pets. He went up casually to them and stroked their backs with every show of courteous attention. Now the truth dawned on the old man. His dream of a lifetime was about to be realized. He understood that the red man was actually making an offer for the goats. He had reared them up in the hope of selling them some day and, with the capital, opening a small shop on this very spot. Sitting here, watching toward the hills, he had often dreamt how he would put up a thatched roof here, spread a gunny sack out on the ground, and display on it fried nuts, colored sweets, and green coconut for the thirsty and famished wayfarers on the highway, which was sometimes very busy. The animals were not prize ones for a cattle show, but he had spent his occasional savings to provide them some fancy diet now and then, and they did not look too bad. While he was reflecting thus, the red man shook his hand and left on his palm one hundred rupees in tens now, suddenly realizing that this was what the old man was asking. "It is all for you or you may share it if you have a partner."

The old man pointed at the station wagon and asked, "Are you carrying them off in that?"

"Yes, of course," said the other, understanding the transportation part of it.

The old man said, "This will be their first ride in a motor car. Carry them off after I get out of sight, otherwise they will never follow you, but only me even if I am travelling on the path to Yama Loka." He laughed at his own joke, brought his palms together in a salute, turned around and went off, and was soon out of sight beyond a clump of thicket.

The red man looked at the goats grazing peacefully. Perched on the pedestal of the horse, as the westerly sun touched off the ancient faded colors of the statue with a fresh splendor, he ruminated, "He must be gone to fetch some help, I suppose!" and settled down to wait.

When a truck came downhill, he stopped it and got the help of a couple of men to detach the horse from its pedestal and place it in his station wagon. He gave them five rupees each, and for a further payment they siphoned off gas from the truck, and helped him start his engine.

Muni hurried homeward with the cash securely tucked away at his waist in his dhoti. He shut the street door and stole up softly to his wife as she squatted before the lit oven wondering if by a miracle food would drop from the sky. Muni displayed his fortune for the day. She snatched the notes from him, counted them by the glow of the fire, and cried, "One hundred rupees! How did you come by it? Have you been stealing?"

"I have sold our goats to a red-faced man. He was absolutely crazy to have them, gave me all this money and carried them off in his motor car!"

Hardly had these words left his lips when they heard bleating outside. She opened the door and saw the two goats at her door. "Here they are!" she said. "What's the meaning of all this?"

He muttered a great curse and seized one of the goats by its ears and shouted, "Where is that man? Don't you know you are his? Why did you come back?" The goat only wriggled in his grip. He asked the same question of the other, too. The goat shook itself off. His wife glared at him and declared, "If you have thieved, the police will come tonight and break your bones. Don't involve me. I will go away to my parents. . . ."

SALMAN RUSHDIE

Indian-British novelist Salman Rushdie was born in Bombay in 1947. He received a BA in history from Kings College, Cambridge, in 1968, remaining in England to work, initially, as an advertising copywriter. His first novel, *Grimus*, published in 1975, is in the tradition of James Joyce, Günter Grass, and South American "magical realism." His 1981 novel, *Midnight's Children*, which takes place during Indian-Pakistani independence, was awarded the Booker Prize in 1981 and, in 2008, celebrating the fortieth year of the award, was voted the Best (Novel) of the Booker Prize.

Notoriety came to Rushdie in 1988 with the publication of *The Satanic Verses*. The novel was banned in India and elsewhere in the Muslim world for its irreverent depiction of the prophet Mohammad, and a *fatwa* (an order of execution) was issued against Rushdie by the Iranian Ayatollah Khomeini, who called the novel blasphemous. The *fatwa* was eventually lifted in 1998.

Among Rushdie's other works are the short story collection *East, West: Stories* (1994), *The Moor's Last Sigh* (1995), *The Ground Beneath Her Feet* (1999), *Shalimar the Clown* (2005), and *The Enchantress of Florence* (2005). Rushdie has received numerous awards and citations from Western countries; he remains a controversial figure in the Islamic world. In 2007, he was knighted by the Queen of England for "services to literature." In that same year, Rushdie began a five-year term as Distinguished Writer in Residence at Emory University in Atlanta, Georgia. In 2008, he was elected to the American Academy of Arts and Letters.

Good Advice Is Rarer Than Rubies

On the last Tuesday of the month, the dawn bus, its headlamps still shining, brought Miss Rehana to the gates of the British Consulate. It arrived pushing a cloud of dust, veiling her beauty from the eyes of strangers until she descended. The bus was brightly painted in multicoloured arabesques, and on the front it said "MOVE OVER DARLING" in green and gold letters; on the back it added "TATA-BATA" and also "O.K. GOOD-LIFE." Miss Rehana told the driver it was a beautiful bus, and he jumped down and held the door open for her, bowing theatrically as she descended.

Miss Rehana's eyes were large and black and bright enough not to need the help of antimony, and when the advice expert Muhammad Ali saw them he felt himself becoming young again. He watched her approaching the Consulate gates as the light strengthened, and asking the bearded lala who guarded them in a gold-buttoned khaki uniform with a cockaded turban when they would open. The lala, usually so rude to the Consulate's Tuesday women, answered Miss Rehana with something like courtesy.

"Half an hour," he said gruffly. "Maybe two hours. Who knows? The sahibs are eating their breakfast."

The dusty compound between the bus stop and the Consulate was already full of Tuesday women, some veiled, a few barefaced like Miss Rehana. They all looked frightened, and leaned heavily on the arms of uncles or brothers, who were trying to look confident. But Miss Rehana had come on her own, and did not seem at all alarmed.

Muhammad Ali, who specialised in advising the most vulnerable-looking of these weekly supplicants, found his feet leading him towards the strange, big-eyed, independent girl.

*   *   *

"Miss," he began. "You have come for permit to London, I think so?"

She was standing at a hot-snack stall in the little shanty-town by the edge of the compound, munching chilli-pakoras contentedly. She turned to look at him, and at close range those eyes did bad things to his digestive tract.

"Yes, I have."

"Then, please, you allow me to give some advice? Small cost only."

Miss Rehana smiled. "Good advice is rarer than rubies," she said. "But alas, I cannot pay. I am an orphan, not one of your wealthy ladies."

"Trust my grey hairs," Muhammad Ali urged her. "My advice is well tempered by experience. You will certainly find it good."

She shook her head. "I tell you I am a poor potato. There are women here with male family members, all earning good wages. Go to them. Good advice should find good money."

I am going crazy, Muhammad Ali thought, because he heard his voice telling her of its own volition, "Miss, I have been drawn to you by Fate. What to do? Our meeting was written. I also am a poor man only, but for you my advice comes free."

She smiled again. "Then I must surely listen. When Fate sends a gift, one receives good fortune."

He led her to the low wooden desk in his own special corner of the shanty-town. She followed, continuing to eat pakoras from a little newspaper packet. She did not offer him any.

Muhammad Ali put a cushion on the dusty ground. "Please to sit." She did as he asked. He sat cross-legged across the desk from her, conscious that two or three dozen pairs of male eyes were watching him enviously, that all the other shanty-town men were ogling the latest young lovely to be charmed by the old grey-hair fraud. He took a deep breath to settle himself.

"Name, please."

"Miss Rehana," she told him. "Fiancée of Mustafa Dar of Bradford, London."

"Bradford, England," he corrected her gently. "London is a town only, like Multan or Bahawalpur. England is a great nation full of the coldest fish in the world."

"I see. Thank you," she responded gravely, so that he was unsure if she was making fun of him.

"You have filled application form? Then let me see, please."

She passed him a neatly folded document in a brown envelope."

"Is it OK?" For the first time there was a note of anxiety in her voice.

He patted the desk quite near the place where her hand rested. "I am certain," he said. "Wait on and I will check."

She finished the pakoras while he scanned her papers.

"Tip-top," he pronounced at length. "All in order."

"Thank you for your advice," she said, making as if to rise. "I'll go now and wait by the gate."

"What are you thinking?" he cried loudly, smiting his forehead. "You consider this is easy business? Just give the form and poof, with a big smile they hand over the permit? Miss Rehana, I tell you, you are entering a worse place than any police station."

"Is it so, truly?" His oratory had done the trick. She was a captive audience now, and he would be able to look at her for a few moments longer.

Drawing another calming breath, he launched into his set speech. He told her that the sahibs thought that all the women who came on Tuesdays, claiming to be dependents of bus drivers in Luton or chartered accountants in Manchester, were crooks and liars and cheats.

She protested, "But then I will simply tell them that I, for one, am no such thing!"

Her innocence made him shiver with fear for her. She was a sparrow, he told her, and they were men with hooded eyes, like hawks. He explained that they would ask her questions, personal questions, questions such as a lady's own brother would be too shy to ask. They would ask if she was virgin, and, if not, what her fiancé's love-making habits were, and what secret nicknames they had invented for one another.

Muhammad Ali spoke brutally, on purpose, to lessen the shock she would feel when it, or something like it, actually happened. Her eyes remained steady, but her hands began to flutter at the edges of the desk.

He went on:

"They will ask you how many rooms are in your family home, and what colour are the walls, and what days do you empty the rubbish. They will ask your man's mother's third cousin's aunt's step-daughter's middle name. And all these things they have already asked your Mustafa Dar in his Bradford. And if you make one mistake, you are finished."

"Yes," she said, and he could hear her disciplining her voice. "And what is your advice, old man?"

It was at this point that Muhammad Ali usually began to whisper urgently, to mention that he knew a man, a very good type, who worked in the Consulate, and through him, for a fee, the necessary papers could be delivered, with all the proper authenticating seals. Business was good, because the women would often pay him five hundred rupees or give him a gold bracelet for his pains, and go away happy.

They came from hundreds of miles away—he normally made sure of this before beginning to trick them—so even when they discovered they had been swindled they were unlikely to return. They went away to Sargodha or Lalukhet and began to pack, and who knows at what point they found out they had been gulled, but it was at a too-late point, anyway.

Life is hard, and an old man must live by his wits. It was not up to Muhammad Ali to have compassion for these Tuesday women.

But once again his voice betrayed him, and instead of starting his customary speech it began to reveal to her his greatest secret.

"Miss Rehana," his voice said, and he listened to it in amazement, "you are a rare person, a jewel, and for you I will do what I would not do for my own daughter, perhaps. One document has come into my possession that can solve all your worries at one stroke."

"And what is this sorcerer's paper?" she asked, her eyes unquestionably laughing at him now.

His voice fell low-as-low.

"Miss Rehana, it is a British passport. Completely genuine and pukka goods. I have a good friend who will put your name and photo, and then, hey-presto, England there you come!"

He had said it!

Anything was possible now, on this day of his insanity. Probably he would give her the thing free-gratis, and then kick himself for a year afterwards.

Old fool, he berated himself. *The oldest fools are bewitched by the youngest girls.*

"Let me understand you," she was saying. "You are proposing I should commit a crime . . ."

"Not crime," he interposed. "Facilitation."

". . . and go to Bradford, London, illegally, and therefore justify the low opinion the Consulate sahibs have of us all. Old babuji, this is not good advice."

"Bradford, *England*," he corrected her mournfully. "You should not take my gift in such a spirit."

"Then how?"

"Bibi, I am a poor fellow, and I have offered this prize because you are so beautiful. Do not spit on my generosity. Take the thing. Or else don't take, go home, forget England, only do not go into that building and lose your dignity."

But she was on her feet, turning away from him, walking towards the gates, where the women had begun to cluster and the lala was swearing at them to be patient or none of them would be admitted at all.

"So be a fool," Muhammad Ali shouted after her. "What goes of my father's if you are?" (Meaning, what was it to him.)

She did not turn.

"It is the curse of our people," he yelled. "We are poor, we are ignorant, and we completely refuse to learn."

"Hey, Muhammad Ali," the woman at the betel-nut stall called across to him. "Too bad, she likes them young."

That day Muhammad Ali did nothing but stand around near the Consulate gates. Many times he scolded himself, *Go from here, old goof, lady does not desire to speak with you any further.* But when she came out, she found him waiting.

"Salaam, advice wallah," she greeted him.

She seemed calm, and at peace with him again, and he thought, *My God, ya Allah, she has pulled it off. The British sahibs also have been drowning in her eyes and she has got her passage to England.*

He smiled at her hopefully. She smiled back with no trouble at all.

"Miss Rehana Begum," he said, "felicitations, daughter, on what is obviously your hour of triumph."

Impulsively, she took his forearm in her hand.

"Come," she said. "Let me buy you a pakora to thank you for your advice and to apologise for my rudeness, too."

They stood in the dust of the afternoon compound near the bus, which was getting ready to leave. Coolies were tying bedding rolls to the roof. A hawker shouted at the passengers, trying to sell them love stories and green medicines, both of which cured unhappiness. Miss Rehana and a happy Muhammad Ali ate their pakoras sitting on the bus's "front mud-guard," that is, the bumper. The old advice expert began softly to hum a tune from a movie soundtrack. The day's heat was gone.

"It was an arranged engagement," Miss Rehana said all at once. "I was nine years old when my parents fixed it. Mustafa Dar was already thirty at that time, but my father wanted someone who could look after me as he had done himself and Mustafa was a man known to Daddyji as a solid type. Then my parents died and Mustafa Dar went to England and said he would send for me. That was many years ago. I have his photo, but he is like a stranger to me. Even his voice, I do not recognise it on the phone."

The confession took Muhammad Ali by surprise, but he nodded with what he hoped looked like wisdom.

"Still and after all," he said, "one's parents act in one's best interests. They found you a good and honest man who has kept his word and sent for you. And now you have a lifetime to get to know him, and to love."

He was puzzled, now, by the bitterness that had infected her smile.

"But, old man," she asked him, "why have you already packed me and posted me off to England?"

He stood up, shocked.

"You looked happy—so I just assumed . . . excuse me, but they turned you down or what?"

"I got all their questions wrong," she replied. "Distinguishing marks I put on the wrong cheeks, bathroom decor I completely redecorated, all absolutely topsy-turvy, you see."

"But what to do? How will you go?"

"Now I will go back to Lahore and my job. I work in a great house, as ayah to three good boys. They would have been sad to see me leave."

"But this is tragedy!" Muhammad Ali lamented. "Oh, how I pray that you had taken up my offer! Now, but, it is not possible, I regret to inform. Now they have your form on file, cross-check can be made, even the passport will not suffice.

"It is spoilt, all spoilt, and it could have been so easy if advice had been accepted in good time."

"I do not think," she told him, "I truly do not think you should be sad."

Her last smile, which he watched from the compound until the bus concealed it in a dust-cloud, was the happiest thing he had ever seen in his long, hot, hard, unloving life.

VIKRAM SETH

Born in Calcutta in 1952, Vikram Seth lived in many cities as a child, including Patna and London. He attended Corpus Christi College at Oxford and entered the doctoral program at Stanford University in California, where, in his own words, he spent "eleven years not getting a degree." While enrolled there he also became the William Stegner Fellow in Creative Writing from 1977 to 1978. He did extensive field work in China for his economics dissertation. Returning to India overland, he gathered material for a memoir, *From Heaven's Lake: Travels through Sinkiang and Tibet* (1983), his first popular success.

His first novel, *The Golden Gate* (1986), was written in rhyming tetrameter sonnets. His second novel, *A Suitable Boy*, is the story of a mother's search for a husband for her wayward daughter, set against the turmoil of 1950s India. It runs to 1,471 pages and took Seth ten years to complete. Among other awards, it received the 1994 Commonwealth Writers Prize for Best Book. Of *A Suitable Boy*, the novelist Khushwant Singh has said, "I lived through that period and I couldn't find a flaw. It really is an authentic picture of Nehru's India." In 1999 Seth published *An Equal Music*, set in contemporary Europe. His latest work, *Two Lives* (2005), is a memoir about the marriage of his great-aunt and -uncle. He is also the author of six volumes of poetry.

Excerpt from

A Suitable Boy

While his mother-in-law was playing patience and his sister-in-law was fending off Malati's leading questions, Dr. Pran Kapoor, that first-class husband and son-in-law, was battling with the departmental problems he was reticent about burdening his family with.

Pran, though a calm man by and large, and a kind man, regarded the head of the English Department, Professor Mishra, with a loathing that made him almost ill. Professor O.P. Mishra was a huge, pale, oily hulk, political and manipulative to the very depths of his being. The four members of the syllabus committee of the English Department were seated this afternoon around an oval table in the staff room. It was an unusually warm day. The single window was open (to the view of a dusty laburnum tree), but there was no breeze; everyone looked uncomfortable, but Professor Mishra was sweating in profuse drops that gathered on his forehead, wet his thin eyebrows, and trickled down the sides of his large nose. His lips were sweetly pursed and he was saying in his genial, high-pitched voice, "Dr. Kapoor, your point is well taken, but I think that we will need a little convincing."

The point was the inclusion of James Joyce on the syllabus for the paper on Modern British Literature. Pran Kapoor had been pressing this on the syllabus committee for two terms—ever since he had been appointed a member—and at last the committee had decided to agree whether to consider it.

Why, Pran wondered, did he dislike Professor Mishra so intensely? Although Pran had been appointed to his lecturership five years ago under the headship of his predecessor, Professor Mishra, as a senior member of the department, must have had a say in hiring him. When he first came to the department, Professor Mishra had gone out of his way to be gracious to him, even inviting him to tea at his house. Mrs. Mishra was a small, busy, worried woman, and Pran had liked her. But despite Professor Mishra's open-armed avuncularity, his Falstaffian bulk and charm, Pran detected something dangerous: his wife and two young sons were, so it seemed to him, afraid of their father.

Pran had never been able to understand why people loved power, but he accepted it as a fact of life. His own father, for instance, was greatly attracted by it: his enjoyment in its exercise went beyond the pleasure of being able to realize his ideological principles. Mahesh Kapoor enjoyed being Revenue Minister, and he would probably be happy to become either Chief Minister of Purva Pradesh or a Minister in Prime Minister Nehru's Cabinet in Delhi. The headaches, the overwork, the responsibility, the lack of control over one's own time, the complete absence of opportunity to contemplate the world from a calm vantage point: these mattered little to him. Perhaps it was true to say that Mahesh Kapoor had contemplated the world sufficiently long from the calm vantage point of his cell in a prison in British India, and now required what he had in fact acquired: an intensely active role in running things. It was almost as if father and son had exchanged between themselves the second and third stages of the accepted Hindu scheme of life: the father was entangled in the world, the son longed to separate himself into a life of philosophical detachment.

Pran, however, whether he liked it or not, was what the scriptures would call a householder. He enjoyed Savita's company, he basked in her warmth and care and beauty, he looked forward to the birth of their child. He was determined not to depend on his father for financial support, although the small salary of a department lecturer—200 rupees per month—was barely enough to subsist on—"to subside on," as he told himself in moments of cynicism. But he had applied for a readership that had recently fallen open in the department; the salary attached to that post was less pitiful, and it would be a step up in terms of the academic hierarchy. Pran did not care about titular prestige, but he realized that designations helped one's designs. He wanted to see certain things done, and being a reader would help him do them. He believed that he deserved the job, but he had also learned that merit was only one criterion among several.

His experience of the recurrent asthmatic illness that had afflicted him since childhood had made him calm. Excitement disturbed his breathing, and caused him pain and incapacitation, and he had therefore almost dispensed with excitability. This was the simple logic of it, but the path itself had been difficult. He had studied patience, and by slow practice he had become patient. But Professor O.P. Mishra had got under his skin in a way Pran had not been able to envisage.

"Professor Mishra," said Pran, "I am pleased that the committee has decided to consider this proposal, and I am delighted that it has been placed second on the agenda today and has at last come up for discussion. My main argument is quite simple. You have read my note on the subject"—he nodded around the table to Dr. Gupta and Dr. Narayanan—"and you will, I am sure, appreciate that there is nothing radical in my suggestion." He looked down at the pale blue type of the cyclostyled sheets before him. "As you can see, we have twenty-one writers whose works we consider it essential for our B.A. students to read in order for them to obtain a proper understanding of Modern British Literature. But there is no Joyce. And, I might add, no Lawrence. These two writers—"

"Wouldn't it be better," interrupted Professor Mishra, wiping an eyelash away from the corner of his eye, "wouldn't it be better if we were to concentrate on Joyce for the moment? We will take up Lawrence at our session next month—before we adjourn for the summer vacation."

"The two matters are interlinked, surely," said Pran, looking around the table for support. Dr. Narayanan was about to say something when Professor Mishra pointed out:

"But not on this agenda, Dr. Kapoor, not on this

agenda." He smiled at Pran sweetly, and his eyes twinkled. He then placed his huge white hands, palms down, on the table and said, "But what were you saying when I so rudely interrupted?"

Pran looked at the large white hands emanating from the grand pulp of Professor Mishra's round body, and thought, I may look thin and fit, but I am not, and this man, for all his slug-like pallor and bulk, has a great deal of stamina. If I am to get agreement on this measure I must remain calm and collected.

He smiled around the table, and said: "Joyce is a great writer. This is now universally acknowledged. He is, for instance, the subject of increasing academic study in America. I do think he should be on our syllabus too."

"Dr. Kapoor," the high voice responded, "each point in the universe must make up its own mind on the question of acknowledgement before acknowledgement can be considered to be universal. We in India pride ourselves on our Independence—an Independence won at great expense by the best men of several generations, a fact I need not emphasize to the illustrious son of an even more illustrious father. We should hesitate before we blindly allow the American dissertation mill to order our priorities. What do you say, Dr. Narayanan?"

Dr. Narayanan, who was a Romantic Revivalist, seemed to look deep into his soul for a few seconds. "That is a good point," he said judiciously, shaking his head sideways for emphasis.

"If we do not keep pace with our companions," continued Professor Mishra, "perhaps it is because we hear a different drummer. Let us step to the music that we hear, we in India. To quote an American," he added.

Pran looked down at the table and said quietly: "I say Joyce is a great writer because I believe he is a great writer, not because of what the Americans say." He remembered his first introduction to Joyce: a friend had lent him *Ulysses* a month before his Ph.D. oral examination at Allahabad University and he had, as a result, ignored his own subject to the point where he had jeopardized his academic career.

Dr. Narayanan looked at him and came out suddenly in unexpected support. " 'The Dead,' " said Dr. Narayanan. "A fine story. I read it twice."

Pran looked at him gratefully.

Professor Mishra looked at Dr. Narayanan's small, bald head almost approvingly. "Very good, very good," he said, as if applauding a small child. "But"—and his voice assumed a cutting edge—"there is more to Joyce than 'The Dead.' There is the unreadable *Ulysses.* There is the worse than unreadable *Finnegans Wake.* This kind of writing is unhealthy for our students. It encourages them, as it were, in sloppy and ungrammatical writing. And what about the ending of *Ulysses*? There are young and impressionable women whom in our courses it is our responsibility to introduce to the higher things of life, Dr. Kapoor—your charming sister-in-law for example. Would you put a book like *Ulysses* into her hands?" Professor Mishra smiled benignly.

"Yes," said Pran simply.

Dr. Narayanan looked interested. Dr. Gupta, who was mainly interested in Anglo-Saxon and Middle English, looked at his nails.

"It is heartening to come across a young man—a young lecturer"—Professor Mishra looked over at the rank-conscious reader, Dr. Gupta—"who is so, shall I say, so, well, direct in his opinions and so willing to share them with his colleagues, however senior they may be. It is heartening. We may disagree of course; but India is a democracy and we can speak our minds. . . ." He stopped for a few seconds, and stared out of the window at the dusty laburnum. "A democracy. Yes. But even democracies are faced with hard choices. There can be only one head of department, for example. And when a post falls open, of all the deserving candidates only one can be selected. We are already hard-pressed to teach twenty-one writers in the time we allot to this paper. If Joyce goes in, what comes out?"

"Flecker," said Pran without a moment's hesitation.

Professor Mishra laughed indulgently. "Ah, Dr. Kapoor, Dr. Kapoor . . ." he intoned.

"Pass not beneath, O Caravan, or pass not singing.
  Have you heard
That silence where the birds are dead yet something
  pipeth like a bird?

James Elroy Flecker, James Elroy Flecker." That
seemed to settle it in his mind.

Pran's face became completely impassive. Does he believe this? he thought. Does he really believe what he is
implying? Aloud he said, "If Fletcher—Flecker—is
indispensable, I suggest we include Joyce as our twenty-
second writer. I would be pleased to put it to the committee for a vote." Surely, thought Pran, the ignominy
of being known to have turned Joyce down (as opposed
to merely having deferred the decision indefinitely)
would be something that the committee would not be
willing to face.

"Ah, Dr. Kapoor, you are angry. Do not get angry. You
want to pin us down," said Professor Mishra playfully. He
turned his palms up on the table to display his own help-
lessness. "But we did not agree to decide the matter at
this meeting, only to decide whether to decide it."

This was too much for Pran in his present mood,
though he knew it was true.

"Please do not misunderstand me, Professor Mishra,"
he said, "but that line of argument may be taken by
those of us not well-versed in the finer forms of parlia-
mentary byplay to be a species of quibbling."

"A species of quibbling . . . a species of quibbling."
Professor Mishra appeared delighted by the phrase,
while both his colleagues looked appalled at Pran's in-
subordination. (This is like playing bridge with two dum-
mies, thought Pran.) Professor Mishra continued: "I will
now order coffee, and we will collect ourselves and approach the issues calmly, as it were."

Dr. Narayanan perked up at the prospect of coffee.
Professor Mishra clapped his hands, and a lean peon in
a threadbare green uniform came in.

"Is coffee ready?" asked Professor Mishra in Hindi.
"Yes, Sahib."

"Good." Professor Mishra indicated that it should be served.

The peon brought in a tray with a coffee pot, a small jug of hot milk, a bowl of sugar, and four cups. Professor Mishra indicated that he should serve the others first. The peon did so in the usual manner. Then Professor Mishra was offered coffee. As Professor Mishra poured coffee into his cup, the peon moved the tray deferentially backwards. Professor Mishra made to set down the coffee pot, and the peon moved the tray forward. Professor Mishra picked up the milk jug and began to add milk to his coffee, and the peon moved the tray backwards. And so on for each of three spoons of sugar. It was like a comic ballet. It would have been merely ridiculous, thought Pran, this display of the naked gradient of power and obsequiousness between the department head and the department peon, if it had only been some other department at some other university. But it was the English Department of Brahmpur University—and it was through this man that Pran had to apply to the selection committee for the readership he both wanted and needed.

This same man whom in my first term I considered jovial, bluff, expansive, charming, why have I transformed him in my mind into such a caricature of a villain? thought Pran looking into his cup. Does he loathe me? No, that is his strength: he doesn't. He just wants his own way. In effective politics hatred is just not useful. For him all this is like a game of chess—on a slightly vibrating board. He is fifty-eight—he has two more years until he retires. How will I be able to put up with him for so long? A sudden murderous impulse seized Pran, whom murderous impulses never seized, and he realized his hands were trembling slightly. And all this over Joyce, he said to himself. At least I haven't had a bronchial attack. He looked down at the pad on which he, as the junior member of the committee, was taking the minutes of the meeting. It read simply:

Present: Professor O.P. Mishra (head); Dr. R. B. Gupta; Dr. T. R. Narayanan; Dr. P. Kapoor.
1. The Minutes of the last meeting were read and approved.

We have got nowhere, and we will get nowhere, he thought.

A few well-known lines from Tagore came into his head in Tagore's own English translation:

Where the clear stream of reason has not lost its way
*   into the dreary desert sand of dead habit;*
Where the mind is led forward by Thee into ever-
*   widening thought and action—*
Into that heaven of freedom, my Father, let my coun-
*   try awake.*

At least his own mortal father had given him principles, thought Pran, even if he had given him almost no time or company when he was younger. His mind wandered back home, to the small whitewashed house, to Savita, her sister, her mother—the family that he had taken into his heart and that had taken him into theirs; and then to the Ganges flowing close by the house. (When he thought in English, it was the Ganges, rather than the Ganga, to him.) He followed it first downstream to Patna and Calcutta, then upstream past Banaras till it divided at Allahabad; there he chose the Yamuna and followed it to Delhi. Are things as closed-minded in the capital? he asked himself. As mad, as mean, as silly, as rigid? How will I be able to live in Brahmpur all my life? And Mishra will doubtless give me an excellent report just to see the back of me.

But now Dr. Gupta was laughing at a remark of Dr. Naraya-nan's, and Professor Mishra was saying, "Consensus—consensus is the goal, the civilized goal—how can we vote when we might be divided two votes against two? There were five Pandavas, they could have voted if they chose, but even they did everything by consensus. They even took a wife by consensus, ha, ha, ha! And Dr. Varma is indisposed as usual, so we are only four."

Pran looked at the twinkling eyes, the great nose, the sweetly pursed lips with reluctant admiration. University statutes required that the syllabus committee, like depart-mental committees of any kind, should consist of an odd number of members. But Professor Mishra, as head of the department, appointed the members of each committee within his purview in such a way as always to include someone who for reasons of health or research was likely to be indisposed or absent. With an even number of members present, committees were more reluctant than ever to bring things to the climax of a vote. And the head, with his control over the agenda and the pacing of a meeting, could in the circumstances gather even more effective power into his hands.

"I think we have, as it were, expended enough time on item two," said Professor Mishra. "Shall we go on to chiasmus and anacoluthia?" He was referring to a proposal, put forward by himself, that they eliminate too detailed a study of traditional figures of speech for the paper in Literary Theory and Criticism. "And then we have the question of symmetrical auxiliaries proposed by the junior member of the committee. Though this will, of course, depend upon other departments agreeing to our proposals. And finally, since the shades of night are falling," continued Professor Mishra, "I think we should, without prejudice to items five, six, and seven, wind up the meeting. We can take up those items next month."

But Pran was unwilling to be dissuaded from pressing on with the unresolved question of Joyce. "I think we have now collected ourselves," he said, "and can approach the issue under discussion quite calmly. If I were willing to accept that *Ulysses* might be a bit, well, difficult for B.A. students, would the committee agree to include *Dubliners* on the syllabus as a first step? Dr. Gupta, what do you think?"

Dr. Gupta looked up at the slowly circulating fan. His ability to get speakers on Old and Middle English invited to the departmental seminar depended upon Professor Mishra's goodwill: outside speakers entailed incidental expenses, and funds had to be approved by the head of the department. Dr. Gupta knew as well as anyone what "as a first step" implied. He looked up at Pran and said, "I would be willing—"

But he was swiftly interrupted in his sentence, whatever that might have been. "We are forgetting," Professor Mishra cut in, "something that even I, I must admit, did not bear in mind earlier in this discussion. I mean that, by tradition, the Modern British Literature paper does not include writers who were living at the time of the Second World War." This was news to Pran, who must have looked astonished, because Professor Mishra felt compelled to explain: "This is not altogether a matter for surprise. We need the distance of time objectively to appraise the stature of modern writers, to include them in our canon, as it were. Do remind me, Dr. Kapoor . . . when did Joyce die?"

"1941," said Pran sharply. It was clear that the great white whale had known this all along.

"Well, there you are . . ." said Professor Mishra helplessly. His finger moved down the agenda.

"Eliot, of course, is still alive," said Pran quietly, looking at the list of prescribed authors.

The head of the department looked as if he had been slapped across the face. He opened his mouth slightly, then pursed his lips together. The jolly twinkle appeared again in his eyes. "But Eliot, Eliot, surely—we have objective criteria enough in his case—why, even Dr. Leavis—"

Professor Mishra clearly responded to a different drummer from the Americans, reflected Pran. Aloud he said, "Dr. Leavis, as we know, greatly approves of Lawrence too. . . ."

"We have agreed to discuss Lawrence next time," Professor Mishra expostulated.

Pran gazed out of the window. It was getting dark and the leaves of the laburnum now looked cool, not dusty. He went on, not looking at Professor Mishra: ". . . and, besides, Joyce has a better claim as a British writer in Modern British Literature than Eliot. So if we—"

"That, my young friend, if I may say so," cut in Professor Mishra, "could be considered a species of quibbling." He was recovering quickly from his shock. In a minute he would be quoting Prufrock.

What is it about Eliot, thought Pran irrelevantly, his mind wandering from the subject at hand, that makes him such a sacred cow for us Indian intellectuals? Aloud he said: "Let us hope that T.S. Eliot has many more

years of life, of productive life. I am glad that, unlike
Joyce, he did not die in 1941. But we are now living in
1951, which implies that the pre-war rule you mentioned,
even if it is a tradition, could not be a very ancient one.
If we can't do away with it, why not update it? Surely
its purpose is that we should revere the dead above the
living—or, to be less skeptical, appraise the dead before
the living. Eliot, who is alive, has been granted a waiver.
I propose we grant Joyce one. A friendly compromise."
Pran paused, then added: "As it were." He smiled: "Dr.
Narayanan, are you for 'The Dead'?"

"Yes, well, I think so," said Dr. Narayanan with the
faintest of responding smiles, before Professor Mishra
could interrupt.

"Dr. Gupta?" asked Pran.

Dr. Gupta could not look Professor Mishra in the eye.

"I agree with Dr. Narayanan," said Professor Gupta.

There was silence for a few seconds. Pran thought, I
can't believe it. I've won. I've won. I can't believe it.

And indeed, it seemed that he had. Everyone knew
that the approval of the Academic Council of the university was usually a formality once the syllabus committee
of a department had decided matters.

As if nothing in the least untoward had occurred, the
head of the department gathered together the reins of
the meeting. The great soft hands scuttled across the
cyclostyled sheets. "The next item . . ." said Professor
Mishra with a smile, then paused and began again: "But
before we go on to the next item, I should say that I
personally have always greatly admired James Joyce as
a writer. I am delighted, needless to say—"

A couple of lines of poetry came terrifyingly unbidden
to Pran's mind:

Pale hands I loved beside the Shalimar,
Where are you now? Who lives beneath your spell?

and he burst into a fit of sudden laughter, incomprehensible even to himself, which went on for twenty seconds
and ended in a spasm of coughing. He bent his head

and tears streamed down his cheeks. Professor Mishra rewarded him with a look of unfeigned fury and hatred.

"Sorry, sorry," muttered Pran as he recovered. Dr. Gupta was thumping him vigorously on the back, which was not helpful. "Please continue—I was overcome—it sometimes happens. . . ." But to offer any further explanation was impossible.

The meeting was resumed and the next two points discussed quickly. There was no real disagreement. It was dark now; the meeting was adjourned. As Pran left the room Professor Mishra put a friendly arm around his shoulder. "My dear boy, that was a fine performance." Pran shuddered at the memory. "You are clearly a man of great integrity, intellectual and otherwise." Oh, oh, what is he up to now? thought Pran. Professor Mishra continued: "The Proctor has been badgering me since last Tuesday to submit a member of my department—it's our turn, you know—to join the student welfare committee of the university. . . ." Oh no, thought Pran, there goes one day every week. ". . . and I have decided to volunteer you." I didn't know the verb was transitive, thought Pran. In the darkness—they were now walking across the campus—it was difficult for Professor Mishra entirely to disguise the active dislike in his high voice. Pran could almost see the pursed lips, the specious twinkle. He was silent, and that, to the head of the English Department, implied acceptance.

"I realize you are busy, my dear Dr. Kapoor, what with your extra tutorials, the Debating Society, the Colloquium, putting on plays, and so on. . . ." said Professor Mishra. "The sort of thing that makes one deservedly popular with students. But you are comparatively new here, my dear fellow—five years is not a long time from the perspective of an old fogey like me—and you must allow me to give you a word of advice. Cut down on your unacademic activities. Don't tire yourself out unnecessarily. Don't take things so seriously. What were those wonderful lines of Yeats?

She bid me take life easy as the leaves grown on the tree,
But I being young and foolish with her did not agree.

I'm sure your charming wife would endorse that. Don't drive yourself so hard—your health depends on it. And your future, I dare say. . . . In some ways you are your own worst enemy."

But I am only my metaphorical enemy, thought Pran. And obstinacy on my part has earned me the actual enmity of the formidable Professor Mishra. But was Professor Mishra more dangerous or less dangerous to him—in this matter of the readership, for instance, now that Pran had won his hatred?

What was Professor Mishra thinking, wondered Pran. He imagined his thoughts went something like this: I should never have got this uppity young lecturer onto the syllabus committee. It's too late, however, to regret all that. But at least his presence here has kept him from working mischief in, say, the admissions committee; there he could have brought up all kinds of objections to students I wanted to bring in if they weren't selected entirely on the basis of merit. As for the university's selection committee for the readership in English, I must rig this somehow before I allow it to meet—

But Pran got no further clues to the inner working of that mysterious intelligence. For at this point the paths of the two colleagues diverged and, with expressions of great mutual respect, they parted from each other.

KHUSHWANT SINGH

Born in 1915 in Hadali, Punjab (now part of Pakistan), Khushwant Singh received a BA at Government College in Lahore, India, in 1934, and became a barrister-at-law in England after studying at London's Inner Temple and King's College, where he earned an LLB in 1938. A noted novelist, short story writer, editor, and journalist, he practiced law at Lahore's High Court in the 1940s, as well as working for UNESCO in Paris in the 1950s. He has been a visiting lecturer at Oxford University, the University of Rochester, Princeton University, and Swarthmore College.

His two-volume *History of the Sikhs* (1962) was commissioned jointly by the Rockefeller Foundation and Muslim University in Aligarth. His best-known work in the West, the novel *Train to Pakistan* (1956), depicts a pair of lovers from different religious backgrounds, one a Muslim, the other a Sikh, caught up in the 1947 partition. Critic Vasani Anant Shahane (in *Khushwant Singh*) has commented that the novel is characterized by "its stark realism, its absolute fidelity to the truth of life, the trenchant exposition of one of the most moving, even tragic, events of contemporary Indian history. . . ."

Among his other works of fiction are *I Shall Not Hear the Nightingale* (1959) and *Delhi* (1989). His story collections include *The Mark of Vishnu and Other Stories* (1950) and *Black Jasmine* (1971). In 2002 he published his autobiography, *Truth, Love and a Little Malice*.

In 1984, in protest against the government's sending of armed troops into the Golden Temple at Amritsar, he returned the Padma Bhushan Award, which he had received a decade earlier. However, in 2007 the government of India awarded Singh the even more prestigious Padma Vibhushan.

The Bottom-Pincher

I am not a bottom-pincher, but I would like to be one. Like some people are granted freedom of a city I would like to be granted freedom to pinch female citizens' bottoms. Pinching is not the right word. If the bottom is nicely rounded, I would like the freedom to caress it in the cup of my palm. If it is very large or very small, I would like the freedom to run a finger up its crevice. Only if it sags would I want the freedom to take the sagging flesh between my thumb and index finger and tweak it. However, no city has yet conferred such freedom on me.

I am a law-abiding citizen. My employers think well of me. I belong to the best club and am on the governing body of the YMCA. In short I am a respected member of the community. This inhibits me from taking liberties with females' bottoms save with my eyes. As soon as I get close to one I would like to stroke, I warn myself of the consequences. I tell myself that the lady may not like my interfering with her bottom. She may start a shindy. She may collect a crowd and some sanctimonious type, though he be a bottom-pincher himself, may take the law into his hands and beat me up. Such thoughts bring beads of sweat to my forehead.

For me bottom-pinching has been a spectator-sport. Again I use a wrong expression. The sport is limited to watching bottoms. I have never had the privilege of watching anyone pinching them.

A crowded city like Bombay provides ideal conditions for bottom-watching. And the garments in which Indian female bottoms are draped are infinitely more varied than anywhere else in the world; *saris, gararas, lungis,* skirts (Indian style *ghagra* as well as the European full lengths and minis), stretch pants, bell-bottom trousers, *churidars*—you can encounter all varieties in fifteen minutes any time any place. My favourite beat is the half-mile stretch from my office to a conjunction of five roads at a statuary called Flora Fountain. The best time is the lunch hour when it is most crowded. It is not much of a walk, it is more like an ant's crawl, dodging people, bumping into them, brushing off beggars, grinning past whores soliciting for a "nooner," snarling at touts who want to exchange foreign money. However, I like this bit of the bazaar precisely because it is so damnably crowded. There are many roadside book-stalls. The pavements are lined with all variety of smuggled goods: French perfumes, cosmetics and chiffons; Japanese tape-recorders, cameras and transistors playing at full blast. And inevitably a large number of women-shoppers. One has to be very careful not to brush against their bosoms or bottoms. Who wants to be very careful?

It was one such lunch hour that I witnessed a memorable performance of bottom-pinching. I was browsing at a pavement book-stall alongside the Dadyseth Parsi Fire Temple. My attention was attracted by a sudden convergence of beggars towards the iron-grilled gate meant to keep out non-Parsis. From the Fire Temple emerged a thin, tall gentleman, in his sixties, wearing a light-blue suit, solar hat and thick post-cataract glasses. He dipped into his pocket and dropped a coin in the hand of every beggar. It was apparent that they knew the gentleman and the time he made his appearance; in the crowd were lepers who had to drag themselves and a blind woman carrying a child on her shoulder. Although I have very strong views on giving money to beggars I could not help admiring one who must by any reckoning part with a small fortune every afternoon.

The gentleman proceeded to walk in the direction of my office. I followed a few paces behind. His charity did not end outside the Fire Temple. He continued to dip in his right-hand pocket and drop a coin in every out-stretched hand. Then I noticed that as he passed a group of three women bending over some article at a stall, his left hand brushed the bottom of one of them. By the time the woman straightened up to see who had done it, the gentleman was a few paces ahead in the crowd. He did not look back but walked on, ramrod erect. So it went on. Right hand to give alms to the needy, left hand to stroke or finger unguarded, unwary female bot-

toms. What a character! What tremendous risks he ran
of being caught, exposed, man-handled!

Next afternoon I was back at the book-stall. I had one
eye in a magazine, the other on the gate of the Fire
Temple. The beggars had already collected displaying
the capital of their trade; lepers their stubby fingerless
hands and toes, men on crutches, the blind woman with
her babe at the breast. The gentleman emerged from
the prayer house; same light-blue suit, solar topee and
behind the thick lenses a pale, sexless, expressionless
face. He went through the same motions; disbursing his
pocketful of coins to outstretched hands. For the blind
woman he had more; a rupee note which he insisted
on handing to the babe. He said something to the
mother which I could at best guess was, "This is for
the little one." In the process he had a nice brush with
the young woman's bosom. He was rewarded with a
smile. What is a little touch on the breast if you get a
rupee for it!

He proceeded on his triumphal march through the
milling crowd. It was easy to keep him in sight because
of his height, the solar topee bobbing above the sea of
heads and the sudden surprise with which women turned
to see who had laid a left-handed compliment to their
bottoms.

I followed him all the way. He turned in the massive
Chambers of Commerce building. The commissionaire
saluted him. There was a long queue for the elevator.
He went straight into the lift without anyone protesting.
He was obviously a big shot.

Some weeks later I was walking back from my office
past the Chambers of Commerce building. I saw a
cream-coloured Mercedes Benz parked alongside the
kerb. Inside were two women—one squat and grey-
haired lady bunched up in a corner of the rear seat,
the other a teenage girl apparently her daughter. The
chauffeur opened both the doors on one side of the car.
The commissionaire deposited a brief-case and a stack
of files on the front seat. Our hero of the Fire Temple
came out trailed by two men who looked like his assis-
tants. The girl bounced out of the car, ran across the

pavement and embraced him shouting "Daddy!" She couldn't have been more than sixteen. Very lovely too! Nut-brown hair falling on her shoulders. Healthy open-air type. And a figure right off the walls of some ancient Hindu temple; large bosom bursting out of her blouse, narrow waist and again a bottom—large, protuberant and so provocative, as if it were cocking the snook at the world and saying "I don't give a fart!"

No wonder our hero had such an obsession with bosoms and bottoms. Constant exposure to such temptation! Constant frustration because of not being allowed to touch them!

The next evening I got to know his name. This time the Mercedes Benz was there without its lady passengers. I pretended to admire the car and casually asked the chauffeur who it belonged to.

"The Burra Sahib."

"Which Burra Sahib?"

"Lalkaka Sahib, who else!" he replied truculently.

There were fourteen Lalkakas in the Bombay Telephone directory. All the first names down the list were Parsis—Cyrus, Darius, Framroze, Jal, Jehangir, Nausheer. Then to Ps. One alongside the address Chambers of Commerce Building: the other against "Residence Lalkaka Mansion, Malabar Hill." My repertoire of Parsi first names beginning with P was limited to one, Phiroze. Next morning at eleven when the chances of any member of the family being at home would be minimal I dialled the number. A servant took the call. "Phiroze Lalkaka Sahib *hai*?" I asked.

The servant replied in a Goan English accent. "Here not Phiroze Lalkaka. Residence of Pesi Lalkaka. He gawn ophiss."

"Is Miss Lalkaka at home?"

"Also Missy Baba gawn college. Mem Sahib awt. No one home. Who calling?"

I hadn't thought of the answer to that question. On the spur of the moment I told the servant to take down my name. I spelt it out slowly for him: "Mr. Bottom-pincher."

"What number?"

"He knows my number."

Pesi Lalkaka was not at the Fire Temple the next day. Nor for the whole week following. The beggars assembled at the trysting hour and dispersed with their palms empty. I felt sorry for them. I felt sorry for the good man whose indulgence in a harmless pastime I had put an end to. I had been a spoil-sport.

I wondered how Pesi Lalkaka had reacted to the telephone message. Maybe his wife or daughter had got it first. "What an odd name! Bottom-pincher! Who is he, daddy?" Pesi Lalkaka must have turned pale and stuttered, "I don't know." They might have questioned the servant. "He say Sahib know number." They might have scanned the telephone directory. There wasn't even a Bottom or a Bottomley in the Bombay telephones. They must have dismissed the matter. "Somebody trying to be funny." But poor Pesi Lalkaka! What agonies he must suffer knowing that he had been spotted!

A fortnight later Pesi Lalkaka was back at the Dadyseth Fire Temple. He looked uncomfortable. He dropped money in the hands of the few beggars who accosted him. He looked around to see if he could recognize anyone. Then proceeded towards his office. I followed him. He continued to dole out money with his right hand. But this time his left hand was firmly embedded in his coat pocket. Each time he passed a woman, he turned back to look if he was being followed. Poor, poor Pesi Lalkaka!

He resumed his lunch hour routine of prayer followed by alms-giving on the way back to the office. But now his left hand was always in the coat pocket. And each time he passed by a woman he turned round to look over his shoulder like one pursued by a ghost. So it went on for some time. Pesi Lalkaka seemed to be getting the better of his obsession. He was becoming a commonplace bore.

Not so. It appeared that Pesi Lalkaka had assured himself that the man who had spotted him in *flagrante delicto* once had disappeared from the scene.

One afternoon he was threading his way through the crammed pavement with me trailing a few yards behind

him. I saw three women ahead of us examining some
merchandise at a stall. Their bottoms presented a tempt-
ing variety of sizes and coverings. One was a young girl
in blue skin-tight jeans; her buttocks were like two nicely
rounded, unripe watermelons. Beside her was an older
woman in a bright red saree. She was massive like one
big pumpkin. The third in the row was a twelve-year-
old Lolita in a white and so mini a skirt that when she
bent down it exposed all her thigh and a bit of her bottom as well. I could see Pesi Lalkaka's left arm twitch.
The triumvirate of bottoms thus served up proved too
powerful a temptation to resist. His hand came out of
the pocket and caressed the three in quick succession.
By the time the women straightened up and turned
round Pesi had gone ahead and I was directly behind the
three. The old woman glowered and swore, *"Badmash—*
rascal." Her younger companion hissed, "Mummy, don't
create a scene." I had a narrow escape.

I was determined to teach Pesi Lalkaka a lesson. As
soon as I got to my office I rang up his residence. It was
the same voice at the other end. "Sahib gawn ophiss. Mem
Sahib resting. Missy Baba gawn college. Who calling?"

"Mr. Bottom-pincher."

"Give number please!"

"Tell him I will ring again in the evening."

That would fix him! It did.

Pesi Lalkaka was not at the Fire Temple for many
days. When ultimately he did appear his left arm was in
a sling. He looked paler than ever before. I was sure he
had cut himself deliberately. Poor Pesi Lalkaka!

The beggars made solicitous enquiries. He simply wag-
gled his head. As usual I followed him through the
crowded corridor. In the few days he seemed to have
developed a stoop. He plodded on without turning back.
Whenever he came to a woman looking the other way
his pace slackened. He inclined his head, gave her buttocks a brief, mournful look and proceeded on his way.
This time I really felt sorry for him. Or did I? Why
didn't he use his right hand to do what his left hand
could not? I had read some sociologist's opinions that
Indians only used their left hands to caress the genitalia

of their women, never the right because they ate with it and did not want it polluted. I wondered if it was that which inhibited Pesi Lalkaka. The curiosity got the better of me.

That evening I rang him up. It was the same servant at the other end of the line.

"Hullo! Who calling?"

"The doctor. I want to speak to the Sahib."

A few seconds later a voice identified itself: "Pesi Lalkaka this side."

"How's the left hand, old man?"

"Who is it?" he demanded in a faltering voice.

"Never mind. Try using your right hand. It's more fun." I slammed down the receiver.

I saw no more of Pesi Lalkaka at the Dadyseth Fire Temple for many weeks. Perhaps he had changed his lunch hour place of worship. Perhaps he had found an alternative route where no one trailed behind him. I felt it as a personal affront. I wasn't going to let him get away with it.

The next few days I took my post-lunch hour stroll round the block of the Chambers of Commerce building. I saw Pesi Lalkaka return to the office by different routes. I tried to get him on the phone in his office. He never picked it up himself. I refused to communicate through his secretary. I tried him at home. Here too it was his servant, wife or daughter who took the call. Every time they asked me who I was, I replied I would ring later. It never occurred to me that the fellow might get Bombay Telephones to keep a check on his incoming calls.

Came the Parsi New Year's Day, Navroz. It was a sectional holiday only for Parsis. I had a feeling that Pesi Lalkaka would visit his old haunt, the Dadyseth Fire Temple, at his usual hour to be able to give alms to the expectant beggars. I was as usual at the neighbouring book-stall glancing over pages of a magazine with an eye on the temple gate. Standing beside me was a man also turning over the pages of a magazine. He had one eye on me.

There was quite a throng of beggars outside the tem-

ple. Parsi gentlemen were dressed in their traditional
spotless white muslin caps, starched shirts and trousers.
Their ladies wore their saris in the Parsi style, draped
straight over their shoulders. The sandal-wood seller beside the doorway was doing brisk business.

My hunch was right; Pesi Lalkaka was there. This time
accompanied by his wife and daughter. He looked very
different in his all-white outfit. His arm was not in a
sling but both arms were engaged. His right hand rested
on his wife's shoulder; his daughter held the left to help
him down the temple steps. On Navroz it was Mrs. Lalkaka who dipped into her handbag to dole out coins to
the beggars. Many complained that they had not seen
the Sahib for a long time and made enquiries about
his health.

The trio turned their backs towards me to walk in the
direction of his office. It was then I noticed that the
Missy Baba was wearing a pleated mini-skirt. Fat thighs.
And what a tail. Her buttocks swayed as if keeping beat
to a tango. I cast aside the magazine in my hand and
followed them.

Walking three abreast through the crowded pavement
was slow business. I walked close behind Missy Baba
with my eyes glued to her posterior and languorous
music ringing in my ears. By the time I came to the
parting of ways I was in a high state of exaltation. When
would I ever get such a chance again! The desire to
caress overcame discretion. I quickened my pace, came
alongside the Missy Baba and let my right hand give the
silken contour of her behind a loving caress. A voice
behind me called "Mr. Bottom-pincher!" I turned back.
It was the man I had seen beside me at the book-stall.
He took me by the arm. "Come with me to the police
station. Please follow us," he said to the Lalkakas.

If I had protested the crowd would have given me a
rough time. But I could not help pleading innocence,
asking my captor what all this was about. "You will find
out. I've been watching you for some days," he said. I
went like the proverbial lamb to the slaughter-house.

What a fool I had been! What would the people say
when they read about it in the papers? "Who could have

believed it of him? The old lecher . . . It often happens to men in late middle-age," etc. I'd be sacked from my job, removed from all committees and expelled from my club. I'd never be able to face the world. Should I kill myself? Or just disappear from Bombay, take the vows of a Sanyasi and spend the rest of my days in some sadhu ashram in the Himalayas?

At the police station I was given a few moments to compose myself. The sub-inspector opened a large yellow register to record my statement. I said, "I have nothing to say. I don't know what it is all about. You have made a big mistake." It did not impress him. "No mistake, mister! We checked your telephone calls and what you did I saw with my own two eyes. You better come clean."

I refused to come clean. I refused to speak to the fellow. He said, "If you want to consult a lawyer, you can send for one. Otherwise, I'll put you up before a magistrate."

"I don't want to see any lawyer for anything," I replied. "But I would like to see Mr. Lalkaka."

"*Aha!* so you admit to knowing him!" he exclaimed, very pleased with himself. He recorded that in his register.

I had put the noose round my own neck.

"Perhaps you would like to see Miss Lalkaka too!" the sub-inspector said with a nasty sneer. "She will be the material witness to the kind of things you do."

That was too much for me. I lost my temper and retorted, "Has she eyes behind her head to see who pats her bottom?"

"*Aha!* So you admit somebody did pat her bottom," he replied triumphantly. And wrote it down in his register. I had put yet another noose round my neck. I tried to extricate myself. "No, I don't want to see Miss Lalkaka. I want to see her father."

"Why? He has nothing to do with this case."

"If he has accused me of harassing him, I want to confront him. He has made a terrible mistake."

"Let's keep Mr. Lalkaka out of this. He is a respectable citizen."

"So am I," I said stubbornly. "I am every bit as respectable as he."

We sat glowering at each other. If my reputation was to go down the gutter, I was determined to take Pesi Lalkaka's with me. After a while the sub-inspector gave in. He pressed the bell on the table. A constable came in. "Ask the Sahib to come in."

After a while, the constable came back and whispered something in the ear of the sub-inspector. Then both left the reporting room. I could hear the voices of sub-inspector and Pesi Lalkaka, but could only catch a few stray words like confession . . . water-tight case . . . not compoundable . . . Then a long silence. The sub-inspector re-entered and sat down in his chair. He fixed me with his eyes. "This time I will let you off with a warning. But if I catch you again doing anything or harassing respectable people, you will go to gaol. You can go now."

I did not want to prolong the agony by protesting my innocence. I got up quietly and left the room.

The cream-coloured Mercedes Benz was parked outside the police station. I turned my face away as I walked past it. I heard a voice call "Gentleman! Gentleman!" It was Pesi Lalkaka. A very doleful-looking Pesi it was. "Gentleman," he pleaded, "can I drop you anywhere?"

SHASHI THAROOR

Shashi Tharoor was born in 1956 in London, educated in India, and received a BA in history from St. Stephen's College, Delhi. He earned two master's degrees and a PhD at the Fletcher School of Law and Diplomacy at Tufts University.

Since 1978, Tharoor has worked in various capacities at the United Nations. On June 15, 2006, the Government of India announced its backing of Tharoor as Kofi Annan's successor for the post of U.N. Secretary General. Tharoor served as Under-Secretary-General until February of 2007.

Tharoor began his literary career at the age of six, writing stories to entertain himself in pretelevision Bombay while bedridden and recovering from asthma. His World War II novel about the adventures of an RAF fighter pilot, *Operation Bellows,* was serialized in the *Junior Statesman* starting a month before his eleventh birthday. His best-known novel, *The Great Indian Novel,* published in 1989, used the narrative method and themes of the Indian epic the *Mahabharata* to tell a satiric story of modern India. His second novel, *Show Business* (1992), was made into the film *Bollywood* in 1994.

The Five-Dollar Smile and Other Stories (1990) is a collection of short stories written, according to Tharoor, "in a spate of collegiate creativity." He says of this youthful effort, "I was writing to be published and read, not to pursue an obscure literary aesthetic. This in turn helped define the nature, and the limitations, of my work."

The Five-Dollar Smile

"Make this child smile again," the black type on the crumpled, glossy newsweekly page read. "All it takes is five dollars a month."

Joseph stared at the picture sandwiched between the two halves of the caption. He had seen it a thousand times—the tattered clothes, the dark, intense, pleading eyes, the grubby little fingers thrust tightly into a sullenly closed mouth. The photo that had launched the most successful, worldwide appeal in HELP's history, four years ago. His picture.

As usual, he viewed it once more with that curious detachment that had come to him during those last four years. He could not see it as a photograph of himself, a record of his past, a souvenir of his younger childhood. It was not personal enough for that; it was in the public domain, part of an advertisement, a poster, a campaign, and now an aging magazine clipping in his hand. The little boy who stared out at him was not him, Joseph Kumaran; he was part of a message, defined by a slogan, serving a purpose, and the fact that he was Joseph Kumaran did not matter. It never had.

Joseph looked once more at the picture, as he had five times already during the flight, as if to reassure himself that he knew what he was doing on this large, cold, humming monster hurtling him towards a strange land he had known only in postage stamps. That's what this is all about, he wanted the picture to say. That's who you are and the reason why you are on an unfamiliar thing called an airplane and why your feet don't touch the ground but your toes feel cold and you have to put a belt around your waist that stops you from leaning forward comfortably to eat the strange food they expect you to get at with plastic forks and knives, sealed impossibly in polyethylene, while you wish you could pluck up the nerve to ask the poised, distant, and impossibly tall, white lady to help you, help you with a blanket and two pillows and some real food you can eat without trying to gnaw at sealed packages of cutlery. . . .

He folded the picture again and pushed it into the pocket of the tight little blazer he had been given the day he left the HELP office with Sister Celine to go to the airport. It had been sent with a bundle of old clothes for the disaster relief collection, he had learned, and though it was a little small for him it was just the thing to smarten him up for the trip to the United States. "Always be smart, Joseph," Sister Celine had said. "Let them know you're poor but you're smart, because we knew how to bring you up."

Joseph sat back, his feet dangling from the airplane seat, and looked at the largely uneaten food on the tray. When he thought of food he could remember the day of the photograph. He had been seven then: that was the day he had learned he was seven.

"How old's that little kid? The one in the torn white shirt?"

"He's about seven. No one's really sure. He came here when he was a little child. We couldn't really tell when he'd been born."

"About seven, eh. Looks younger." *Click, whirr.* "Might be what I'm looking for. Get him away from that food, Sister, will you please? We want a hungry child, not a feeding one."

Suddenly, a large, white hand interposed among the tiny, outstretched brown ones crowded at the table, pulling Joseph's away. "Come here, Joseph. This nice man wants to see you."

"But I want to eat, Sister." Desperation, pleading in his voice. He knew what could happen if he was too late. There would be no food left for him: it had happened before. And today was his favorite day, with crisp *papadams* in the *kanji* gruel. He had watched the cooks rip up and fry the *papadams* from behind the kitchen door, and he'd tried to get to the table early so he wouldn't miss out on his share. He'd had to fight the bigger boys to stay there, too. But what determined resistance had preserved, Sister Celine was taking away.

"Please, Sister, please."

"Later, child. Now behave yourself." He was dragging his feet and she was pulling him quite firmly by the left hand. "And if you don't walk properly I shall have to take the cane to you." He straightened up quickly; he knew the cane well and did not want it again.

Would the stewardess take a cane to him if he asked her for a fork and knife? Of course she wouldn't, he knew that. He knew his nervousness was silly, unnecessary. He was suddenly hungry, but he didn't know how to attract her attention. She was giving a man a drink several rows in front of Joseph.

"Miss!" he called softly. His voice came out huskily, tripping over dry obstacles in his throat. She didn't hear him; he wished desperately that she would catch his eye, and he trained his look on her with such fearful intensity it was unbelievable she should not notice. "Miss!" he called again, waving his hand. She was sticking a pin into the headrest of the man who'd bought the drink, and she still didn't hear.

"Miss!" This time it was too loud. It seemed to Joseph that everyone in the plane had turned to look at him, as if he had done something very odd. There were a couple of smiles, but for the most part people looked disapproving, frowning their displeasure at him and making comments to their neighbors. Joseph's dark cheeks flushed red with embarrassment.

The stewardess straightened up, controlled her irritation, and smiled sweetly but briskly as she walked down to him. "Yes, what is it?"

"Can-I-have-a-knife-and-fork-please?" The words came out in a rush, Sister Angela's diction lessons forgotten in his anxiety.

She hardly seemed to pause in her stride. "It's on your tray—here, on the side, see? In this packet." And she lifted the packet, placed it on top of the napkin for him to see, and before he could say anything more, strode off down the aisle.

"Hold it there, kid." Joseph, seven, wanting *papadams,* confronted American slang for the first time in the person of a large, white man with a mustache and a camera. To little Joseph, everything seemed large about the man: his body, his mustache, his camera. A large hand pushed him back a little and a voice boomed: "Seems rather small for his age."

"Infant malnutrition. Mother died in childbirth and his father brought him through the forest alone. These tribals are astonishingly hardy. God knows how he survived without any permanent damage."

"So there's nothing really wrong with him, right? I mean, his brain's okay and everything? I've gotta be sure I'm selling the American public poverty and not retardation, if you see what I mean. So he's normal, huh?"

"Just a little stunted." Sister Celine, quiet, precise. *Click, whirr.* Lights exploded at him. His eyes widened.

"Let's take him outside, if you don't mind. I'd like to use the sun—I'm not too sure of my flash."

"Yes, of course, Mr. Cleaver. Come, Joseph."

He squirmed out of the nun's grasp. "But, Sister, I want to eat."

"Later. Now if you're difficult there'll be no lunch at all for you."

Resentfully, he followed them out into the courtyard . . . stood there sullenly, staring his quiet hatred at the large man. *Click, whirr, click.* "Move him to this side a bit, won't you, Sister?"

It was being pushed around that made him thrust his fingers into his mouth, as much in self-protection as in appeasement of his palate. The photographer clicked again.

Joseph turned to look at the stewardess' retreating back in profound dismay. Why hadn't he told her that he knew he had a knife and fork, but he didn't know how to get at them? Why hadn't he made clear what exactly was the help he needed? Why had he been so scared?

He drew himself even more deeply into his seat and looked around nervously. His neighbor, staring out the window, smiled briefly, mechanically, at him. Joseph could not ask him to help. Or could he? The man turned from the window to a magazine he was reading over dinner. Joseph's resolution faded.

That day, after the photographs, there had been no *papadams* left for him. Only cold *kanji*; the *papadams* were already finished.

"See—I told you you could have lunch later," the nun said. "Here's your lunch now."

But I wanted the *papadams,* he wanted to scream in rage and frustration. And why did you need to take me away from my *papadams*? What was so important about that man with the camera that you had to deprive me of something I've been waiting a month to enjoy? But he did not say all that. He could not. Instead, the lump in his throat almost choking him, he flung the tin plate of gruel to the ground and burst into tears.

"Good heavens—what's the matter with him today? Very well, no lunch for you then, Joseph. And you will clean this mess off the floor and come to my office as soon as you have done so, so that you may be suitably punished for your ingratitude. There are many little boys not as fortunate as you are, Joseph Kumaran. And don't you forget it."

Sniffing back his misery, Joseph knew he would not forget it. He would have six strokes of the cane to remember it by.

How could he ask his neighbor to help open the packet? He was so engrossed in his magazine. And he was eating. It seemed so wrong, and so embarrassing. Joseph tried to speak, but the words would not come out.

At the head of the aisle, another stewardess was already bringing tea or coffee around. The other passengers seemed to be finishing their meals. They would take his tray away from him and he would not even have eaten. A panic, irrational but intense, rose to flood him.

He struggled with the packet. He tried to tear it, gnaw at it, rip it open. It would not give way. The cutlery inside the packet jangled; at one point he hit a cup on his tray and nearly broke it. Joseph's attempts became even wilder and he made little noises of desperation.

"Here," his neighbor's strong voice said. "Let me help you."

Joseph turned to him in gratitude. He had hoped his

desperation would become apparent and attract assistance. It had worked.

"Thank you," he managed to say. "I didn't know how to open it."

"It's quite easy," his neighbor said.

The first copies of the photographs arrived at the HELP Center a few weeks after the photographer had left. Joseph had almost forgotten the incident, even the caning, though the frustration of the *papadam*-less gruel remained. One of the nuns called him to Sister Eva's office excitedly.

"Look, Joseph—these are the pictures the nice man took, the day you were so bad," Sister Celine told him. "This is you."

Joseph looked at the black-and-white image without curiosity. He would rather not have seen it, rather not have been reminded of their perverse cruelty to him that day. He stared at the picture, made no comment, and looked away.

"It's going to be used in a worldwide appeal," Sister said. "Your picture will be in every important magazine in the world. Helping us get money to help other children. Doesn't that make you happy, Joseph?"

He had learned to be dutiful. "Yes, Sister," he said.

The man in the seat next to him turned the polyethylene packet around, slipped out a flap, and deftly extricated a fork and a knife. He handed them to Joseph with a cordial smile.

"There—you see, easy."

"Thank you." Joseph, taking the implements from the man, felt his ears burning with shame. So there had been no need to try and tear open the packet after all. There was a flap. He turned single-mindedly to the food, wanting to shut the rest of the world, witness to his humiliation, out of his sight and hearing.

The first MAKE THIS CHILD SMILE AGAIN poster was put up in the HELP office just behind Sister Eva's desk, so those who came in would be struck by it as soon as they entered and looked for her. It was put up without any fuss or ceremony, and Joseph only knew it was there because the door to Sister Eva's office had been open when he and a group of boys had been walking down the corridor to their daily classes. It was one of the other boys who had noticed it first and drawn everyone else's attention to it.

The slogan soon became a joke. "Smile, Joseph, smile," his friends would tease him. And if he was in a particularly angry mood, one of the boys would ask with mock gravity, "Has anyone got five dollars?" Sometimes Joseph would only get angrier, but sometimes he would be provoked to smile at them. They used to call it the five-dollar smile.

The food was terrible. It was totally unfamiliar to Joseph's taste buds, anyway, and he did not enjoy it. There was, however, a bowl of fruit salad on the tray that contained little diced apples. He ate those, spilling some on the seat and the floor. He did not know whether to be happy about the pieces he had eaten or sad about the ones he had lost. He looked around to see if anyone was watching him. No one was. He tried to pick up a little piece of apple from the floor, but the tray was in his way and he couldn't reach down far enough. It was frustrating. On balance, he felt miserable.

The stewardess swished by to collect his tray. Would he like some tea? Joseph said, "Yes." Actually he wanted coffee, but he was scared that if he said "no" to the tea he might not be offered any coffee either. Why couldn't they have offered him coffee first? he thought, as the pale, brown liquid filled his cup. It was so unfair.

He was, not surprisingly, the first child to be "adopted." Other people who responded to the campaign had sent in their five dollars for the first month, and their pledges for a year or two years or a decade or a lifetime, for any child HELP wanted to rescue. But three couples insisted their money go to one specific child—the child in the photograph. They had seen his sad, little face, and they wanted to make him smile again. No one else. Their five dollars were for Joseph Kumaran's tiny little fingers to come out of his hungry little mouth. And they insisted on being allowed to adopt him alone.

The nuns had sighed when those letters came in. "Oh,

what a nuisance some people are," Sister Eva said. "I have half a mind to return their money to them. It's none of their business to tell us where their money should go." But Sister Eva had kept the money and the pledges anyway—from all three couples. Joseph Kumaran's five-dollar smile was actually netting HELP fifteen dollars a month.

So every month Joseph would have to sit down and, in his neat, strained little hand, write a letter to each of his foster parents, thousands of miles away, telling them how good and grateful he was. "Today we had catechism, and I learned the story of how Lot's wife turned into a banana tree," he would write to one couple. (Salt was an expensive commodity in those parts, and the nuns didn't want the children to derive the wrong lessons from the Bible.) Then he would copy the same line out neatly onto the other two letters. As he grew older, Sister Celine would no longer dictate the letters, but let him write them himself and correct them before they were mailed. "Sister Angela has told me about America," he wrote once. "Is it true that everyone is rich there and always has plenty to eat?" Sister Celine did not like that, scored it out, and was later seen speaking sternly to Sister Angela.

The steward was coming down the aisle selling headphones. Joseph had seen him doing that as the flight began, and though he did not know what headphones were, he had discovered that they cost money and that people put them into their ears. He shook his head vigorously when asked whether he wanted one. But his anxious eyes rolled in curiosity as his neighbor, who had also declined the first time, looked at the movie handbill in approbation, produced green notes and silver coins, and was rewarded with a polyethylene packet. From this emerged a contraption even stranger at close quarters than it had seemed from a distance.

The curtains were being drawn across the airplane windows; a screen was lowered at the head of the cabin; images flickered on the whiteness ahead. Joseph stared, transfixed, rapt. His neighbor had plugged in his headset and was obviously listening to something Joseph could not hear. Titles began to appear on the screen.

Joseph desperately wanted to hear the movie, too.

He would get letters in reply from his foster parents. Initially, they were as frequent as his monthly letters to them, but later their interest seemed to flag and he would get only occasional replies. One couple seemed the nicest—they would always apologize profusely whenever their letters were too late, and they would always ask about him, his schoolwork, his games. At Christmas they would send little gifts that Sister Celine would let him open but which he would have to share with the other children. Joseph liked their colored notepaper, the lady's handwriting, which was so easy to read, and the lingering smell of perfume that still clung to each sheet of stationery. Frequently he would hold it up to his face, smothering his nose in it, smelling America.

One day, after several letters to this couple, he became bolder. "It is very hot here at this time of year," he had written in the version approved by Sister Celine. "I suppose it is cooler in America." But while copying the corrected draft out neatly on to an aerogram, he added: "I think I would enjoy America very much." He told no one about the addition, sealed the aerogram, and waited excitedly for a reply.

When it came, there was no reference to what he had written. But Joseph did not give up. "I often wonder whether America has trees like the ones in my drawing," he hinted while enclosing a precocious crayon sketch. And in the next letter, "If I came to America, do you think I might like it?" He was so enamored of this approach that he copied that line into each of his three letters and sent them away.

It worked. His favorite "parents," the ones who sent him Christmas presents, wrote to Sister Celine to say that they'd often wanted to see the little boy they'd "adopted" but they'd never been able to manage a trip to India. Would it not be possible for young Joseph to be sent to America instead? As soon as they heard from Sister Celine, they would be happy to enclose a plane

ticket for the little boy. Of course, they were not sug-
gesting that he should stay with them always. Obviously,
his place was among "his people" in India, and "with
you all at HELP." They would send him back, but they
did so want to see him, just once.

Sister Celine seemed a little taken aback by the letter.
It was not customary for foster parents to evince such
an interest in their protégés. When they were old enough
the children were simply taught an elementary trade and
packed off to earn their keep. Foreign trips, for however
short a duration, were highly unusual.

Sister Celine showed Joseph the letter and asked,
"You haven't been up to anything, have you?" To his
excited protestations she merely responded, "We'll see."
And then she went to talk to Sister Eva.

Joseph had only seen one movie before. That was a
documentary about HELP's activities among orphan
children in the wilds of Bihar, and it had been shown
one evening after dinner by the man who made it, so
that the nuns could all see what the outside world was
being told about their work. Sister Eva, in a spirit of
generosity, had suggested that the boys, at least those
over five, be permitted to sit on the ground and watch
it too. It might teach them a few things, she told the
other nuns, make them realize how much we do for
them, maybe instill some gratitude in them. Joseph had
fallen asleep halfway through that movie. He didn't want
to see starving Adivasi children and warm-hearted nuns;
he saw them every day. The black-and-white images, the
monotonous, superimposed voice of the commentator,
blurred in his mind; the nuns danced tiptoe through the
crevices of his brain, and the pictures pulsed and faded
in his eyes. Firm but gentle hands were rousing him.

"Get up—it's time to go to bed."

In the background, Sister Eva's high-pitched voice
rang through the clear night: "Look at them! Give them
a special treat like this and half of them go off to sleep!
Don't ever let me catch any of you asking to see a movie
again. I mean it!"

But what a movie this was. Bright, vivid colors, pretty,
white women in short dresses, fast cars racing down

broad, foreign streets. It was like nothing he had ever seen before. And he wanted to hear it; hear the loud roar of the car engines, the soft, tinkling laughter of the women, the shouts and the screams and all the sounds of bullets and people and whizzing airplanes.

"Sir." The steward who had dispensed the headphones was standing at the end of the aisle, just behind Joseph, watching the movie too.

"Yes?"

"May I have some headphones too?"

"Of course." The steward disappeared behind the partition and emerged with a polyethylene packet. He handed it to Joseph.

Joseph reached out to take it with an ineffable feeling of awe, wonder, and achievement. He pushed aside the flap, put in his hand, and touched the cold plastic. The sensation was indescribably thrilling.

"Two dollars and fifty cents, please."

"But . . . but . . . I don't have any money," Joseph said miserably. His eyes pleaded with the steward. "Please?"

The steward had a why-are-you-wasting-my-time-you-dumb-child look on his face. "I'm sorry," he said, taking the packet out of Joseph's hands, "IATA regulations."

And then he was gone, having invoked an authority higher than Joseph's longings, more powerful than philanthropy. When he reemerged from the partition it was on the other side, on the aisle away from Joseph's.

Sister Eva had taken some time to decide. It was not that she minded in principle, she told Sister Celine, but this could set a dangerous precedent. The other children would be wanting to go too, and how many had rich American foster parents who would be willing to mail them plane tickets?

In the end, however, to Joseph's great relief, she agreed. She would write personally to the American couple making it clear Joseph was not to be spoiled. And that he was to be back within a month, before he could become entirely corrupted by American ways, to resume his place among those as unfortunate as he was. Unless they wanted to keep him in America for good, which they showed no intention of doing.

The next few weeks passed in a frenzy of preparation. The ticket had to arrive, a flight had to be booked, a passport had to be issued to Joseph, a visa obtained. He was given a little suitcase for his clothes, and he swelled with pride at his tangible evidence of possessions. He had things, he was somebody. With a passport, a suitcase, a ticket, he was not just a little brown face in a crowd around the gruel bowl; he was Master Joseph Kumaran, and he was going somewhere.

And finally, wearing the tight blazer he had been given on the morning of his departure, its pocket stuffed with the news-magazine clipping he had hoarded since it had been shown to him by Sister Celine four years ago, his passport nestling next to a glossy color photo of his hosts sent to him so that he would recognize them at the airport, Joseph was put on board the plane. Sister Celine was there to see him off; she smiled at him through misty glasses, and Joseph felt the wetness on her cheeks when she hugged him at the departure gate. But he could not cry in return; he was a little scared, but more excited than upset, and he certainly was not sad.

The man sitting next to him did not seem to care particularly for the movie after all. Twice, Joseph caught him dozing off, his eyes closing and his chin sinking slowly to his chest; twice, with equal suddenness, his neighbor's head would jerk awake, prompted no doubt by some startling sound on the headphones. The third time this happened, the man pulled off his headphones in disgust and strode off, clambering over Joseph, in quest of a sink.

Joseph could not resist this opportunity. It was too good to be true: headphones plugged in, next to him, unused. He eased himself out of his seatbelt and sat in his neighbor's chair. Then, tentatively, looking around him to make sure no one had noticed him, he raised the tips to his ears. Almost immediately he was assaulted by the sounds of the movie: brakes screeched as a car drew to a halt; a man dashed down some stairs with a gun in his hand; there was some panting dialogue; the gun went off, the bullet's report a deafening symphony in Joseph's ear; a woman screamed. And his neighbor returned from the toilet.

Joseph looked up, almost in agony. His pleasure had been so brief.

The man smiled down at him from the aisle. "Mine, sonny," he beamed.

Joseph had been well brought up. "Excuse me," he said, gently removing the headphones and placing them on the seat. He slid into his place again, his neighbor returned to his chair, the earplugs went back on, and Joseph found he could not see the screen through his tears.

Hoping his neighbor would not notice, he dabbed at his eyes with the clean, white handkerchief Sister Angela had pressed into his hand that morning. That morning—it seemed so long ago. He returned the handkerchief to his pocket, feeling once again the magazine clipping that, four years ago, had started him on this journey. Resolutely, he refrained from pulling it out. That was not him: he had another identity now. He took out his passport, and his eyes caressed each detail on the inside page, from the fictional birthdate ("It's easier than going through the entire 'birthdate unknown' business," Sister Eva had declared) to the inventory of his characteristics ("Hair: black; eyes: black; skin: brown") to the new, awkward photograph, Joseph staring glassy-eyed into the studio camera. And then, returning the passport at long last to his inside pocket, he touched the other photo, the glossy, color portrait of his new, albeit temporary, parents. After some hesitation, he took it out: these were the people whose house he would call home for the next month.

But would he really? He stared at their forms in the photograph. They had sent Joseph their picture so he would recognize them, but they had not asked for his. "We're sure we'll spot him as soon as he gets off the plane," the wife had written to Sister Celine. "We feel we've known him all our lives." Joseph had felt flattered then, deeply touched. Then one day, in a fit of temper, Sister Eva had threatened to replace Joseph with another little dark-skinned boy from the orphanage. "Do you think they'd be able to tell the difference?" she had demanded.

In silent, desperate misery, Joseph had not known what to say.

Looking at the photograph, Joseph tried to think of the magic of America, of things there he had heard about and dreamed of—movies, parties, delicious food of infinite variety, outings to the beach and to Disneyland. But his eyes dilated and the photograph blurred. He did not know why he felt suffused with a loneliness more intense, more bewildering in its sadness than he had ever experienced in the gruel crowds of HELP. He was alone, lost somewhere between a crumpled magazine clipping and the glossy brightness of a color photograph.

On the seat next to him, his neighbor snored peacefully, chin resting in surrender on his chest, headphones embedded into his ears. On the screen, the magic images flickered, cascaded, and danced on.

Anthologies of fiction from diverse cultures and classes

Other Voices, Other Vistas
STORIES FROM AFRICA, CHINA, INDIA, JAPAN, AND LATIN AMERICA
Edited by Barbara H. Solomon
This collection of contemporary multi-cultural fiction brings together the works of such writers as diverse as Bessie Head, Charles Mungoshi, Ngugi wa Thiong'o, Wang Anyi, Wang Meng, Chen Rong, Lu Wenfu, Anita Desai, Mahasweta Devi, Ruth Prawer Jhabvala, Khushwant Singh, Kobo Abe, Sawako Ariyoshi, Yasunari Kawabata, Yukio Mishima, Yuko Tsushima, Carlos Fuentes, Nadine Gordimer, and Isabel Allende.

The Haves and Have-Nots
30 STORIES ABOUT MONEY AND CLASS IN AMERICA
Edited by Barbara H. Solomon
How does money—or the lack of it—affect our lives? What happens when the rich meet the poor, when status comes with a price tag, when personal desires do battle with financial concerns? This unique anthology offers a mosaic of answers, with stories by Francine Prose, F. Scott Fitzgerald, Jack London, Kate Chopin, Gloria Naylor, Sandra Cisneros, O. Henry, Theodore Dreiser, Stephen Crane, Kate Braverman, James T. Farrell, and many others.

Available wherever books are sold or at signetclassics.com

READ THE TOP 20
SIGNET CLASSICS